WHISPER OF MAGIC

UNEXPECTED MAGIC SERIES

Patricia Rice

Whisper of Magic

Patricia Rice

Published by Rice Enterprises, Dana Point, CA, an affiliate of Book View Café Publishing Cooperative

Formatter: Vonda McIntyre

Cover design by Killion Group

Book View Café Publishing Cooperative

P.O. Box 1624, Cedar Crest, NM 87008-1624

http://bookviewcafe.com

ISBN: 978-1-61138-586-1 ebook

ISBN: 978-1-61138-587-8 trade

Author's Note

Those of you familiar with my magical Malcolms and scientific Ives know that I'm playing with possibilities more than I'm using magic. Centuries ago, flying machines would have been magic and a scientific impossibility. Today, we know they aren't magic at all.

Of course, since I'm not dealing with fantasy magic but elements of humanity, what my protagonists are really learning is to use what they are given for the betterment of all—a lesson we should all take to heart.

So in Erran's book, I'm playing with the possibility of levitation—a psychic gift reported by spiritualists over the centuries and even in the Bible. I'm also flirting with persuasion and Mesmerism—persuasive voices have long been the basis for the success of everyone from snake oil salesmen to politicians. Why else would perfectly sane people do exactly what a particularly eloquent speaker tells them to do, even though they ought to know better?

So as Hamlet says: *There are more things in heaven and earth, Horatio, Than are dreamt of in your philosophy.* - **Hamlet (1.5.167-8)**

One

June 1830

LORD ERRAN IVES, barrister, glanced back at his client's shadow of a wife. The babe in her lap sucked at its fist, but even he could tell the child was ill, and the children sitting quietly beside them were undernourished. The family shouldn't even be here, but they had nowhere else to go. His sense of injustice burned like a flame in his chest as he waited for the other barrister to finish speaking.

Once it was his turn, incensed by the half asleep judge's inattention to a poor family's welfare, Erran drew himself up to his full intimidating height and released his outrage in his closing statement. "To allow the monstrous greed of the defendant to deprive a hardworking man and his family the roof over their heads is an injustice so foul that all Britain must stand and *cry for reparations!*"

As if in agreement with this impassioned speech, a gavel rose and banged against the bench—startling the half-asleep judge whose hand wasn't on it. The judge jerked awake and stared in astonishment as the gavel flew from the bench and slammed to the floor.

Hiding his puzzlement at this bizarre flight, knowing he'd indulged in unseemly theatrics, Erran tightened his jaw and squared his shoulders for the scolding to come. He'd be lucky he wasn't thrown out of the courtroom on his first case.

Behind Erran, the baby howled and the crowd awoke, first with a low grumble, and then with increasingly agitated murmurs of "He's right!" and "*Hang all landlords!*"

Surreptitiously studying the now inert hammer on the floor while he waited for the judge to establish order, Erran let his mechanic's mind calculate the possibility of his shouts vibrating the bench enough to bounce off inanimate objects.

Instead of quieting at the judge and clerk's commands, the audience started stomping and chanting louder. They'd found a rhythm in a word Erran couldn't quite discern.

Wondering what fresh nightmare this was, he refrained from glancing over his shoulder again or he would most likely blow a gasket. Were they chanting at him? Why?

Prepared to face his punishment, Erran focused on the bench. His head itched beneath his newly-acquired wig. Swallowing a lump in his throat, he squared his shoulders and stiffened his spine. He hadn't the wherewithal to fix his clients' problem on his own. The court was their only resource. If Erran lost his plea, the man, his ill wife, and their three very young children would be on the streets.

He had been their only hope. Now he would be their undoing.

The judge nodded in what appeared to be approval.

Disconcerted, Erran lurched back from his self-flagellation. What did that nod mean? Why wasn't the judge shouting at the bailiffs to haul the noisemakers from his courtroom? Or throwing Erran out for inciting a riot?

Beside Erran, his normally apathetic clerk embraced their openly weeping client. *What the deuce?*

Erran regretted becoming more heated than was suitable for a courtroom, but he certainly hadn't said anything new or different to make grown men weep. Everyone despised greedy landlords. No one ever did anything about them. They were part of the landscape like sky and trees. Why tears and sympathy for stating a basic fact?

While waiting for the axe to fall—or another gavel—he finally sorted out what the crowd chanted: *Reparations, reparations!*

The half-asleep audience had picked up on his speech? Erran had observed a lot of cases in his years of study. He had never seen or heard anything of this sort. He glanced across the aisle. His client's criminally abusive landlord and his solicitor were conversing nervously.

What the devil was going on? His stomach clenched and his throat locked. If the judge didn't act soon, Erran thought he might collapse in a puddle of sweat. And the mob behind him was likely to take the courtroom apart.

The audience continued stomping and shouting, while the bailiffs did nothing and one of the new policemen ran in from the street, looking confused at the hubble-bubble.

The judge was going to throw him in jail and leave him to rot. His brothers probably wouldn't miss him for a year or two if he ended up in chains.

He'd told them to cry for reparations—and they'd obeyed. Why?

With no gavel to restore order, the judge finally shouted, "Let the court record state that Mr. Silas Greene must forfeit the entirety of the building at 16 Foxcroft to Mr. Charles Moore and his family in perpetuity. And if said Mr. Greene should ever face this court again, he shall be fined every cent in his possession. Court adjourned."

The crowd roared jubilantly, threatening to bring down the rafters from the vibrations.

"What does that mean?" Mr. Moore asked anxiously, wiping at his eyes.

"That the whole damned world has gone insane," Erran replied, but the noise was too loud for his client to hear, although his clerk sent him a strange look.

"You're possessed of the *devil*," Silas Greene, the landlord, snarled as he passed their table.

The devil, what a load of crockery . . .

Appalled, Erran shuddered as he recalled that term applied to his Cousin Sylvester—the Ives with a silver tongue who'd repeatedly sold fraudulent investments until forced to escape to the Americas. This wasn't the same at all, he told himself. He had right on his side.

It was just rare for right to triumph over wrong. And for gavels to fly, but that had to be a coincidence of vibrations and atmosphere. Devils did not exist.

Uneasy, but refusing to accept *evil* as an explanation of how an honorable suit over an eviction had become a triumphant melee, Erran stalked out of the chambers, discarding his robe and wig into the hands of his clerk before he escaped from the building.

"The house is mine?" Following in his wake, timid Mr. Moore stumbled in confusion as they reached the less noisy street. The Moore family huddled together, confused and waiting to be told what to do.

"The house is yours," Erran agreed, not believing it either. "The clerks will draw up the papers and deliver them on the morrow. Tell your wife she may move out of your employer's cellar and back home."

Moore was weeping again, this time in apparent relief as he gave his family the verdict even Erran hadn't expected.

Granted, the landlord had been a greedy bastard who'd thrown the young family out when offered twice the rent by a neighboring merchant—but that was business as usual for London. Erran had simply taken the case to practice in a real courtroom now that he'd passed the bar.

He'd *shouted* at a judge, and instead of rightfully being thrown out on his noggin—he'd won the case in spectacular fashion.

The cloud darkening the previously bright summer day seemed an ominous portent.

A crowd of his fellows swarmed up to congratulate him, and Erran tried to shake off his apprehension. Jestingly, letting himself be momentarily buoyed by triumph, he climbed up on a mounting block and made a grandiose gesture. "All bow before your new lord and master!"

His jaw dropped as his fellow students, clerks, and friends removed their tall hats and bent in half before him.

Worse, everyone on the crowded street—businessmen, urchins, and timid Mr. Moore—all performed awkward gestures of obeisance. And looked extremely confused a moment later after Erran jumped from his pedestal and fled into the nearest tavern.

September 1830

HUNTING for dry ground for his polished Wellingtons, Erran didn't see the mud ball until it knocked his black beaver hat into a puddle. *Bloody hell.* Erran stalked into the mews in pursuit of the miscreants while his ten-year-old nephew Hartley Ives-Weldon ran to rescue the expensive D'Orsay.

These days, Erran kept his formidable voice to himself, but that didn't mean he didn't have fists to shake a few louts into next week. In the narrow mews, he caught sight of the troublemakers taunting a slender woman striding through the rutted mud. Realizing his hat hadn't been their intended victim didn't quell his temper. More mud splattered the woman's long black wool cloak and hood as she marched toward the reprobates without flinching.

Abandoning his nephew, Erran ran after her, hoping to scare the ruffians off with his greater size. He despised his preposterous delusions about his voice, but he was taking no chances in a public venue. To this day, most of his friends steered clear of him.

And once he'd returned to his senses, the judge had banned him from his courtroom.

"You will take your mud balls and run or the wrath of all the gods will rain upon your unworthy heads." The woman berated her mockers in mellifluous accents that sounded more like song than curses.

The beauty of her voice almost made up for the damage to his new hat.

The rain of rocks and mud balls abruptly ceased. Stunned, Erran watched as the lads vanished into doorways and alleys— terrified by a song?

Apparently unsurprised by their retreat, the woman opened a service gate into the yard of one of the substantial houses lining the left side of the alley. Erran strained to catch a better look at the producer of such a marvelous sound, but she didn't turn around. Instead, she slipped into the yard beyond the gate and shut the panel firmly.

Realizing what gate she'd just used—Erran would have flung his hat in a puddle again, if he'd been wearing it.

Bloody damn hell—he'd been trying to get into that house for a week. No one ever answered the door. He'd thought no one was home.

"Miss!" he called over solid English oak topped by wrought iron. He had learned to modulate his voice, but making it carry would require shouting if she got too far away. "Miss, if I might speak with you!"

For a moment, the black cloak hesitated. A head turned, and over the top of the gate, he caught a glimpse of an oval face tinted by the rich hues of a tropical sun, long black lashes, and a frown. Then she hastened her pace and vanished behind a hedge of greenery.

"Drat." Erran rubbed at the soiled hat that Hartley handed him, rattled the barred gate, and kicked an errant stone.

Not tall enough to see over the panel, Hartley tried to peer between the cracks. "Why were they throwing rocks at her?"

"It's a puzzlement," Erran said, scowling at the damage to his boots. "I've not seen so much as a ghost in the place all week. At least we now know there are servants in there, even if they don't answer the door."

Even as he said that, Erran wasn't convinced he hadn't seen a ghost. She had glided with the elegant grace of a lady, head high, steps delicate, skirts swaying with expensive layers of petticoats. But no lady would have brown skin, wear an ugly black cloak, or use the servants' entrance. It was *all* a puzzlement.

It was his own damned house he was trying to get into.

His whole accursed life had become a mystery, even to him. He blamed his brother Theo for marrying a witch—although Lady Aster had merely been a thorn in their collective sides at the time the courtroom incident had happened.

Her family research had simply prompted the notion of inheriting the bad strains of prior generations. Just because Cousin Sylvester had persuaded thousands of pounds out of the hands of wealthy investors didn't mean Erran had inherited his relation's deceitful streak. Erran considered himself to be a man of education and science, not a superstitious peasant—or a thief.

But with judges unwilling to take his cases, he was an *unemployed* man of education.

"How will we get the house back for Papa if we can't move out the tenants?" Hartley inquired anxiously. Hartley was the worrier of Ashford's illegitimate twins. The catastrophic summer had turned the boy's usual cheerful smile upside-down as the weeks passed and it became evident his father would never be the same. "We'll never persuade him into town otherwise."

Erran had his doubts that they'd persuade the marquess to town even if they gained the townhouse, but the family home was the only suggestion his newly-blind brother had shown an interest in. It should have been a simple task to find the tenants new accommodations and help them to move out. Unfortunately, the tenants had proved remarkably unavailable for moving.

Legally and morally, he could do nothing to evict them. The tenants had a proper, paid contract and no obligation to open their doors to him. He had been hoping to persuade them by offering a better house in recompense. He might have more success battering down doors, but that would make him as reprehensible as the landlord he'd taken to court.

These days, he was working hard to stick to a moral, as well as a legal, high ground, in hopes he would one day be employable again. Being arrested for battering down his own family's door would set tongues clacking and guarantee disbarment.

"It's time to make more inquiries," Erran concluded, steering his nephew toward the tavern now occupying the former stable.

In this street just off St. James Square, the once formidable stone and granite mansions built in the prior century were showing signs of deterioration. Many had been subdivided and turned into shops and taverns or bachelor flats. The Ives town house, however, remained a solid square occupying the entire space between the street and the mews.

"Hunt down those ruffians and find out why they're throwing stones at our tenants' servants," Erran ordered. "I'll be in the tavern making inquiries. Don't take too long. We have to return for dinner at Theo's."

Obediently, Hartley ran off to find the neighbor lads. That there were vast differences in their stations didn't occur to the son of an actress and a marquess. Well, for all Erran knew, the ragged ruffians could have been the bastard sons of dukes. The Crown owned half the property around here.

He entered the smoke-filled dark room to put his lawyerly skills to work—praying he would have no use for the dangerous Courtroom Voice that had caused him to lose his profession and question his sanity.

CELESTE Malcolm Rochester removed her muddied cloak with a trembling hand and hung it on a hook by the back door. She'd had enough experience at these misadventures lately that she no longer collapsed beside the door, shaking and crying. She'd learned to take deep breaths and go on.

But the gentleman—he was a new development, and he'd rattled her badly. His mellow baritone had promised a security she hadn't known since they arrived in London—which was entirely ridiculous. She hurried up the stairs to find a window overlooking the mews. Rubbing her elbows, trying to calm herself, she peered through a gap in the drapery.

The formidable gentleman who had followed her wore a fashionable gray frock coat, the kind with a redingote collar. He'd topped it with a handsome black muffler and held an expensive tall hat. He was no ruffian, although she questioned the origin of the child to whom he was speaking. Were they the instigators of these episodes?

The boy ran off while the gentleman studied the windows where she stood. Dark curls and slight sideburns framed an arrogantly square jaw and high cheekbones, before he slammed the muddy hat back on his head and retreated to the tavern, out of her sight.

"Why do they hate us?" she asked, attempting to expel her fear and despair. "We have harmed no one."

"People fear what they do not know," her African nanny said prosaically, glancing up to verify Celeste was unharmed, then returning to pedaling the machine they'd brought with them.

Nana Delphinia had been with them for as long as Celeste could remember. The older woman had loyally accompanied them to London, leaving behind her own grown children in the process. Therein lay the true tragedy of their lives, and another reason Celeste spent her sleepless nights in tears.

Their faithful servant's hair was turning gray, and lines of worry marred her face, but Nana had lost none of her strength of character. "What happened this time?"

"They've escalated to mud flinging. I'll have to scrape my cloak once it dries. I'm not certain what the gentleman had to do with the attack, if anything." Celeste dropped the old velvet panel back in place. "If he's a solicitor, he's more elegant than the others they've sent. I may actually have to talk to him."

Celeste's younger sister hurried to look and frowned at seeing only the empty alley.

Her younger brother glanced up from his schoolbook with alarm. "Unless we've miraculously found the coin to hire a solicitor of our own, talking to him isn't wise," Trevor counseled. At seventeen, he was the image of his great-grandfather in the portraits their great-grandmother had painted—tall, dark-haired, brown-skinned, and handsome, now that he was growing into his bones.

"The lease is ours," Celeste assured him, trying to convince herself. If they lost the roof over their heads along with everything else, she didn't know what she would do. "They can't take away our home. We'll have a solicitor of our own soon enough. I have a new order for shirts. Sewing in the pleat has proved popular. Young gentlemen lack servants who can wield crimping irons."

"Popular, but tedious," Sylvia complained, returning to her

chair and her hand sewing. Unlike her older siblings, Sylvia was blond and petite, more like their mother than their father. "I was so hoping for grand parties and elegant gowns and . . ." She let her voice drop off at Celeste's pointed glare.

"We're in mourning, and you're still too young." And Celeste was too old and too unsuitable, but their father had cheerfully refused to acknowledge that. He had paid for his foolishness with his life and quite possibly the lives of others, but that couldn't have been predicted. "Your time will come, but first we must earn the funds to find a good lawyer. Be grateful for what we have." Celeste hunted for her sewing basket.

"Be grateful for a cousin who has appropriated our inheritance?" Trevor asked bitterly. "Or for a half-sister who won't acknowledge our existence? Or for our father's unfortunate demise on a miserable ship that nearly took our lives?"

"For being alive with an excellent situation and food in our bellies," Nana scolded. "You have seen how those back home fare. It will be your duty to help them one of these days. Now study."

It would be Trev's duty to save the servants—like Nana's family—from their cousin's greed was the admonishment they all heard. Trev paled and dipped his head back to the schoolbook.

Celeste swallowed back tears and picked up her own sewing. If only she'd been born a boy . . . But it would be four more years before Trevor would be of a legal age and could assume their father's estate. Four years in which their father's cousin, the Earl of Lansdowne, could sell off all their father's assets, along with the people who had served their family for decades. *Free* people, not slaves—although without access to their father's papers, no one could prove that.

Celeste couldn't imagine any English court of law giving a woman the right to take care of her family, not any more than she could imagine them giving Nana her freedom if the Earl of Lansdowne chose to challenge it. He'd already usurped their father's estate by having himself declared head of the family.

Hiring a solicitor was scarcely one small weapon in their puny arsenal.

Hiding for the next four years didn't seem like a brilliant plan, either, but it was the best she had. It wasn't *all* she had, but anything else was built on fairy dust and magic.

Two

HAVING CLEANED the worst of the mud from his boots and brushed off his coat, Erran settled at his sister-in-law's dinner table knowing no one but he would notice if he sat down in shirt sleeves. Fashionable, his brothers were not, despite their wealth and lengthy aristocratic history. Theo's eccentric new wife was cut of similar cloth.

Wearing another of her unfashionable peacock-colored gowns, Lady Azenor signaled one of her footman trainees to serve the first course. "Hartley says neither of you had any luck at discerning the whereabouts of the townhouse's tenants?"

Accustomed to the blunt speaking of his brothers, Erran had no difficulty adjusting to Lady Aster, as she'd asked them to call her. "We've only seen servants," he acknowledged. "As the lease indicates, the tenants are Jamaican, and they've brought foreign retainers with them. If I'm to believe half the tales told in the tavern, they have giants and ogres as well. Hartley says the boys throwing mud balls swore the servants are witches."

Lady Aster immediately lost interest in her soup. "Witches? Why ever would they say that?"

Short, plump, and copper-haired, his sister-in-law might not look much like a witch, but she came from a long line of women who'd once been vilified with that epithet. The women might have a few uncanny talents, but Erran didn't count them as more than the application of illogical conclusions to scientific principles. Although lately . . . He squirmed uneasily, preferring not to consider his own brush with the Wyrd. "The ruffians were incapable of communicating any story that made sense."

He glanced at the footman serving his soup. "James?" he asked, diverting his unease by trying to determine if this was the same footman he'd seen here last.

"Smithson," the servant corrected. He shut up quickly at a frown from the lady, nodded, and moved back to the buffet.

"We're informal," his brother Theo said after Erran's faux pas.

"But Aster is trying to train servants for more formal houses. Presumably, elsewhere, they are expected to only occasionally be seen and never heard."

"Better to train them to suit ourselves." Erran tasted the soup and approved. "I still need a valet. Pascoe can't keep a nursemaid. And Dunc will drive those few people he has left insane, so we can use a steady flow of servants at the estate."

"I'd thought of that," Theo agreed. With his neckcloth already coming undone and his overlong chestnut hair falling across his brow, he reached across the table for the bread rather than waiting for it to be served. "Aster can train them so Dunc can dismiss them. Some sort of poetic justice. But then we can give them references from the house of a marquess."

Erran knew they made light of a tragic situation. His all-powerful older brother had been blinded in an accident that had been no accident, as they had discovered when Aster had overheard their neighbor's son and a band of hired rogues. The son had fled the country, and there was no one to give evidence or identify the hirelings—not that convicting anyone would give the marquess back his sight.

Erran ground his teeth, sipped his soup, and contemplated how to move the newly-blind marquess into his city home, where Duncan might recover part of his former authority—and possibly restore Erran's reputation.

The alternative was Erran forfeiting his education to become a tinker. And Dunc could lose his brilliant mind cooped up inside four walls, refusing to emerge from his misery.

"If we can retrieve the townhouse from the tenants, we'll be able to employ even more of my aunt's workhouse rescues." Aster glanced inquiringly at Erran. "Does the place appear to be in good condition? Will it be worth converting the ground floor for Ashford's use?"

Erran knew she wasn't rubbing in his failure. Aster was too oblivious to reality for that, so he merely shrugged and posed another possibility. "Hard to say what's been done on the interior. The tenants—wherever they are—aren't complaining about leaking roofs anyway. The *location* is what Dunc needs—only a few blocks from Parliament. Perhaps we could lease another place in the area."

The lady glared at him. "It is *that* house he needs. Astrogeographically, it's ideal since he was born there. There are strong power points running through that lot. If anything could cure him, it will be that house."

There were dozens of reasons the marquess needed the family London town home, but *power points*—whatever they were—weren't high on Erran's list. Dunc needed to return to Parliament for his own sanity. The vote on the next prime minister would affect the entire reform movement, including the labor laws and other bills crucial to their family and to the entire country. As Marquess of Ashford, Duncan had influence and responsibility the rest of the family could only aspire to.

As a newly blind man, Ashford refused to leave his chambers. He had ceded his responsibilities to his heir, a reluctant Theo—who was more scientist than politician. Erran accepted that Duncan needed familiar surroundings just to tackle each day, but leaving him to rot in his room wasn't healthy for anyone.

"Perhaps you should take me over to the town house," Aster suggested. "I could talk to the women in the area. Surely there are neighbors who gossip? We need to find out where the tenants have gone."

"Or you could set up as a Gypsy woman on the corner and offer to read their fortunes," Theo suggested wickedly.

Aster frowned thoughtfully, as if she were actually considering his suggestion. "It's an expensive neighborhood, but my aunts know everyone. I could obtain an introduction to the neighbors and hold one of my parties. I won't really read their fortunes, of course, but with their birth dates, I can tell them about their sun signs. People talk at parties. If the tenants have gone to Scotland for the hunting season, perhaps someone will have an address."

Considering the mysterious cloaked visage he'd observed for that one brief moment—and the flying mud balls in the mews and the insults he'd heard in the tavern—Erran didn't believe Aster would have much luck questioning the neighbors.

He'd have to find another way in—if only for their tenants' protection.

"OLD-FASHIONED AND DIRTY." The Honorable Emilia McDowell sniffed in distaste as she, Lady Aster, and Erran walked down the street beyond St. James Square to study the Ives' London home.

Wealthy and attractive, as Lady Aster's relations often were, Miss McDowell was also independent enough to decline the offer of Erran's arm. With her thick black hair and pale complexion, she looked the part of witch that the riotously-colored, cheerful Lady Aster did not.

"Ives House is one of the wider lots, with a yard in the rear," Erran explained. "There should be sufficient space on the ground floor for Duncan's chambers, and there may even be room for expansion in back."

"Only if you remove the tenants," Lady Aster pointed out pragmatically, studying a chart she'd removed from the capacious bag she always carried with her. "This is even a more auspicious location than I'd realized. It should enhance Ashford's already copious powers."

"To the point of healing him?" Miss McDowell asked with interest.

Erran noted she didn't ask *what powers*, like any sensible person. The women talked in a language all their own. Dunc's power was in his wealth and authority. The house's location had little to do with that except as a display of his heritage.

"One never knows about healing. Perhaps if you have herbs that will work for him and grew them here . . ." Aster sighed. "The herbs would be more powerful, too, but asking plants to heal blindness does not seem realistic."

Miss McDowell studied the four-story stone exterior. "It is a very plain structure, not a pilaster or column in sight. But I do feel energy emanating from it. I wonder if it has an herb garden?"

Well aware that Lady Aster was attempting to match him with her wealthy but unconventional cousin, Erran attempted not to scoff at their idiocies. He wasn't ready for a wife, but at the rate he was headed, he might need her wealth. Without the career he'd been trained for, he was existing on his allowance and his brother's goodwill. Neither were sufficient to afford rooms, much less an office and a clerk.

Gardens, however, he could answer to. "There is a large yard in the rear with plenty of room for a garden. I believe one of the greats grew herbs."

"The Malcolm connection," Lady Aster reminded him. "Your great-grandmother was a brilliant Malcolm herbalist and healer.

You said the tenants are Jamaican. We have ancestors who lived in the Caribbean. Perhaps we should research your tenants. They may have been drawn to this house for the same reasons we are—the earth energies beneath it."

"The chances of someone from Jamaica both knowing the house and being from the same family as ours are about as good as curing Duncan." Unable to contain his skepticism any longer, Erran spoke more sharply than he'd intended and regretted it instantly. His normally smiling sister-in-law cast him a narrowed look that did not bode well for future peace.

Pretending oblivion, he studied the mansion's tall windows. Every one of them had the draperies drawn. "There's a better chance that they're vampire monsters who never come out in day. That place has to be darker than Hades with all the windows covered."

The women laughed and returned to discussing nonsensities. Disgruntled, Erran studied the busy street. Expensive bays pulling crested carriages trotted past gas light posts. Inside the carriages sat ladies sporting their wealth with the feathers and finery of the latest fashions. The vehicles stopped at columned mansions to be greeted by liveried footmen or rattled on to the more fashionable shops in Mayfair. Despite its age, the area was still respectable.

The pedestrians pushing and shoving along the cobblestones were mostly men in top hats, foreign ambassadors and their staff at this time of year. In another few weeks, the aristocratic residents might return for the parliamentary session that had just been called to replace the prime minister, and the streets would be even more crowded.

Urchins still swept street corners. In the evenings, prostitutes would hug the walls of the taverns. Tailors had shops just around the corner, convenient for the government staffs that passed to and fro who had need of mending, new coats, or orders for uniforms.

Erran thought the neighborhood safe enough for a blind marquess—but not if ruffians were attacking servants. The whole incident bothered him, but he could not quite put his finger on why.

He escorted the ladies to the entrance of the old house, where they insisted on sending their footman up the stone stairs to rap despite the lack of knocker. When no one answered, as usual, Erran led them down the street to the house of one of their acquaintances, where they would begin the business of gossip.

Leaving them with a promise to return in an hour, Erran excused himself from the company. Out of all the foolishness the women had spouted, he'd found one gem—he should have researched their tenant more thoroughly. A man who could pay the exorbitant lease on a house like this for the next five years should be a man known in the business community.

Erran didn't possess enough wealth to traverse the rarified clubs where affluent industrialists discussed business, or even the clubs designated for the sons of aristocrats. That put him at a disadvantage for researching their tenant.

Rendered useless by his weird courtroom encounter—and the embarrassing aftermath—he'd been avoiding his usual clubs lately. Wielding a silver tongue, or vibrating inanimate objects, wasn't how he wanted to win his cases—or influence friends.

Unfortunately, if he meant to help Duncan, he would have to return to his clubs for information. The temptation to test his Wyrd Theory was great, but every moral fiber in his body resisted.

Reaching his club, Erran sighed as his path crossed that of one of his inveterate gambler friends.

"I have a pony on you marrying into your sister-in-law's witchy family before year's end," the gambler cried in delight at seeing Erran.

Well, at least he didn't need magical persuasion to counter that idiocy. Pounding his companion on the back, Erran climbed the stairs. "And I have a pony that says you're a horse's arse."

Maybe if he was rude enough, he would restore his reputation.

STACKING NEATLY FOLDED shirts into a box, Celeste called, "Is the coast clear?"

"No one at the front," Trevor answered from the drawing room.

"I haven't seen anyone in the mews," Sylvia announced from her bedchamber at the back of the house. "Perhaps the gentleman scared off the ruffians."

"The *gentleman* has been making inquiries about the neighborhood," Jamar intoned in his deep bass with only a hint of wryness as he shrugged on his frock coat. "I will escort you."

Celeste cast him a concerned gaze. Jamar was nearly seven feet tall and very black, more African than Jamaican. He had not met with politeness in these months in London. As Nana said, people feared what they did not know, and unfortunately, they acted very badly when afraid.

"It won't be dark for another hour. I should be safe enough just walking down the street," Celeste argued, hiding her fear of walking these city streets alone—as she had hidden all her fears these last months. "I am just another servant carrying her employer's packages."

She truly didn't mind being reduced from privileged lady to servanthood for her family's sake. But she utterly despised being afraid every minute of her life.

"I will go with you." Jamar straightened his neckcloth and buttoned his coat.

There had never been any arguing with her father's majordomo. If she tried her charm, Jamar narrowed his eyes and muttered in an incomprehensible patois until she gave up. He was probably praying to devils and saints and placing a curse on her. She hoped he was happy that his curses had worked.

She wouldn't encourage his bossiness by letting him see her relief.

"Fine, then. Take a big stick." Huffing in impatience, she threw on her cloak, hid her un-English complexion beneath her hood, and picked up her box. If Jamar intended to be her security, he needed his fists free. She wasn't risking all their hard work.

Knowing how far he could push her, Jamar didn't fight over the box, but merely followed her down the stairs and out the kitchen garden. The September days were growing shorter, and a light fog was moving in, casting the bushes into gray shadow. They would have to adjust their hours soon. She wasn't about to run to the tailor shop at dark. That could mean one less shirt a day—or burning more candles. She'd have to think about raising prices.

Frowning, fretting over new ways of keeping their small household running without access to the wealth to which they had always been accustomed, Celeste hurried down the muddy alley. At her side, Jamar kept his huge fist on the knife beneath his coat and vigilantly studied the shadows.

"Watch out!"

The commanding bellow so startled her that she nearly dropped the precious box of shirts. While Jamar glanced around for the danger, a well-dressed gentleman grabbed her cloak and shoved her against a brick wall. He shielded her with his big body as noxious liquid splashed where she'd just been walking.

Crushed between the wall and the bulk of a masculine stranger, Celeste stupidly noticed his spicy scent more than the stench rising from the street. Her next frantic thought was not to crush the box in her arms. She struggled to push free from an obstacle as solid as a brick wall.

Before she could react more sensibly, the gentleman gagged on a growl of surprise as Jamar wrapped a brutal arm around his spotless neckcloth and lifted him off of her.

Shakily, she straightened and tried to puzzle out what had just happened.

"Put...me...down," the gentleman said precisely and threateningly, even though Jamar had his head pulled back and could have broken his neck in a single jerk.

Those handsome dark curls looked familiar, as was the expensive tailoring. She thought the stranger's intonation a little constrained, but she applauded his courage under fire. "Jamar, I believe the gentleman prevented a very unpleasant drenching. Put him down, please."

Once Jamar obeyed, both men reached for the weapons beneath their coats, but they refrained from drawing them while they studied each other with male belligerence. Celeste thought the haughty stranger might be the one who had called after her the other day, the one who had come knocking with the ladies yesterday. He was taller than she by half a head—and she was of above average height. Muscular, broad-shouldered, and thick-chested as a boxer, he was still no match for Jamar, despite his defiant stance. She had to admire him for not backing down from a fiercer opponent.

But apparently satisfied he would not be attacked again, the stranger removed his hat and bowed stiffly, revealing a visage as handsome as the rest of him. "I saw the wretch in the upper window with a pail. I did not mean to frighten you. I apologize for the presumption."

Dragging her gaze from his taut, angry jaw and compelling dark eyes, Celeste glanced up at the tall brick building they stood below. All the windows were shut and blank now. The only evidence of what could have been a damaging attack to her hard work was the malodorous smell of the slop pail's contents running down the street.

She would have asked if London was still so primitive as to use slop buckets, but she knew better—this had been another personal attack. Remembering her role, Celeste tugged the cloak tighter, nodded without speaking, and hurried on her way. The persistent gentleman followed. Irritatingly, Jamar did not chase him off but began watching the windows of the buildings they passed.

"I do not mean to impose," the gentleman said, matching his stride to hers, "But I need to speak with Bardolph, Lord Rochester. It's a matter of immense urgency. If I could importune you to let me know of his return . . ."

The mention of her father's name startled her almost as much as his thrusting her against a wall. London had been a difficult learning experience these past horrible months. She was rather tired of the constant need to adapt to new circumstances. She didn't need arrogant gentlemen pushing their way into her life. What could he possibly know of her origins?

She cast him a sideways glance, but beneath his polished exterior, he seemed most earnest. He really did want to speak with her father.

That meant he wasn't from her father's cousin or the estate solicitors.

She sighed as she followed that thought—it probably meant he was from her *landlord's* solicitor. The letters from them had been far more frequent than any communication from her wretched conniving relation.

Trying to maintain a subservient demeanor, she kept her face hidden and applied her repelling vocalization beneath her most melodious tones. "We do not know, sir. I should not speak with strangers. You must leave. Good day to you, sir."

She hurried toward the safety of the tailor's shop around the corner, fully expecting him to go away as she'd commanded. As further warning, Jamar placed himself at her back.

She started in surprise as the audacious gentleman circumvented Jamar, not put off by her voice or a giant. What manner of devil was this? She halted to glare at him before he discovered her destination.

She had to admit that having an elegant gentleman addressing her with intensity was pleasing, as were his features. He had long-lashed dark eyes beneath slashing dark eyebrows, eyes that studied her with the same interest as she studied him. Blatantly, she let her gaze drop to his very masculine nose with a bit of a crook in it, his supple lips, and his dimpled chin. She adored dimpled chins, even worn on a visage frosty with determination. Still, she did not speak.

"I know you do not understand this country," he said.

That he had not obeyed her command immobilized her with confusion. Men always obeyed her voice. Despite her pleasure at his looks, her loss of control of the situation made it difficult to comprehend his words.

"You have no cause to sympathize with the problems facing my family," she heard him say, "but perhaps you are familiar with the fight to free the slaves in places such as your home? What I have to say affects that fight as well."

Had he just addressed her deepest fear—right here in public? Was he a mind reader? Celeste nearly stumbled in shock.

He reached to catch her before she fell, but she was quick on her feet and righted herself, still in an appalled daze.

Could he really be speaking about the anti-slavery bill that might stop her uncle's predations? And what would this stranger have to do with her late father?

Three

ERRAN HAD NEVER been reduced to begging, especially from beautiful women. But he was too caught up in the urgency of this opportunity to recognize any loss of dignity. Obtaining his brother's town house was the most important goal in his rotten life right now. If he must implore servants to gain access to the tenant, he would bow down on bended knee.

Besides, it was no hardship to study this mystery woman who did not scream assault when attacked or retreat to hysterics when confronted. He had his suspicion that she was no simple servant. From what he could see beneath her concealing hood, she had long-lashed eyes, lush lips, and a complexion as rich as her accent—all of which spoke of foreign aristocratic refinement.

Somehow, he had to breach the lady's rather formidable defenses to resolve the problem at hand. An armed, seven-foot tall Nubian was a rather daunting obstacle—although perhaps not so much as the lady's refusal to speak.

At her nod of dismissal, her bodyguard stepped around Erran to open the door of the tailor shop. The lady hastened inside, and the servant closed the door, blocking Erran from following. Servants did not have servants.

Erran studied his adversary. "You saw what happened back there. You know the lady has enemies."

Garbed in the formal, if old-fashioned, attire of a gentleman, the towering African remained stoic, staring over Erran's head.

"I can find out who would want to harm her and why, but only if I know for certain that she is who I believe she is. It would be rather futile to search for her enemies if she's someone else." He didn't even know if the other man spoke English, but he had to assume he did since the lady had addressed him that way.

No response. Erran contemplated testing his Courtroom Voice on the irritating Colossus, but temptation was addictive and dangerous, not to mention illogically superstitious, and he refused to give in to it. If that meant demeaning himself before a footman or butler, so be it. It wasn't as if an Ives existed who stood on formality.

"I'm Lord Erran Ives, brother to the Marquess of Ashford," he said stiffly. "My family owns the house in which you're living. If the lady is not safe there, we can arrange better, safer accommodations."

He noted a flicker of interest. Before he could find a more persuasive argument, the lady returned, empty-handed. If she really was a lady, why would she be running menial errands to tailor shops? And yesterday, she had been doing so without the accompaniment of any servant.

Determined to solve the puzzle, Erran refused to be pushed aside. He fell in step with them as they returned the way they'd come. "My sister-in-law has been doing some research," he said.

In actuality, after he'd given Aster all the names he'd acquired, she'd fallen into near fits of ecstasy. But describing Malcolm weirdness was beyond him. He stayed with the facts he understood. "She says that the Rochester family and hers are distantly related, if Lord Rochester is from the same branch. She is a genealogist and would very much like to meet the family, if that's possible."

The lady said nothing, merely hurried toward the mews as if he were no more than a talking lamp post.

"As I've told your friend here, the family of a marquess could be very influential in dealing with those who might threaten your household." Erran considered that a fairly persuasive argument—until the lady finally spoke, decisively turning his own words against him.

"And they can be equally dangerous enemies," she replied in honeyed tones that did not seem to match her meaning. "How do we know *you* aren't the ones causing us grief? I would rather you left us alone."

For a brief moment, she turned almond-shaped, spectacularly blue eyes to him with what appeared to be expectation. He was so startled at the juxtaposition of light eyes, dark lashes, and bronzed complexion that he almost forgot to reply.

Dismissively, she turned to escape into her hidden garden.

He recovered his tongue. "If a marquess wants to harm you," he retaliated, "he'd march an army to your door and haul you out. He wields that kind of power but has refrained from using it."

For some reason, his argument seemed to alarm her. She shoved anxiously at the garden gate.

Her bodyguard halted her. "I think we should listen to him."

At that, she tensed and straightened her shoulders, obviously preparing a rejection. She was tall for a woman, but Erran could tell little else about her beneath the concealing cloak. It was hard to imagine a lady taking suggestions from a servant, but he had no better means of reaching her.

"We do not *know* him," she said in a tone reflecting hesitation and . . . fear? Why would she fear him?

"How does one come to know anyone without talking to them?" Erran asked. "I can bring my sister-in-law here. I can bring you references from dukes and judges. What do you require?"

"A message from God," the giant said with wryness.

"He does not respond to my vocalization," the lady whispered. "I cannot trust anyone that unpredictable."

Erran raised his eyebrows. "I respond to spoken words just as everyone else. That illogic sounds like my sister-in-law and her relations. Do I have the honor of meeting Miss Celeste *Malcolm* Rochester?" He repeated the name Aster had given him, almost hoping he was wrong. Malcolms were impossibly irrational.

She peered at him from beneath her hood. "You say that as if it's a bad thing."

He winced. "Sorry. The Malcolm ladies sometimes have windmills in their heads, and I do not fully comprehend their rationale. It would be better if I could speak with your father, but I'm a desperate man. I'll bring Lady Aster to translate woman-speak for me, if necessary."

"Woman-speak," she said in an expressive tone that probably reflected eye-rolling, if only he could see her eyes again, but she'd retreated beneath her hood. "Yes, it would probably be better if I spoke with this Lady Aster, except you are here and she is not. I cannot imagine how we can help you."

"You *are* Miss Rochester?" Erran asked, trying not to show his disbelief that Aster had been right. "Then by all means, we must speak. I think we can help each other."

CELESTE DOUBTED that anyone could help her, but this haughty aristocrat had saved her—and their valuable shirts—from a particularly nasty misadventure. That cautious Jamar was willing to listen said much about their desperation.

She was terrified of letting anyone new into their precarious lives, and someone resistant to her . . .charms . . .seemed especially risky.

Jamar would not understand that she needed every little bit of control she possessed to hold herself together. If she could not influence this powerful gentleman by using her voice—as she did everyone else—she would never be rid of him until he had what he wanted. Without her shield, she had no backbone at all. A man like this would walk right over her.

She craved the influence and security she had lost with her father's death. Still, a man who knew a marquess and who had relations who might be distant family . . . offered some small hope.

Crushing her terror at trusting the unknown for the millionth time these past months, she opened the gate and allowed him inside. A wind greeted them as if recognizing an invader, and she shivered with the rustle of her petticoats.

Dusk had fallen, and the air was exceedingly damp. She could not, in all good conscience, leave a gentleman standing in the overgrown garden. Reluctantly, Celeste led him to the kitchen door. She wasn't about to lead him into their lives.

His Arrogance raised a noble brow as she passed by the ground floor door, but he did not comment when she led him down the mossy stone stairs instead. Inside the kitchen the fire blazed, eradicating any lingering cold and damp from outdoors. She might never become used to England's gray fogs, but the lovely hearth with its crackling flames helped immensely.

Nana had apparently been watching from the upper story and hurried to join them—fortunately, without Trevor and Sylvia. Garbed in the printed red and blue cottons of home—not the dull black uniforms of English servants—the cook and kitchen maid they'd brought with them glanced up, but accustomed to Celeste's ways, they returned to their chopping and stirring on the far end of the large cellar.

Celeste was too nervous to care how her colorful company looked in the eyes of a dignified London aristocrat. They were Jamaican, not English. He'd have to accept them as they were.

At least by bringing these few servants with her, she'd been able to save them from the earl's greed—for now. She prayed the dastard didn't know of their presence here, which was why she had insisted that Jamar stay inside. But in his male arrogance, he had refused, time and again.

She slipped off the cloak's hood and waited for the gentleman to introduce himself. To her surprise, Jamar performed the courtesy.

"Lord Erran Ives, brother to the Marquess of Ashford, our landlord," the majordomo intoned. "Miss Celeste Rochester, daughter of the late Baron Rochester." He nodded at Nana. "Miss Delphinia, our housekeeper. I am Jamar, the baron's estate manager in better times."

Brother of a marquess! This was even worse than she feared.

"Delphinia and Jamar are family to us," Celeste said stiffly. "They were given the name Rochester when they were given their freedom, as were all our people, unless they had names of their own already. If you'll have a seat, we can have coffee. We have not yet learned your custom of tea."

To his credit, his lordship pulled out chairs for both her and Nana and gestured for them to sit first. She rather missed such niceties. With a sigh of resignation, she hung up her concealing cloak. She knew her mourning gown wasn't the latest fashion and that she hadn't the buxom hourglass figure so admired by handsome gentlemen like this one. Those things no longer mattered. Survival did.

She waited until the kitchen maid set out cups and saucers and brought the coffee. It wasn't as if she knew where to start.

"Your father is deceased?" Lord Ives asked as she poured the steaming beverage and before she could summon a single opening sentence.

Her tears of grief at any mention of her beloved father had become those of self-pity, so she fought them. "On the voyage here," she acknowledged, adding cream to her coffee but not the expensive sugar. "There was a terrible storm. The crew lost men. Since Father had sailing experience, he helped out, probably saving the lives of everyone aboard when one of the masts broke, and he knew exactly how to react. But he was injured in the process, and there was no ship's surgeon. Despite every effort, we did not have enough knowledge to save him."

And still, after all these months, she choked back a sob—of

sorrow and of exhaustion. Her sheltered life had not prepared her for these months of tribulation.

"That was in spring," Jamar said, taking up the story when she could not speak further. "The baron wished to bring his daughters out in London society and give his son an Oxford education. His executors have other ideas."

Sipping her coffee to steady her nerves, Celeste watched Lord Ives' dark eyes narrow, as if he saw an opportunity. She feared the advantage would be all his and none of theirs. She was discovering that was how this gray, clammy world worked.

"And your mother?" he inquired with caution.

"Deceased, several years past," Jamar answered for her.

His lordship nodded. "Leaving the burden on your shoulders, I understand. If I might suggest . . .I often act as a solicitor for my family. If you give me the name of the firm handling your father's estate," Lord Ives said, "I can carry out any dealings with them that you require. Sometimes, men of business are not amenable to persuasion from females, but they *will* listen to authority."

Celeste didn't even bother testing her charm but spoke bluntly. "His executor is my father's cousin, Quigley, the Earl of Lansdowne."

His lordship covered his shock well, but she could tell by the way he sat back and sipped his coffee before replying that he saw the obstacle, even if he didn't know the goal.

"The earl is . . . a trifle strapped for cash, I hear," he said in a far more polite tone than Lansdowne deserved.

"For all I know, the earl is a degenerate who has gambled away his estate," she said flatly, tempering her anger. "He has stolen my brother's inheritance for his own purposes and is at this moment arranging to sell all my father's free people, claiming there is no proof of their freedom. That is a lie."

Lord Erran glanced at Jamar, who nodded once. That he turned to a *man* to verify her declaration irritated her even more. She bit her tongue, knowing she could not expect more of this starched and stiff nobleman.

"I witnessed the signing of the freedom papers and the baron's will," Jamar said. "You must understand that on the island, we do not have access to your courts of law. The papers should have been properly registered with authorities on the island and a copy sent to solicitors here in England for filing, but we have no proof. We have sent for additional copies, but the earl has placed his people in control of the plantation. They will not give our representatives access to the baron's office."

"This does not explain why Miss Rochester is being attacked in the streets," his lordship said, drawing out his words as if he was thinking while he spoke. "Do you think the earl is to blame for that?"

"Unless you believe in coincidence," Celeste replied frostily, reminding them of her existence. "We were shattered and lost when we first arrived. Hoping for direction, we sent messages to the earl and to our half-sister, who had promised to bring us into society. We received notes of condolence only. A month later, the attacks began."

Nana finally spoke. "They were *cruel* to my little ones. Instead of sympathy, these cold English send unkind notes saying they are not in town, without saying when they might return or offering aid. We know *nothing* of this city, and they cannot even give advice. Jamar and Miss Celeste make repeated requests for allowances, for visits, for information, and we hear nothing. These are bad people. We want to go home to our families and friends, but we cannot."

Celeste patted Nana's hand, knowing her fear went deeper than expressed. The earl might sell off Nana's sons while their mother was helpless here in England.

"Lansdowne is a powerful political figure," Lord Erran said with a frown. "He may be strapped for cash, but I have not heard that he is so degenerate as to ignore his own relations."

"Why would my father allow a bankrupt to be executor of his will?" Celeste cried in frustration. "I do not understand how this earl we do not know can control our property and lives!"

"Your father may not have named him executor," his lordship explained. "If there is no formal document filed with English courts, he would be appointed executor simply as head of the family. You have not received the documents from the island authorities either?"

She shook her head. "I do not understand the delay. We wrote as soon as we realized there was a problem, months ago. There has been time enough for a reply. I fear Lansdowne's hired help has intercepted them."

"Do you know your father's solicitors here in London?"

She was terrified he was simply another swindler out to deprive them of what little they had. She despised living in fear, but she'd lost all her security when her father died. If her persuasive voice had failed her too . . .She had *nothing*. Catastrophe loomed a single word away, no matter how she looked at it. She didn't reply.

Jamar gave his lordship the name of the firm. He'd been handling Rochester affairs for decades. He knew these things better than she anyway.

"It's a decent firm," Lord Erran acknowledged. "I'll draw up a statement that you can sign appointing me as your man of business in your father's London affairs, and I'll see what I can find out. Sometimes, it's simply a matter of who is standing in the office at the time a question comes up. If Lansdowne stepped up, they might take an earl's word over a dead man's."

"Sign papers?" Celeste panicked, fearing anything that might give him authority over her. "Why can you not simply take me to these solicitors and let me speak with them? What do you expect in return for helping us?"

Nana squeezed her hand, but Celeste was not reassured. She could tell from his lordship's hesitation that he most definitely wanted something—and this was his family's house.

A commotion on the stairs interrupted any reply their visitor might make. Already on edge, Celeste rose to meet whatever calamity had arrived on their doorstep now.

"Celeste, there are soldiers out front!" Trevor shouted before he'd even reached the kitchen.

Every chair at the table scraped back.

Four

ERRAN HELD HIS HAND up to prevent his hostess from fleeing up the stairs. "London doesn't have an army. We do have a fairly new and inexperienced police force. Let me handle this."

The sad story their tenants had recited of thieving executors wasn't uncommon. The Chancery Court was buried in similar civil complaints, and it could take years to untangle lost or unregistered documents. Usually, only the lawyers came out ahead, so Miss Rochester had every right to be suspicious of him.

But *Lansdowne* . . . The irony of the earl's relations landing in an Ives' residence didn't escape him. The Whig party needed Lansdowne's support in this next election. Lansdowne was playing the reformists and Tories against each other, no doubt in an attempt to fill his coffers. Antagonizing the man at a politically sensitive time like this— would not aid Ashford's candidate for prime minister.

The whole point of gaining this house was so Ashford could come to London and twist the arms of men like Lansdowne.

Erran took the kitchen stairs two at a time, passing a lanky youth resembling the woman below. With her striking eyes and lush lips, the lady had an expressive countenance that had almost caused him to lose the path of his thoughts several times. The boy was less prepossessing and more terrified.

Erran could hear the rustle of petticoats as Miss Rochester followed him up. Of course the woman hadn't stayed behind. And from the sounds of it, the others were on her heels.

From the top of the back stairs, he could hear pounding on the front panel. The racket echoed in the nearly bare, dark-wainscoted corridor. He had vague recollections of this house from his childhood, but it had been leased to tenants for decades. He didn't recall the emptiness. Or if a knocker had ever existed on the door. The pounding was quite loud enough without one.

"Don't answer it," Miss Rochester whispered, grabbing Erran's arm and nearly upsetting his balance with the proximity to her lush scent. "They'll go away. Everyone always does."

"And then they throw rocks and chamber pots at you," he responded in disgust. "Hiding is no solution."

She held his arm with long fingers and pressed close enough that her skirts brushed his legs. "It's *my* solution. I have not given you permission to run our lives."

He'd never backed down from a challenge in his life—except from his inexplicable, potentially dangerous vocal ability. *I will not shout, I will not . . .* he chanted internally.

Keeping his tone even, he replied with patience, "They will simply keep coming back. At some point, they will batter the door down. Let me handle this while I am here. You and your siblings stay out of sight. This is my family's house. I do not have to tell them you are in residence."

That seemed to satisfy her. She studied him through wide, up-tilted eyes that jolted his pulse, then ushered her brother, Jamar, and a young woman he hadn't seen earlier into a front chamber. She closed the heavy dark oak door to the foyer, and he could hear the click of a latch.

He'd like to think she was a woman of sense, but most likely, she would come after him with a tomahawk if he failed. He straightened his neckcloth, checked his buttons, and ran his hand through his disheveled hair. Donning his best glare, he opened the door.

A rotund bailiff Erran recognized from the courts stood on the step, his waistcoat stained with gravy and his outdated overcoat open to make room for his paunch. Behind him stood two trim policemen in their new uniforms, looking vaguely uncertain. Erran doubted they were accustomed to knocking on the doors of the wealthy.

He crossed his arms and glared down at the shorter bailiff. "What the devil do you mean by raising this rumpus? Do you wish to disturb the entire neighborhood at this hour?"

"We're to evict these here tenants," the bailiff said with an air of accomplishment, pointing at a battered document he produced from his pocket.

Erran prayed his hostess couldn't hear that or she'd never speak to him again. "Then you have the wrong house. I am the brother of the marquess of Ashford, and we *own* this place and have so for a century. You cannot evict us from our own home."

He snatched the document from the bailiff's grubby hand while the young policemen looked even more uncertain. Shaking the paper open, Erran peered at it in the fading light, finding the name of Lansdowne's solicitors on the last page.

Damn. Duncan was going to despise knowing a potential political ally was a bully and a thief. He could hope this was the solicitor's work and that the earl didn't know about it.

"This is a fraud," he said, looking over the bailiff's head to his uniformed escort. "The marquess would not evict himself, and these papers are not penned by his solicitor. Ashford is ill and is not to be disturbed, which is why the knocker is *not* on the door," he said pointedly. "Should you trouble us again with this taradiddle, we'll have all of you arrested!"

"It's not for his lordship," the bailiff tried to protest. "It's for these here foreigners that been walking our decent streets! Look at them names. It don't say Ashford."

Erran forced down his desire to experiment with his courtroom bellow. He was a civilized lawyer, not a beast who menaced the stupid. "It says *Rochester,* a very proper family who happen to be our guests and our cousins. That's *Baron* Rochester to you, and they're as English as I am. I have my doubts about your origins, however."

While the bailiff flapped his gums incoherently, Erran glanced back to the policemen. "If you good sirs would remove this repugnant piece of filth from our doorstep, the marquess will show his appreciation later."

Bribery, they understood. Nodding respectfully, they grabbed the bailiff's elbows and led him off, protesting, into the dusk.

Erran shut the door. Before he could completely process the pure brutality of such fraud, the drawing room door opened and the Rochesters rushed out. Their dignified majordomo merely watched over them without expression.

"You should have shown us that document," the lady said angrily. "How do we know that it didn't come from the marquess and you were simply covering up the bad timing?"

"Dashitall, you're a suspicious wench." From his pocket, Erran produced the document he'd pilfered. "Here. Take it somewhere with light. I merely glanced at the names, but I recognize the earl's solicitor."

The boy held out his hand. "We have not been introduced, sir. I am Trevor, Baron Rochester."

He could not be older than sixteen, much the same age of the blond girl beside him. The boy had his older sister's dark coloring but lacked her extraordinarily light eyes. His as yet unformed features promised his sister's handsomeness, but the plump bottom lip looked more petulant than pretty at the moment. His blond sister possessed the blue eyes but not the dark coloring or the striking cheekbones of her siblings. Still, she was pleasant enough and would do well when it came time to present her.

Erran shook the boy's hand and introduced himself while keeping an eye on the older sister. Miss Rochester lit a candle and was perusing the eviction notice with more care than he had.

"He is saying the rents must be returned to the estate, and we must move by the end of next month! Is this at all legal?" she asked in dismay.

"Not in the least," Erran said with assurance. "If you'll return the paper to me, I'll show it to our firm and have them respond appropriately with threats of lawsuits and criminal trespass. My assumption is that—if Lansdowne is truly behind this—he wants the cash your father paid to lease this place. Such a sum would stave off the worst of his debtors."

She slumped dejectedly onto an old wooden settle. "Our own family wishes to throw us into the streets?"

"He doesn't even know us," the younger sister said, patting her on the shoulder. "If he cares at all, he may assume we can go to Mother's family or our half-sister."

"Your mother has family here?" Erran asked, consumed with curiosity. He really needed to be encouraging them to run to any other family, so Dunc could have his house back. But their executor's dirty trick had raised his unholy need to fight injustice.

For all her strength in the face of adversity, the lady looked frail and vulnerable. Erran wasn't in the habit of taking care of others, but her defense of her siblings appealed to his better instincts.

"Distant family, possibly," she finally replied. "Mother was born in Jamaica. We lost her to an epidemic a few years ago. She used to correspond with people here, but we never met them, and from what little she said, she had never met them either."

Erran rubbed his hair. "I don't suppose she kept journals, did she?"

All three of the siblings stared at him. The young blonde was the first to respond. "Why, yes, as do we. It is a family tradition."

"Malcolms, of course," he said in resignation. "As I mentioned, my sister-in-law believes you're related to her family, although I thought the *Malcolm* in your family name was from your father's side. I will return with Lady Azenor on the morrow, if I might, and leave you undisturbed for the rest of the evening." He bowed.

"Wait a minute!" Miss Rochester leapt up and caught his arm again.

He liked the way she touched him so easily. He also approved of the way her head rose past his shoulder. Her lips would be right where he could lean over and...

He had to *evict* her. Prurient thoughts were inappropriate. He waited patiently in the glow of the one candle.

"You did not tell us your urgent matter. If you are to help us, how might we help you?" she asked in concern.

"You can't," he said curtly. "I doubt anyone can. I'll let Lady Azenor explain. It involves more mumbo-jumbo than I'm prepared to relate."

And he was fairly certain that telling them he needed them out of his brother's house immediately would not go over well. He should bask in the lady's approval for this one brief moment, before she returned to regarding him with well-deserved suspicion.

BITING HER BOTTOM LIP, Celeste pulled back the faded drapery to watch his handsome lordship stride down the road as if he hadn't a care in the world. She knew better. She'd seen the weariness in his eyes and heard the worry in his voice.

"He saved us from the earl's treachery," Sylvia said hesitantly. "He's a good man, yes? We can trust him?"

"We can't trust anyone," Trevor responded angrily. "They're all as bad as pirates in this place.

"It's not as if we can trust everyone in Jamaica," Jamar said with his usual complacency. "Our neighbors will jump at the opportunity to buy our people even knowing they are free."

"Papa protected us from seeing the evil," Sylvia said sadly.

As Celeste could not. She hadn't the strength to carry this

burden alone, so she had inflicted her fear on Trevor and Sylvia. She regretted that. "Let us see about fixing supper, and then we must hurry and finish more shirts. I have told Mr. Taylor we must raise our prices or sell them ourselves. He has agreed to pay more, but only if we can continue producing in the same quantity. We cannot let him down."

"I should be doing more to help," Trevor grumbled. "We cannot afford Oxford now, so studying is wasted time."

There was her real hope in inviting Lord Erran into their household. The brother of a marquess would surely know how one went about teaching a boy to be a baron and the owner of a vast plantation—

One that would be bankrupt and without field hands before Trevor came of age, if the earl had anything to say about it.

She would fight until her dying breath for their home and her family, but she rather suspected a man as evil as Lansdowne was capable of arranging that too.

"Let us see what his lordship's family can do to help," she replied with more equanimity than she felt.

"It's rather like choosing the devil you know or the one you don't, isn't it?" Trevor asked, sensing her hesitation.

"Yes, rather," she agreed, without adding that Lord Erran's devils must be great for him to agree to help complete strangers. "Except we don't really know Lansdowne any better than Lord Erran, do we? So it's in ourselves that we must trust. We have this home, and we have our talents. Let us put them to the best use."

What worried her most was that her best talent apparently did not work on the very autocratic Lord Erran. His family *owned* this house, and she could say or do nothing that would stop him from taking it if he wished.

Losing another home would shatter her—and her family. She could not let that happen, if she must cause rioting in the streets to prevent it.

And she could. She'd done it before.

Five

LATE THAT EVENING, Erran slammed his fist into a heavy canvas punching bag, relishing the release of frustration. He followed with repeated blows using both fists, working up a sweat and hoping to clear his head.

He could still smell Miss Rochester's floral scent, feel her slender waist close to his and the softness of her breasts crushed against his chest. He wanted to beat Lansdowne's solicitors and half the world into a pulp for harming such a delicate blossom.

And he needed to put her out of her home—Ashford's home.

He whacked the heavy bag again, until it slammed into the wall behind it.

"Natural aggression is a good thing," his Uncle Pascoe's voice said from the cellar doorway. "But it ought to be channeled into more useful pursuits."

"Right." Erran wiped his brow on his drenched shirtsleeve. "I'll punch a few boneheads, shall I?"

"Personally, I prefer chasing women for release of tension, but you apparently have different tastes. Does this have anything to do with removing the tenants from Ashford's house?" Dressed in frock coat and pleated linen, still wearing his gloves from outdoors, Pascoe leaned his broad shoulder against the wall and twirled an affected walking stick.

His uncle was only in his early thirties and as hale and hearty as Erran, but Pascoe's political role required that he play the part of effete gentleman.

"Your multi-talented valet has learned to use a crimping iron?" Erran asked, nodding at the pleated shirt, unwilling to discuss his reason for pounding the sawdust-filled bag. "I've admired them but I'm not about to learn to crimp them."

Pascoe glanced down at his shirt. "There's a tailor near St. James that sells them with the pleats neatly sewn in. Merritt is most appreciative that he needn't learn crimping. Besides, the brats would only rip up anything not sewn down."

Pascoe had twins still in the nursery, with no wife to care for them. Erran admired the man's ability to deal with household, politics, and family—except it made Erran look like a milksop for not being able to handle the one job he'd been given.

He grabbed a towel to wipe himself down. "Useful to know. I'll look for him next time I'm down there."

"And the reason you're beating a bag into submission?" Pascoe pushed.

Erran had hung the bag in an unused portion of Pascoe's wine cellar so it was available when the boxing salons weren't open. They had no audience and could speak plainly here.

"It has everything to do with the world being a rotten core inhabited by worms," Erran said in disgust, not acknowledging that a woman was at the core of his particular apple. "I need Lady Aster's genealogical charts. Have she and Theo left for Surrey yet?"

"Surely you jest?" Pascoe said with a laugh. "You have given her new material with these New World arrivals. She's frothing at the bit. If you do not introduce her, she will introduce herself. She told Theo to hie himself home for the harvest, if he needed, but she was staying here. And this from newlyweds. It's a wonder Theo isn't over here staving in your head."

"Poor thug, torn between duty and a woman. Rather him than me." Except, by Jove, that was exactly where he was. Disgruntled, Erran yanked his waistcoat over his damp shirt. "I don't know how much of the tale Lady Aster should be given. It involves Lansdowne and filthy tricks. Theo won't appreciate involving his bride, and Dunc won't appreciate our interference."

"Ah, now I see the difficulty. This is not a task you can punch your way out of, and finesse with ladies is not your style." Pascoe nodded understandingly. "From all reports, the election date will fall in November. It's more important that we have Duncan in place than worrying about one earl's favor. Shall I attend Lady Aster in her visit with her new relations? Will that persuade them from the house any faster?"

"Nothing will persuade them from that house, I'm convinced." He should be grateful for his uncle's offer, but Erran wasn't a shirker who could send a busy man like Pascoe in his place. "There are a number of legal matters involved. Lansdowne is head of their household. They claim he has usurped their inheritance and is trying to drive them out of the house and into the streets. At the moment, he's merely using trickery, thinking they're easily frightened naïfs. He'll escalate to warfare, if necessary, to drive them out and demand the lease money back from Dunc for his own coffers. That would be our simplest solution."

Pascoe frowned, either hearing his reluctance or understanding the lack of scruples involved.

Erran sighed in resignation. "If Lady Aster can prove the tenants are related to us, I'll have better leverage with the estate solicitors. Lady Aster it will have to be. Once their funds are safe, perhaps we could find them a smaller place for less cost."

Pascoe frowned. "I don't like it. Lansdowne could be testing Ash. Montfort and Caldwell are wooing the earl's favor for the Tories and have shown themselves willing to join in his schemes."

Sir George Caldwell and Lord Henry Montfort were Ashford's country neighbors, staunch conservatives who opposed everything Ives represented. Their scruples were questionable. Erran smacked the bag again.

"If that pair were truly behind the attack on a man as powerful as Duncan, what might they do to ladies if Lansdowne asks it of them?" Pascoe asked.

"Ladies who have no power? Nothing besides threats," Erran said with a shrug. "If Lansdowne is truly at fault, he's after cash. It takes wealth to buy votes, and he has exhausted his. Montfort and Caldwell are far more likely to come after *me* if they believe I am intervening between the earl and the Rochester money."

"I dislike playing our hand too soon." Pascoe twirled his stick thoughtfully. "We need to install Ashford discreetly, so the Tories won't realize he's back in play. Any chance your ladies and the young baron will be willing to share the house?"

Erran tried to imagine the terrified Rochesters dealing with Duncan's roars of fury and frustration and couldn't. But then, he was a lawyer and better at strategy than understanding a woman's nature. "That's one solution. I'll call on Lady Aster and we'll see what can be done," he said noncommittally.

Perhaps his sister-in-law could talk Miss Rochester into signing papers so he could take himself off to the executors and courts and places where he knew what he was doing—far, far away from seductive scents and mysterious females with eyes the color of peaceful seas.

***

THE NEXT MORNING, after receiving a note from Lady Azenor Ives requesting a visit, Celeste dithered in front of the old-fashioned cheval mirror that had come with the furnished household. Her hair was the dismal color of blackened walnut and refused to curl into feminine ringlets. All she could do was pin her thick braids into an elaborate chignon and pretend she was fashionable.

Sylvia waltzed in, sporting her best lavender silk, wearing her blond tresses in charming curls to frame her face. "Lavender is suitable for mourning, is it not?" she asked with a frown. "I don't want the lady to take a distaste for me."

"It has been almost six months. I think you'll be fine. It's not as if anyone knew Father or cares when he died," Celeste said, hiding the pang of grief at this huge hole in their lives. "I am simply amazed that she responded so quickly after Lord Erran told her of us."

She feared they would merely be a subject of dinner table gossip for the next week and no more, but she had to take the chance. Risk-taking had ruined their lives, but sometimes, one had to take risks or surrender.

"Wear your cashmere shawl," Sylvia recommended. "It is very elegant and makes your eyes even more blue. At least we will not look like poor relations."

No, they would look like old-fashioned colonial relations, but that could not be helped. Their talents for sewing had to be applied to projects that provided an income. Adding wide sleeves and lowering hems to fit more petticoats didn't fit into their goals.

"Do we entertain them upstairs or down?" Sylvia asked worriedly. "The parlors are so very drab."

"If we bring them upstairs, there's a chance they might see our fabrics and machine and realize that we're working for a living. Let us keep visitors to the downstairs and attempt to maintain the pretense that we're genteel. Although I hate to open the draperies on the street to brighten that room. It will let people know we're home and make the disrepair more obvious." Celeste glanced out the upstairs parlor window at the busy street below, fretting over the decision.

"Let's open them just a little," Sylvia pleaded. "We can't burn oil in the middle of the day!"

That would be an additional expense, so Celeste reluctantly nodded agreement. "We've dusted and cleaned as much as possible. They're our landlords, after all, they should realize the state the house is in."

Jamar had installed a door knocker for the occasion. The rap at the door ended any further fretting. Celeste shook out her skirt over all the petticoats she owned, sent up a prayer of hope, and hurried down the stairs. Jamar played the part of butler, waiting for them to enter the front drawing room before opening to their guests. Sylvia hurried to tug the drapery back just enough to allow in a ray of morning light.

Garbed in her usual plain gray broadcloth, Nana arrived to arrange a tea tray as the guests were introduced into the front room.

Lord Erran was dressed in a faultless tailored black coat and starched linen. His dark curls were a little less wind-blown today, and he'd shaved recently. Celeste could see a glisten of moisture in his sideburns, which almost made him human today. To distract from that unwelcome notion, she curtseyed for the lady he introduced as Lady Azenor, his sister-in-law.

The lady wore an extraordinary silk gown of an iridescent peacock hue with only a minimum of petticoats and no elaborate full sleeves. Her hat, however, was the height of extravagance, with ribbons and feathers and straw . . .stars? She carried a large tapestry bag crammed with papers that she instantly set on a faded chair and rummaged through.

"It is an amazing delight to meet you," the lady said with excitement. She was short and plump and not the least bit intimidating as she unrolled papers. "I am so eager to confirm our charts . . . But all of you look just like portraits in the family gallery. My father collects them, you see."

Celeste didn't exactly see, but she managed a smile. "Please, have a seat. Sylvie, if you'd pour . . ." She glanced at his towering lordship, who stood with hands behind his back, studying the aging room as if prepared to deconstruct it. "Do you prefer coffee or tea, sir?" They'd purchased tea for the occasion. She hoped they'd bought the preferred kind.

Lady Azenor happily settled on a broad horsehair sofa and spread her charts out on a low table. "Tea with milk would be lovely. I think this is the family line you descend from." She pointed her gloved finger at a paper.

Lord Erran paced the parlor on his long legs, frowning at the damp spots under the windows and glancing up at the peeling paint on the molded plaster ceiling. "Coffee will be fine, thank you. Are you having problems with roof leaks?"

Wearing his Sunday frock coat and neck tie, Trevor spoke up. "In the north corner, sir. We've put buckets in the attic."

His lordship muttered and looked as if he was prepared to take on the attics, but Lady Azenor interrupted. "Here it is, Sir Trevelyan Rochester and Lady Lucinda Malcolm. Are these your ancestors, do you know?"

Celeste nodded. "Our paternal great-grandparents. Lady Lucinda was a well-known artist in the islands, and Sir Trevelyan eventually became Lord Rochester, a baron in his own right due to some service for the Crown. We have portraits of both of them over the mantel at home." She bit her lip and tried not to worry that their uncle might sell even their precious family portraits.

Lord Erran absent-mindedly sipped the coffee Sylvia had poured for him and examined the floor boards. Perhaps he did not approve of his sister-in-law's interest in their family relationship?

In any case, Lady Azenor reacted with delight. "Do you paint as Lady Lucinda did? She was said to have the gift of foresight and painted her predictions on the canvas."

Celeste could answer that honestly. "I've not a drop of her talent." She didn't need to mention any other, although it was interesting that the sophisticated lady knew the family legend and seemed to believe in superstition and magic.

The lady didn't express disappointment. "My genealogies list Malcolm descendants back to the 1600s, and they all have different abilities. Your great-grandmother, Lady Lucinda Malcolm Childe, the prescient artist, was a cousin of Ninian Malcolm, the wife of the fifth earl of Ives and Wystan. Ninian was a talented healer and herbalist. Our current Marquess of Ashford and his brothers are her direct descendants. So they are your distant cousins," she exclaimed with all the triumph of a conquering general. "My relationship is a trifle murkier and not as direct, but who cares about a few centuries? We are all family!"

Celeste wasn't certain she followed all the names, but she understood the lady's excitement—in some way, no matter how distant, they were all related. She had *family*—and they were willing to claim the relationship. She couldn't explain even to herself how much it meant not to be alone. But what could the connection mean to their aristocratic visitors?

"We are *all* in the way of cousins?" Celeste asked tentatively. Even Sylvia and Trevor sat up straighter, waiting for an answer.

"Probably more distant than most royalty, but we are all cousins, even Lord Erran. One assumes the Earl of Lansdowne is head of your father's *paternal* branch, but we are your great-grandmother's branch. And Malcolm women control their own destinies."

The lady sat back and gave Lord Erran a look of satisfaction. "There will be Malcolm documents giving Miss Rochester control of her grandmother's portion, beyond any shadow of a doubt. We tie up our dowries tighter than any male entail, and they descend through the generations. So if part of Sir Trevelyan's property came from Lady Lucinda's dowry, then the funds set aside for their descendants could be substantial, and Lansdowne cannot touch them."

"The courts will want documents," his lordship said forbiddingly, draining the lady's excitement. "Until we lay hands on those, all we can do is offer our protection."

"Oh, we'll do much more than that," Lady Azenor corrected, rolling up her charts. "There are a great many of us, after all, and we are all very well-connected. You men can play with courts and papers and official business. The women will ram our willpower down Lansdowne's throat."

Celeste thought the large, authoritative gentleman looked as if he might strangle on his own tongue at that pronouncement.

Abruptly, the heavy brass vase on the mantel toppled to the hearth with a thud loud enough to mean damage to both hearth and vase.

Six

ERRAN WINCED at the toppling vase and leaned over to retrieve it. A substantial dent marred the base. "The mantel is no doubt tilted," he said aloud, quelling his own superstitious theories. Surely raging with frustration didn't affect inanimate objects. "Perhaps the floor vibrates."

The ladies frowned, then shrugging, returned to their insane discussion of ramming their wishes down Lansdowne's throat.

Just the thought had Erran vibrating—but he could do nothing. Until proven otherwise, the earl had to be considered both a possible ally—and a dangerous enemy.

To keep his vexation to himself, Erran counted off steps in the front chamber. He calculated the approximate depth of the house and multiplied it by the width to determine if there would be sufficient space for Duncan's apartments.

Most of the family, including himself, had hoped they'd be able to use the upper stories for their own quarters so they needn't pay the exorbitant rents elsewhere. Jacques, his half-brother, in particular, was hoping to move out of Theo and Aster's city house.

But it appeared that Lady Aster meant to treat the Rochesters as long-lost relations and leave them installed here while the women connived in matters over their heads. Erran had no power to overrule her. Desperate heir or not, Theo had attics to let for marrying into a family as manipulative as Lady Aster's.

It simply wouldn't suit to leave unchaperoned single ladies in the same house with unrelated bachelors—especially Duncan, who was the whole point of this venture. The Rochesters *had* to leave.

Restless, Erran pondered a means to explore the remainder of the house. A leaky roof meant he needed to call in construction workers immediately. With one ear, he listened to the discussion of Malcolm documents. He was not yet inured to the notion of women managing their own affairs and couldn't imagine their documents would amount to anything.

When the excited chatter fell to a natural silence, Erran spoke up. "As I mentioned earlier, I'll draw up a paper for you to sign, Miss Rochester, authorizing me to deal with your father's solicitors. As you are unmarried and the legal age of majority, you have the authority to act on your own. You could potentially assume guardianship of your siblings, but we really need your father's will before we can assume you inherit any portion of his property. The land will otherwise fall to your brother, who is a minor, and Lansdowne can fight for his guardianship."

"Why can I not deal with my father's solicitors directly?" Miss Rochester asked. "I have written to them here and in the islands, but so far the only response I've received is that they need permission from Lansdowne. I just cannot imagine that."

She had a voice that rivaled the best orchestra he'd ever heard— not that he attended musicales with any frequency. Still, her every word was a song. He could see everyone in the room waiting, entranced, for his reply.

Which was when he realized it was unlike Lady Aster to remain silent for long—as if she were truly *spellbound.*

Erran raised a quizzical eyebrow at this oddity but nodded to acknowledge the question. "You have the right to question the solicitors directly, certainly. But as the eldest male in the family, Lansdowne is asserting his authority by refusing to give you access to the documents. If they exist, they should be a matter of public record. The question is whether or not the will exists or has been filed with the courts. If there is no will, then Lansdowne has strong rights in the matter. I can search court records, but while I'm at it, I would like to make our case to appoint you as guardian."

"May I go with you?" she asked in a voice that sounded sweet as chimes—but concealed a demand.

Again, Lady Aster raised no objection—although she had to know there were dozens of reasons Miss Rochester could not accompany him. What on earth was wrong with the woman? Did she *want* the Rochesters to hate him for rejecting all their pleas?

Stifling his irritation and maintaining a composed tone, he replied, "Of course you can accompany me. There won't be another lady within a mile of the City, your reputation will be shattered, and any chance of winning the case will be lost, but I have no other objection to your accompaniment. Ladies do not have the same freedom in England as in the colonies."

Her frown was ferocious. Oddly, that made Erran smile inside. She looked so damned fragile and vulnerable with all that heavy mahogany hair balanced on such a slender neck.... But her spirit was indomitable.

"I see," she said coldly.

As if a spell had been broken, Lady Aster spoke up. "Let us have Ashford demand that the solicitors come here."

Miss Rochester looked almost as surprised as Erran felt. Something dodgy was happening here. He wouldn't have noticed— except for his own experience with the Wyrd. Hands behind his back, he rocked a bit on his boot heels, watching—and listening—to the ladies at work. He deliberately ignored the errant brass vase.

Now addressing Lady Aster instead of himself, Miss Rochester chatted excitedly in melodious tones, arranging his day—and probably his future. His damned sister-in-law didn't find it in the least odd that he'd been excluded from the conversation that essentially involved him carrying out their plans. She was indulging every word Miss Rochester spoke, without argument.

He glanced at the siblings. Miss Sylvia appeared pleased simply to follow the conversation. The boy looked bored and discontent.

"Let us inspect the attics, shall we?" Erran asked the lad, with deliberate intent. He watched to see if the ladies took notice. They did not.

Gratified to be acknowledged, Trevor eased from his chair, keeping one eye on his sister as he followed Erran toward the door. Completely focused on their plotting, neither lady paid attention to their departure.

Erran mentally measured the front hall and peered into the foyer's anteroom on the far side of the wide staircase. He didn't think it would take more than a general refurbishment to make the front rooms suitable for a marquess who needed to entertain his political allies. He needed to see the area behind the stairs for suitability as Duncan's private chambers. The stairs were too dangerous for his brother for now.

Trevor led Erran up the dark oak staircase—it should probably be painted to brighten the hallway. On the family floor, the carpeting was threadbare and would need removing. Lady Aster would no doubt be delighted to take charge. Erran followed the boy toward the back of the house, glancing in each room with an open door.

He halted at the sound of a machine whirring behind a closed panel.

It took a moment before Trevor noticed he'd stopped following. The boy looked uneasy at seeing where Erran stood.

"The stairs to the attic are at the far end." Trevor nodded in the direction he'd been heading.

"I like working with machinery," Erran said, honestly. If there had been any money in patenting his hay baler, he would have enthusiastically given up law. But he didn't have the ability to sell his ideas, and instead, indulged his mechanical aptitude with experimenting when he had the chance. "May I see what you're operating in here?"

He didn't give the boy time to object but pushed open the door.

The plump African lady who had served their tea earlier sat at a machine that she worked with her foot. She appeared to be pushing pieces of linen beneath a needle that pumped up and down as she pedaled.

At his entrance, she instantly stopped and folded her hands in her lap, so it took him a moment to realize what she'd been doing.

She'd been sewing! With a machine.

"It's just something Papa put together to help the women make shirts," Trevor whispered anxiously. "Nana doesn't like to be disturbed. Please, let us go."

"If it works, it's ingenious," Erran said with genuine admiration, ignoring the boy's warning. "You could make your fortune selling this to tailors and seamstresses." He addressed the disapproving older woman waiting for them to depart. "Might I take a look at the machine?"

"It is old," she said stiffly. "It will soon wear out."

"Not if the parts can be replaced," Erran said cheerfully, crouching down to examine the mechanism when the woman pushed her chair away. "He used screws to hold it to the cabinet! Where did he find them? This one should be tightened."

He produced a knife from his pocket and proceeded to twist the metal head back into place.

ONCE SHE and the delightful Lady Azenor had worked out the

details of how she might keep control of her family's affairs rather than hand them over to Lord Erran, Celeste realized the men had left the room.

Alarmed, she glanced around. Sylvia reminded them of the attic leak conversation.

"Erran loves fixing things," Lady Azenor said with a dismissive wave. "Not only does he enjoy fixing legal puzzles and injustices, he mends plumbing and machines. He'll have repaired the roof and will be looking for more things to do. Shall we see what they have found?"

Celeste was terrified of what he could have found. Since the lady was already rising and heading for the door, she had no choice but to follow. It had been a relief finding that she hadn't lost her ability to persuade, but just as she'd thought she'd reclaimed her authority, his wretched lordship had stolen it again.

He hadn't been at all swayed by her voice, drat the man. How would she ever induce him to go along with what she and Lady Azenor had planned?

To her utter horror—but not surprise—they found Lord Erran sprawled beneath her father's sewing mechanism. His lordship had grease on his linen and a knife in his hand and bits and pieces of everything all over the floor. Nana stoically looked on as Trevor fashioned a circle from wire while his lordship gave instructions.

Celeste remembered her father doing exactly the same, and she fought a wave of nostalgia—and admiration. "Really, my lord, it is not necessary for you to fix everything in our lives."

He didn't even bother looking up, although his once-immaculate clothing was now rumpled and dusty. "This is a rare pleasure. Consider it payment for my legal services, such as they are."

She glanced to Lady Azenor. "Is he quite mad?"

The lady laughed. "Ashford will not let him near the mines or the steamships for fear he will take apart all the equipment and not be able to put it back together again. But Erran has been quite clever in installing gas lighting in my parlor."

"It would be simpler if I could rip out the walls," the gentleman said from beneath the table. "I'm thinking that needs to be done here, but there isn't time for that amount of repair."

He backed out and took the wire ring from Trevor. Glancing up at Celeste, he actually grinned. The sardonic gentleman with the disapproving glare actually *grinned.*

"I'll have this right in a trice. I need better parts, but these will do for now. I can draw up a patent application, but it would be best to keep it to yourself until Trev is old enough to sell the idea to people who can manufacture it." He slid beneath the table again.

He didn't mind that they were sewing shirts for strangers? That they were essentially in trade? Celeste bit a fingernail and tried hard to believe that. What was a patent application?

"First, we must retrieve the Rochesters' plantation and fortune from thieves," Lady Aster reminded him, tapping his boot with her shoe. "Patents are for those with leisure time. We have developed a strategy, if you'll come out from there so we might explain it."

"I'll go to the city, search for the registered will, take a letter from Ashford to the solicitors demanding that they appear here where they might be interrogated by the marquess's representatives, including Miss Rochester," Lord Erran recited. "Child's play."

Celeste refrained from rolling her eyes. She had wasted half the morning on charming Lady Azenor into this plan when she could have been sewing pleats, and his arrogant lordship had it all mapped out without her having to say a word. Having her wishes anticipated was most distressing, perplexing, and just a trifle . . . exhilarating.

Behind all that lordly linen, Lord Erran was a scarily dangerous man.

"In return, Miss Rochester has agreed that we might start fixing up the lower floors for Ashford's use," Lady Azenor explained with cheer. "The arrangement will be convenient for all of us. We have been quite busy while you've been painting yourself black."

"I have returned the machine to proper working order so Miss Delphinia might work easier," Lord Erran retorted, sliding back out again and tucking his knife away. "I'll hire an architect to begin work. I have a good man in mind, one who would delight in having his name known in these parts."

"He means one of his cousins," Lady Azenor explained. "Ives' talents are manifold. They are all dangerously intelligent, practical, and scientific, and there are far too many of them. There is always one with empty pockets who can do what's needed."

"As if you don't already have *your* cousin ready to putter in the garden," his lordship retorted, wiping his greasy hands on what had once been a pristine handkerchief. He turned to Celeste. "The lady's family are a meddling lot. Once you allow them into your life, you will never be left alone. Be certain of what you wish for."

"I wish beyond all things to have meddling family," Celeste admitted fervently. "It has been exceedingly difficult these last months of managing on our own in a strange city."

"The hard part comes when you want one thing and they insist on another," he warned.

"No, not at all." Celeste smiled. Lady Azenor had responded to her voice and acknowledged her wishes without a single objection. She was certain the rest of the lady's family could be as easily manipulated. It was only Jamar who frowned and muttered about curses when she used her charm. Celeste couldn't see any harm in persuasion when it was her only defense. "I think it only takes a little discussion for all parties to find an amicable middle ground."

She hoped and prayed the marquess would merely stay long enough to cast his vote and return to the country, leaving them alone with an improved home where she could eventually bring out Sylvia. But the return of some of their rent would ease a few of their money woes.

"You may have to find a middle ground over Lansdowne's dead body," Lord Erran reminded them. "I'll have to find out what that's about or some of his cohorts are likely to escalate to arson."

That was not the pleasantry she wished to hear, and Celeste shivered in her shoes. She would not allow her family to go homeless, ever, even if she must use her skill to persuade the earl to leap off a high cliff.

Seven

"I SWEAR TO YOU, your damned tenant is another Malcolm witch," Erran declared in disgruntlement, putting his boots up on the marquess's desk and swilling the brandy offered. "I don't know if it's wise to put you in the same house with her. She'll have you voting for women's emancipation."

Ashford sipped from his glass and stared—blindly—at the wall above Erran's head. "Emancipation would not be all bad except for the battle necessary to accomplish it. I'd rather fight a war I can win."

"That's not the point!" Erran swished the brandy, searching for more goads. "Miss Rochester is devious, manipulative, and apparently dabbling in trade. We would fare better moving her out of the house entirely, but the women are resisting. They think the house is enchanted or some such rot."

The marquess snorted. "Lady Aster reads her family's journals. They're packed with such idiocy. It gives the women something to talk about. I'm less concerned with the ladies and more concerned with Lansdowne. I was hoping to sway his vote, but if we take the Rochesters under our wing and threaten his income, he's likely to turn against us. I suppose I'll have to move in just to keep security on the place."

Erran slammed his hand down on the desk so Dunc could hear his exasperation—even though his brother was saying exactly what Erran wanted to hear. Manipulating Dunc didn't set well, but dammit, a brilliant mind shouldn't be left to rot.

"Fine, then. Have eggs flung at you and the roof fall on your head in the next hard rain." Erran meant every word he said, knowing his obstinate brother would do exactly the opposite of what he suggested. "The Rochesters will probably burn voodoo charms in the kitchen. Which is another thing . . . I'm not certain we can remove their servants and replace them with ours."

Ashford's mouth quirked. "Our *what*? Non-existent servants? Have Lady Aster magically summon a very large butler and two strong footmen to guard the doors. We'll sort the rest later."

"They have no proper chaperone," Erran argued, keeping his tone dispassionate. He intended to influence his brother, but not with any kind of . . .what? Silver tongues weren't magic, but what was the difference if he lashed out or twisted words? Either way, he was manipulating Dunc. He needed to examine his morals at a better time. "You'll ruin their reputations!"

The marquess snorted. "I'll call them my wards. No one will believe a blind man could compromise two perfectly healthy females accompanied by their brother and Nubian giants."

Erran sat up, rocking his chair to indicate surprise. "You really mean to go through with this—just move into that aging mausoleum with a flock of lunatics?"

Ashford drew a sour face. "It's no worse than sitting here moldering. At least there I can rot while talking to men with influence."

"It's on your head then," Erran declared, standing, hiding his triumph. By jingo, he could see where the power of persuasion could go to the head. "I have to head back and start digging through files to see how much Lansdowne's solicitors have destroyed or if they've ignored the courts entirely. I shall be pleased to call on you once you're installed in London so I may say I told you so."

"Go to hell," Ashford answered complacently as Erran opened the door wide enough for him to hear the hinges creak.

The blind marquess had finally agreed to leave the house! Duty accomplished—to his own amazement—Erran took the Iveston stairs to the ground floor two at a time. At the bottom, he found Theo waiting for a report. Erran slapped him on the back. "He's agreed to move to London, warts and all. Aster just needs to summon a burly butler and two giant footmen."

Theo snorted. "I could talk to him logically and explain all the reasons he needs to go to town, and he'd throw his snifter at me. You go in and tell him all the reasons he shouldn't go, and he decides town's the place to be."

Erran shrugged uncomfortably and sounded out his theory on his more scientific older brother. "I apparently possess a lawyerly ability to twist phrases to my advantage."

Theo snorted in disbelief. "Right-o. You were always a silver-tongued little mongrel. How did an uncommunicative scientist like me get stuck in this family?"

That wasn't what Erran had wanted to hear, but he played it nonchalant. "Luck, pure luck, old boy. Except you're the madman who married into your wife's witchy clan. There is no accounting for taste."

It was the damned witchy family causing his confusion. He ought to quit worrying about Cousin Sylvester, silver tongues, levitating gavels and vases, and go back to what he did best—twisting words. That's what lawyers did, right?

Erran donned his redingote and hat and pulled on his gloves. "I've sent word to Cousin Zack to meet me at the house tomorrow to look at the repairs, so I need to ride back tonight. Do you think Aster can summon servants from nowhere?"

"She has two suitable footmen trained, but she'll have to raid the staffs of her family to find a butler. She'll make it happen. She's quite taken with Miss Rochester and her family."

So was Erran, but he wouldn't admit his fascination. Women were fine in bed when one had the wherewithal. He seldom did. And he certainly had no home in which to install a wife. He had a future to build before he could even consider it. He touched the brim of his hat and set out into the dusk.

A good long ride back into the city should shake off his need to see how Miss Rochester spent her evenings.

UPON ERRAN'S RETURN to London, rioters were marching past Westminster, drunkenly smashing windows and stoning carriages. The new police force had been set up only a year ago, with this kind of commotion in mind, but they'd had a rough year and lacked experience. The mob flung stones and curses in the direction of any blue uniform, cursing Robert Peel and rudely calling them *bobbies*. Erran didn't blame the force for playing least-in-sight.

Mobs weren't uncommon, but the direction of the marchers toward the park worried him. Erran urged his horse past the relative quiet of St. James and down the side street.

He could see lights in the upper story of the townhouse, so the Rochesters were home. This back street had little activity except for people avoiding the protestors approaching the square. Recalling how Duncan's enemies had hid their depredations behind rural rioters, Erran stopped at the stable across the mews from their townhouse, boarded his horse, and entered the tavern for ale and gossip. The inhabitants were boisterous and loud but didn't appear to be violent.

Carrying his tankard to the lane between the tavern and the house, Erran lurked in the doorway, studying pedestrians hurrying through the unlit space. Oddly, lantern light glinted through the gates of the townhouse. What were the Rochesters doing in the yard at this hour?

And then he noted the darker shadow leaning against a building farther down the alley, seemingly appraising the back gate. The noise of the rioters came closer, and the shadow straightened in response, crouching down to pick up objects at his feet. *Damn.* This was no idle drunk. Erran tensed with anticipation.

At some point, bullies would have to learn that Ives protected their own.

He had grown up in an all-male household that excelled at all manner of creating havoc—it was either that, or regularly beat the stuffing out of each other. He couldn't punch an entire mob, but he knew how to distract. And his legal training had taught him a great deal about how people reacted to fear.

Besides, thrashing a lackwit was too easy and inspired only retaliation. He'd rather put fear in the lout and any of his companions.

Swinging his tankard erratically, Erran faked a drunken stagger and proceeded toward the shadow. He pretended to stumble and sloshed ale on the spy. "Oops, sorry ol' chap, tryin' to steer clear of the lion," he said in a loud sing-song.

The smaller man shoved him away in disgust. "You've wits to let. What lion?"

Erran flashed a white smile and didn't keep his voice down. He had a suspicion the light in the back yard was there for a reason. He wanted to give them warning. "The lion them furriners keep in the yard. Ain't you heard it? Sounds like it'd bite a man's head off."

"I ain't heard a thing." But he inched away from the gate.

"Sometimes, they don't feed it," Erran said knowledgeably, louder than necessary. He didn't need his impassioned Courtroom Voice to fool a fool. "That's when it growls. But I ain't goin' near.

Don't never know if the gate is barred or if it can leap over if it likes my smell."

As if on cue, a loud thump rattled the gate. Erran staggered back, as if in fear. His companion took several more steps toward the end of the mews. A low, almost realistic growl emanated from the yard. Erran had never heard a lion and wouldn't know what one would sound like, but he was pretty certain the maggot in the alley hadn't either.

Another harder thump and louder growl followed.

"It's comin' after us!" Erran hollered, shoving the man between his shoulder blades. "Run!"

The spy didn't need more encouragement. He sprinted down the alley, leaving Erran in his dust—probably because Erran was leaning against the building, downing his ale and chuckling.

"That you, Jamar?" he called quietly once the lurker was gone.

The gate slid open and the towering African gestured for Erran to enter. "He has been there for nearly an hour. The ladies were frightened by the torches and shouts down the road, so I said I would watch."

"Excellent thinking." Before crossing the mews, Erran scattered the pile of throwing-sized rocks where the lurker had stood. To his horror, he found an unlit torch among them. Surely no one meant to torch the house with people in it?

The day's weariness escalated to fury—and he kicked the pile of stones. They scattered with unusual velocity, as if shot from a cannon. Levitation involved lifting objects, did it not? Not rolling them? He must have hit them harder than he thought. Maybe the *power points* added force to his swing, he thought sardonically.

More worried about arson than stones, Erran stalked through the open gate with a sense of urgency. "Whoever is behind the alley scalawags is not a gentleman if he's capable of hiring thugs under cover of the rioters. Does it sound as if the mob is coming closer?"

Jamar frowned worriedly and hastened his step. "They have turned this way."

Damnation. He had only the one pistol and a pouch of lead shot with him. Good for close range but no more. "Don't suppose you have a shotgun?" he asked, following the giant into the back hall.

"We have swords." Jamar confirmed their lack of modern weaponry.

"Keep the ladies upstairs or in the kitchen. Shattering glass is a favorite pastime of mobs. Bring me a sword, if you can spare one. If the ruffians are out there, they may attempt rushing the house." Erran refused to believe an earl would be behind these depredations, but if Duncan's new enemies, Montfort and Caldwell, were trying to curry favor—nameless rioters were just their sort of tactic.

"If there are only a few of the ruffians, I can stop them," Erran added. Not if they came at the house with torches, but he'd have to hope they wouldn't be that daring. "Just in case, let's bring some buckets of water up here."

Looking horrified as he caught the direction of Erran's fears, Jamar took the kitchen stairs two at a time, reappearing with buckets.

Trevor raced from the upper floor a little later carrying a rapier and a short sword—the weapons of Georgian courtiers. Loading his pistol, Erran counted the blades as one step better than nothing.

"I am a dead aim with a pistol but not good with a sword," Trevor said, eyeing the long barrel of the one Erran was loading.

"I've modified this one to hold more than one round." Erran sighted along the barrel. "I cannot verify its accuracy."

Trevor waited silently for his decision. With resignation, Erran handed it over, knowing he had more strength for sword wielding than the lad.

The raucous shouts grew louder. It would be damned expensive replacing the glass windows. They'd probably been there a century or more.

The boy expertly checked the loading and sight and nodded his approval. "Thanks." A man of few words.

Erran doubted a silver tongue could persuade a mob, especially if he couldn't be heard over the drunken shouts. But if he was to test his theory and experiment, now was the time.

Before he could step outside, he winced at the sound of shattering glass up the street. Women screamed in terror. He yanked back a drapery panel, and in the torchlight, he saw the mob rocking a carriage. The terrified horses reared while the mob jeered. He didn't see a policeman anywhere.

Rage filled him. Protesting was one thing. Harming the innocent was quite another. And if this was the work of Lansdowne to drive his relations out of their home . . . he would remove the man's head—slowly and with great relish.

"Stand here," he told the boy, pointing at the front foyer. "If anyone comes in through the windows or the door, you have only five shots. Use them wisely."

The boy nodded, looking more determined than fearful.

Erran clutched the hilt of the sword, knowing the folly of going up against a drunken mob alone. But as an Ives, he never turned away from a challenge. He couldn't allow those innocent women in the carriage and their horses to suffer.

Holding both sword and rapier upright like torches, he marched down the steps and into the streets. He had no chance of being heard without shouting. If ever there was a time to experiment, it was now.

"Cease and desist!" He didn't use his courtroom fury but his bellow reverberated loudly in his own ears.

Only a few of the marchers even glanced in his direction. The others continued shouting and rocking the carriage containing the shrieking women.

Feeling like a right bloody fool marching on a mob with a sword, Erran stalked down his street like an avenging warrior. His expertise was in *building* mechanical weapons, not wielding old-fashioned swords, but he knew the basics. Stick 'em and they bleed. Rather unsporting when it came right down to it.

But he was furious enough to use the flat side of the sword to swat aside a man who approached him with fists upraised. *"Cease and desist!"* he shouted again. The man fell back, startled. That was satisfying, but not particularly unusual. Erran knew he was big and dressed like a gentleman. Most working men followed orders.

More of the cowards at the carriage turned in his direction. The ones who were merely shouting slogans began to dart uneasy looks toward the alleys. The rock-throwing lot reached for their pockets.

Erran smacked the sword against the ear of a drunk who dared fling a handful of pebbles scooped from the street. The drunk stumbled and fell, but more of the mob grew brave enough to heave their artillery at the windows high above the streets. Glass broke.

The horses screamed as the traces tilted with the carriage.

Stopping a mob by himself was futile.

Erran's sense of justice *required* that he test his damned stupid superstitious theory. Praying his fury wasn't getting the better of good sense—he lifted his sword and allowed his rage at injustice to boil over into the full power of the terrifying voice he'd used to command a courtroom. *"Drop that carriage!"*

This time, the villains halted and glanced around in panic.

The first time he'd released that peal of sound, he'd shocked himself. This time, it felt devilishly good, which probably meant he was going to hell. But the ladies and horses were still in danger. Concentrating on the carriage, Erran aimed his anger and his sword at the men with torches. *"Set the carriage down!"*

The rioters abruptly dropped the carriage in mid-push. The nearly-overturned vehicle rocked from its precarious position to miraculously fall back on its wheels.

Could he possibly have levitated a carriage?

Before Erran could sort out his next action, a sweet voice called from an upper story window in the house he'd just left. "Your families need you. Go home before anyone is hurt!"

Beneath the sweetness, Erran heard bitter anger. He glanced back to see the window open, and Miss Rochester's slender form perched on the sill. Her almond-shaped eyes had narrowed and her lips tightened in an expression that reflected a fury as great as his own. But her voice was a melodious siren call.

"Run, run before you're caught," she cried with deceptive sweetness.

And they did. With guidance now, half the mob fled. Stumbling drunkenly, they melted into the shadows. Whatever their voices were doing, it seemed to be dissolving the riot. Erran was too enraged to be amazed. Torches still advanced in this direction—the real ringleaders?

If so, he needed to know who'd hired them. Erran strode into the street, rapier in one hand, sword in the other. "Halt!" he thundered, the sound echoing off the walls.

There were more of them than him, and still they hesitated—as if he were a conquering army loaded with weaponry. Fearing for his own sanity, Erran had to force his feet to stay planted where they were. "Who sent you?" he demanded.

Before his stunned audience could respond, Celeste's celestial voice called, "There's a tankard waiting for you at the tavern!"

The torch-bearers rightfully looked confused. Was her voice

actually countermanding his? Erran glared up at her. "Go back inside," he ordered.

She didn't. So much for his Courtroom Voice if it wouldn't command one damned female.

"Tell me who sent you!" Erran roared at the ringleaders before they escaped.

"Go away, little boys," Celeste sung from on high.

Erran clutched his sword, but he didn't dare shout at her to shut up. He had no notion of what in hell was happening here, but if there was any chance he had tilted a carriage, he wasn't risking her falling out of a window because he was furious with her.

With Erran's attention diverted, his audience chose to follow Celeste's siren call. They threw down their torches to smolder in the gutter and sauntered off down alleys. The stragglers, without their leaders, threw a few punches at each other and drunkenly marched off—theoretically in the direction of a tavern.

Down the street, a servant raced out of a house to soothe the frantic horses. Two uniformed policemen finally appeared to help the women in the carriage. Only the stench of guttering torches and spilled ale remained of the riot.

Furious, Erran stomped into the house, slammed and bolted the door, and headed up the stairs, more out of instinct than logical decision. When Trevor started to follow, Erran pointed at the foyer. "Stand guard until the streets are quiet. We don't know if they'll be back."

With the boy's nod, Erran continued up the stairs. The silent African housekeeper stood in front of a closed door, a fireplace poker in hand and a fierce expression on her broad features. She searched his face a moment, then relaxed and slipped back into the room she'd been guarding.

Erran knew for fact that he wouldn't find the older Miss Rochester sensibly behind closed doors. He stalked down the corridor to the front salon—where he'd specifically told her *not* to go.

Miss Rochester was still seated in the window. At his entrance, she watched him warily.

"What did you just do?" he demanded. He wanted to yell and shout and call her three kinds of fool, but now that disaster had been averted, he was too confused.

He'd stopped a mob? Or had she? And the carriage?

Abruptly drained of all his avenging need for justice, he dropped on the bench beside her—a mistake. He inhaled her delicate fragrance and had to fight the urge to take her into his arms and shake her. Or kiss her. His rage had become a boiling stew of confusion. Lust was simple and easier to act on.

The most logical conclusion was that he was losing his mind.

She wrapped her slender fingers around his hand, the one holding the sword. He hadn't even realized he still carried it. He released the hilt, and the weapon dropped to the worn carpet. He tossed the rapier down beside it. She didn't release his hand. He didn't know what that meant and was too dazed to care.

"I'm not certain what happened," she said softly. "All I've ever done before is ask for pretty lace or scare bad little boys. Although once I caused a minor riot when all the boys scrambled to fetch me the last orange from a tree."

Erran pondered a few swear words at that admission. She used her siren call on little *boys*? And they'd responded?

He was to believe she persuaded a mob to depart with her *voice*?

He'd label this Malcolm madness and walk away . . . except he wasn't entirely certain that he hadn't just commanded a mob to disperse. And she'd beat him at his own game. Only he'd bellowed and she'd sung; he'd ordered, and she'd entreated. *Madness*.

"You ask nicely and you are given lace and oranges and little boys run away?" Erran asked sarcastically. Needing solid reality, he leaned against the wall, circled her waist, and tugged her back with him.

To his astonishment, she rested her head against his shoulder as if she needed this contact too. "Only Jamar notices when I do it. He told Papa that he gave in to my wiles too easily. It was never intentional at first."

"You just ask, and people give? You could walk up to the bank and ask for your father's money, and they would hand it over?" Erran was tired and confused enough to appreciate the sound of that, even though he knew in the light of day, it wasn't right or just. That was temptation speaking. Just because one could do something, didn't mean he should—as Cousin Sylvester's case proved.

"I've always had anything I wanted," she admitted. "I've never needed to ask for what might not be given freely. And *you* don't respond when I try to tell you what I want. Neither does Jamar now that he knows of my persuasion. So how can I know a banker would listen? I've never really tested myself. What about you? I've never *ever* heard a voice like yours. You spoke with the power of gods," she said in what almost sounded like awe.

Erran wanted to gather her in his arms and kiss her for not calling him a monster. That would end this impossible conversation in a more comprehensible manner.

He didn't want to consider what they'd just done because it was bloody damned spooky. He could write it off as coincidence that they'd shouted just as the mob decided they'd gone too far and shrank away in shame after they struck the carriage.

But he knew better, just as he knew that crowd hadn't turned down this side road by accident. Mobs kept to the main streets where they could summon the most notice. He didn't blame them. Without a vote, it was the only way poor men could make their voices heard. But the spy with his torch in the mews warned that this was no ordinary mob led by the usual troublemakers. Their route had been planned.

"Whatever we did, it was wrong, and doing it again would make us more evil than the rioters," he said angrily.

"Are you calling me evil?" she asked in surprise, shoving away.

"You drove away the villains I needed to talk to. You might as well have been in league with whoever sent them." He said it as disparagingly as possible so she wouldn't fall into his arms again.

He needed to get away from a woman who could counter and possibly exceed his Courtroom Voice. He couldn't trust her any more than he could trust himself.

She smacked his whiskered jaw and stalked out. The smack stung, and he almost felt better for it.

LEAVING THE ROCHESTERS to themselves, Erran located a few of the miscreants in a tavern on a back street off St. James. The first lot he talked to weren't drunk enough to do more than growl at him to back off. He needed to change into something less . . . tailored.

He returned to the house, left his coat in the kitchen, and borrowed one of Jamar's old ones. It hung on him so badly that it looked as if it came from a second-hand store. By this time, he was tense enough to need a few pints of his own.

When he stopped in the next tavern, the men were drunk enough to include him in their revelry. While Erran guzzled his ale, he listened.

Among the usual uneducated diatribes against politicians, government, and aristocrats, he caught the puzzled murmurings of men who had marched with different goals in mind. Even in their drunkenness, they were trying to work out how they'd been diverted. Erran edged in their direction.

"We ain't gonna get paid," one mourned. "All this work for naught."

"Ain't no work," another scoffed. "Bit o'fun is all. Why'd you run when the toff shouted? There was more of us."

"I didn't run," the first speaker protested. "But the lady promised us a tankard. I thought we was done."

"Ain't natural," one of the less drunk said in puzzlement. "He yells at us to stop, and the fools stopped as if he were the king."

A fellow in a knit cap snorted. "We wouldna stopped for no king. Thought it was the fellow who paid us, myself. Did you see them swords? He coulda skewered us right proper."

"The lady had the voice of me own mama," one drunk said rapturously.

The argument descended from there into inebriated reminiscences. The chances of finding out *who* had promised payment weren't high.

Erran questioned them a time or two as the night wore on, but it became apparent they had taken coins, threats, and promises from men no better than themselves. Whoever had set the rioters loose had sent minions who would be difficult to trace.

After ascertaining no actual harm had come from their venture into the Wyrd, Erran gave up, drank his ale, and dismally contemplated his future as a mute.

Eight

THE NEXT MORNING, Celeste did her best to pretend it was a perfectly ordinary day, rather than consider herself evil as Lord Erran had suggested.

She had slapped a gentleman! She had never in her life been so . . . so rude.

Of course, no one had ever made her feel as furious, or as lonely.

She yanked her hair into a braid, pinned it at her nape, covered it with a dark bonnet, and picked up the satchel of newly-sewn shirts. Lady Azenor's visit yesterday had interrupted their routine and put them behind schedule.

Trevor met her in the hall. "Did Lord Erran explain how he held off a mob?" he asked in wide-eyed anticipation. "He confronted a mob with nothing more than a sword and rapier!"

She had stayed awake all night fretting over Lord Erran's behavior. Such bravery was beyond her experience. That somehow they'd managed to disperse a mob still caused her to shiver, but she refused to believe what they'd done was *evil*.

She had wanted to shower him with kisses of gratitude when he'd returned, whole and unharmed. There for a brief moment, he had held her against his big body and made her feel safe. And then he'd shattered her brief peace by calling her *bad*.

She sniffed in disdain. "I'd rather box Lord Erran's ears for explaining nothing. For all I know, he instigated the attacks to scare us into accepting his aid."

"He wouldn't do that," Trevor said in indignation. "You just don't like anyone disturbing your boring routine." He stalked off down the hall, leaving her to hurry down the stairs alone.

If she was to put food on the table, she must put one foot in front of the other and march onward, not fret over impossibilities.

At least Nana had said the machine was running more smoothly, and she should make better time now that she didn't have to rip out bad stitches. Celeste need only convince the tailor that the rioters were at fault for their not finishing the order.

Wrapping her cloak around her, she entered the kitchen. She stumbled to a halt at finding Lord Erran ensconced at the table, sipping coffee and filling his plate with bacon and toast. He rose at her entrance and bowed as if they met at this hour every day. Her heart thumped so hard, she feared everyone heard it. He called her evil, then usurped her home!

He hadn't shaved. His dark beard shadowed a square chin and the hollows beneath his strong cheek bones. His usually immaculate linen was rumpled and dusty, but he wore his frock coat buttoned and had made some effort to brush off the dirt. He'd slicked his unruly black curls with water, but they were springing back up as they dried. One fell over his sardonic eyebrow as he regarded her dreary attire.

"Good morning, Miss Rochester. Were you intending to go out without an escort at this hour? I don't advise it." He used a modulated baritone far different from last night's that still managed to reflect his irritation.

Deciding it was easier to suspect his motives than accept his aid, she tightened her bonnet strings and crossed the kitchen to the door. "I am capable of walking around the block without guard dogs. I have been doing so for a considerable amount of time without incident."

"She bites anyone who approaches," Jamar added with humor, setting down his coffee. "Do not underestimate her."

"This is London. A lady does not go about unescorted, especially after last night's events. Jamar hasn't finished his breakfast, so I'll be happy to attend you." Lord Erran removed his high-crowned hat from a hook and opened the door for her.

When Jamar didn't object, Celeste pressed her lips tight in disapproval and hurried out. They had been imposing on Jamar's good nature by requiring that he behave as a menial instead of the educated businessman that he was.

It was Lord Erran to whom she objected, but he seemed immune to her persuasion. She wouldn't waste energy arguing with the deaf. She stayed silent when he took the satchel and opened the back gate. She lifted her skirts from the muck and hurried faster.

She should never have allowed this man into their lives.

They could have been burned out of their home if they hadn't.

She gritted her teeth against her own inadequacy.

"I will insist that the solicitors release funds for your family's support," he said as they walked through the morning fog. "It is unconscionable that Lansdowne should leave you sewing shirts for a living—although the pleats are a nice touch. I mean to buy one of those when my allowance permits."

He was fishing. He could not possibly know what was in the satchel or that she was the one who sewed the pleats. She had spent these last months doing her best to hide the fact from their aristocratic neighbors that they were in filthy trade. And now their landlord was about to find out. She continued her silence.

She shivered in unease when he opened the tailor's door before she could do so.

Looking like a disreputable rake in his expensive clothes and beard shadow, Lord Erran arrogantly set the box of shirts on the counter, looming over the small man behind it. The tailor looked nervous and reached for his coin pouch without counting and examining the detail of every single shirt, as he'd done in the past.

Her landlord gazed in noble disdain at the amount the shopkeeper held out. "You'll have to find another source. That's scarcely sufficient for the quality of these shirts, and you know it. You've been charging your customers four times that amount."

Celeste's eyes widened, and she just barely kept her mouth from dropping open. How did he *know* that? Or did he? Here she'd been horrified at revealing their occupation, and instead, his noble lordship took them one step better by *negotiating* as if he were a shopkeeper!

Head bent, she watched him surreptitiously from beneath her lashes. Lord Erran seemed perfectly comfortable with whatever tale he was spinning.

The tailor hastily doubled the amount of coin on the counter, even though she'd brought him fewer shirts. "I had no idea . . . . Certainly. Of course. For the exclusive sale of these shirts, we can pay a trifle more."

The tailor wasn't demanding that she double her supply as he had last time. He was simply ingratiating himself with a gentleman. That grated even worse. She'd been using her most persuasive charm to wheedle a higher price, but his lordship simply waltzed in and got what he wanted by demanding it. And she was fairly certain he wasn't even using that dreadful voice he'd used to terrify rioters. That was so unfair!

Lord Erran took the coins, handed them to her, and held the door open without a word to her. Celeste wanted to stomp his boot as she passed all that big male body . . . but he'd more than doubled their earnings! That would halve the time it would take to earn funds for a solicitor.

"How did you know how much he was selling those shirts for?" she asked, finally gaining sufficient control of her tongue to speak.

"My uncle wears them. I wanted one. Every bachelor I know covets them, but his prices are beyond our means. You could set up your own shop and make a fortune," he replied curtly, placing her hand on his arm and striding down the street.

"We've considered it," she admitted, finally opening up in the astonishment of knowing her work was valued. "We had ordered fine linen for delivery to Jamaica so we might teach some of our people to sew as Nana does. We thought we could set up a shop on the island where they could sell the shirts to other planters. But after Papa died . . ." She fought to keep the grief from her voice for fear she would make everyone within hearing weep. "We didn't pay attention to the return cargo manifests. The ship sailed without the linen, so we had it sent here."

"Another triumph over the estate executors," he said in approval.

Approval. He wasn't about to scold her for ruining the family reputation by engaging in mercenary commerce! Or tell her she was ruining her siblings' chances of making their way in society. Celeste didn't know how to respond.

"The executors may have tied up your bank accounts," Lord Erran continued, "but they cannot lay hands on what's in your possession. It must be driving them mad, although I suppose the solicitors have little inkling about linen shipments."

Celeste allowed herself to relax into a small smile. "Now that I understand what type of man the earl is, I am not sorry that we've stolen from the estate."

"I should think not. It's pure genius. But from now on, you'll send a footman to the tailor. Lady Azenor will be sending two over today, along with a butler, I hope." He stopped at the back gate and bowed over her hand. "I will leave you here. I'll be visiting the city today, and we'll see what comes of it. I'll try to be back in time to introduce my Cousin Zack, who will be overseeing the repairs."

How did he *do* that? She wanted to box his ears all over again for taking charge of her entire life . . . and hug him for calling her a genius and sending her footmen and looking after her family. While she was still feeling the glow of flattery, she placed a hand on his arm to prevent his departure. "Tell me about your voice. I have never met another who possessed such a gift."

He made a noise deep in this throat and glanced up and down the mews, but it was early, and no one lingered. Looking uncomfortable, he clenched his gloved fingers. "The first time I used it was shock enough. I'd rather not discuss last night. It's not the act of a gentleman to use a weird aberration to influence others."

"It's the act of a lady?" she asked with sarcasm. "Am I beneath you now?"

"That's different," he argued. "Women have no other defense. I should be able to use my fists and weapons and logic without resorting to mumbo-jumbo."

If she said what she thought now, she would inflict harm. She didn't wish to hurt a man who had offered his aid. Biting her tongue, she merely made a polite curtsy and allowed him to go.

How did one argue with a force of nature who did not respond to even her most convincing voice?

Sadly realizing a plain beanpole like herself could never make a man like Lord Erran listen to her when he was appalled by her one gift, she trailed back to her sewing. She would simply try to be grateful that he was condescending enough to notice their plight.

Nine

WEARING HIS BEST black business coat, Erran rode back from the city in an ill temper. One of the less pecuniary reasons he had gone into law was that he'd admired the way the rules of law worked in the same way as the rules of physics—cause and consequence.

The Court of Chancery, on the other hand, followed no rhyme or reason much less anything resembling *rules*. The equity courts were so overburdened that only corruption produced results, and the decision of judges often depended on what they ate for breakfast that day.

He'd almost unleashed his unholy Courtroom Voice this morning and was regretting that he had not. How much longer could he resist the temptation to make grown men weep?

He'd like to blame last night's episode on the very tempting Miss Rochester, but he couldn't lie to himself. He was irritated that her charms seemed to work better than his commands. And still, he'd taken her in his arms and might have done more if his over-developed conscience hadn't intruded.

How long could he hold out against Miss Rochester's charms *and* the infuriating urge to demand justice? Something had to give or he would explode.

He arrived in St. James just as his cousin was dismounting from his horse. Zack was one of the rare light-haired Ives, lighter than even Theo's brown. Wide of shoulder but not as broad in chest as Erran, Zack dressed in tradesman's tweed and a countryman's knee boots, without regard to fashion.

"So that's where our ancestors sank all their money," Zack said in greeting, studying the stone façade. "And we proceeded to let it run to rack and ruin."

"Not entirely, but close enough. The tenants have kept it up better than we would have, I suspect. Homemaking has never been an Ives' trait." Erran flipped a coin to a street boy who ran up to watch the horses. "But Ashford means to move into the ground floor, so we need to adapt it for him."

Zack made sympathetic noises as he examined the front walk and step. "I've never attempted to construct an apartment for someone who can't see. We'll probably need his instructions, although a railing from gate to door might be beneficial."

"He'll tell us all to go to hell and he doesn't need anything special," Erran said in resignation, rapping the knocker. At least they'd made enough progress that the Rochesters trusted leaving a knocker on the door to let people know they were in town. And the front draperies were partially open.

Erran stifled his disappointment that the lad opened the door and not Miss Rochester. On a day as rotten as this one, he shouldn't expect the brief pleasure of her reluctant smile. "This is my cousin Zack Ives. He's an architect and can help us determine what changes need to be made in the house. Zack, this is Trevor, Lord Rochester, a distant branch of the family."

Jamar joined them in the narrow foyer. Erran knew he could explain the result of his courthouse search to the Rochester's imposing man of business, but he wanted the lady to hear what he had to say as well.

She wouldn't be happy, but he needed to see her reaction. Or so he told himself.

He'd spent the night in the downstairs office he thought would suit Duncan for a bedchamber. It was windowless, but Duncan would scarcely notice. As they tramped through the back corridor, Erran pointed out the need for a chamber for a valet adjoining the study, and Zack measured the rooms behind the stairs to draw up plans.

"I would like to see stronger bars on the entrances," Jamar suggested. "We cannot have guards sitting at all the doors, all the night. And if the ladies are to take the next floor, there should be a wall down this back hall so they might enter and leave without disturbing the marquess."

"Perhaps we should discuss this with Miss Rochester?" Erran suggested, while pretending interest in testing the lock mechanism on the study door. "We do not wish to make the ladies feel uncomfortable."

He could hear the rhythmic thumping of the sewing mechanism and assumed they were sewing to make their daily quota, which irritated him beyond all reason. He had no way of subverting their ambition and no funds to replace the tailor's trade.

Before Jamar could reply, the knocker rapped. Erran glanced questioningly at the majordomo. "Has Lady Aster sent over the footmen yet? Could that be them?" Even as he asked, he knew the footmen would have gone to the back door.

"The lady sent a note saying they will arrive before evening. We have been arranging suitable accommodations," Jamar said, striding toward the foyer.

Erran followed, interested in seeing who dared knock and how they would react to a black giant in gentleman's clothes opening the door. A footstep from above caused him to glance up the stairs.

The lady was hesitating on the landing, frowning as she, too, waited. She'd most likely been watching from the front window and had seen their visitor arrive. Dressed in drab gray—although of excellent cut on her slim figure—she caught his eye and flattened her lips in disapproval again. His cheek stung in memory of last night. Would he ever land on her good side?

Jamar opened the door. A woman shrieked as if the house had fallen on her, and a man exclaimed in irritation. Erran stepped up, allowing Jamar to retreat into the foyer, out of the public eye.

On the doorstep, a footman in elegant livery cursed and attempted to hold up a beribboned and frilled lady of larger girth than himself—who had apparently fainted at sight of Jamar. Erran was reluctant to lay hands on a woman he didn't know, but he felt sorry for the poor fellow dealing with foolish vapors.

"One would assume the populace of a city as large as London would be a little more sophisticated," he muttered under his breath, taking the female's other arm and lifting her upright. Aloud, he asked in annoyance, "Shall we escort her back to her carriage?"

"No, no, I'll be fine. I just need to sit down." The new arrival abruptly straightened, taking her weight off the young footman, much to his evident relief. She waved a lace handkerchief under her nose. "Where is Lily? My smelling salts, please."

A tiny, terrified maid peered from behind the hedge. Apparently relieved that no foreign entities darkened the doorway, the maid scurried to help her mistress.

Feeling mean, Erran released the lady's arm and blocked the doorway with his bulk. "Perhaps we could provide you with direction?" he inquired in his coldest, most aristocratic tones.

"I'm here to see my dear, dear sisters and little brother," the lady protested. "Lily, give this person my card. I'm sure they will be eager to see me."

"This is the home of the Marquess of Ashford," Erran informed them with hauteur. "He has no sisters." He took the card proffered and added with disdain, "Mrs. Guilford."

At last, Miss Rochester joined him at the doorway and elbowed him to one side. Erran rather enjoyed the intimacy her touch produced—he thought she must be feeling more comfortable in his company to dare strike him again. He inhaled her delicate floral scent as a reward for his rotten day, and fought a proprietary urge to place his hand at the small of her back.

His hostess wasn't smiling in welcome, however, as she snatched the card from his hand. "Come in, Charlotte," she said curtly. "We may call you Charlotte, may we not, since we are sisters? I am Celeste. We have corresponded."

The difference in the ladies was so striking that Erran had difficulty believing there could be any relation at all. Mrs. Guilford was obviously older, with the plumpness of childbirth and fine dining. But she was also built sturdier and closer to the ground than the taller, more willowy Miss Rochester. The older sister had frizzed her yellow hair to disguise the pasty roundness of her face. Whereas Miss Rochester's sleek mahogany hair was drawn severely back, deliberately exposing sun-browned high cheekbones and those wicked, slanted, blue eyes.

Accepting the invitation, the newcomer deliberately ignored the amused Jamar in the hall and waddled in the direction of the front parlor.

"Oh, no, Charlotte, dear. We must go upstairs to the *family* parlor. The front is for the marquess's *distinguished* guests," Miss Rochester said in polite tones that Erran could swear hid a solid streak of derision.

"Shall I join you, Miss Rochester? I have news from the city that should be discussed. Perhaps Mr. Jamar could join us?" Erran couldn't resist adding that, just to detect the direction of the social wind.

"I shall stay here and discuss renovations with the architect," Jamar said in his dry Jamaican lilt. "Miss Rochester will catch me up later."

Mrs. Guilford was too busy huffing and puffing and dragging herself up the stairs by the railing to take notice of the undercurrents. "A nice coze with family," she gasped. "That's just what we need."

Miss Rochester, looking a trifle exasperated, met Erran's gaze in a manner he could not quite interpret. "If you would not mind joining us, please, I would be appreciative."

"I will happily tear her to shreds if you require," he murmured, relishing the thought of taking apart a woman who would abandon her bereaved siblings without a single offer of aid.

Relief, delight, and a hint of mischief lit the lady's lovely face. "Oh, you may simply witness that event. But detecting truth of matters we know nothing about may be needed."

"Indeed." Bowing his agreement, Erran carried his ruthless mood up the stairs, but this time it was in defense of a lady and not because the world did not comply to his sense of order.

PHYSICALLY AWARE of Lord Erran's sturdy frame brushing entirely too close on the way up the stairs, Celeste nervously put a distance between them on the way to the parlor.

Now that their long-lost half sibling had showed up on their doorstep well after they needed her help, Celeste wasn't certain whether to rail at the fates or be wary of treacherous shoals. Since learning to survive in London had taught her suspicion, she was inclined toward the latter.

She watched with interest as Charlotte glanced around the shabby family parlor. After they'd seen this stranger alight from a carriage outside their door, Trevor and Sylvia had hidden the linen bolts and sewing baskets in spare bedrooms. Celeste deliberately opened the draperies enough to reveal the faded upholstery and threadbare carpet. She wanted to rub their sister's face in the poverty they'd been left in.

"I would have thought a marquess's establishment would be a little more . . . fashionable," Charlotte mused in dismay, taking a sofa that had probably been new during the reign of the first King George in a prior century.

"Our father would have brought in new furnishings, had he

survived," Celeste said sweetly. Curious to know how much their half-sister knew about their circumstances, she didn't expound further.

Lord Erran stood near the window behind Charlotte, apparently keeping an eye on the street while listening to their conversation. She liked that he'd accepted that she would lead the attack, if attack was necessary. But she dared not rely on him as she had relied so heavily on her father. She wasn't about to be left helpless again.

But his lordship's aristocratic hauteur and imposing physique lent an air of . . . security . . . that she would not have had otherwise. Every time she glanced at his glowering visage, her insides did a little dance of glee that so handsome and intelligent a gentleman was willing to linger in their company.

That was very definitely a rash and irrational reaction. He was still the enemy who would oust them from their home if he could.

"Of course," Charlotte said with a bewildered note. "I had assumed the estate would be sufficient . . . Is that why I heard nothing from his executors? There was no estate left? I am so sorry that I did not come sooner . . ."

A year ago, Celeste would have believed her. These days, she believed few. Worse yet, she thought she detected a layer of artifice beneath the lady's protestations. She'd never particularly noticed levels of emotion in other people's voices . . .

She widened her eyes. Was her gift actually increasing with their residence in this house as Lady Azenor had suggested?

Celeste glanced around but no one else seemed to notice. Lord Erran merely lifted a sardonic dark eyebrow, uninfluenced by Charlotte's sympathy. Of course, even Celeste's own charm didn't affect a man who responded only to logic, so he was not a reliable indicator.

"The solicitor says our father left no will, although we have witnesses who can attest otherwise." Celeste used her best polite and helpless voice. "Until the document is located, our father's cousin has taken charge of the estate. Do you know the Earl of Lansdowne?"

"Oh, yes, of course," Charlotte said vaguely, waving a chubby hand. "My husband is an acquaintance. We are very rural, however, and don't go about much in society. I'm sure Lansdowne will do everything that is proper. Perhaps my husband should apply to him to determine if we inherit anything of my precious Papa's belongings. You say there was a witness? Could he say? I do so miss Papa's letters."

Or his money. He'd often sent her funds when she requested them. Celeste looked up to Lord Erran. Good thing he was standing behind Charlotte. The frown on his sun-browned visage was dark enough to scare crows. He didn't trust their visitor either?

"I don't believe I explained," Celeste addressed his lordship sweetly, without answering Charlotte's questions. "Papa married here in England when he was still at Oxford. He took Charlotte's mother with him to Jamaica. She objected to the primitive society and returned to London when Charlotte was very young. Papa provided support until Charlotte married, but she has never visited with us."

Their half-sister dabbed at her eyes with her lacy handkerchief. "Charles and I had hoped to visit this year, but the children were ill and with one thing or another, it just could not be helped. And now I'll never see dear Papa again."

"You cannot possibly remember seeing Papa at all," Sylvia said with puzzlement. "You could not have been out of nappies when your mother took you back to England."

"He will be very much missed," Celeste said, covering Sylvia's protest with a layer of honey. She needed as much information as she could obtain, and as lovely as it would be to shred deceptive Charlotte into snowflakes, she wasn't in a position to burn bridges. "The Earl of Lansdowne has not been very forthcoming. Like you, he has ignored our pleas for advice." She inserted the last malicious statement under the same tone of honey, wondering how Charlotte would react.

Interestingly, Charlotte heard only the honey. The lady continued dabbing at her eyes. Celeste sneaked another peek at Lord Erran. He was fighting a snicker. The man heard her meanness despite her charm!

If he could hear the truth behind her sweetness, that wasn't just interesting, but frightening.

Charlotte finally looked up from her handkerchief-dabbing and widened her eyes. "Couldn't Ashford speak with the earl? Surely his influence would persuade Lansdowne to release our funds?"

Our funds? Celeste hid a smirk of her own. Now she understood the sudden reason for a visit—the lady needed money.

"The marquess is more likely to shoot the earl than speak with him," Lord Erran said in the same pleasant tones that she'd been using. His deep baritone, however, rumbled the walls and did not exude charm. "I'd suggest that you hire a solicitor if you think you were named in the will, but unless you think you're due more than five-hundred pounds, the solicitor will cost more than you'll gain."

Five-hundred pounds! It would cost *five-hundred pounds* to fight for their inheritance and save Nana's family? They could live for a lifetime on five-hundred pounds! It was Celeste's turn to look wide-eyed, while Charlotte returned to sniffing.

Nine

ERRAN WATCHED in disgust as the useless bird-wit escaped without once offering to help the bereft Rochesters. He wondered if Lansdowne might have sent the female here to find out what she could about witnesses and documents. Erran was more than pleased that clever Miss Rochester had given away nothing—which improved his humor.

He waited until he saw Mrs. Guilford depart in her carriage, then raised an expectant eyebrow at his hostess. Miss Rochester looked serene with her hands folded in her lap and her expression such that one would assume butter wouldn't melt in her mouth. But he heard the emotion beneath her controlled voice.

"*Five-hundred pounds*?" she asked in disbelief and horror. "We cannot possibly find a sum so vast. How are we ever to go home and save our people from the earl's greed?"

As if attuned to this question, Jamar quietly arrived in the doorway. As much as he would like to console his hostess, Erran had to be practical. He addressed her man of business. "You said you were a witness to the will, sir. Did Lord Rochester leave anything to his eldest daughter?"

"A small sum and a portrait of her mother," Jamar answered promptly. "He said he'd already provided her dowry and more. The rest was needed to keep the plantation running and provide for his other daughters. There *is* a will. I have seen it. Can I not swear to it?"

"Would your testimony stand up in a Jamaican court?" Erran asked, hoping the island would be a simpler place with better understanding.

The silence that followed said it all. If they could not win in a Jamaican court, they had no chance in a British one. An African would not hold leverage against an earl—not in that corrupt morass that was the equity court.

"The executors have filed nothing with Chancery," Erran said into the despairing silence. "Lansdowne has merely had his solicitors draw up documents as head of the family and presented them to the banks. As eldest male and with no will to express otherwise, he has a strong claim. Do you have any idea at all where Lord Rochester would have left copies of the will?"

"Just with our Jamaican solicitors," Miss Rochester replied sadly. "There might have been a copy in his desk." She looked inquiringly at Jamar.

"Possibly," Jamar agreed. "But if our solicitors on the island cannot or will not provide their copy, who can we trust to search for another? And will anyone believe it should we present it to the court?"

"If a representative of a marquess presents it, they'll listen," Erran assured them. "It will be more difficult here where we cannot call on your island solicitors who wrote the will or any other witness but you, but I can begin the correspondence and ask for affidavits. It will just take time."

"We do not have time," Jamar said sadly. "The earl's man has already begun selling off the estate's assets."

"He means his son and Nana's family, as well as the others." Trevor spoke up. "The bloody British may have made *shipping* slaves illegal, but it did not make slavery itself illegal. Freedom papers are easily destroyed, but black skin isn't. That's all the thieves need to convince others that our workers are slaves, when they *aren't*."

"They will hide," Jamar said. "Noah knows all the caves. And there are those who can smuggle them off the island. But the land will suffer for it."

The steward did not mention how hard that life would be for children and old people, but Erran could picture the horror of cold caves and no food.

Such tragedy put his bad day sharply in place. "This is Friday, and most men leave for their rural homes so they may celebrate Sunday services with their families. So I've arranged for one of your father's London solicitors to visit here on Monday. I've advised him to bring all documentation giving Lansdowne control over your inheritance. With your permission, I'll bring in Ashford's estate solicitors to insist that Miss Rochester should be legal guardian of her siblings. A will expressing your father's wishes would be beneficial, but perhaps Jamar can be more influential in a private setting than in a courtroom."

"We cannot afford five-hundred pounds," Miss Rochester protested. Her lovely complexion had grown pale these past moments.

Erran wished he could reassure her, but he could only offer his services. "Ashford pays his solicitors a retainer. Lansdowne will have to pay his. And if it comes down to bribing court clerks, Ashford will owe you rent if you allow him to occupy the lower floor. Money is not as important as people," he concluded decisively.

And given the anarchy he'd seen in the courts today, he might as well call on his barmy sister-in-law's stars and planets too. Moon magic was just as likely to find justice as logic and fairness.

And there was that temptation to use undue influence again. Erran gritted his teeth.

"MY LORD, this is . . . unusual." Charlotte Guilford tugged at the bunched up folds of her gloves and glanced nervously around the coach interior. The curtains had been drawn against the last rays of sun. Her footman waited outside the closed door. The suave old man in his fashionable coat on the forward-facing seat didn't appear dangerous. She knew him vaguely from her husband's entertainments. She allowed her eagerness for recognition from an aristocrat to overcome any fear and waited to hear what his message had meant.

"Some things require confidentiality," the earl of Lansdowne said in the plum tones of authority. "I hear you have met with my young cousins, the Rochesters. How did you find them?"

"Well, my lord," she said, trying to conceal her curiosity. "The eldest is rather plain-faced and unfashionably dark, but the others will do respectably when they're of an age."

"Good, good," he said, tapping a walking stick across his knees. "The eldest is probably not legitimate, you realize. Your mother was most likely still alive when she was born, as I understand it. I cannot think it best for them to remain in society. They haven't the funds in any account."

Startled, Charlotte nodded, taking her time to digest this news. "I had not realized, my lord. I've been told my father was a proper gentleman . . . ."

"Well, that is all water under the bridge. I understand they've had a bit of trouble. Will you be taking them under your wing?"

That, Charlotte didn't need to think more about. "Good heavens, no. They're perfectly set up as they are, and Charles and I haven't the wherewithal to take on any more burdens. I had hoped my father would have left us a little something to get by on, but there seems to be no funds left."

"There is the unusually large lease payment for that monstrosity of an old house," the earl said. "It represents an outrageous sum. My men of business could arrange to have those funds returned to the estate if the Rochesters could be removed. Most of it would have to be kept in trust for the young baron, of course, but I'm sure they could arrange for a living expense to anyone looking after him."

"Do you know the cost of raising a young man?" Charlotte asked acerbically. "That alone takes a substantial sum. And I should imagine he would go nowhere without his sisters. If you are asking me to take on that chore, my answer is a firm *no*."

"Your husband has a rural property in Yorkshire, does he not?" Lansdowne continued, taking a different direction instead of giving up. "It would be no great expense to set them up there, as a personal favor to me. The eldest could go as a governess and companion, I'm certain. That's the most she can expect. If the younger one is well-looking, you can marry her off in a year or so. Would a living of a hundred pounds per annum cover the burden?"

Charlotte narrowed her eyes and tried to puzzle through what he was asking. Surely he did not think those very peculiar young people and their servants would go anywhere they didn't like? She had so many arguments against such a challenge that she didn't even know where to begin. So she stuck with the simple.

"You honor me, my lord, but I must think of my own family first. A hundred pounds will scarcely buy linen and put food on the table. The boy will want education. No, my lord, I fear we simply cannot take on so large an encumbrance. My husband works day and night as it is to keep our own children fed and housed."

The earl's stick bounced a little harder. "What if I arranged for Mr. Guilford to take a better position in the Home Office? It would mean a substantial raise in income."

The hair on the back of her neck prickled. An earl as powerful as Lansdowne could arrange many, many outcomes—some of them unpleasant. Dear Charles was barely holding onto his position as it was. One word from an earl . . . She heard the threat, even if it wasn't voiced.

"I see, my lord. And why would the Rochesters wish to give up their palatial home in favor of mine?" She knew *she* couldn't hold out against an earl. But perhaps her half-siblings had resources beyond hers. One could always hope.

"They need to eat, don't they?" he asked jovially. "They have no funds. They can't have much more to sell off. They'll see reason when it comes time."

Gloomily, Charlotte understood the truth of this. "May I have time to discuss this with my husband? Would we have to take that horrible darkie giant they have for a servant?"

"The servants would be returned to the estate where they belong," the earl said smoothly. "You may have no fear about that. Send word to my office on Monday. I'm sure you will see the benefit of looking after your young siblings."

Charlotte saw only trouble and woe in her future, but she was already calculating the benefit of her husband's superior position with the Home Office and realizing their rural estate in Yorkshire was a very long way from London. If she and Charles could afford to stay in London . . . she needn't trouble herself much at all.

LADY ASTER sent word that the new servants were on their way. Jamar stationed himself at the barred back gate to let them in. Erran took Zack into the yard to examine the possibility of inventing a better means of notifying the household when someone wished to enter.

"Wouldn't it be simpler to just bar the house doors instead of the gate?" Zack inquired, studying the solid stone posts and the heavy oak. "We don't need medieval fortresses any longer."

"In this case, we do," Erran said, studying the distance from gate to house. "We have every reason to believe there are unsavory elements who wish the Rochesters gone, and their assaults have been escalating. And with Duncan moving in . . . His accident was no accident. If someone still wants to kill him, I'd rather opt for caution."

"I'll have to bring my workmen in and out through the gate," Zack reminded him. "It will delay construction if they have to wait for someone to hear them knock every time they wish to enter."

"It will be complicated," Erran agreed. "Perhaps after our meeting with the solicitors, the family might trust us enough that they can be persuaded to visit Iveston. I'm not certain that anything short of sending an army to Jamaica will satisfy them, but I'll see what I can do."

Sending the Rochesters anywhere was his devout desire. Perhaps then his life could return to the humdrum pursuit of justice through legal means, once he persuaded the judges he wouldn't throw more tantrums.

Erran was measuring the yard for a bell pull when the servants arrived. He stopped to watch how Aster's newly trained men reacted to Jamar. They merely doffed their caps, hefted their boxes of belongings to their broad shoulders, and followed the giant into the house.

"They seem . . . polite," a soft voice said from the shrubbery.

Erran swung around to find Miss Rochester sitting on a bench in the barren rose garden behind a hedge. The woman moved with the graceful silence of a butterfly.

"Lady Aster will have grilled them for their birth dates," he said, "then drawn up their zodiac charts to be certain they are reliable, and trained them to a standard of her own. The ones she's introduced to Iveston seem to think for themselves—a good thing since *we* never know what to do with them."

Her sky blue eyes turned up from her sewing to study him quizzically. "Surely your housekeeper knows how to employ servants?"

He fought the urge to take the seat beside her and discuss any subject on earth but the ones they must adhere to. Tearing his gaze from her entrancingly pursed lips, he jotted figures down in his notebook as a distraction.

"The Iveston housekeeper has taken to tippling after lunch and is incoherent by dinner," he explained as he tucked his notebook away. "But she has been with us forever and none of us is capable of casting a female into the cold. Ives are not . . . *normal* by society's standards. I will warn you now that the marquess is subject to fits of temper and flings things at anyone who stands in his way. Servants tend to disappear regularly on us, so we don't dare remove the few who linger."

"So Lady Aster has found servants of independent minds who learn how to avoid the marquess and your housekeeper? Quite enterprising of her, I'm certain." She sounded amused as she returned to applying tiny stitches to the pleats in the linen.

"Well, she's stuck living at Iveston most days, so it's a matter of self-defense. Until she came along, we'd been an all-male household. It was like living in a pig sty inhabited by savages. I've been avoiding the place like the plague for years."

She chuckled. "And here I've always thought of noble estates as stuffy and boring. I suppose I must go in and meet our new butler. Will he get along with Nana? She's been in charge of us forever."

"As if I have any notion of the hierarchy of servants." Erran held out his hand. "Come along. I need to be assured that they know how to secure the doors and windows and keep out blackguards."

The moment she placed her ungloved hand in his, he knew his mistake. He'd removed his gloves to write. With her soft flesh pressed into his rough palm, his instinct was to wrap her hand tightly and not let go. Skin-to-skin contact was electrifying, and he inhaled sharply at the shock.

She tried to slip her fingers away, but he couldn't have released her if he'd been paid all the gold on earth. She did not protest but let him lead her into the house. She seemed as short of breath as he. This wouldn't do.

But he didn't know how to make it go away. Swallowing, he hid his shock by calling roughly to his cousin. "I'll be back shortly. Don't do anything interesting until I return."

To his horror, Zack froze in the process of hammering a loose board.

Celeste giggled and called, "The gate is not interesting, Mr. Zack. Please, return to beating it up."

Zack enthusiastically began beating nails into wood again.

"That did not just happen," Erran muttered as they entered the garden door.

"Evil, my lord," she said sweetly. "We are evil, remember?"

Damnation! Before Erran could wring her neck, Jamar led his new charges to meet them. The majordomo didn't blink at the sight of their clasped hands. He merely introduced the servants Ashford had hired and allowed Miss Rochester to question them.

Erran wanted to scratch under his collar and flee, but he forced himself to study the new staff. Lady Aster had found three burly, seemingly intelligent men to protect the household. He recognized one who had served dinner at Theo's. Multi-talented servants were excellent. Ones who could survive having rocks and shoes thrown at their heads would be beneficial.

Seemingly unfazed by the weirdness in the garden, Zack entered through the back door, donning his hat and gloves, as the servants were being led off to become acquainted with their duties. "I'll bring you plans and estimates in a few days." He hesitated when he realized the lady lingered. "I don't wish to be alarming, but you might want to employ one of the new men in watching that gate until you can add a more substantial bar."

Miss Rochester placed her slender hand on Erran's coat sleeve in a gesture indicating uneasiness. He resisted covering it with his own hand. Instead, he bunched his fingers. "More ruffians lingering in the mews?"

"No, someone has sawed half way through the bar. A few good shoulders pounding against the gate will snap the wood in two."

Damn.

Erran turned to the lady. "I'll send one of the men to pick up a few clothes and my gear. I'll be staying here until this is settled."

He couldn't tell if her look of apprehension was for him or the knowledge that their enemies were more dangerous than petty ruffians.

Ten

BITING HER LIP, Celeste hesitated in the doorway of Nana's sewing room.

The aristocratic Lord Erran with his expensively tailored clothes and polished boots had transformed into another man during the last twenty-four hours. He had slept in the study again, despite her protestations that he should take one of the empty beds upstairs. And this morning, he was sprawled on his back like a workman across the floor, fitting bits of metal beneath a table.

He was in stocking feet and shirtsleeves—an intimacy that had her wallowing in admiration at his manly physique, plus other feelings not quite so admirable—especially since his position revealed a great deal of his . . . masculine proportions.

She glanced up at Nana for guidance, but her arbiter of propriety was simply sewing and ignoring the man on the floor.

"I have made teacakes, if anyone is interested in stopping for morning coffee or tea," Celeste said in a diffident whisper. She hated to disturb them. She was so far out of her depths these days, she might as well be living with penguins and wondering if they ate fish with their tea.

Lord Erran's head popped out from beneath the old table he'd dragged down from the attics. He had dust in his dark curls and a smudge on his nose. "I need a strong elastic band, two preferably, so I can repair the other machine. I don't suppose you have anything in your sewing baskets?"

Celeste feared her mouth gaped open for a moment too long. She'd asked if he'd like teacakes. And he wanted *elastic*? Penguins might be easier.

"You look in your father's box," Nana advised in her raspy little-used voice.

Even Lord Erran glanced up at the normally silent woman in surprise. "Thank you, ma'am," he said politely, before glancing back to Celeste. "Your father's box?"

"I'm not sure where it is," Celeste admitted. "Perhaps with the trunks in the attic. He always had a chest of tools and mechanical bits, and none of us knew what to do with them."

Lord Erran sat up and brushed himself off. "Tell me what the chest looks like, and I'll hunt for it. I'd love to see the workbox of a man who built this machine."

"I suppose I might show you," Celeste said, glancing at Nana for approval. She'd never spent time with a man, unchaperoned, but the elderly woman didn't even look up from her sewing to glare. Perhaps she felt out of place too. "Shall I have someone bring up cakes for you, Nana? Or will you be going downstairs?"

"Go, child," Nana said brusquely, turning the linen on the table to start a new seam. "You are the lady of the house now."

What was *that* supposed to mean? She'd had to step into her mother's role years before, but she'd always consulted Nana before making any decisions. She supposed teacakes weren't important, but she felt still even more lost by Nana's dismissal.

His lordship loomed over her expectantly, and she retreated to the corridor. "It is a large, long wooden box. If you would go up and start searching, I'll have someone fetch cakes for Nana." She thought perhaps the "lady of the house" would look after loyal family retainers, and Nana deserved a rest, even if it wasn't for tea.

"She's frightened," Lord Erran said unexpectedly. "She has every right to be. It takes months for us to send word and hear from anyone in the islands. I have an uncle in the shipping business sending me ship schedules so I know which ones will take my letters soonest and fastest. We know people who know people all over the world. It may look as if I'm doing nothing, but my family is doing everything they can to protect your servants and tenants."

Hearing his concern, overwhelmed by his earnestness, Celeste touched his coat sleeve. "I trust almost no one these days, but I believe you in this. I don't know what we've done to deserve your support, but I hope someday we can repay you."

And she meant it. She felt lighter for knowing someone else shared her burdens, even if that someone was so far beyond her experience that she could not imagine the world he walked in . . ..

Except for his voice, which left her very confused but on familiar grounds. They really needed to talk about their shared oddity, but she thoroughly disliked being considered evil.

"You'll take back any desire to repay us once Ashford moves in,"

Lord Erran said with dark humor, before trotting off to the attic door.

More unwelcome change, but if it meant her family would be out of danger, she wouldn't argue. This shabby London mansion was a far cry easier to live in than the caves and fields where the plantation's workers must be hiding now. It felt safer staying with a mad marquess until they could go home. She hoped they might help each other until then.

She sent one of the new footmen to carry a tray to Nana, then hurried up the stairs to the attic storage room under the eaves. Lord Erran was collecting more dust by crawling around under the low roof, attempting not to bang his head while he sorted through old trunks and boxes. He already had an assortment lined up for her perusal.

"I didn't want to open anything that might be private," he explained, pointing at the row of old boxes. "I thought you might recognize your father's tool chest."

"Most of those should belong to your family. We're living out of the trunks we brought with us. But father's things . . ." She swiped angrily at an escaping tear and pointed at a wooden box with carvings and a leather-bound trunk. "We couldn't bear to part with them."

"I don't suppose he kept documents in any of them?" his lordship asked without hope.

"Nothing useful." She opened the trunk. "This only contains the lease, introductions to family and friends, letters to the bankers and solicitors . . . no will. He was young and hadn't planned on dying."

"Or having Lansdowne usurp his assets," Lord Erran said grimly, glancing through the papers. "Might I take these down and go through them? It might give me some insight in how best to fight this battle."

"Please, if you would. All we did was cry as we read through them, which admittedly, is not a very constructive reaction."

"But a perfectly normal one. Counteracting grief-stricken families is the reason we have cold-hearted lawyers like me." He flashed her a bleak smile. "And this other box is the workbox? I have your permission to use the contents?"

"Absolutely." It felt very odd to be in this narrow enclosed space with a gentleman, no matter how unlike a proper gentleman he currently appeared. She wasn't certain of the etiquette, or even of what to do with her hands.

He stood up, his head bending to accommodate the low rafters. The space became even smaller. "I'd like those teacakes now, especially if they come with your delicious coffee." He hefted the heavy workbox to his shoulder. "I'll come back for the trunk before I join you, if that's all right."

Lord Erran seldom smiled, but he sounded almost content at the moment. Or pleasant, at least, and Celeste felt another tickle of excitement. She almost rather he would return to calling her immoral so she didn't have to like him. Recalling what she planned, she wouldn't have to worry about him much longer.

"In the main drawing room?" she asked, leading the way down the stairs.

"Only if I don't have to clean up too much to sit on the furniture. I want to go back to building another of those machines while I am here," he said.

While he was here—confirming that he meant to move on after settling in his brother. It was a good thing her goals were the same.

"You could have a healthy business if you hired several seamstresses," he continued. "You'll need to charge enough to put money away to buy more linen, though. You need a business manager."

"We hadn't planned on running a manufactory," she said, returning to the practical. "We were dreaming of gowns and balls for Sylvia and Oxford for Trevor. Jamar had planned on starting the shop on the islands."

"The shirts you're making are too expensive for a small market. Better to ship a few finished products to the island and sell the rest here." He stopped at the sewing room to deliver the workbox.

"Are you sure you're not a tradesman instead of a lawyer?" she asked. She was unaccustomed to bantering with the nobility, but it was hard to take him seriously when he had a dead spider on his neckcloth.

"In our family, we do everything. There are too many of us for any one to be idle. A lazy Ives would be bounced on his ear and flung in the pond and left for the fish to nibble. So drop any preconceptions you might have of idle aristocrats. Or even polite ones. Ashford would as soon throw a shoe at your head as bow over your hand, although admittedly, that is a more recent development."

He was actually *talking* to her, man to woman, as if they were equals. He wasn't making demands or arguing but was actually being self-deprecating, and she didn't know how to respond. Telling herself it wouldn't matter shortly, Celeste nodded and left him to play with his workbox while she ran to set up a tea tray.

MISS ROCHESTER was the most reticent woman he'd ever encountered, Erran decided as he took the stairs down to the ground floor after moving the boxes. Most women chattered incessantly, but this lady kept her thoughts to herself. He couldn't determine if he appreciated the difference.

The new footmen had set up a basin and pitcher in the study for his use, and he took advantage of them now to wash up, pondering the mysterious ways of women.

He preferred the challenge of the fascinating sewing mechanism to analyzing women, but that was probably because he was avoiding the lady's questions about their mutually weird abilities.

Drawing a deep breath to conceal his discomfort, he checked that his neckcloth was straight and his coat buttoned, and proceeded to the front drawing room.

All the siblings had gathered around the tea tray, looking every inch the proper English family except for their darker coloring.

That's when Erran nearly fell over his feet with a full-blown idea that even his insane sister-in-law couldn't duplicate—although he'd need her cooperation, and he knew how to accomplish that, too.

He just didn't know how to approach this solemn, grieving family. He already knew their arguments, because they'd be his own in their place.

"Lord Erran, have a seat, please." Miss Rochester gestured at an armchair next to her brother's.

At least with others around, they wouldn't be having any weird discussion on the topic of voices. Erran took another, less comfortable, chair that kept all three of them in his sight. The boy looked as uneasy as he felt. So they had something to say, as well. Teacakes had just been an excuse.

"We have been talking," young Lord Rochester said,

uncomfortable with his new role of family head. "We wonder if we might break the lease and be returned some of the rent monies so we might return to our home. It's possible we might stop some of the depredation if we are there."

That was so exactly opposite of his own suggestion that Erran quit reaching for a cake to readjust his thoughts. Every instinct clamored against their plan, but instincts were unreliable. He needed to understand why he objected since it was the perfect solution to his problem.

"An interesting proposition," he admitted, giving himself time to think. It didn't take long to grimace at the ramifications of such a move. He was a practical man, but his one goal in life had always been to serve justice.

Sending the family back to Jamaica might solve his problems, but it would only make theirs worse. He chafed at the choice, but even Dunc would have to agree. "Unfortunately, I fear you will meet with worse aggression there than you have met so far here. The executors have already installed men in your home, men who will not give up their position without a fight."

He thought he was on firm ground when he saw all three Rochesters frown. He hurried to continue before they could formulate arguments. "If the estate executors—and I still don't have proof that your father's cousin is personally involved—are determined to sell your servants, then that means they also intend to sell the land. You will not be allowed in your home. Worse yet, you will be more vulnerable staying with friends than here, in the protection of the marquess. I would not advise returning just yet."

"Sell the plantation?" the boy asked in dismay. "That is our only income!"

"Exactly." On firm ground now, Erran sipped his coffee. "The executors have rendered you helpless, with no ability whatsoever to fight, proving your well-being is not their goal. I haven't had time to think this through, but I think you should turn the tables and become the aggressor."

The younger siblings gasped and stared at him as if he had started speaking in tongues. Aggressiveness was obviously not in their vocabulary. He hadn't thought it in Miss Rochester's lexicon either, but she merely sipped her coffee and regarded him with her usual wariness until she'd prepared her speech.

"We are not exactly assertive people, as you may have noted," she said dryly, confirming his conclusion. "Have you found documents in our father's trunk that we didn't? Ones with which to take the executors to court?"

"No documents," Erran acknowledged. "But the executors have no documents either. All they have is the earl's place on the family tree. The Ives family is more powerful and wealthier than Lansdowne. We will declare Ashford as your guardian. As his wards, you will be presented to society. We will begin making demands on the banks, forcing them to stop handing out your funds to the earl, if nothing else."

"This is how you will approach the solicitors on Monday?" Miss Rochester asked, still not expressing excitement or approval.

"From a position of strength, yes. We'll bring in my brother, Lord Theo, to act as Ashford's personal representative, and Lady Aster, who is the daughter of a powerful earl. We can point out that instead of using your father's funds to feed and clothe his young relations, the estate has grossly neglected you. Then we can offer to take the responsibility from the estate to sponsor you in society ourselves. We will demand an allowance for Lord Rochester's education and your clothing. We will threaten to sue the estate if an allowance isn't forthcoming." Erran didn't think anything would come of a suit, but often, just the threats of a lengthy, expensive lawsuit forced a settlement. Chancery was a headache everyone wished to avoid.

"And how will this help save the plantation and our people?" the boy demanded. "An education avails me nothing in their defense."

Erran approved of the elder sister not interfering while the young baron attempted to step up to his father's role. Why did he suspect she was just biding her time?

"What Lansdowne has done is called asserting authority," Erran explained. "The British have conquered entire countries by stepping in and using bullying tactics to restore order over people who haven't the ability to fight back. First, however, you have to establish your authority. By taking your place at Oxford as a baron, you will be connecting with others of your station and higher, making the kind of connections that present a powerful front."

This idea hadn't come to Erran earlier because his family had seldom bothered to wield their influence in society. Their interests lay in scientific and business pursuits, scorning frivolity. But after Duncan had been attacked, Theo had told them the family needed a united front to fight the malefactors, and Erran realized the same tactic would work here.

He turned to the ladies. "Women create power in ballrooms— you build formidable alliances to aid and abet your family's goals. If Ashford sponsors you, you will be in a position to aid him, and all and sundry will know that he will return the favor. It will become apparent that opposing you will be the same as opposing him."

"And you think to influence *judges* by this behavior?" Miss Rochester asked incredulously.

His reaction exactly, and it still stuck in his craw, but using society was a more civilized method than bullying and bribing his way through the court. "Wielding power is the only way to win in a civil case, short of beating judges about the head with a big stick," he said with cynicism. "There is always bribery, of course, and some amount of that will have to happen, which is why I said the case would be expensive. But right now, the earl's solicitors are the only ones leaning on the court—and Lansdowne doesn't have the family we have. He has gone about this entirely wrong—he should have enlisted you from the start, instead of driving you away."

Erran watched as this sank in. It wasn't the immediate solution they wanted, he knew. Miss Rochester was looking particularly mutinous, but the other two seemed hopeful. There were enormous hurdles, of course. He didn't possess a magic wand. His all male family hadn't wielded social influence in generations.

But Erran had watched Lady Aster and her family in action, and they worked together like a well-oiled machine. He didn't see why Ives couldn't duplicate that social command as well or better.

Once Erran presented his plan, Theo would have a fit as thorough as one of Duncan's—but even his big brother would ultimately concede it had to be done. After Lady Aster's family heard of the predicament of the African servants, they'd be sending armies of women to Jamaica unless provided alternatives.

And this way, Erran could provide Duncan with the impetus to rejoin the society he needed, without using deception.

Eleven

After Lord Erran outlined his outrageous battle plan, Celeste was ready to chew off her fingernails and possibly her toes. And she still wanted to flee to her sunny home, where she knew where she belonged. If she couldn't be pretty, she could excel at practical, and she'd been running the household for years. She couldn't smile and enchant a room full of strangers, but she could feed hundreds of workers.

Except—as much as she loathed admitting it, Lord Erran was correct. If the earl controlled the plantation, the home she wanted to return to was gone, along with everything else familiar. Her whole world felt ready to shatter and she with it.

Sylvia and Trevor were more enthusiastic about conquering new worlds. So much so that Celeste had to wonder if Lord Erran didn't employ some charmed voice that she couldn't hear—as he couldn't hear hers.

"He says I could take finishing classes with the daughters of dukes!" Sylvia said excitedly once they'd returned to their sewing.

"I cannot imagine how we can repay the marquess for the lessons if we don't win access to our funds," Celeste said dampeningly.

But nothing would quell Sylvia's high spirits, and after all they'd been through, Celeste hated to be the spoil-sport. Her siblings were young and accepted their helplessness. They needed hope and a little joy to keep them looking to the future.

Trevor needed to be in school. He had an exceptional mind when he applied it.

It was only Celeste who longed for home and felt the weight of responsibility for what was happening. She understood better than her siblings that once the marquess moved in, this house would no longer be theirs—it would be his.

She had never needed to be strong. Until her father's death, she'd had little experience at it. These last months, she'd learned survival, but that wasn't sufficient. To protect the people like Jamar and Nana, who had taken care of her all her life, she needed to be brave and bold. She couldn't imagine saving anyone by wearing nice clothes and dancing—which left her feeling even more helpless than before.

She never wanted to be helpless or dependent on a man again.

She was relieved when Lord Erran rode off to discuss his grandiose plans with his family. Perhaps they would put some sense into him. Surely, if they could just send her home, there was something she could do once she was on familiar ground again.

He returned just before dark with some contraption he installed on the back gate. Celeste watched the men working on it from her bedroom window. His lordship had doffed his long-tailed coat. Since the evening air was chilly, he presumably did so to avoid damaging it. In shirt sleeves and waistcoat, he still looked the epitome of elegance, and she couldn't stop her erratic heart from pounding with an excitement she didn't want to feel. For just a moment, she wished circumstances could be different.

Still, she wanted to go home, and he belonged here. A man like that would marry a beautiful heiress. She had no claim to beauty or wealth—and he thought her only asset was *evil*. She needed to stick to her sewing and not develop impractical notions—even if he did occasionally hold her hand as if he enjoyed the sensation as much as she did.

Sunday did not improve the situation. Lady Aster and her intimidating Aunt Daphne arrived to escort them to church. The wife of a viscount and daughter of an earl, Lady McDowell used her formidable Junoesque frame to simply carry all obstacles in her way with the force of a tidal wave. Lady Aster's younger cousins followed in her wake, and Celeste admitted she enjoyed their lively company—especially since Lord Erran managed to elude the swelling tide.

But once they returned to the house, the horror began again.

"Lord Rochester will need new clothes if he's to attend school with Kenan," Lady McDowell asserted as if she had been making lists of announcements all through the sermon. "The teachers will make certain he's up to snuff before he's thrown into the rigors of Oxford."

"I thought perhaps a tutor . . ." Celeste suggested. "Oxford is out of the question unless we regain our inheritance."

"Nonsense. He needs to meet people just as you do," the lady said imperiously, gesturing for the footman to set the tea tray down in front of her. "You need maids!"

Celeste blinked at this abrupt change of topic and glanced to copper-haired Lady Aster for explanation. Short and well-rounded, Lord Erran's sister-in-law had a mischievous smile that dazzled when her family's apparent lunacy prevailed.

"Aunt Daphne is intent on saving women from the workhouse by finding them employment," the younger lady explained. "My city household is small and can only take a few. And there are only so many I can train at once in Iveston. I don't suppose your housekeeper would be willing to train inexperienced maids?"

"Ashford will need them," Lady McDowell proclaimed, before Celeste could reply. "If only to keep coal in the scuttles in this drafty old house."

"Nana is elderly," Celeste said hesitantly. "I suppose she could use helping hands so she needn't run up and down stairs so much. I just don't know . . . . She's trained maids at home, of course, but they're . . . not English." And Nana needed to be sewing shirts, but money didn't seem to be a consideration in Lord Erran's world.

"The Rochesters have African servants," Lady Aster explained to her aunt and cousins. "Even in the kitchen."

"Better yet," Lady McDowell decided, after a moment's thought. "We have several mixed bloods who can't find employment. Indian, I believe, not African. Will that be a problem?"

Celeste shook her head. "Of course not, if it isn't a problem for Lord Ashford." Who couldn't see, she remembered. He threw shoes at all and sundry, without regard to race or gender. She bit back a smile at her own foolishness.

Lord Erran wandered in after having some discussion with Jamar. With his solid, impressive build clothed in the finest tailoring, he could have been the marquess instead of simply his brother's solicitor. He helped himself to a sandwich and raised his dark eyebrows. "If what is a problem for the Beast of Iveston?"

The ladies explained, and he shook his head with an impolite snort. "The maids just need to stay out of his way and keep objects from his path and they could be green three-eyed Martians for all Dunc will care. It might be interesting to see how his guests will react, but we can cross that bridge when we come to it. *If* we come to it. Prying him out of the country comes first."

"He knows how important the election is," Lady McDowell said with a sniff. "We'll see that he comes to London." Straight-backed and regal, she rose from the old chair as if it had been a throne. "Come along, girls. We'll return in the morning to begin the round of modistes, and a tailor for Lord Rochester."

Alarmed, Celeste jumped up with far less grace. "Modistes?" She glanced anxiously at Lord Erran, who didn't seem at all surprised. "But the solicitors are coming tomorrow," she protested, although that wasn't her only concern.

"They'll be here mid-afternoon. There's plenty of time for a round at the shops," he said with a dismissive air—as if spending a fortune on clothing for impoverished relations was of no moment whatsoever.

Sylvia was practically drooling and watching them hopefully. Trevor . . . needed new everything. He'd outgrown almost all his clothes this past year. It was all too much, too fast. Celeste wanted to weep her frustration.

"United front," Lord Erran said with a wave of his sandwich. "You'll be entering the wars as Dunc's troops. He can provide the uniforms."

Uniforms! Celeste thought hysterics might be appropriate, were she given to such excessive display, which she was not. She had just established a new normality, and now he would throw all her routine into disarray again. She opened her mouth to argue, but no words would emerge. She, who had wielded her voice to good purpose for a lifetime, was speechless.

From beneath a rumpled cap of dark curls, Lord Erran winked. He *winked*. As if this were all a grand jest and not their lives! Now she not only wanted to weep, but to pound her fists against his broad chest in hopes of beating sense into him.

Instead of railing like a shrew, she smiled graciously at her guests, escorted them to the door with promises to look forward to the morrow, then stomped up the stairs without returning to the parlor.

HAPPILY OBLIVIOUS to his surroundings while working out the

intricacies of the sewing mechanism, Erran installed the elastic to improve the working machine. If his formidable intellect couldn't be applied to a courtroom, he could study machines for ways to better society, and this mechanism would be a boon to the overworked eyes and fingers of tailors and seamstresses.

Earlier, he had sorted through the late baron's workbox and found tools but little else, not even drawings for the mechanism. He'd started reading through the various documents in the other trunk, but as the lady had said, they were mostly letters of introduction. Lord Rochester had attended schools in England and lived with relations here for a large part of his life. He had an extensive collection of acquaintances, and if Erran did not mistake, some were related to Lady Aster's family. The Rochesters might not recognize all the names, but he had a good memory for connections. He'd have to ask Aster later.

Without a defined direction for his energy, he played mechanic.

Still under the table, Erran sensed more than saw Jamar's arrival. The majordomo wasn't in the habit of visiting the sewing room. Erran scooted out and looked up questioningly as he dusted himself off.

"There are two young women pulling the bell at the back gate. Will the ladies have sent over maids this quickly?" Jamar asked in his lilting English.

"The bell works, does it?" Pleased, Erran stood up. "The Malcolm ladies have magic wands which produce servants in the blink of an eye." He bowed before Nana to catch her attention.

She gave him a wary look and stopped sewing.

"I should have told Lady McDowell that you needed help with the sewing. I'll rectify that error instantly, if you would be so kind as to take charge of the maids she has sent over. They're new. They'll need training. There will be more to follow, so we'll leave it up to you as to what positions need filling first."

The gray-haired housekeeper rested her hands in her lap and studied him as if he might be a curious specimen of insect. "You and she are two peas in a pod," she said slowly, frowning. "The power in this house is very strong. Use it for good and not evil."

Without further explanation, she rose and sailed from the room. With a shrug, Jamar followed after her.

Erran fought a shiver of foreboding. Evil? Had she really said that?

Having feared that his mysterious verbal ability to bully came straight from the devil, he'd rather consider her comment about *two peas in a pod*. What did that mean? And was it a good thing? Because the only "she" he could think she meant was Miss Rochester, and he didn't think it very fortunate to resemble a woman, no matter how lovely.

Thinking of Miss Rochester made him restless. He should go to his club, lift a few mugs, learn the drift of the political winds— perhaps hit the streets in search of the latest beauty of the night.

Instead, insanely, he was more inclined to walk around the block, looking for any sign of miscreants. He didn't want to believe the influential earl of Lansdowne had sent rogues to drive his relations out of the house just to reclaim the rents. He preferred to believe it was his own family's enemies.

Perhaps he could enlist a few troublemakers of his own to find out. That would get him out of the house, and he could lift a pint in the tavern while doing so.

Dropping his tools into the box, Erran returned to the study where he'd left his valise, retrieved an old coat he'd meant to wear while working, and set out for the newly improved back gate. While he was verifying that the new iron bolt operated properly, the young baron approached him.

"If you are going out, sir, might I ask to walk with you awhile?"

Hiding his surprise, Erran slipped the bolt and gestured for the boy to precede him. "You might actually help me on my enterprise. Shall we discuss it over a tankard?"

Lord Rochester's dark eyes registered surprise and pleasure. "Thank you. My sisters do not believe in strong spirits."

"Ladies generally don't," Erran agreed, fastening the bolt with a turnkey before leading him across the mews to the tavern. "They don't understand that a man's tongue only loosens over a mug of ale. Tea isn't quite the same."

The tavern wasn't crowded at this early hour. Erran bought two mugs of ale and took a table where he could keep an eye out for the young lads he'd talked to before. "What's on your mind, Rochester?"

"Trevor, please, sir. It's too hard to be my father just yet." The boy tasted the warm ale and grimaced. He brushed a dark lock off his bronzed face and sighed as if all the world weighed on his shoulders. "I cannot think tutoring will help me run an estate.

Oxford was a fine idea while my father was alive, and I had no other responsibility, but now it's important that someone manage the plantation. If Jamar and I could return home, we might recruit aid from some neighbors—"

Erran shook his head. "I understand that you prefer immediate action. We all do. If I had command of an army, I'd ship them out now to protect your workers. But we're civilized these days, and we don't hire privateers anymore. Information and who you know will accomplish the same, although admittedly, it is slow going from this distance."

The boy took another drink. Wiping the froth from his mouth with his coat sleeve, he chose his words carefully. "I know people on the island. I know no one here. I cannot see how I can be of any use when your family is in a better position to do so. At home, I could at least see that the women and children are cared for."

Erran sympathized, but the lad didn't have the experience to know what he was up against. "I have had Ashford's solicitors send letters to your governor and to your men of business in Jamaica, warning that the executors have no legal right to sell anyone or anything. If you know good neighbors who can be trusted, you might write them and implore them to keep your people safe. I can have the letters sent out with official document carriers so they arrive swiftly. Anything else is likely to end in bloodshed."

Trevor scowled. "They're *family*, can't you see? They'll think we've abandoned them, especially if they receive word that we're flitting about London, having a good time, while they starve."

"Jamar won't allow them to think like that," Erran argued. "He's already in communication with his son and will let him know what we're doing. In the meantime, there is something you can do here besides flitting about ballrooms."

"There is?" the boy asked in suspicion.

Erran hoped Miss Rochester wouldn't boil him in oil for this, but the boy had every right to want to protect his holdings, and he needed to be included in their plans. "Someone has evidently paid local ruffians to harass your family in hopes of forcing you to leave. It takes only a few ha'pennies to buy anyone around these parts. Do you think you could occasionally step over here, talk to the younger lads, give them a few coins and tip them off that their help would be appreciated, that kind of thing?"

Trevor glanced around the tavern at the slouching, ill-dressed occupants. He swallowed hard, then nodded. "I can't stay cooped up inside all day, can I?"

"You've been doing a fine job of it until now," Erran said without rancor. "And it's been smart to do so, not knowing your enemies. But now that we have some idea where we stand, I'll introduce you to a few to get you started. They're plucky lads, and they're more likely to work for people who are good to them, than to work for ill-bred bullies."

Trevor nodded with a little more confidence. Erran assumed he would be accused of aiding and abetting in the dissipation of a minor or some such, but the young baron had to start somewhere if he was to hold his own at Oxford.

Ives knew how to raise boys. The real puzzles were women.

Twelve

LADY ASTER arrived early on Monday morning, escorted by a sturdy footman, a lady's maid, and two bedraggled, terrified children.

"I am desperate," she announced as Celeste hurried down to meet her in the foyer. "Aunt Gwendolyn says the village will not accept any more maimed children, that their families must care for them. But their mothers must work to put food on the table, and there is never enough to go around . . . ." She halted to catch her breath.

The child in a shabby dress was balancing on a walking stick. The boy in trousers too short for him had only one hand, and the stub was still wrapped in a dirty bandage. With dismay, Celeste needed no explanation. "And these two have been helping feed their youngers by working in the factory?" The ladies had described the horrors they fought against in the mills—some of which her father's horrible cousin, the earl of Lansdowne, owned as part of an investment consortium.

"Exactly. And they have been injured in the process. We have *laws*, but no one to enforce them." The lovely copper-haired lady wore an expression of despair—and anger. "They ought to be receiving an education, but their families need their wages or the whole lot will end up in the workhouse. And if they end up in the workhouse, the beasts who sell children out to farmers as little more than slaves will take them. I thought perhaps Marie could learn sewing, but I'm at a loss with what Tommy might do."

"We used to have a potboy with a crippled arm. He managed just fine." Faced with a problem she might handle, Celeste gained a little more confidence. "If you don't mind, let's take them down to the kitchen. Cook just made bread, and we have some fresh jam." Celeste hoped the lady wouldn't be insulted by suggesting the kitchen, but she needed to introduce the children to her unusual staff on grounds they all understood.

The two new half-Indian maids sent over by Lady McDowell were shy, but eager to learn. Celeste had hopes the children would adapt just as easily.

Lady Aster didn't hesitate but ushered the children ahead of her. "Bread and jam sound perfect. Marie, Tommy, you're not to gawk but speak politely to those who are about to feed us. A house like this is different from the factory, but you will be safe here."

Celeste swallowed hard as the little girl limped down the stairs on her little stick without a whimper of complaint. She couldn't see beneath the child's overlong skirt to see how damaged her foot might be, but she'd heard horror stories.

"They were caught under the machines?" she asked Lady Aster as they trailed after the children.

"Yes," the lady hissed with fury. "In the mills. They work the mothers from dawn to dusk—as long as there is daylight. And the mill pays pennies for the children to slide beneath those monster machines to gather the cotton bits that fall out. If they don't move fast enough . . ." She took a deep breath to calm herself. "We need laws that can be enforced!"

"And that is why it is so important to have Ashford return to London?" Celeste asked, using her serene voice to aid the lady in regaining her control.

"Yes, among other things," the lady agreed with less hysteria. "The Tories and their kind would rather repeal the laws we already have. They claim the laws interfere with private industry, and the government has no right to tell managers how to run their businesses. This is why the nobility should not be in commerce!" she replied in outrage. "They must rule the country for the best of all, not just themselves and their business partners!"

"But Ashford is in commerce, is he not?" Celeste asked as they reached the kitchen.

"Yes, to the extent of investing in steam engines and trains," the lady admitted with a sigh. "It's a new world, and I cannot say I like all of it."

"The laws must change to keep up with the times. Perhaps the government must change, too." As she must, however reluctantly, she admitted to herself. "Isn't reform what the election is about?" Celeste took the hands of both children when they stopped to gawk at the enormous cellar kitchen. They shrank back against her skirts in fear when they spotted the kitchen's colorful occupants. She supposed the exotic turbans must seem as strange to the rural children as dark complexions.

Celeste put a firm hand on each skinny shoulder and used her best soothing tones. "Marie, Tommy, I'd like you to meet Cook and our two Marys. They are from Jamaica, a country on the other side of the world. Can you make your bows?"

Their regal, African cook barely looked up from the pot she was stirring as the children performed their awkward obeisance. The two young mulatto kitchen maids, who had come to London for the adventure of traveling, studied the children with interest but offered no greeting.

"If you don't mind, we would like some toast and jam and a bit of tea while we discuss where Marie and Tommy will fit in best." Celeste used her persuasive voice and was relieved to see the maids respond as they would have at home. So far from her normal life, she feared everything she had ever known had changed, but apparently she could still rely on her charm to some extent.

Persuasion was not *evil*, she told herself.

Alerted by whatever secret signal traveled through the house, Jamar arrived to take charge of the latest arrivals. The household would soon be bursting at the seams with untrained servants—as Lord Erran had warned.

"Oh, thank goodness," Lady Aster murmured as duties and beds were duly found. "We will need a staff just to sew uniforms for everyone at this rate. Theo is threatening to burn down the mills, but that will scarcely solve the problem. And the Luddites failed in that endeavor already," she added with her usual humor.

"As you said earlier, education is the answer," Celeste said, leading the way out of the kitchen. "We will see that Marie and Tommy learn to read and write. Your Lord Ashford must write a bill that requires all children be able to read and do sums before they can work. How can we expect the poor souls to make a living if they can't even count their wages?"

"Yes, that is it exactly!" Lady Aster said with enthusiasm. "We owe you for being so willing to accept our impositions. I think this is the beginning of a perfect working relationship. I looked up your zodiac chart the other day. We are both on the part of cooperation right now, very strong in the family sector."

"Zodiac chart?" Celeste asked warily. Practical problems, she could solve, but they were treading the unknown again.

"Yes, of course. I am the Malcolm family librarian. I keep the genealogy of all our families. Your birth and that of your siblings was conveyed to us before my time, but my predecessor had already started basic charts for all of you. I amplified yours."

That explanation only confused her more, but they had reached the upper hall where Trevor and Sylvia awaited their shopping trip. Rather than ask more questions, Celeste called for her cloak so they might start out on the dreaded expedition.

Just as they were about to step into the cool morning air, Lord Erran strode up from the back of the house, settling his top hat on his dark curls. "The construction men have arrived. An excellent time for an outing!"

Celeste was fairly certain he'd slept in the study again last night. He apparently thought staying here was improper, so she bit her tongue about his abrupt arrival in front of his sister-in-law. As much as the gentleman's arrogant assumptions annoyed her, she welcomed the extra security his presence offered. For some reason, she felt certain the alley ruffians would not attack a gentleman as they might Jamar.

"Oh, most excellent," Lady Aster exclaimed. "You may introduce Lord Rochester to your tailor. He will need a complete set of everything, and you have better taste than Theo."

"Beasts in the field have more taste than Theo," Erran said, offering his elbows to Aster and Celeste. "But he never emerges from his cave, so he doesn't offend anyone with his execrable choices. I'm confident Lord Rochester will know precisely what suits him best, so don't think we'll dally long at the tailor. We'll have plenty of time to criticize your bonnet choices and if you aren't too cold, buy ices while we're at it."

Celeste wrapped her gloved fingers around his elbow with the fear that she was walking to her execution. She could not imagine London modistes would take to the oddity of her ungainly stature and too-dark features.

"AH, THE MADEMOISELLE is exquisite," the modiste exclaimed, tilting Miss Rochester's chin to the gray light from the window. "The color, it must be bold to show off these eyes! And the cut . . ." She rummaged in a drawer for a fashion doll, clucking excitedly.

Assured that Aster's choice of modiste had the good sense to rave over the lady's exotic beauty, Erran turned his attention to more serious matters than colors, fabrics, and his disturbing need to shower the lady in all she desired.

He had a notion that his little party was being observed by more than the usual bored matrons. The hulk in ill-fitting gentleman's clothes on the corner looked out of place, and the beggar lad who had surreptitiously trailed after Trevor to the tailor shop wasn't behaving in character.

As a precaution, Erran sent the carriage back to the house with a call for two sturdy footmen to join them for guard duty. There wasn't a great deal more he could do except stay alert.

It was possible that he was overly suspicious, but he was relieved when the ladies finally declared themselves too exhausted to linger over ices, especially since it was starting to rain. He ushered the ladies and Trevor into Ashford's equipage and mounted his steed, noting the young baron's wistful glance at the mare. The boy needed his own stable, but there was only so much Erran could appropriate from the estate's coffers for this project.

And that's what it had to be—a project. He'd restore as much of the Rochesters' inheritance as he could, send them back to Jamaica if they liked, move Ashford in, and then he'd figure out what he could do with himself besides become a mechanic—or an evil bully. Perhaps before all that happened, he could attend a dinner or two to see Miss Rochester in that cream silk she'd so reluctantly purchased today.

Imagining the lady in a low-cut dinner gown instead of her stiff, high-collared mourning gowns, Erran wasn't paying attention to the crowded road as he should have. He glanced up just in time to see a ragged beggar darting around a fruit cart in the direction of Ashford's carriage—with a flaming object in his filthy fist.

Too much knowledge was a terrible thing. As Erran kicked his mare into action, his mind ran wild through all the ramifications of dynamite, gunpowder, and flame beneath a fragile carriage pulled by skittish horses.

Aiming for the narrow passage between urchin and carriage, he spurred his mount faster, splashing mud across the well-dressed crowds on the walks. Fixated on his goal, the boy didn't look up until Erran was nearly upon him. The ruffian shrieked and stumbled backward. Erran's horse reared. And the carriage team panicked, nearly trampling an elderly pedestrian in their haste to escape.

The homemade bomb fell to the wet stones, the wick still burning.

Coachmen roared curses as they reined in their teams. The fruit cart took the corner too fast, dumping its fragile cargo on the street for others to crush.

Erran struggled to bring his spooked mare under control—not before nicking the boy's arm with sharp hooves. The would-be terrorist collapsed, screaming, into the mud—not bothering to reach for the burning bomb rolling away.

Focused on the flame, Erran noted nothing but the seconds it would take to dismount and stomp the wick before the bomb blew him and all around him into bloody pieces. He could have galloped away and left it to explode, but every cell in his body rejected that solution.

"SNUFF IT," he shouted instinctively at the moaning boy writhing on the ground, holding his broken arm.

The burning bottle rattled faster, reversing direction toward the boy.

Weeping, the boy rolled over the bottle, quenching the flame in the rain-slick street.

The bottle had reversed direction.

And the boy had risked his wretched life to *snuff* a bomb.

Too shaken to think, Erran simply gulped air. A bobby grabbed the injured boy and hauled him from the gutter by the scruff of his neck.

That's when Erran noted the pedestrians swarming out of the street back to the walk—after they had all run to snuff a flame they hadn't noticed until Erran had bellowed his orders. They'd apparently obeyed his shout without even knowing why.

Gorge rising at the horror of what had almost happened—and what he'd done—Erran didn't stop to watch the outcome. He galloped after the carriage fleeing down the street.

CELESTE CLUNG to Trevor as the closed coach careened through the crowd, cracking against other vehicles, causing pedestrians to flee and cursing horsemen to wheel their horses out of the way. On the forward-facing seat, Lady Aster was pale and gripping a strap while holding on to Sylvia.

By the time Lord Erran caught up with them, the team was slowing down, but Celeste wasn't certain she could return to breathing.

She had seen what had happened and had to watch helplessly, fearing the worst. At seeing his lordship in one piece, she inexplicably wanted to weep and fling her arms around him. Losing their father, plus the burden of coping these last months, had apparently made a watering pot of her.

She watched as Lord Erran rode past them to settle the team. Instead of stopping to speak with the passengers to see if they were all right once the vehicle quit rocking, he merely rode beside them, observing their surroundings with a cold gaze, his square jaw set in anger.

She had seen him nearly trample a small boy carrying a flaming object. From the furious stiffness of his lordship's posture, Celeste had to assume the boy had meant harm. This time, it had not just been Jamar or herself, but her siblings and Lady Aster who had been threatened.

If Lansdowne was behind this, he did not mean for them to have friends.

After the laughter and excitement of their shopping trip, it was a grim reminder of their precarious situation. She glanced at Lady Aster, who had her arm around a weeping Sylvia.

"I know Lord Erran doesn't wish to believe an earl would be so dastardly, but I see no one else who would benefit from terrifying us. And if our enemy could be so callous about harming you as well as us, then it's quite possible it is not just us he wishes out of the way, is it? Is he a danger to Lord Ashford?"

Lady Aster shrugged. "From what I have learned of his birth date, the earl's horoscope is very black, admittedly. He is not a man who likes to be crossed. We have reason to believe Ashford's accident was caused by men who object to reform, but we have no proof of more."

"I would give him our dowries if he would leave us alone, but we cannot let him have the estate and our people," Celeste said, as much for her siblings' sake as her own.

Trevor looked grim, and Sylvia looked frightened, but neither argued with her assessment.

"Spoken like a true Capricorn," Lady Aster said with a small smile. "Let us hope the solicitors will give us enough rope to hang him."

Celeste clenched her fingers and vowed that she would use every ounce of her persuasive gift to ensure that the solicitors did exactly what she wanted of them.

Remembering the night of the riot when Lord Erran had apparently used his bellows to counteract her charm . . . she shivered. She must hope they had the same goals.

Thirteen

IN A BLACK HUMOR after the bomb incident, Erran watched grimly until the ladies were inside the house, then rode around to the mews to stable his horse. With the animal in good hands, Erran stalked in the direction of the gate, just as Trevor darted out of it.

"What happened?" the boy demanded.

"Nothing," Erran snarled, pointing to indicate that Trevor return to the yard.

Workmen had piled construction materials along the path. The bags of Portland cement and stones would make excellent obstacles to trip up intruders, but the piles of lumber would aid an arsonist. He despised thinking like this.

"The team spooked. That's not nothing." The young baron looked almost as shaken as Erran felt. "Are my sisters in danger? Do we need to move them elsewhere?"

"That's precisely what someone wants." And what they were likely to get, because Erran couldn't think of a way to keep them safe in the city. But then, it wouldn't be safe for Ashford either, and his brother would never come to London if he couldn't have his own home.

And without Dunc here to whip the Whigs in line, the Tories would win again. *Filth and bother!* Was that the whole point of this torment? Someone was trying to make Duncan stay away?

"Dressing up and going to parties won't be enough, will it?" Trevor asked, speaking what Erran was thinking.

"We'll talk to the solicitors first." He couldn't see a positive outcome, but he needed to know where they stood. He needed the solid ground of law beneath his feet before deciding on action.

No man should be above the law. If a law was wrong, then it should be changed, not trampled beneath the feet of men powerful enough to escape punishment. Righting wrongs was what he'd wanted to do with his life.

He hadn't wanted to *bellow* people into submission. That was the same as bullying and totally, irrevocably wrong.

Although Miss Rochester thought it was perfectly fine to *charm* people into compliance, Erran realized later as they gathered in the study with the solicitors.

Theo had arrived with documents from Ashford allowing Erran to speak on the marquess's behalf. Their Uncle Pascoe had shown up just to intimidate with his official, imposing presence. On the surface, Pascoe dealt in transporting goods, but anyone with connections to government knew he had influence with the king and others in the cabinet. Erran suspected his uncle transported more information than goods.

The Rochester estate had sent Mr. Herrington, a plump older gentleman who kept nervously polishing his spectacles. Erran thought Mr. Luther, Lansdowne's solicitor, looked more like a card shark than a man of the law. Balding, narrow-eyed, and skinny, he appeared to be gauging the other players and arranging his documents in order like a hand of cards.

Lady Aster had insisted that she and Sylvia stay out of the crowded study, but she hadn't been able to dissuade Celeste or Trevor from taking part in their fate. As Erran listened to Celeste speak with the compelling voice of angels, he wished he'd locked her in the cellar. The damned female was trying to *charm* hard-headed lawyers.

"It is only a matter of time until my father's will is found," she said with crystalline sweetness that had the idiot solicitors actually bobbing their heads and hanging on to her every word. "His majordomo was witness to the document and has provided an affidavit attesting to our father's wishes. I am of an age to take charge of my share, and the marquess has generously offered to act as guardian for my siblings. I think this is a very simple matter, if you'll agree."

"Yes, yes, of course, Miss Rochester," Herrington, her father's lawyer, agreed, crossing his hands over his paunch in satisfaction. "The baron gave all indication that he meant for the three of you to share the estate. We've read your letters and seen the affidavit. It's all very proper and in order."

Theo sent Erran a look expressing his surprise at this easy capitulation. This was the solicitor who had handed the estate over to the earl without a qualm. Unable to explain what Celeste was doing in terms even remotely logical, Erran shook his head and waited for the axe to fall.

Luther, the rat-faced solicitor from Lansdowne's firm, was looking as if he'd eaten lemons, even though he'd nodded agreement.

Erran suspected *charm* only went so far. He watched with interest as Luther clenched and unclenched his fists and moved papers about on the desk as if fighting a compulsion.

Which he could very well be doing. It would take strength and determination to overcome Celeste's persuasive tones.

"Your father . . ." Luther shoved forward one of his documents, stumbling for words. "The firm you say drew up the will, has no record of it. This is their affidavit."

Pascoe's thick eyebrows raised, but he waited for Erran to speak.

Erran snatched the letter, made note of the firm's name and Jamaican address, and compared that to the papers he'd found in the baron's trunk. Without holding one against another, he could not immediately determine if the signatures were identical.

"The majordomo . . . is an African slave belonging to the estate," Luther said sluggishly, searching for words as if shaking off a spell and needing to find his argument again. "His testimony is . . . irrelevant. The law is clear. As head of the Rochester family, the earl must act in his cousin's place."

Celeste seemed set to argue. Erran slapped a hand over her arm and shook his head at her and his uncle. He wanted to hear the entire argument before she began twisting words and heads.

Apparently finding his way again, Luther picked up speed. "Unfortunately, Miss Rochester's birth outside of legal wedlock prevents her from inheriting any part of the estate. Her father was still married to another woman at the time she was born. The earl would like to place the younger siblings in the proper schools and have their half-sister, Mrs. Guilford, preside over their household until they come of age. Miss Rochester, of course, being of the age of consent, may choose her own way."

Celeste and Trevor gasped. Pascoe almost looked amused, so he saw through the ruse too. Good.

Without questioning Luther's scandalous assertion, Erran merely placed his hands over the documents on the desk. Letting the Jamaican one fall to the floor where he could collect it later, he crumpled the others, and said, "No."

He tossed the papers at the grate. "As marquess and head of the baron's maternal family, Ashford has greater jurisdiction. We will take the case to court. Until such time, the children, including Miss Rochester, are under his protection. I have already filed documents with the banks preventing anyone from access to their funds until this matter is settled."

The injustice and outright fraud of naming Miss Rochester a bastard almost had him bellowing with his Courtroom Voice, but Erran's sense of fairness prevailed. He was in the right. He didn't need to savage a bonehead. Yet. "Should the earl dispose of *any* assets, we can and will sue the earl for everything he owns. The plantation and its inhabitants are the property of the estate until such time as this matter is settled, and the courts will appoint a neutral executor. We have notified the Jamaican authorities accordingly."

"You have no basis for this wholesale takeover of the earl's responsibilities," Luther shouted.

"But he does, sir," Celeste said sweetly. Erran could hear her fury but she had marvelous control. "We are of Malcolm descent, and as such, the property passes through the female line. I do not believe the earl is female."

Erran almost choked on surprise and laughter. She was feeding him Aster's nonsense, and both the men of business were willing to eat it up—because of her damned voice and not any logic that he could discern. Female line! As if such a thing were possible under British law.

Caught in her spell, without any prepared document or counter-argument, Luther spluttered incoherently. Even Theo and Pascoe didn't protest the idiocy.

"We'll provide the proper credentials to the court, of course, gentlemen." Pascoe finally spoke, while standing up to dismiss the company as if he were judge and jury. "The king will stay apprised of the proceedings. Good meeting you, Herrington." He held out his hand to shake the hand of the Rochesters' solicitor. "Keep up the good work. Ashford will be pleased."

Luther looked prepared to protest.

Celeste rose, and etiquette forced all the men to rise as well. "It was lovely clearing the air, gentlemen. I do thank you for your concern. I'm sure we'll remember your kindness when Lord Rochester comes into his estate. It was good of you to come. Jamar will be happy to see you out."

And the solicitors left as if they were puppets on her strings. Erran could barely keep from gaping, even though he knew what she was doing—he could hear her sarcasm beneath the syrup.

Apparently, although her charm didn't work on Erran, his family had soaked it up right along with the solicitors. But after Celeste quit speaking and lapsed into angry silence, Theo and Pascoe shook their heads as if to clear them and watched in disbelief as the angry solicitors filed out without argument.

"What just happened here?" Pascoe demanded once the study door closed on their departing guests. "I came here prepared to take the matter to the Crown, and they just run off as if a hound is on their heels."

Having experienced some of his wife's weird abilities, Theo was a little slower to react. He glanced questioningly at Erran, and then to their hostess.

Who promptly broke into tears. "He called me a *bastard*! My mother and father would never ever do anything improper. How dare that dastard suggest such a thing? How *dare* he!"

The glass on the oil lamp shattered.

Fourteen

SPRAWLED ACROSS HER BED, sobbing, Celeste ignored the timid knocks at her chamber door. Fire bombers, runaway carriages, nasty lawyers, and bastardy had shattered her too-brief joy at walking about shops as the lady she'd once been. While indulging in fabulous fabrics, she'd even allowed herself hope that she might have some small part of her life back.

But the reality was that she would never be her father's pampered daughter again. Her world had irrevocably changed to one of chaos and anarchy. And even though she knew she was engaging in self-pity, she couldn't control her tears of pure terror and loss.

Burying her head in the pillow to hide her weeping, she scarcely heard Lady Aster's worried call through the locked door.

If only she could just shrivel up and blow away! Or go home. She so very much wanted the comforting familiarity of blue skies and warm breezes and the soft murmurs of patois . . . .

But that seemed long ago and far away, in a time when her father had handled all difficult matters and all she had to do was choose menus and gowns. Those days were gone. She cried harder, burying all her bottled up grief and despair into her pillow, where she hoped she couldn't hurt anyone or anything.

She'd shattered glass. She had never, ever used her voice as a weapon of destruction. What had she become?

What was this house doing to her?

She didn't hear the key in the lock but was instantly aware the moment Lord Erran's imposing presence crossed the threshold. She couldn't look up. Her face would be all blotchy and wet from crying. "You don't belong here. Go away," she said, using her most compelling voice.

He ignored her command, as usual. Why was she cursed with the company of a man who couldn't be seduced by her voice?

"You've missed dinner," he said. "The entire household is on edge because of you. I've sent your sister off with Aster and have your brother patrolling taverns. Jamar wanted to break down the door, but I said I'd try civilized methods first."

Celeste scrubbed guiltily at her damp cheek, realizing how she'd let everyone down to indulge in selfish megrims. She refused to look at him, even though it was difficult to keep her head averted when she so much wanted him to *do* something, to make things better—*as her father had once done.*

That realization struck her painfully. She could not, would not sink down that hole again. She must stand strong and on her own— in the morning, after her tears had dried. "Where did you find a key?" she muttered into her pillow.

"I didn't. I made one. Hundred-year-old locks are very crude. I've been unlocking them since childhood."

Of course he had. This man knew no boundaries, as evidenced by his appearance in her room. It wasn't as if anyone, anywhere, *cared* if she lost her reputation! Instead of causing another bout of weeping, that made her angry.

The bed sagged from his weight. She was painfully aware of the incongruence of his masculine size in her dainty surroundings. She'd chosen this room for the rose-printed calicoes and spring green walls. She'd decorated with the gauzy summer bed hangings from home. It wasn't a room meant for men. He would be wearing the black coat that reminded her of mourning, and she couldn't bear the dark cloud of gloom.

"Breaking and entering is more civilized?" she asked with a sniff, forcing herself to focus on his imposition instead of her terror at what she'd done. "Go away. You don't belong in here. I just need to be alone for awhile."

"I understand, and I'm sorry," he said, without really sounding sorry.

He rested his hand near her hip and leaned closer, giving her far more to think about than self-pity.

"I wish I could create a magic bubble that would shut out reality," he continued, "and surround you in sunshine and roses, but I can't. You're the one with the magic to create change, not me."

"Me?" she asked in incredulity, wiping at her face and inching away from his encroaching presence. "*Change* is the very last thing I want. I want everything to go back to the way it was." His assertion terrified her.

"If you can't accept change, you might as well be dead," he countered with scorn. "Being able to wrap everyone around your little finger has made you weak."

"Weak!" Outraged, she wiped at her eyes and dragged herself up to sit against her pillows. He was every bit the black thundercloud she feared, but she had to admit that Lord Erran's chiseled features were magnificently handsome wearing a frown of concern. "I am not weak!"

"You are," he asserted. "You've never had to fight for what you want."

That was true. She glared. "Preferring peace is not a weakness!" He was sitting on her *bed*—as if he had every right to do so. Nervously, she scooted a little farther, but the bed was not large— and he was.

"I heard you the night of the riot," she said, trying to steady her breathing but still nervous at his proximity. "Do not pretend I am the only one with magic. You could have ordered that dreadful mob to go soak their heads, and they would have rushed off in search of a horse trough."

"*I* wanted to talk to them. *You* drove them off so I couldn't," he retorted. "Whatever I did that night is not something I'm proud of, but you did not help." Beneath lashes too long for a man, his dark eyes smoldered, igniting fires she preferred to deny.

Crossing her arms in a protective gesture against his too-masculine proximity, Celeste studied this lordly English aristocrat. His attire was spotless. No wrinkle marred his linen. Every polished silver button was in place. He hadn't shaved, and his stern jaw was dark with stubble, but that didn't detract from his mien of competence and assertiveness—characteristics she found all too attractive and ought to avoid if she meant to stand up for herself from now on.

Weak—he thought her weak. And pathetic, and a weepy clinging vine, she supposed. Worse, he was right in too many ways she didn't want to consider.

"I don't believe you," she said frankly, refusing to back off any further, although the delicious scent of his shaving soap had her wanting to taste him. Perhaps she should have eaten dinner. She took a deep breath and concentrated on his infuriating argument. "You have the ability to command armies with a voice like yours, and you're not proud of it?"

"Women need mystical crutches because they're weak," he said with an expression of disdain. "Men command through respect and intelligence and strength. Not that I'm convinced I've done anything except assert authority, I still maintain that manipulation by . . . weirdness . . . isn't fair play or good for character."

Astonishingly, Celeste punched his muscular arm. She had never done such a thing before. She stared at her fist in disbelief, but the act felt good enough to repeat. That she refrained made her feel even better.

Unharmed, his elegant lordship merely raised his black eyebrows in question.

"If you really believe in fair play, then you're already living in a fantasy world," she said witheringly. "Fair play only exists for the privileged few with the wealth and power to be noble. 'Nice try, little girl,'" she mimicked. "'Let me pat your little head so I can walk all over you again using *my* rules because it's my game.' *Balderdash.*"

He studied her as if she'd just emerged from a wall painting. She nearly leapt off the bed when he brushed her hair behind her ear. Lust as a distraction from weeping worked well, although she thought it might be dangerous.

"So you think I should confront Lansdowne and bellow at him to jump off a high cliff?" he asked without rancor. "Wouldn't that be akin to murder—except no court could convict me?"

She shrugged. "I've found that people do not respond well if it goes against their beliefs. You will notice that the earl's solicitor worked past my charm within minutes. He truly *believes* I'm a worthless bastard! Unless the earl is already suicidal, I doubt that jumping off a cliff would appeal to him."

She was coming out of her despair despite herself, fascinated by discussing the forbidden topic with someone who understood—and even more fascinated with the man nearly leaning over her. Even in the semi-darkness, she could see his beard shadow and longed to stroke his jaw—if only he would give her some excuse.

"There are unanticipated casualties, though," he argued, properly keeping his hands to himself. "If I believed in your weird theory and shouted at the earl where others could hear, we might have an entire rash of suicides. Or today, I could have had carriages colliding as pedestrians ran into the street to snuff the wick. Or had it been evening, they might have attempted to snuff gas lights by smashing them. Even if I should be superstitious enough to believe I wield that kind of unreliable power, I wouldn't use it."

She glared at him. "You halted a riot and stopped a terrorist and still you do not believe you have an . . . ability . . . greater than most? No wonder it's only the Malcolm ladies who talk about oddities, gifts, and talents. Men are too thickheaded to accept what they don't understand—which includes pretty much the entire universe."

"Men like scientific evidence before they believe the ridiculous," he countered.

"Artists are not called *weird* because scientists haven't proved they paint better than anyone else! Priests aren't called weird because they have faith without science. It does not seem extraordinary to me that some people can speak well and influence others. You have surely seen eloquent orators who can sway crowds—are they witches employing magic?"

"That was not your *erudition* seducing hardheaded lawyers," he exclaimed, leaning closer with the intensity of his argument. "As much as I want to believe it's my authority to which people respond, I simply cannot take a chance on such unfair use of my *ability*. It would be akin to practicing Mesmerism."

"*Mesmerism*! Is that how you explain what we do?" she asked in amazement, admiring the flash of his dark eyes as he spoke of this interesting new theory.

"It's the only scientific explanation I can determine," he said, almost angrily, although his hand brushed hers on top of the covers as if seeking reassurance. "I mesmerized an entire courtroom once." He dismissed the discussion with a complete change of subject. "Would you like to come down and have a bite to eat so the household knows you're alive?"

Fascinated despite their disagreement, Celeste didn't ever want to end this moment, but he was right to cut it off. She feared her entire family would be here if they lingered longer. "I don't think I can. I'm not hungry." Not for food, at least. "It's been a horrible day. And I broke an oil lamp. I do *not* want to consider what that means. I think it best if I rest so I have better control."

As if they hadn't just been quarreling, his lordship offered one of his rare smiles—more heart-stoppingly effective because of their rarity. His fingers enclosed hers, offering the reassurance she craved, and she would have swooned, had he not continued with his usual pragmatism. "I had wondered if that was intentional. I've heard of opera singers who can shatter glass. I'll have the maid carry up some hot tea. Perhaps that will help you relax."

Opera singers—she'd like to believe that, but she was a contralto, not a soprano. But if that's what he wished to believe . . . She was done arguing.

"You are upsetting me as much as the lawyers," she admitted, although not clarifying in how many ways he disturbed her. "I wish I could tell you to go away and let me return to my sewing. It's safer."

His expression darkened, and he withdrew his hand. "When this is all over, I promise to leave you in peace. But it's far from over."

She lowered her gaze in acceptance and disappointment that someday, he would no longer be part of her life. Maybe then she could seek normality again. No, normal was being weak. He was right. She must learn independence. "I cannot promise to contain myself if faced with any more days like this one. I'm worn thin as it is."

"I can respect that, although I will not lie to you. Given the circumstances, I cannot promise to bring you peace, but I will work toward that goal." He patted the hand he'd just released. A frisson of electricity passed between them. She froze, and he hastily stood up, as if he'd felt it too. "Good-night, Miss Rochester."

She fell asleep wondering what it would be like if his lordship didn't have to leave her room—if she could have his comforting size and security all night long.

That was the old Celeste speaking. In the morning, the new independent and strong Celeste would scorn him.

WISHING he could simply wrap the glass-breaking, manipulative, fragile Miss Rochester in cotton batting and ship her somewhere safe until this was all over, Erran sought activity to distract him from the woman upstairs. Her beautiful, tear-streaked face had nearly broken his heart. Her refusal to believe that charm and bullying were unfair and a dangerous path to perdition made him want to bang his head against a wall.

So he spent the evening digging through the rest of her father's document trunk. The man collected papers the way squirrels gathered nuts. Why the devil hadn't he included his will?

Because a reasonably young man of strength and good health does not expect to die. And a man of integrity does not expect his relations to be treacherous frauds.

Erran compared the letter purloined from Lansdowne's solicitor with a few of the Jamaican solicitor's letters in the trunk. The handwriting was different, but there could have been a new clerk.

None of the documents in the trunk had the same signature as the letter stating there was no will, however. How many partners were in the firm? Who was authorized to speak for the Rochester estate? Or had Lansdowne simply made up the entire letter?

Finding answers meant sending more letters to the governor's office and court clerks, asking about the discrepancy—months more time lost. Erran's suspicion was that someone in the Jamaican office had been bribed to keep the will hidden and was receiving a commission on assets sold. Preying on the weak was a game to the bullies of the world, morality and legality be damned.

Ashford was depending on Lansdowne's support in the Whig campaign for the prime minister. Without proof, Erran hated to accuse the earl of lies, theft, and fraud, but he was furious enough to confront the man. Better he do so with evidence in hand.

He dug deeper and scanned more papers. Invoices for shipments, journals of daily thoughts and appointments, lists of household items Rochester wished to buy—the trunk was bottomless. And useless.

Beneath all the papers and books was a small package wrapped in brown paper with a note attached—*For the Malcolm library.*

Suddenly wide awake, Erran tore off the wrapper and scanned the contents—more slender journals similar to the one he'd already perused. No wonder the siblings hadn't bothered opening it. They must have seen packages like this regularly, and in their grief, probably respected their father's privacy.

He scanned the dates of these tomes—all from the last few years. There were entries on weather, crops, experiments on the sewing mechanism and other equipment. He noted the sketches of the design, but he'd already drawn similar ones.

Disappointed, Erran looked at the brown paper again—*the*

Malcolm library. Aster only kept genealogical records. She had no room in her small townhouse for a library.

The earl of Lochmas, Aster's father, had spoken of his castle full of moldering old medieval Malcolm volumes from distant, prolific ancestors. But the wrapping paper hadn't specified Edinburgh or even Scotland.

The *current* Malcolm library was in Wystan—one of Ashford's holdings in Northumberland.

Was it possible . . . ?

He would never know without trying. Wystan was much closer than Jamaica.

Fifteen

THE NEXT MORNING, to avoid any chance of running into Lord Erran, Celeste asked one of the new maids to carry her tea and toast to the sewing room. She could hear the construction men pounding on walls below and felt certain he'd be there directing them.

If she had learned nothing else these past months, it was that circumstances changed in the blink of an eye, and she could only rely on herself. The marquess's family could suddenly decide the Rochesters were a liability and all promises of allowances and schools might disappear in a puff of smoke. She would attempt to continue earning her own way, and sewing was the only way she knew to do it.

"This house, it may be too strong for you," Nana said as she took another basic shirt body from her machine. "You should explore your gift, not run from it."

Nana seldom spoke, but when she did, Celeste felt compelled to listen—even if she didn't like what was being said.

"Lord Erran thinks it is wrong to force people to do what I want. And breaking glass . . ." Had she done that because she was stronger here or because she was simply more upset than she'd ever been in her life? "I don't think destruction is a positive use of my gift." She took the loosely pleated shirt body and smoothed the linen creases with her fingers.

"Explore and control," Nana said enigmatically. "Or give it up."

Give up her gift? How would she go on without it? She couldn't, quite simply. A beautiful woman might not even notice she wielded vocal charm. But Celeste knew that without her voice, no one would pay attention to a lanky, unprepossessing spinster. And if society labeled her as a bastard . . . The horror of that appellation branded her as unworthy as surely as if they'd taken a hot iron to her flesh.

She would go from pampered daughter of a wealthy baron to an invisible nothing who must scramble for pennies. She would be a dreadful liability to her siblings and could not risk their futures by living with them. The earl had picked a frightful way of terrifying her this time. Even her voice couldn't save her if the rumor spread.

It was nearly luncheon before Lord Erran sought her out. She'd been nervously awaiting this moment, afraid of what new scheme he meant to perpetrate. He was worse than the ocean winds blowing her about with no means of controlling where she was tossed.

He'd already stripped her of most of her defenses by inviting Trevor and Sylvia to go off on their own. Sylvia had happily returned to the shops with Lady Aster, and Trevor was out exploring. Since there was no longer any reason to hide, she would have been a horrible witch to object.

Without any greeting, Lord Erran set her father's journals on the sewing table accompanied by a torn piece of brown paper. He pointed at the label on the paper. "Did your father regularly send his journals to this library?"

Trying to act as if his presence didn't leave her breathless, Celeste shrugged. "Jamar is more likely to know than I am. Our parents were always jotting notes of recipes and garden knowledge and such and taught us to do the same. I asked about mama's diaries once, and Papa said they were in a safe place. Jamaican weather is not good for books and papers, so I assumed he'd found a dry storage."

"I'll ask Jamar to which Malcolm library they might have gone. Lady Aster says she has not seen them, so I'm thinking it's Wystan." He started out of the sewing room.

"Wait! Why do you ask?" Attempting to assert a little of the authority he'd stolen from her, she set down her sewing.

He opened one of the books to a place he'd marked with a piece of paper. "Your father made notes of important dates and occasions. He'll have noted the date he married your mother and the date of your birth and all the circumstances. If they're in his handwriting, they'll stand up in court better than any Jamaican witness."

She could tell he was excited. For a man who usually expressed only cynicism, that meant he thought he'd discovered something of importance.

She glanced to Nana. "You can tell them when and how Papa was married, can't you? And who was there?"

Nana nodded. "He was lonely for many years. When he learned of his English wife's death, he married a neighbor lady. He was filled with joy that he could finally have the woman he loved. Jamar was there. And the old preacher who died in the hurricane. And a few others."

"There is no doubt of your legitimacy," Lord Erran said emphatically. "Jamar has already given me names of witnesses. But they are all either dead or in Jamaica. It will take months of correspondence to clear up this vicious rumor the earl apparently intends to spread. If Lansdowne is that desperate, Ashford will simply have to do without his influence. I will not have him besmirch your reputation, even for the sake of a damned prime minister."

"Your brother depends on Lansdowne to change the fate of all England," she said, trying to sort out his arguments. "Wouldn't the good of everyone be more important than my birth?"

He waved away her concern. "I'll find another vote. Lansdowne has proved himself unreliable and treacherous."

Her lonely heart swelled with joy that he would place her above the needs of a marquess. She didn't think this wise, but she waited to hear what else he planned.

"Your parents' journals will convince society without need of lawsuits, especially if Ashford declares them sufficient. I am hoping they may contain more information that I can use as well. I'll be off to Wystan directly."

She did not even know where this Wystan was. Celeste glanced dubiously at the pages he showed her. Her father's familiar penmanship warmed her heart, and she smoothed her hand over the page, trying to grasp why his lordship was so excited.

The rap of the door knocker carried up from the foyer. Instead of responding to his lordship's declaration, she hurried toward the front parlor to look out on the street. Very seldom did visitors bring good news.

"It is our sister's carriage," she said when Lord Erran caught up with her. She turned to him in horror. "Will the earl have told her these lies?"

"There is only one way of finding out. I'm of the belief that the more information we possess, the better prepared we are. Do you wish me to leave or stay?"

Her desire for independence warred with her need for safety. It wasn't just her future at stake, but that of her siblings. Reluctantly, Celeste conceded. "Join us after she's brought up, if you please. I don't have Sylvia or Trevor to act as my companions, and I'd rather not ruin my reputation more than necessary."

He nodded and departed, leaving her to settle in the front parlor like a lady of leisure. She was wearing her gray silk with unfashionably simple sleeves, but she hoped her pearls lent an air of modest respectability. She needed all the protective armor she could summon.

Charlotte was huffing and puffing by the time the footman led her up the stairs. Today, she was festooned in pink frills from head to silk slippers. "A butler," she exclaimed breathlessly as she entered. "You have acquired a butler and a footman. How extraordinary. Are they Ashford's?"

"Good morning, Charlotte," Celeste said sweetly, correcting her half-sister's rudeness. "How are you today?"

"Terrible, quite terrible. The rumors are all over town." She glanced up at the footman, waiting for him to depart.

Celeste signaled him to bring tea. He bowed and left the parlor door open, per her instructions. She didn't trust Charlotte and didn't wish her to feel too comfortable. "I'm sorry to hear that," she said without curiosity. "And how are your children? Are they well?"

"Well as can be, considering the scandal!" Charlotte said indignantly, flouncing onto the worn sofa. "My own papa, a bigamist! I cannot believe it of him. I will not. I cannot say what it will do to my dear Charles's position."

As Lord Erran had said, forewarned was forearmed. Celeste bit her tongue and let her sister ramble. Lansdowne had not been slow in spreading the gossip. Bigamy! That was an interesting new angle.

"And you sitting there with butlers and maids as if butter wouldn't melt in your mouth. That will not last once Ashford hears," Charlotte said angrily. "We must remove you from this house at once. My Charles will help find you a position before the scandal grows. It's the least we can do."

"Don't be silly," Celeste said in her sweetest placating tone as a maid arrived with the tea tray. "Papa was the most proper gentleman on earth. Did you hear about our excitement yesterday? An arsonist almost set us on fire." She poured the tea and spoke as if terrorists were a daily occurrence, waiting to see how Charlotte would react.

"The streets are dreadful these days," Charlotte said with a wave of her chubby hand after the maid left. "I cannot live in town with any ease. We will be happy to see the baron and your sister to our home in Yorkshire, where they will be safe. It is best to sever the connection quickly, so their reputations do not suffer. You do not have the understanding of gentlemen as I, a married lady, do. Even our dear papa was capable of sin."

Celeste wondered if the lady always talked in circles or if she was trying to convince herself that what she said was true. Celeste sipped her tea and studied her much older sibling with interest. Charlotte was nearly red-faced with her effort to sound credible.

"I have no notion what you are about," Celeste lied. "Ashford has been all that is sincere. He is providing Trevor with an excellent school and tutor, and Lady Aster is looking for a good finishing school for Sylvia. We have invitations to dine with them next week, after our new wardrobes arrive. Do you have some quarrel with the marquess?" she asked politely, enjoying watching Charlotte writhe in discomfort. Apparently, the conversation was not going as her sister had hoped.

"No, that cannot be," Charlotte said, with less confidence than earlier. "He has not heard of your birth, surely. You must be honest with him. And Lansdowne is most certainly the one to take the baron in hand. He's head of the family, after all."

The maid arrived in the doorway. "Lord Erran Ives, miss."

His arrogant lordship strode in without invitation, just as Celeste had hoped he would. Today, he wore immaculate white pantaloons with an elegantly tailored gray frock coat and what suspiciously looked like one of the pleated shirts she'd sewn, topped by a black linen neckcloth.

The thrill of having him as her white knight would have to stop, but she so admired his willingness to dive into battle that she threw his grim visage a bright smile. "My lord, welcome. I was telling my sister how your family has so kindly taken us under their wing. She keeps prattling about scandal. Have you heard anything?"

Charlotte was practically gaping at the elegant aristocrat gracing the shabby parlor and bowing over her hand.

"A pleasure to see you again, Mrs. Guilford. Will you be staying in town long? I will have my sister-in-law add your name to the guest list, if so," he said smoothly.

Oh, that was good. Celeste watched her half-sister's mouth fall open at the promise of an invitation to a house of nobility.

Charlotte glanced in confusion from the confident Lord Erran to Celeste, who merely smiled and sipped her tea. Whatever her sister had hoped to accomplish by coming here had been knocked awry.

Remembering how terrified they'd been before Lord Erran arrived in their lives, Celeste shuddered at how they would have reacted to such awful news back then. In their horror, they might actually have accepted Charlotte's invitation to flee to the country. She didn't think she would have believed the lies about their parents, but she had been so distraught that she might not have had the confidence to argue. She'd learned hard lessons these past months, and the experience had made her stronger.

"But surely..." Charlotte stumbled over the words. "The scandal... It's all over town. You cannot mean to accept... I mean..." She glanced desperately at Celeste. "Have you not explained to his lordship?"

"That the unscrupulous earl lies and means to steal my dowry by calling me a bastard?" Celeste asked. Beneath her surface cheer, she laced her voice with fury and disdain, just to see if Charlotte could hear her other voice. "Lord Erran is not so foolish as to doubt our father's integrity." Which was one of the many reasons she had begun to accept his presence, despite their many differences.

The cup in her sister's hand rattled, and she hastily set it down. "But... you said... If there's no will... I do not understand."

Celeste couldn't determine if her guest was reacting to her voice or if she was genuinely upset. She let Lord Erran reply for her.

"Lansdowne is deeply in debt," his lordship said sympathetically. "It is a tragedy that he seeks to cover up the fact with falsehoods and by preying on innocent persons such as yourself. You would do well to counter the scandalmongers by telling them that Ashford is in possession of all the necessary documents to protect his wards. I know you were quite young when you lost your mother, but if you will make inquiries, I'm sure you'll find the correct date of her death. Take that to our solicitor, and he will be happy to show you that your father is as honorable as you believed."

Celeste didn't think he was using any influencing charms, but Charlotte seemed to be entranced just by his lordship's presence. Admittedly, those broad shoulders in tailored coat and gleaming linen would overwhelm any woman. Should Lord Erran actually smile instead of frowning formidably, half the female population would be at his feet.

"Oh." Charlotte threw up a be-ringed hand in confusion. "Oh, of course, my lord, I will do that. I did not think . . . The earl is such a commanding man. And he has generously offered to send dear Lord Rochester to school, so I thought . . ."

Lord Erran gave her an impatient look. "He hasn't paid the school for his own son's tuition. The real scandal is that the earl failed to present himself to Miss Rochester and her young siblings immediately upon their arrival and offer to introduce them to their families. Ashford has been ill and did not know of their presence until recently, or all this would have been handled much more discreetly, I assure you."

"I had heard . . . Yes, of course." Charlotte seemed to deflate. "I don't suppose a will has been found? My dear papa . . ."

Celeste leaned over and patted her sister's plump hand. "Left you a beautiful portrait of your mama and yourself and a small token of his affection. But the earl has tied our hands, and we cannot do anything until the courts give us permission."

"Oh, that was kind of him." She produced a handkerchief and wiped a tear. "The earl had promised . . . But I suppose that is lies. It is all very difficult to comprehend. But our home is open to all of you, as I'm sure you know." She cast an imploring look at the gentleman standing behind Celeste. "If you will be so kind as to let the marquess know, we will be happy to help in all ways. I'm sure dear Charles will agree. He works hard, and his position is so . . ."

"Understood, my dear Mrs. Guilford," Lord Erran replied smoothly. "If our families are to be connected, it is beneficial if we all work together to ease the path of our new relations. We look forward to seeing more of you."

Talk about lies! Celeste would be happy if she never saw Charlotte again. The woman was self-serving and much too easily swayed by coin. And she couldn't be trusted not to spread scandal.

If she was to survive in this jungle, she really must develop a backbone. And harsh experience had taught her just where to start.

The moment she was rid of her unwelcome guest, Celeste turned to Lord Erran and said, "I wish to go to Wystan with you."

Sixteen

ERRAN CLAMPED his jaw shut to prevent howling. *She wanted to go to Wystan with him?* Women often had maggots in their brains, but he'd thought this one to be sensible.

Miss Rochester was looking very much like a Spanish princess this morning, with her mahogany hair scraped back from her high cheekbones, highlighting her heavily lashed, almond-shaped eyes. Pearls and a lacy collar draped around her loathsome gray gown added to the image. But the uncanny blue of her eyes was intense and perspicacious and had him wondering if he'd heard her wrong.

"You wish to go to Northumberland?" he asked carefully. "It is a great distance from here."

"Is it very costly?" She refilled her tea cup and offered to fill his. "I can ride, if renting a horse would be cheaper than a carriage. How did you mean to go?"

"Very quickly," he said, taking a seat and helping himself to a piece of toast so he had something to rip with his teeth.

"How long does such a journey take? It's not as if we haven't been here since spring, suffering the slings and arrows of adversity. Could a day or two more matter?"

She looked so damned respectable—while suggesting a highly indecent expedition. "It's far more than a day or two. You can't travel with me. It's not proper."

She tilted her head as if considering that. "I could take Trevor. Or if we're journeying by carriage, a maid."

Erran tried a different tactic. "What can you possibly accomplish by traveling to a moldering tower in the middle of absolutely nowhere? Even if you took a carriage, you'd have to ride the final miles. Ashford has been receiving complaints that the road has washed out again."

"I have heard some of the legends of Wystan. I understand its significance to Malcolm women. Should it come to pass that Lansdowne keeps me from returning to my home, I shall need a place to live. I thought I might be of use there," she said demurely.

That would be one way of moving her out of the house. She was dangling temptation in front of him, but Erran heard the lady's determination beneath the politeness. Her manipulative charm didn't work with him. "Give me truth or you'll have to find your way on your own."

The flash of her eyes warned that he'd gone too far and was already in over his head. Women were much of a mystery to him, but this one . . . spoke too clearly.

"I have been sheltered all my life," she stated frostily. "And that has made me weak. From now on, I want no knight errant, no noble protection, no more being helpless. If Wystan holds the answers to our problems, then I wish to be there to help solve them. My parents wrote hundreds of journals. I am not at all certain I *want* you reading them, but even so, it would take you weeks to peruse them all."

"I had planned on simply looking for the appropriate dates." Erran set down his cup to pace to the window where he couldn't see the plea in her proud visage. "Planning a journey with women and carriages and trunks will take me longer than reading through the journals I need."

"Then I shall dress in Trevor's clothes and ride on horseback. We are not so proper in Jamaica. I'm well accustomed to riding astride. If there is any chance of finding what we need to claim the plantation again, I could go *home*."

There was the argument that could sway him. If he could send the Rochesters back to Jamaica, where they belonged, he would have the townhouse back again. Finally, he would have accomplished a task the way it should be done. He would prove to Duncan that he would make an excellent estate solicitor. With a respectable abode in the house of a marquess, he might even be able to persuade the judge to let him back in a courtroom again.

They would all get what they wanted. He had to keep his mind on the goal—and not on sea-blue, slanted eyes and rich feminine scents.

"I meant what I said about staying in Wystan," she continued when he did not immediately agree to her pleas. "I am not cut out for society. I will not *take*, as you say it. I am too old, too different, too independent to ever want a society marriage."

Startled out of his cogitations, Erran swung around to stare at her in disbelief. "Not *take*? You are the most stunning woman in all London, and you don't believe men will be crawling at your feet? What kind of insects do they breed in Jamaica to leave you believing this?"

She looked genuinely shocked at his idiotic speech. He tried to go back over his words to discover which had shocked her, but he couldn't take back any of them.

She looked as if she'd speak. Then she closed her mouth and set down her cup and blushed. He'd actually made her blush. He'd simply been honest. The house had mirrors, after all. She had to see herself. Her beauty couldn't be a surprise.

"Modistes flatter me so I will spend money. Gentlemen have courted me for my dowry," she said, hunting for words. "But if I wished a particular gentleman to take me to a dance, I had to use my vocalization on him. I was never belle of the ball. Even if I wear no heels, I tower over most men. I am dark, and gentlemen prefer pale English skin. I believe my ancestors had Spanish blood, perhaps native. It's attractive on Trevor, but not on me. But looks are not what I'm talking about. It's *me*. Who I am."

She was beseeching him to understand, but he did not. She was not only attractive, but she had grace and a quiet strength he admired far more than he ought. It was for his *own* safety that he fought. Days in her company, and he'd go stark, raving mad with the need to throw her into bed and possess her—when all he should want was to send her home. He returned to his chair to plead with her common sense.

"I do not comprehend how riding to Wystan with me will prove anything, unless you wish to prove that you have no care for your reputation," he said as disparagingly as he could.

Except in the back of his mind, he was actually trying to figure out a way to let her go with him. He would enjoy her company, yes, but she would also be an excellent buffer to whatever women were currently occupying the castle. The notion appealed to him entirely too much. She was already making him mad.

"Fine, then, go. I will find some other means of traveling on my own," she said stiffly.

Erran wanted to rip out his hair at the thought of this beautiful woman, a stranger to England's ways, traveling alone by coach, staying in inns with treacherous men, innocent of all the dangers.

His teacup rose from the saucer on its own. Hoping she hadn't noticed, Erran swiped the errant china from thin air and pretended to sip from it.

"I'll let Aster talk to you," he said curtly, setting down the cup and rising to head for the door. "She'll make you see sense."

"OH, I WISH I COULD come with you!" Lady Aster cried upon being presented with Celeste's proposal of traveling to Wystan. "My family is only a day's ride from Northumberland. But if Erran is to gallop off and leave the construction project, someone needs to be available to see that Ashford's needs are met. Besides, I cannot desert Theo. He is buried in harvest duties and swearing like a sailor already. I know a perfectly competent companion who can travel with you, and you can take Ashford's barouche. It's most comfortable for distances."

"Not the barouche!" Lord Erran practically moaned. "I hoped you'd speak *sense* to her!"

The frosty gentleman was deteriorating rapidly under their continued pressure, Celeste thought—not with satisfaction. She wanted him to *want* her with him, and that was the very definition of insanity.

He had called her *stunning*. And he'd been sincere. She'd heard it in his voice—a new phenomenon she'd developed since moving here. She could hear the emotions in other people's voices—or she thought she could. She'd almost talked herself into imagining he really wanted her with him but was trying to talk her out of it for the sake of propriety. Just the possibility had given her the courage to stand up for herself.

His flattery had rattled her thoughts. She needed to remember she was no longer interested in a man's approval.

"We cannot find good horses along the way to haul a carriage that large," he insisted, "and that unbalanced monstrosity certainly won't navigate Wystan's narrow lanes. Can't you see this is a mad idea?"

"A post chaise then?" Lady Aster asked dubiously. "That won't be very comfortable."

"Did I not read that the mail coach can reach Edinburgh in two days? I will simply travel that way," Celeste said serenely. "Lord Erran may travel as he wishes."

Both Lord Erran and Lady Aster looked appalled. His lordship ran his hand through his dark curls until they tumbled about his brow, creating a rather dashingly romantic image. Celeste turned her gaze to her tea to avoid falling for everything he said simply because she wanted to please him.

"I have a cousin working with a steamship engineer," he admitted reluctantly. "He wants to develop a transportation route through the North Sea using a steamship combined with sail. I don't know how far north they can take it or where it will port, but even if we only reach Newcastle, we can save several days of travel."

"A steamship?" Celeste widened her eyes in apprehension at this terrifying new development. "It will not explode?"

"Says the lady willing to travel in close proximity with filthy flea-ridden drunks for forty-eight non-stop hours," Lord Erran said disdainfully. "No, it will not explode, or they would not still be alive, would they?"

Celeste set her jaw. If new experiences did not kill her, they would make her stronger. "Then steamship it shall be. When will we depart?"

They could not be any more in debt to Lord Erran than they already were, and she could not bear to sit here for weeks sewing shirts, while he rode off to the rescue. If she was to be labeled bastard and cast out of her home, then she would have time and a little more knowledge to make plans. Penury was horrible enough, but without honor, she would simply wither away in shame.

"Marvelous!" Lady Aster cried, clapping her hands. "Just be certain when you arrive that they give you rooms on separate floors. Legend has it that the first marquess was conceived in Wystan by magic." She smiled happily.

Celeste didn't dare look at Lord Erran after that.

When Celeste explained her intentions later that day, Sylvia and Trevor were appalled. Trevor wanted to take her place, until she explained that Wystan was where Malcolm women went to have their babies. Since Ashford was the property owner, Lord Erran had the excuse of visiting as his brother's representative, but unmarried gentlemen were not particularly welcome.

Apparently a castle of expectant women seemed safe to her

siblings—she didn't mention Lady Aster's mad assertion about magical conceptions—and the argument was surrendered. Lord Erran's brother, Theo, promised to take Trevor, Sylvia, and Nana to Iveston, where they would be protected from any more of Lansdowne's depredations.

"It will look as if we're running from scandal," Trevor said worriedly, even though his eyes had lit with delight at the invitation to the countryside.

"We will simply say the construction crews are causing too much disruption. No one would question that. We can depart in all directions with no one being the wiser," Celeste explained. "Jamar and the workers will be here to protect the house."

"But what about the dinners and parties Lady Aster promised?" Sylvia cried.

Celeste considered Wystan a far better solution than dining among society to prove they weren't afraid of the earl's scandal-mongering, but she answered in terms her sister could understand. "We'll still do that after our wardrobes are complete, and we have proof in our hands. We'll make a grand entrance!"

Her siblings breathed easier, not knowing the exigency of travel ahead for her.

Of course, the noble Lord Erran was barely speaking to her by the time all the arrangements were made. If she must learn not to rely on him, that was probably best, but she missed their often lively give-and-take. That was understandable. She was lonely, she acknowledged. She would find other companionship—perhaps at Wystan. She was rather looking forward to this mysterious outpost.

Unwilling to delay, Lord Erran swiftly arranged their travel. Two mornings later, he escorted Celeste and her new companion, Mrs. Lorna, to a carriage to take them to the docks. He rode alongside, accompanied by a groom. Celeste thought the pistol, whip, and sword he carried a little excessive in civilized London. It wasn't as if they were traveling with jewels or even fat coin purses. All she had was her sewing money.

In the early morning fog, the docks seemed muffled and tamer than the noisy, colorful ones in sunny Jamaica. Of course, in the gray mist, she could not see more than a foot in front of her face as Lord Erran helped her from the carriage.

"You will not rethink this journey?" he asked curtly once she stood beside him. "I can send you back with the groom. Lady Aster will be delighted to have your company while I am gone."

"I am looking forward to steamship travel. The water reminds me of home," she lied, studying what little she could see of the dock to hide her terror. "I am sorry to be a burden to you. If you'll simply tell me what we must do, Mrs. Lorna and I will be out of your way."

His curt tone was painful, but it was better that she not develop notions based on his silly comments about her looks. He had softened her heart in ways no other man had ever done. She could not risk such vulnerability.

She knew the pain of carving someone out of her heart. Her father's death was still too raw.

Celeste clenched his lordship's arm for the scary crossing onto the ship. Once there, a crew member escorted her to the cabin, along with the stout, wide-eyed lady Aster had sent as a chaperone. Lord Erran stayed on deck to discuss the wonders of steamship travel with his friends. Out of the cold damp, with a brazier to warm their feet, it was almost comfortable, despite the bobbing of the water beneath them. Trying to pretend she was in a drawing room, Celeste settled in with her sewing. Mrs. Lorna nervously took out her knitting.

She didn't know where they had taken her trunk, but one of the crew thoughtfully carried in their food basket. Cook knew how to prepare food for long journeys.

Gentleman that he was, Lord Erran stepped in to ask after their comfort before they sailed.

"There is not much light, but we are warm, and the bench cushion is comfortable," Celeste replied. "Do you know how long we will be at sea?"

"If the weather holds, we'll make excellent time, and should make port by nightfall. If we catch the tide, we may even sail into Newcastle, where we can hire a post chaise. But this is not a season for predictable weather, so I can make no promises."

His voice was all that was polite, but Celeste heard his underlying concern. She wished she didn't. Her memories of the storm that had killed her father were painful. She merely nodded acknowledgment without expressing her fear.

"We have plenty of food and lemonade, whenever you need it," she said serenely.

His eyes narrowed, as if he heard the terror she was holding in check. It was bad enough that she couldn't charm him. It was worse if he could actually hear what she tried to hide. Tensely, she forced a smile, letting him believe what he must.

"Thank you. I wish to observe the engine room, but I will join you for luncheon, if you do not mind." He bowed out, leaving them to the cozy cabin.

"He is most particular about our comfort," Mrs. Lorna said in satisfaction. "I am sure all will be well."

That certainty lasted only until the ship sailed from the Thames into the North Sea. At that juncture, Celeste realized the difference between a large ocean-going vessel and a small river-sized one. They felt every surge of the waves, every blast of the wind tilting the small craft about. The roar of the boiler and churn of the paddle seemed to strain as they chugged northward.

Mrs. Lorna groaned, looked decidedly greenish, and set aside her knitting.

At least Celeste had experience with seasickness. She urged her companion to sip ginger root tea with a little honey and when that did not help, took a bucket from the wall. The lavatory facilities were limited to a closet and not what one could want when ill. She wiped Mrs. Lorna's forehead as she lost her breakfast, and resigned herself to treating her for the rest of the journey.

The waves and wind worsened by mid-day. Lord Erran clung to his hat as he blew into the cabin, leaning against the door to close it. Taking one look at the prostrate woman on the bench, he grabbed the foul bucket and struggled outside again.

"We're hoping it's only a brief squall," he said when he returned. "We're still making good time."

Until we crash on rocks, Celeste thought. *Or a wave tosses us over. Or the wind blows us to France or whatever is across this ocean.*

"Would you like a sandwich?" was all she said. Perhaps all that was required for a stiff backbone was the façade of civilization.

"I will not apologize for the conditions," he said stiffly. "I begged you not to come. The ship is experimental."

Celeste glanced down at the woman on the bench, but Mrs. Lorna seemed to have fallen asleep. She met Lord Erran's gaze. "Do you read minds or are you simply assuming that I'm complaining?"

He looked uncomfortable. Rather than answer, he poked through the basket and found a sandwich wrapped in brown paper. He took one of the small lemonade containers and sipped from it, and handed her another.

"You . . . convey what you're feeling when you speak," he said, apparently thinking it through as he spoke. "You have this marvelous voice, one that could soothe babes to sleep or melt a man into a puddle of wax. I'd love to hear you sing. But underneath . . . you are raw emotion. If you sang an unhappy song, I might fling myself into the sea."

Celeste stared. He did not seem pleased to disclose this, so it was not flattery. "No one has ever told me that my voice made them suicidal," she replied, striving to understand.

"I don't think anyone else hears what I hear," he admitted. "And the converse is that when you are happy, it makes me unreasonably pleased. But I think others hear only what you *want* them to hear, which is dangerous."

"If I want people to hear my unhappiness, I have only to voice it?" she asked in doubt. "I have only ever tried to wheedle them into doing what I want."

The ship lurched, and he steadied himself on an overhead beam. "Your family hasn't noticed this? You never experimented to see what else you could do?"

"I'm rather amazed that you know what I do and admit it," she said, somewhat testily. "No, my family never noticed. Jamar and Nana seem to know and mostly ignore me. I don't believe I've ever upset them as you say I can."

"It's good to know that not everyone is affected." He bit into his sandwich as he pondered the preposterous. "It's possible that once people are attuned to you and recognize what you're doing, it's easier to block out the charm."

She frowned and thought about that. "Are you saying our gifts are different, that you must bellow authoritatively to make people do what you wish? I can hear when you really want to shout, and I admire your restraint." Celeste opened a sandwich and nibbled at the cucumber filling.

"I only discovered my oddity this past year, with my first courtroom case." He paced the tilting floor. "I terrified a judge into not only returning my client's home, but into demanding that his landlord pay him damages. I was furious that a scurrilous landlord would evict a poor man with three small children. I fear I was outrageously bombastic in his defense, and it was most certainly not my knowledge of the law that brought the entire courtroom to their feet, shouting, ready to stone the landlord—and the judge, if he did not side with me. It was an ugly scene that could easily have evolved into riot. I wasn't certain if we'd escape with our skin intact."

"I would like to do that," she said fiercely. "I would sue Lansdowne and bring the rafters down about his ears."

His smile was almost fond and caused an irrational flutter beneath her breastbone.

"I don't think it works that way. I think you would bring them to tears with your plight and even the earl would beg to shower you in gold, or whatever you asked. Yours is a rather more gentle persuasion that my riot-inducing ability. And I feel like the veriest sapskull even saying this." He poked around in the basket and produced an apple.

"There have been great orators over the centuries," she said, unconcerned. "It is not real magic. If I had real magic, I'd bring back my father and slay Lansdowne. I don't know why your speaking ability bothers you."

"Oration and what we do are two different things," he asserted. "It is possible that what we do is related to Mesmerism, but I would have to study a science that seems little more than Aster's foolish astrology to find out. Besides, I want to win cases honestly, on their merits, not with an unfair advantage based on emotion or voodoo that is neither just nor logical."

"Politicians win elections by saying things people want to hear," she argued. "There's not a great deal of difference as far as I can see. You believe in your case. Your opponent believes in theirs. Only the future will tell who is right. It would be terrifying if you could stop the wind, but you're only doing what generals have done over the ages—asserting your authority. Generals are not always right."

He didn't look convinced. It was sad that he was the one person she could not persuade, and rather terrifying that he could *hear* how she felt as she argued.

The floor tilted ominously, and bucket and basket slid toward the door.

"Would you rather I stay here through this storm, or should I leave?" he asked, glancing at the stormy clouds through the porthole.

That was a terrible question to ask when he could tell if she lied.

Seventeen

BY EVENING, it became obvious that the ship would not make the mouth of the Tyne at a reasonable hour. Erran gathered up hammocks from below and carried them to the cabin, where Miss Rochester sat on a smaller bench and sewed by the light of an oil sconce. Her useless companion still lay groaning on the larger seat.

Erran seriously regretted letting the lady talk him into this. No matter how much he wanted to succeed at the task of removing the Rochesters to their own home, he *knew* better than to travel with a woman, and still, he'd let her overcome his common sense with female illogic. At the moment, he was just relieved that he wasn't being battered by bitter complaints. Yet. As the ship pitched and night fell, he braced himself for a tirade.

"Even if we can sail upriver and reach port tonight, it will be too late to disembark and find an inn," he explained as he hooked up the hammocks. "We will have to sleep on board."

The storm had mostly passed, but the sea was rough. Miss Rochester cast her moaning companion a look of concern. "I don't suppose there are blankets or pillows to make Mrs. Lorna more comfortable?"

"I'll find blankets. Is there anything in your trunks that might be rolled into a pillow?"

She wrinkled her patrician nose. "My petticoats will have to do. I've more linen in my sewing basket. I can wrap them in that."

Expecting the usual female complaints, Erran was surprised by her calm resilience, but he refused to give her the pleasure of knowing it. He nodded curtly. "I'll leave you to prepare for bed. I trust our crew, but once we're up the river in Newport, the ship will be accessible to thieves. I cannot in all conscience leave you alone. If Mrs. Lorna sleeps on the bench, I'll take this other hammock."

He watched in satisfaction as her eyes widened in alarm, but *still*, she said nothing. He'd really wanted her to speak so he could judge whether she hated the idea or not. But she was perceptive and had learned to stay silent to give him no hint.

After he'd correctly judged her relief beneath her earlier cold declaration that he could leave or stay, she was rightly wary of speaking.

She wanted him near her. To his disgust, Erran was learning how a beautiful woman could inflate his pride. Previously, his only relationships with women had been of the mutually satisfactory physical kind. He'd never tried to please one.

He wanted to please Miss Rochester.

The companion did not do no more than moan while they made arrangements. By the time Erran returned with blankets, Miss Rochester had turned off the lamp so he could not admire the full effect of her slender form without billowing skirts. But he was painfully aware of her as they arranged the hammocks and blankets in such close proximity.

Their chaperone was almost completely useless.

Acting on his urges was a sure way to fall into the parson's mousetrap. Unlike most of his infamous family, he did not intend to support a raft of bastards.

"We will be in Newport by morning?" she whispered as they settled into their respective canvases.

"If the tide is right, we'll be there before midnight. In the morning, I will find transportation north. Lady Aster has given me a list of inns where we might stop for the last few days of our journey. You should sleep better tomorrow night."

"I have not slept well since we left Jamaica," she said sadly. "I will be content to sleep at all."

Erran had no reason to feel guilt at her admission, but he winced at her honesty.

TWO MEN had to haul Mrs. Lorna into the dinghy the next morning.

"I don't think she is well enough to travel further," Celeste murmured in dismay as they climbed up the embankment from the river, with Mrs. Lorna still clinging to one of the crew.

She had passed a restless night with Lord Erran only a few feet away. He didn't snore, but she had been painfully aware of his masculine proximity. He had been the perfect gentleman, though. She had almost been disappointed.

"We'll find an inn to break our fast and discuss what to do next," Lord Erran said grimly, casting about for transportation.

They pried the older woman, moaning, into a battered open carriage. The crew tied on their trunks, and Lord Erran rode with the driver as they traversed pitted roads to the inn that had been recommended. Celeste held up Mrs. Lorna's head and patted her hands and watched their surroundings with interest.

The Jamaica she knew was sprawling green and fields of sugar cane. It had no manufactories, no coal heaps, no burgeoning industry of the likes she saw around her. Coal dust and neglect had left much of the town dilapidated and filthy, but the streets bustled with activity.

This was the world to which Lord Erran aspired with his mechanical friends?

He had never said as much, but she had heard his fascination when he spoke of the sewing mechanism and talked with his friends about the amazing steam engine that had allowed them to travel so swiftly. She liked the notion that the fastidious gentleman didn't mind getting his hands dirty when he was playing with machines. It was an interesting dichotomy of intellect and manual skill—pursuits only a young, unattached man might follow.

She would remind herself of that every time Lord Erran looked at her as if she might actually hold his interest. He no doubt thought of her as a puzzle to be solved and certainly not in a way that might suggest permanence. She needed a real home and security. She would more likely find that in Jamaica than with lordly English gentlemen.

Once settled at the inn in a comfortable parlor with tea and coffee and a large breakfast, Mrs. Lorna showed signs of recovery. She asked to be excused to repair herself, leaving Celeste alone with Lord Erran—not an auspicious sign that her companion had all her faculties about her.

"I hate to mention this," Celeste said as she studied the situation. "But I fear we have somehow convinced Mrs. Lorna that we . . . are above the usual propriety?"

Pacing the small parlor while sipping his coffee, Lord Erran scowled. "She's just not well."

"I will not cast aspersions on Lady Aster's trained employees. A proper companion would insist that I go with her so we could help repair each other. She has left me here as if I am of no moment. My choice is to believe she thinks I'm not a lady or to believe she thinks I am above reproach. I have chosen to believe the latter." Celeste buttered her toast and ate hungrily, undisturbed that he did not understand what she was telling him. He didn't want to believe in his gift, so he wouldn't acknowledge hers.

"She is not well and I cannot see how we can go on," he insisted. "I don't want to leave you here alone for the week or more it might take me to journey to Wystan and search the library. But I cannot punish that poor woman by rocking her about in a post chaise over rutted roads."

Celeste considered her options as she ate. She was fairly certain she would not reach the same conclusions as Lord Erran. Unfortunately, he was not susceptible to her counter suggestions. She would have to work around him.

The merit of clearing her name, establishing the date of her father's marriage, and possibly finding information about where he may have stored copies of his will far exceeded that of propriety, in her opinion.

Rather than argue, she waited for Mrs. Lorna's return. Lord Erran finally took a seat and emptied his plate. She could feel his tension as much as her own. He *knew* what they had to do. He simply would not admit it, stubborn man.

Even after a night in a hammock, he managed to look unrumpled and elegant. Yes, his linen was a little worse for wear, but his tailored coat would not dare possess a wrinkle, it clung so lovingly to his broad chest and slim hips. And he'd already had someone wipe the mud from his boots. On a practical level, he'd donned mud brown for his traveling attire instead of the white and gray he often wore at home. Only his gold vest revealed his dandyish side.

She was starting to understand that Lord Erran presented the casual elegance of wealth to influence the company his brother's business needed. He no doubt needed that image in court as well. On his own—he would have fixed things by grubbing in oily machines.

Mrs. Lorna hurried in, using a damp handkerchief to wipe her brow, pushing at her spectacles, and trying to tuck straying gray curls back under her cap. "I am so sorry. I usually do not do so poorly. I fear I have been a terrible burden on you."

"Dear Mrs. Lorna," Celeste said in her most charming voice. She patted the chair beside her. "You will make yourself ill by fussing so. We have decided that it would be best if you stay here with your feet up, and a maid to look after you until you are well enough to travel again. You deserve every consideration after that horrible steamship."

Lord Erran sent her a sharp look, apparently hearing her persuasion. Celeste ignored him to fuss over the older lady.

"That is very kind, I'm sure," the lady said with some bewilderment, settling into her chair. "I do not wish to be a burden in any way."

Since she was saying exactly what the woman wished to hear, Celeste was confident her charm would sway her. "And you are not a burden! I'm sure dear Lady Aster will approve, if you do not mind staying at an inn. I would not ask you to stay somewhere that you're not comfortable." The beauty of her charm, Celeste knew, was that she meant every word.

"I have an aging aunt," Mrs. Lorna said with eagerness. "She lives close by. Perhaps I could stay with her and be useful."

"That is perfect!" Celeste cried. "We'll arrange for you to see her, then. Perhaps when it is time to take the return journey, you will be feeling hale and hearty, and we'll make a party of it." She turned a smile to his disgruntled lordship. "You will not need to hire a horse, just the post chaise, correct?"

She feared he struggled against bellowing at her in his riot-inducing voice. But this was the only way. Mrs. Lorna might fret later, when not under the influence of Celeste's appeal, but for now, her companion was quite happy to be charmed into doing what she wanted to do anyway.

"I will make the arrangements," Lord Erran all but growled, glaring as if he'd have a word to say to her later.

It was quite freeing not to have to please him, Celeste decided, sipping the inn's horrible coffee. She could learn to enjoy her independence, if she could just overcome her terror.

Eighteen

"YOU CHARMED your companion into staying behind without any consideration to what will happen to your reputation if it becomes known you're traveling with me," Erran said, barely able to contain his fury—and amazement—at the woman beside him in the small post chaise.

"It was necessary," his Spanish princess declared with a regal shrug of her slim shoulders.

Draped in a fur-lined, hooded cloak from Lady Aster, Miss Rochester looked so damned demure, she could be royalty in her chariot, above all common expectations. And apparently, she spoke like royalty, too, to convince the very respectable Mrs. Lorna that a lady could just disappear for a week without anyone noticing.

And worst of all, she was right, he acknowledged grudgingly. The trip needed to be made. No one but themselves would know that they did it without chaperonage.

Miss Rochester, obviously, had no problem being alone with him. He, on the other hand, was crippled by lust. At this angle, he could see nothing of her except the loose cloak and bonnet, but her scent filled his senses, and he was all too aware of her mysterious magnetism. Perhaps he had gone too long without a woman.

He fought against imagining the night to come at a roadside inn.

The horses flung filth as they trotted the muddy road. Once the late September sun emerged, Miss Rochester doffed her heavy wrap. Unaccustomed to England's chilly weather, she kept the cloak nearby, but Erran had the pleasure—and discomfort—of admiring the glory of her supple figure as the team pulled them north at a good pace.

The jarring ruts made it impossible for him to read a book, or for her to sew, but she was a pleasant conversationalist. She asked questions about the surrounding countryside that Erran did his best to answer. She happily chatted about Jamaica, when he inquired.

They were laughing over the dreadful names of foods: *toad-in-*

the-hole in England, *jerk chicken*, and *cowfoot* on the island—when the horses clattered into the yard of the designated inn for the evening. Erran hadn't wanted to risk being on the road too close to dark, so he'd ordered a shorter journey than he would have made on his own. It was still daylight, and the inn wasn't overcrowded.

"Keep your hood pulled around you," Erran suggested as they rolled to a stop. "I will try to pass you off as my sister so the innkeeper doesn't think we're running off to Gretna or something disreputable."

She turned a blinding smile to him. "Or I can go in without the oh-so-lovely cloak, looking like myself, and say I'm her ladyship's maid and ask to inspect the room. Later, I will appear wrapped in furs and pretend to be me."

"No one but a sapskull will believe you're a maid, no matter how dull your gown," he said in irritation, climbing down.

"That's exactly what everyone thought for all those months before you arrived. That is what people will *always* think when they see me. It is why I'll never take in London society. I do not *look* English or aristocratic." Without waiting for him to extend a hand, she climbed out the wrong side, leaving the cloak behind.

She lifted out her sewing bag and came around the carriage as if she'd been on the postilion seat. Annoyed, Erran stalked inside where the innkeeper was waiting.

"How may I help his lordship?" he asked, gauging Erran's coat and casting Celeste a suspicious glance.

Erran grumpily realized he wore expensive tailoring not simply because he enjoyed it, but because of just this reaction—clothes forced people to recognize his place in society. He had never considered how it felt to be on the other end of the spectrum—being judged as a servant. He wanted to slug the proprietor for doing exactly as expected—judge his clientele by their clothing.

"My sister and I would like two rooms for the evening, if my sister's maid approves of the accommodations." Calculating the distance to the next inn, Erran waited stoically to be flung out on his ear for corrupting a young lady. A man perceptive enough to judge Erran's coat surely must see through this foolish charade and know that Celeste carried herself as a lady, despite her grim attire.

"It must face east, sir," Celeste said meekly. "The lady is very particular. I can replace the linens and scrub the china, but I cannot move windows." Her Jamaican accent sounded foreign enough to fool the uneducated into believing she was Continental.

Apparently that was all that was needed, Erran noted with exasperation. She hadn't even used her persuasive voice. The old fool bowed, wrapped his hands in his apron, and led them upstairs to examine his best chambers.

"*Oui*, that is much perfect," Celeste said in a sweet voice that made Erran want to strangle her. *He* heard her laughter and triumph. The innkeeper heard only meekness.

She accepted this insult with laughter instead of fury? Erran wanted to howl at the idiocy, but he bit his tongue. They had the rooms they needed, and that was what mattered.

They returned to the carriage, where Erran ordered the grooms to carry the baggage after the hotelier. Once the innkeeper's back was turned, Celeste donned her cloak. When she re-entered the inn, she swept the velvet and fur around her—in full regal princess mode—even though the cloak was too short and stopped before the hem of her gown.

With her hood concealing her face, she inspected her chamber under their host's anxious gaze, nodded curtly, said a frosty "thank you," and gestured imperiously for everyone to leave.

Outside her closed door, the proprietor nearly fell over himself in his desire to please. "Your sister is all that is gracious, my lord. It is a pleasure to serve you. I will have hot water sent up at once, and more coals for the fire so she need not suffer a chill."

"Most kind, I'm sure," Erran said absently, thinking that if it had been left to him, he'd send the devious lady ashes, bread, and water for that performance.

But again, she had accomplished exactly as she had said she would. He was gaining some insight into how Miss Rochester had lived all these years—not being herself but only what people imagined her to be.

Surely that had affected how she saw herself.

He shouldn't care. He ordered himself not to care. He wondered if he could shout himself into not caring. He had an assignment to accomplish. Her presence might speed the task along. He needed to protect her as part of his duty—no more.

Which was why he dined in her company that evening instead of repairing to the tavern. And why he slept with his door open so he could hear anyone who might approach her chamber.

And of course, it was only polite to keep her entertained as they drove northward the next day. He showed her sketches of the improvements he would like to make to her father's sewing mechanism. Since it might be used by women, it only made sense for a woman to approve the design.

"If you don't mind," he suggested at one point, "I might see if any of my family can produce a machine like this in quantity. Once we have a prototype, I can patent your father's invention. The profit from sales may be negligible for all I know, but I can take a small commission for the improvements and filing the patent and the rest will go into his estate."

"We could make money from selling a machine?" she asked in wonder. "How very amazing. I had hoped we might have one or two more built so I could set up a dress shop on the island."

"Imagine that multiplied by hundreds," he said. "A large factory could produce basic shirts and undergarments for everyone in England and maybe the Continent! Machines are our future."

"It will be a sad future if they are all run by men like Lansdowne," she said curtly. "Children will be ruined by the hundreds. I do not think I like the idea of this machine used in such a way."

"Progress has its pitfalls," he admitted.

A point they argued until they reached the last posting inn before Wystan.

EXHAUSTED by travel but exhilarated by lively discussion, Celeste gazed in dismay at the derelict tavern sign and muddy carriage yard of the next night's inn. She had enjoyed the company of Lord Erran this past day. But this inn . . .

"How much farther is it to Wystan?" she whispered as Lord Erran assisted her from the post chaise.

"Too far to reach before dark," he said apologetically. "We will have to ride the last miles on horseback unless there's an oxen cart available."

The inn was not a prosperous one. The men lounging outside did not appear to be of the reputable sort. She clasped Lord Erran's arm and murmured, "Perhaps you ought to call me your wife. I think we had best leave the rich cloak bundled up."

She had left it off in order to play the part of maid, and she was shivering already in the cool dusk. Even Lord Erran's look of concern could not warm her. That he listened to her was a miracle and eased her fear somewhat as he negotiated with the innkeeper over the inn's one available chamber.

Instead of abandoning her in the room while he oversaw the baggage unloading, Lord Erran gave coins to the post boy to make certain all the bags were carried up.

Celeste grimly studied the small chamber, then set to work. She unpacked the clean linen, ordered a maid to bring fresh blankets, and stripped the bed.

Taking the stack of old woolen blankets reluctantly provided by their landlord, Lord Erran shut the door and leaned against it. "There are bugs?" he asked warily.

"I will take no chances with slovenly housekeeping. Help me turn this mattress."

He flipped it easily. She covered the fresh side with a layer of blankets and her own clean linens. She threw the graying flowered coverlet on a laundry heap with the old sheets and replaced it with the clean blankets. She wrinkled her nose over the flat pillows. "I suppose we shall have to use my petticoats again."

"I apologize for the accommodations," he said, still watching her with caution. "The place has apparently deteriorated since any of us have been up here."

"Is this part of your brother's estate?" Knowing they would have to share that bed, Celeste couldn't quite meet his eye but busied herself with examining the threadbare drapery for spiders.

"On the outskirts, I believe. Until Duncan's accident a few months ago, none of us but him has had reason to visit. We're still learning the extent of his holdings and attempting to deal with them. I'm to be his eyes and ears while we're here."

"Well, it's not to be expected that an outpost as rural as this would be profitable. But if Ashford entertains guests with any frequency, this doesn't appear to be a hospitable introduction, especially if your guests are expectant mothers."

"I'll make note of that and see what Dunc suggests. It's quite likely Lady Aster will ask to come to Wystan someday, and she's not one to remain silent," he said with a hint of humor.

Unable to think of any further excuse to study a window, Celeste steadied her pulse and turned around. Lord Erran was leaning against the doorframe, arms crossed, looking windblown and elegant. "It is good to know that some English ladies are willing to speak out. We do not have that so much on the island. We are too isolated, I believe."

"Do not think that English women are much different. I sometimes think it's only Malcolm women who operate independently of men and believe they have an equal right to be heard. I disagree on many levels, but my thoughts on the matter don't count."

She dared cast His Arrogance a scowl. "Because your thoughts on the matter are worthless. Perhaps women are more than equal, and men are the boors who don't realize it."

"Apparently, anything is possible," he said with a verbal shrug, continuing to lean his wide shoulders against the frame. "I don't wish to leave you alone in here. I've ordered supper and warm water and more coals. What can I do to make you comfortable with the situation?"

"I brought it on myself, so I cannot complain." In fact, she was so amazed that he asked, that she almost suggested she be the one to sleep elsewhere. Except she really didn't want to be parted from the annoying gentleman. That was weak of her, she knew, but she had limits. "I'll be fine. Perhaps you could teach me one of your English card games?"

HAVING WATCHED the lady defrost and relax over a reasonably edible supper and a watered jug of ale, Erran played his last card, literally.

Celeste studied her hand, looked at his, and laughed in a manner that would have stirred his lust even if he couldn't see her. But after these days in close proximity, Erran could see her with his eyes closed—and he wanted her more than anything else in his life, no matter how hard he tried to push her and her nonsense out of his mind.

He was a doomed man.

She moved her last button toward the center of the small table holding the cards. "I lose. What is my forfeit?"

"Forfeit?" As if he could think clearly when a mahogany strand of hair brushed her rosy cheek, white teeth flashed behind ruby lips—and a clean bed waited three feet away.

"You do not do forfeits if you lose a game?" she asked, tilting her head with a curiosity that appealed to him too much.

With any other woman, he would have considered the question flirtatious, and he would have responded outrageously. But this one—while looking like all the temptations of Eve—was wearing governess gray and buried in three layers of shawls with a heavy cloak over her knees. Besides, she was an innocent and had no idea how seductive her velvet-lashed, blue eyes could be.

"I cannot take money from a lady who has just learned the game," he protested. "That would be the same as cheating."

He didn't *think* he'd influenced her with his voice when he'd taught her the rules, but he wouldn't be comfortable taking her few coins even if he knew for certain that he hadn't. He said the first thing that came to his overworked brain. "How about a kiss as forfeit?"

He regretted that insane response the moment he said it. He would start believing in the devil shortly and swear Old Nick had made him do it.

To his shock, she shrugged and leaned over the table. "One kiss for five buttons seems fair," she said.

Not waiting for a second offer, Erran leaned over and pressed his mouth to her primly pursed one.

The explosion was as powerful as he'd feared—and hoped. She gasped. He touched a hand to her jaw and guided her closer to sip from ruby lips and tease them into parting.

The table between them kept anything but their mouths and hands from touching. Erran kissed her tenderly, stroking the beautiful cheek he'd longed to touch from the moment he'd seen her. Unsteadily, she caressed his sideburns and whiskered jaw—and pressed her mouth closer.

He inhaled her unusual floral scent, tested the silken texture of her skin, and nearly knocked the table over to get at her. He touched his tongue to hers, and she moaned, then grabbed his shoulder for support.

He did knock the table over then. It tumbled to one side, and he circled his arms around a waist so slender he feared she'd break if he squeezed too hard. He felt broad and blocky and no more than a crude ruffian against her willowy grace, but that didn't stop him. Celeste was in his arms, at last, and instead of fighting him, she wrapped her fingers around his neck and tugged him down to her height.

She was tall enough that he didn't need to lean far. He plundered her mouth and felt her breasts rising and falling rapidly against his waistcoat. He ran a hand over the soft curve of her buttocks, crushing skirt and petticoats. She didn't hesitate but inched closer, until his arms were full of heaven.

He took a step toward the bed.

A knock pounded on the door.

Nineteen

AT THE RAP on the door, Lord Erran hastily released her, and Celeste stepped away, horrified at what they'd just done. What *she* had done.

Covering her bruised lips, still shaking with the desire he'd ignited, she hurried behind the dressing screen while his lordship answered the door. She heard the maid offer hot water and ask if there was a problem with the table. She flushed, knowing others had heard the crash. After his curt reply, the door shut again, but she hadn't pulled herself together sufficiently to dare step out of hiding.

"I shall go down to the tavern and give you time to wash and prepare for bed," he said curtly from the other side of the screen.

He behaved as if what they had done was nothing, a momentary aberration easily forgotten—a forfeit, as he'd asked. Celeste couldn't find her tongue to reply.

She'd always considered herself a pragmatist without a romantic bone in her body. She'd allowed boys to kiss her just to see what it was like, but mostly, it had been silly and sometimes unpleasant. Those had been boys. Lord Erran was very much a man, and she shivered with the sensuous pleasure he'd initiated.

After she heard the door close again, she took a deep breath and stepped out to find the water pitcher while it was still warm. She had survived worse disasters. She would muddle through this night somehow, no matter how deeply she had embarrassed herself.

Her saving grace was that she was pretty certain his noble lordship had enjoyed that kiss too.

By the time Lord Erran returned, smelling slightly of ale, Celeste had yanked her hair into a loose braid, wrapped in her warmest nightshift and robe, and cocooned herself in linen and wool covers. She'd set aside another sheet and blanket on the other side of the narrow bed for her companion.

She had left a lamp burning behind the screen and lay in bed with her back to the room to give him privacy. She heard him struggle out of his coat and move a chair to hang it over. He'd had his linen washed and starched at the last inn, but it had been sadly rumpled this past day. She was fairly certain they had no such services in this outpost, so he'd be draping his neckcloth over the coat, and possibly his waistcoat.

She tried not to conjure images of his muscular frame in only shirtsleeves and trousers, but it was impossible not to. A chair creaked as he sat down to tug off his boots. He'd worn short ones, which she assumed were easier to remove without a valet.

She heard him splash water into the basin. She'd scrubbed the cracked china clean and had left him half the water. She hoped it was enough. Did gentlemen shave in the evenings? Probably not when sleeping alone. But tonight?

He didn't spend long behind the screen, so presumably, he hadn't attempted shaving in the dark. She held her breath as she heard his unshod feet treading the creaking floorboards. To her puzzlement, after flinging more coal on the grate, he crossed to the door and seemed to be knocking about with the fire poker.

She peered over her shoulder. "What are you doing?" she had to ask.

He'd propped their table against the door and jammed one end of the poker into the door opening beneath the bar. The table supported the other end. "The door crack here is wide enough for a blade to slide through. I don't want anyone lifting the bar from the other side. The poker prevents them from reaching the bar."

"Oh, I'd never have thought of that."

"Precisely." He turned off the lamp and started rooting about in the dirty blankets and sheets she'd thrown to the floor. The maid hadn't offered to remove them, and Celeste feared the servant fully intended to put them back on the bed in the morning.

"What are you doing now?" she whispered.

"I'm not testing my willpower," he said gruffly.

Celeste had to study this before translating, then felt a lamentable thrill at this acknowledgment that he was as stirred by base desire as she was. Still, she could not let him suffer for her insistence on sharing this journey. "Then test mine. You cannot sleep on that cold floor. I've put pillows down the middle and given you your own blankets."

She could feel his towering physique looming over the bed. Rather than quiver in fear, she daringly turned over to look up at him. She could just make out his broad outline in the dark, but she realized her error. He was not as small as she, and the bed was very narrow.

He seemed to still be wearing shirt and breeches as he lifted the covers. "Thank you, I think. I am not accustomed to sharing any bed, except briefly, under circumstances I will not describe to a lady. I do not know what a lady expects."

She could well imagine what he didn't describe. She was thankful he came to bed smelling only of ale and not of the cheap perfume of the women in the tavern. "I don't want it to be awkward between us, if that's still possible. I've never had a gentleman friend, and you've made me feel at ease."

He grunted as he tried to fit his broad body into the narrow space. "I do not cultivate lady friends," he said with a hint of exasperation. "There is no purpose in it. Ladies expect marriage, and I cannot even offer them a home. Beyond that, I grew up in a male household. I have no idea what ladies expect of me."

His heavy weight bent the mattress and Celeste savored the nearness of his solidity. She felt sheltered enough to consider what he was telling her rather than feeling afraid. "You grew up with no ladies about at all my lord?"

"None respectable," he admitted. "And I think you could drop the title under these circumstances."

"Erran?" She tried the intimacy of it and liked it. "And I am Celeste, please. I have too few people to call me so these days. Your mother died young?"

"My mother died before I had any memory of her. My grandfather had all sons, legitimate and otherwise, as did my father, and there was quite a collection of boys at Iveston when I was in the nursery. You've met my Uncle Pascoe, he's only about six years older than I am, so he and other uncles and cousins were still at home, many of them young bachelors. At some point, my father gave up on hiring nannies and nursemaids and hired tutors. The upstairs maids gradually departed. It became a family joke that any woman looking for employment at Iveston was hoping to better herself by becoming a mistress. Aside for brief visits from ex-fiancées, Aster is the first lady in decades who dared descend on our household and stay."

"My word," Celeste murmured. "It's a wonder you didn't all turn out like beasts in the field. You must have had good tutors."

"They pointed our studies in the direction of our interests to keep us tame. Dunc had the estate, of course, and our father kept him busy. Theo always had his head in books and was good at mathematics and was dreamer enough to study the stars. That kept him occupied, and so forth. We didn't know anything different."

"And you?" she asked. "How did they tame you?"

"I was the youngest." His voice conveyed a verbal shrug. "I just followed the others around. I liked taking things apart, but tutors couldn't help me put them together again. As the baby, I couldn't fight boys bigger than I was, so I learned to argue instead of punch. You need to be getting some sleep. Tomorrow is likely to be a miserable, long day."

There were so very many things she'd like to ask. . . . But she feared the questions would only stir this longing their kiss had set aflame. "Thank you for not hating me," she whispered. "Good night."

He reached across the pillows and found her hand. "I have no earthly reason to hate you. I just cannot be what you need."

She clasped his rough hand and felt a melting away of so many fears . . . that alone should have made her fearful. But she didn't push him away. "I don't need a man to take care of me," she whispered back. "But I need a friend."

He squeezed her hand but released it quickly.

He'd already made himself clear—he wasn't the marrying sort and he didn't have lady friends. She'd have to cast aside any hope of more kisses—that way lay certain disaster.

WITH NO GOOD means of appeasing his arousal, Erran barely slept and woke in the same state. Rather than shock his lady *friend,* he grabbed his coat and boots and slipped out to wash in cold water at the pump.

She wanted to be *friends!* No wonder men and women shared little more than beds. He glared at his whiskered face in the bent metal mirror and attempted to scrape off the worst of his stubble. Men were furry, lust-crazed beasts. Women were . . . obviously oblivious to beasts.

They saw pretty coats and shiny boots and heard flattery and dreamed romantical notions. Ladies needed a basic education in the Care and Feeding of Men and Other Animals. That would discourage them from owning man or beast.

He ordered breakfast sent up for the lady but ate his downstairs. When he thought he'd given her enough time, he rapped on the door before entering. At her call, he stepped inside to help carry out their trunks.

She was still brushing out her hair—her waist-length, shimmering waterfall of mahogany tresses. Erran nearly swallowed his eloquent tongue.

She glanced guiltily up at him. "I didn't braid it properly last night and now I'm a mess and we'll be meeting the Malcolm ladies today and I thought—"

Impatiently, he crossed the room and grabbed the brush. "The ladies will be so busy talking that they won't notice if you walked in upside-down." He buried his crude hands in smooth silk and was as aroused as he'd been before he'd doused himself in cold water. Gritting his teeth, forcing himself not to hold tight and tip her head back so he could kiss her again, he stroked out the last of the knots. He began braiding, when all he wanted was to feel all that glorious silk falling across his naked chest as he crushed his mouth against her lush lips.

"What are you doing?" She tried to take away the brush, obviously not following the path of his lust. "I can't go in braids."

"We will be riding sorry nags in rotten weather for miles. Braids are the only thing that will hold. How many of them do you want?" He sounded grouchy but couldn't help it while fighting the need to stroke her slender throat and drag her into his arms.

She grabbed a hank of thick tresses and began separating out strands. "Whatever it takes," she said in frustration. "I'll just pin it all together and secure it with ribbons. I should just chop it all off."

"Don't you dare!" he roared in horror, torturing himself by running his fingers through the softness to start a smaller braid. "I've never seen hair so rich and thick. It doesn't even curl about in wisps but lies just where you put it. It's enchanting." And he knew he was fully insane to say any such thing, except he was appalled at the thought of all that beauty falling on a barber's floor.

"It is a nuisance without a maid. If you can wear mufflers instead of starched linen when traveling, then I should have better ways of managing. I am sorry to delay the start of our journey." She began another braid.

Apparently she'd noticed that he wasn't wearing a starched collar this morning. How much else did she notice? That she'd been observing him as he observed her stirred him almost as much as their kiss last night. Almost.

He'd never been kissed with such gentleness and genuine passion in his life, and he was starved for more. Maybe he should have kissed more ladies and fewer maids. Whores never kissed at all. He hadn't thought ladies would either.

"If I had known the difficulty, I would not have allowed you to come," he said curtly, to distract himself. "But I wasn't thinking of hair at the time." He had been thinking of exactly what had happened last night. And what he wanted to do tonight.

"Neither was I," she admitted. "I've always had Nana or Sylvia to help me. I had the maid at the inn yesterday, but I didn't want to ask here."

"I've made note of the condition of this place to tell Duncan when we return." He finished off the braid and reluctantly let her pin and tuck the ends into a chignon.

He couldn't prevent visions of how all that glorious dark silk would look hanging over bare breasts. He wasn't even certain a bruising ride would cure what ailed him—not that the nags the inn provided would manage more than a trot. They'd sent the post boy away in favor of a cart and horses that might better traverse the muddy lane through the woods ahead.

Celeste tied a cap over her hair and let him help her into the cloak. Even buried in layers of wool and fur, she had the power to arouse him just by her subtle scent. Erran heaved a trunk to his shoulder, put a hand to her back, and escorted her out to their waiting mares.

It was too early for most of the vagrants to be hanging about. Erran loaded the trunks into the small pony cart he'd hired for their baggage, making certain his pistol and sword were visible to discourage any brigands who fancied the lady's cloak. *Celeste's* cloak. He wanted to savor the intimacy of her name and knew he was in deep trouble.

She handed a coin to the boy holding the horses' reins. "I would appreciate it if you would tell your friends that I do not have any more coins," she said in that throaty tone that could make grown men weep. "But if we travel safely, the marquess will reward those willing to do an honest day's work. I can see you're a hard worker, and I shall tell him that once we see him again."

On the surface, this was pure silliness, Erran knew. No thief would care about an honest day's work. But she was weaving spells again, convincing the boy that it would be dangerous to follow them and beneficial to leave them alone. Erran hoped the message reached those who needed to hear it. He glanced at the few loungers by the door. They'd heard.

The pony cart driver merely looked stoic. Dunc had recommended him, so Erran had some hope the baggage would ultimately arrive at Wystan.

"Perhaps we ought to experiment sometime to see who is seduced into behaving and who responds to the threat of weapons," Erran said dryly as he lifted her into the saddle.

"The power here is different," she said, revealing her bewilderment. "It's more . . . feminine . . . somehow than the house in town. I think experimentation requires controlled circumstances, correct?"

He snorted his disbelief. "Correct, if one understands what needs to be controlled. *Power* that cannot be measured or seen or heard is not a tangible control."

More loudly, so anyone listening could hear, he added, "My pistol fires five shots. You do not need to worry, my dear. Thieves have no chance against it."

He could not interpret the look she shot him as he helped her into the side saddle, then mounted his own nag, and led the way into the forest around Wystan.

Once they were far enough down the road, she rode close enough to ask, "Do you really have such a horrible gun?"

"I do. It was mostly a matter of balancing the percussion level and gunpowder amounts so it wouldn't blow up."

"Can you not patent such an invention as you said you might the sewing mechanism?" she asked in curiosity.

Erran glared ahead. He'd had this argument before. "I could. I won't. Can you imagine what these roads would be like if every thief had a weapon like that?"

He waited for her to jump on him as his brothers had, saying honest men could better protect their homes, soldiers could win wars, and the world would be a safer place.

Celeste didn't say anything. She frowned and worked his argument through that frightening female mind of hers.

"You have given up the chance for great wealth in order to keep more people from dying," she said in what sounded like honest wonder, and not her magic vocalization. "A gun like that would be a killing machine in the wrong hands, and it would mostly be the wrong hands that it would fall into—people who like killing and think human life can be wasted."

Erran wanted to hug her. He wanted to more than hug her, but fortunately, they were on horseback. "Thank you," he said in relief. "I know it is only a matter of time before someone else does what I have done, but I'd rather not be known as the father of modern murder."

She turned those intriguing light blue eyes up to him in wonder. "It would be easy to love a man as wise as you."

Twenty

CELESTE knew she had erred by mentioning *love,* but she had not been able to help herself. He had invented a gun that could kill five people at once—and he refused to sell it! Lord Erran's mind was a fascinating place she would like to explore more. But they rode along in silence after that. She debated all the other things she could have said, but how else did one express such admiration?

It didn't help that this damp forest in the midst of a glorious autumn felt more like spring. She could feel the earth's burgeoning fecundity here. Or perhaps she was just remembering his kiss and how it had felt sleeping beside him last night. She seemed compelled to do stupid things around this brilliant, honorable, annoying man.

They kept their horses to the pace of the baggage cart. Lord Erran . . . *Erran* . . . rode back and forth, keeping an eye on their surroundings but not leaving her out of his sight, as she feared he might do. As he probably wanted to do, she admitted. He looked dashing in his tall hat and caped redingote, every inch the nobleman. Just watching him was cause for excitement.

Fortunately, that was all the excitement they encountered. They rode into the village about noon. Enchanted by the neat cottages, nodding Michaelmas daisies, and a few late roses, Celeste exclaimed in pleasure. "I thought this would be a dismal place! It is lovely. Your family should visit more often!"

Erran rode up beside her, pointing out a cottage almost inundated in rose canes and surrounded by aromatic herbs. "That's my great-granny's home, the Malcolm who was a cousin of your ancestor. I don't know who is living there these days. This was all owned by Malcolms once, according to family legend, until they made the mistake of marrying into the Ives family."

"The mistake?" she asked in amusement. "From rural anonymity to marriage to nobility is a mistake?"

He shrugged. "I don't pay much attention to the stories. But after the fifth Earl of Ives and Wystan married my great-grandmother, she gave birth to my grandfather, who became the first Marquess of Ashford. There are those in the family who claimed he had magical talents as strong as his mother's, and that was the reason he was so successful. You can ask the ladies when we reach the tower."

Magical talents. Celeste was wary of talking about magic. Native magic was often associated with evil intent, and her own might be used that way. She'd rather just call it *talent*. She didn't know if she dared ask anyone anything so personal as to what kind of *talents* they possessed.

"Why do you call it the tower?" she asked, skipping over the question his reply had opened.

"It was once a medieval fortress, but we've only maintained the original hall—which was quite a large tower for the time. The bailey walls have crumbled and been carried off to build the village. Once upon a time, this must have been a bustling little town that supported a busy fort of knights and courtiers and their households, but that's all gone now. There is not much here now that we have no need to guard against Scots barbarians."

The road wound through more woods, along a stream, and into a meadow surrounding a hill topped by an enormous stone structure. At first glimpse of a real medieval castle—or its remains—Celeste halted her horse and sat back to study it.

"It is very tall," she said in awe. Several rows of windows indicated a number of floors topped by crenellations and a guard tower.

"The better to see the enemy. I was told my great-grandfather enjoyed astronomy, like Theo, and he set up his telescopes on that top floor. I suppose in earlier times, height was the best way of studying the stars as well as the countryside. If it hadn't been for Duncan's injury and all the women staying here, Theo might have settled up here with Aster. We're a little over a day's ride from her home."

"If all the Malcolm ladies are as nice as Lady Aster, I shall enjoy this visit." She pressed her mount into a walk again.

"The ones I've met range from rude and overbearing to sweet and giggly. I don't think they're much different from anyone else, except they like to pretend they're witches."

She reached over to swat him, but he rode ahead.

"What do they call male witches?" she called after him.

"Insane," he called back.

***

E<small>RRAN</small> <small>CONSIDERED</small> his off-hand comment later and thought perhaps he hadn't been too far off the mark—he must have been insane to come here.

There were only three enceinte females in residence, but they'd come accompanied by an assortment of maids, sisters, mothers, children, and midwives. The arrival of fresh fodder for the gossip mill filled the ancient hall with a swirl of high-pitched voices, fragile females, and delicate frippery. Feeling uncomfortably like a bull in a china shop, Erran wanted nothing more than to escape to the library with a decanter of brandy.

He introduced Celeste to the only vaguely familiar relation and let her be swept off in a gaggle of women, all talking at once. She didn't seem unhappy with the attention.

He consumed a platter of sandwiches and other bite-sized comestibles while he waited to be assigned a room. He could probably make a bed on the top floor, but he had the need to know where they'd place Celeste.

Which was foolish of him, he realized, swallowing a tiny cake and discovering the tray to be empty. He had no need to protect her in his family home while she was surrounded by other females. She was perfectly safe here.

If he could not retrieve her inheritance, she would be quite happy here, he suspected. She didn't need him. She'd said so.

She only needed a friend.

Since he had no notion of how to be a friend to a lady—although he was pretty certain it didn't involve making mad, passionate love to her—he would do best to try to find the information they sought and send her back to Jamaica, where she would be even happier, and justice would be served. Then Duncan could have his whole townhouse back and Erran could take rooms there in hopes of finding some place for himself on his brother's payroll.

Or he could bellow and send all these frippery females scurrying and take Celeste up to bed and be the bully his size allowed him to be. A pity he was too civilized for that. He should have been born in a different century.

Imagining shining armor and ladies swooning at his feet—no doubt in horror—he set down his lemonade, located the nearest exit, and strode into the next room. From there, he worked his way through the maze to the library. He was studying the index to discover the filing system when a familiar scent wafted around him.

"Thank goodness," the lady said, studying the towering walls of shelves with interest. "I thought we'd never make it out alive."

He almost laughed, if only because he was relieved to have her with him again. That way definitely lay madness, but he couldn't be less than honest with himself. He enjoyed her company. And he'd rather be anywhere than explore a Malcolm library. He'd studied law more in the courtroom than in books, preferring action to sitting still. Her presence made his task more agreeable.

He pointed at the catalog. "I found the page where they've indexed your family's journals." He gestured at towering, two-story walls of books. "It just may take me a while to determine their filing system."

"Oh, my." Obviously entranced, she tilted her head back to admire the layers of walnut shelving, books, railings, and ladders. Stained glass windows offered the only natural light.

Erran had lit oil lamps on the table to better read the index's penmanship. The glow illumined Celeste in a halo, and he could scarcely tear his gaze away. He was in deadly danger here. She'd said she could *love* a man like him. What the devil did that mean? He couldn't remember anyone ever bothering to love him, so he didn't grasp the concept.

It didn't matter what it meant. He had no means to marry, no other talents than working in English law—from which he was currently banned—and she wanted to return to an island where he would be useless. He had no interest in taking up sailing and trade or even raising cane. And if he ever did create a useful invention, the patent courts and industries were here, not half way around the world.

He didn't even know why he was thinking like this. Maybe he should start believing in Aster's foolishness about magic castles.

Celeste lit another lamp and carried it to the first section of ground floor shelving. "What are the catalog directions?"

"Eccentric," he muttered, tearing his gaze from her slender form and back to the book. "We must look for family branch name—from the sixteenth century, apparently. In your case, that would be Hermione Wystan Malcolm if I'm following these charts. Then we trace down through Hermione's descendants until we reach the one who married a Rochester."

She cast him a look of dismay over her shoulder, arching her lovely brows. "How does one find anything with a catalog like that?"

"If one isn't the family librarian, like Aster, one starts on the Hermione bookcase, presumably." Erran consulted a library map and pointed at the fourth case to the right. "Logically, the oldest volumes will be on the bottom shelf, and the more recent ones at the top." He pointed up the ladder to the balcony tier.

She crouched down to examine the volumes on the bottom shelf. She had to pull one out to read the title page. "I fear you are correct," she said in awe as she turned yellowed pages. "This is in Latin, I think. Hermione must have been a scholar."

"Hermione had any number of descendants named after her, so presumably she was a decent sort. If you'll read down this list, I'll climb up to the top and try to find your shelf. It may spread over more bookcases as it goes higher."

Staring up at shelf after shelf of their ancestors' books, she shook her head in awe. "Does anyone ever read these?"

"We're about to. Libraries are repositories of information and collected wisdom. Aster claims the journals are here so history needn't keep repeating itself, so we can learn from the past. Unfortunately, no one has come up with a subject list for journals other than the name of the author." He pointed out the column he was following on the page of her family's tomes as she returned to his side. They both smelled of horses, but he could still detect that subtle exotic scent that was all hers. His hunger for her hadn't abated. He needed to step out of the reach of temptation. Ladder climbing should do it.

"Well, if we're dealing with magical families, I'm certain there must be someone who can magically locate the required volume, if necessary," she said with amusement, placing her slender fingers on the page near his.

Erran clenched his thick fingers rather than reach to cover hers. He backed off in the direction of the ladder. "Aster calls herself a librarian, so she must assume that's her task. But she's mostly interested in genealogy and astrology."

She glanced up at him with those velvet-lashed eyes that haunted him. "Perhaps if she and Theo were allowed to live here, she might do more. Usually, one must *practice* talents for them to improve."

Erran felt the impact of that declaration like a blow below the belt. He wasn't about to practice voice manipulation or levitation. Refusing to acknowledge what she was telling him, he climbed the ladder to the next level and started checking dates on the upper shelves.

"If I'm reading this correctly, the year of my father's second marriage is the fourth level down in the second block to the left," she called up to him as he reached the balcony.

Holding up the oil lamp, Erran began scanning volumes until he found the year. "I'm going to take out all the volumes from that year, the one prior, and the one after. From the looks of it, your parents had a lot to say. This could take forever." He set the lamp on a shelf and gathered up an armload of slim volumes.

"If I my memory doesn't fail, my father rewrote his will after my mother's death," she said, scanning the catalog. "Shall we check that year to see what he says about it? That shelf should be two shelves above where you are now."

Erran grabbed that stack as well. As he began carrying down his prizes, the housekeeper rapped and entered.

"Your rooms are prepared, my lord, miss." She bobbed a curtsy. "The spirits are in a turmoil, so we expect Lady Octavia to have her lying-in during the night. We have taken the liberty of placing you in the guest rooms on this floor so you won't be disturbed by the coming and going."

"The spirits?" Celeste whispered as Erran reach the bottom of the ladder with the last load of books.

"Malcolms," he whispered back, holding a stack of books under one arm and offering his other so they might follow the housekeeper. "Expect the weird."

She lifted another stack of books instead of taking his arm. "That makes *us* weird. You may reject this fascinating family, but I do not." she said curtly, striding off ahead of him.

Which left him to admire the graceful sway of her hips as they traversed the insane maze of public rooms back to a quiet corner behind what appeared to be a billiard parlor/game room and a small sitting room littered with books and papers and various needlework projects.

"I hope this will be satisfactory," the servant said, opening a heavy panel door for Celeste. "I'll send Abigail to help you dress for dinner."

She took Celeste's stack of books and set them on a table inside, then nodded down the corridor. "If you would, my lord, the next chamber is prepared for you. I fear we don't have a valet in residence."

Celeste raised her eyebrows in warning—reminding him of Aster's accursed admonition about sleeping on different floors. He would be damned before he listened to such foolery. He was reluctant to abandon Celeste in this towering hall of emptiness. He pretended not to understand her question and waited outside her door until he saw that she was settled.

"If you don't mind," she told the housekeeper, opening one of the books. "I'm very weary from the journey. I would much rather have a bath and a cold collation in here than join the ladies. Could you make my apologies?"

By Jove, she was a woman after his own mind! Relieved that he did not have to argue over the rooms, Erran imagined an evening reading through this muddle of journals. With any luck at all, they'd have what they needed by morning.

"I'll give you good evening then, Miss Rochester," he said, bowing.

Immersed in the book, she nodded dismissively, and the housekeeper closed the door between them.

Directed to his own room, Erran immediately noted the connecting door. Insanely, he felt better knowing he could reach her easily.

All he had to do was resist the temptation to open it unless she invited him in.

Twenty-one

CELESTE COULD barely wait for the maid to empty the last bucket of hot water into a tub, help her with her gown, and depart. She stripped off the rest of her clothing and slid into the warm water with relief.

She ached. She smelled. She had barely been able to tolerate herself as they worked in the library. Thank goodness Erran had been almost as disreputable as she or she'd never be able to hold her head up in his presence again.

She smiled at the realization that he'd forgotten his wilted attire—apparently an intellectual challenge overcame his preference for pristine fashion.

The maid had carried off her riding garb with a promise to clean it. Unfortunately, they still had the return journey, and after that horrible inn, she knew she couldn't count on bathing again until they were home. She savored the luxury while she had it.

She really was spoiled, as Erran had so impolitely pointed out. How would she learn to live in poverty if they didn't find evidence of her father's will or her birth? She wouldn't have maids to bring her baths or pretty soaps to wash with.

She could *survive*, she knew. They had learned to live without many things these past months. She was proud that they had done so, but Erran's aggressive approach to life showed that there was much more to living than survival. She needed the ability to go into society without shame, to make a difference, and the independence to go her own way. Without those, she would be worse than worthless. She might be weak, but there wasn't a subservient bone in her body.

Without the authority of her wealth and good name, she could not return to Jamaica to save the plantation and their people. That thought was too depressing to consider.

So she enjoyed the hedonistic luxury of soaking her hair clean before wrapping it in a towel and abandoning this momentary pleasure for the work ahead.

She donned the nightshift and robe the maid had left out. A tray of meats and cheeses awaited, and a kettle boiled over the grate. She settled into a wing chair prepared to spend the entire evening reading through journals.

Outside her door, the house seemed peculiarly... *busy*... wasn't quite the right word. Astir, possibly. The wind had picked up, and it carried voices on the drafts through the old stone walls and down the chimneys. There were apparently stairs nearby, and she could hear feet pattering up and down. She hadn't met Lady Octavia but hoped her lying-in was comfortable.

She did her best to pretend she'd never heard Lady Aster's warning to sleep on a separate floor from Erran. That was superstitious nonsense, although these drafty, medieval, stone walls opened themselves to old tales and legends.

Restlessly, she sorted through the journals stacked on the table beside her tray. She stroked pages of her mother's penmanship with a pang of longing, remembering long ago days when they'd both sat in the sunny parlor, writing their thoughts. She missed her parents dreadfully and would always associate them with sun and warm breezes. Would she ever see her home again?

Fighting loneliness and an impractical homesickness, she nibbled from her supper tray while skimming through the journals. Erran had distracted her from moroseness these last nights. Perhaps that was why she enjoyed his company so much.

The wind whistling under the door said she lied to herself.

She wrapped a blanket over her shoulders and kept reading.

She had the early books, the ones that spoke of courtship, marriage, and pregnancy. She sighed in longing over the words of love in the writing of both her parents. She marked the pages with dates of their marriage. She couldn't find the earlier tome mentioning how her father learned of his first wife's death. She'd have to go back to the library to find that date.

Her birth was almost nine months to the day from their marriage. Their mutual joy spilled onto the pages. How could anyone doubt her father's integrity or her mother's virtue? It was all right here.

When she encountered mention of sending the journals to Wystan, she read closer.

The knock on the door at the rear of the room startled her, and she nearly dropped the book. Before she could gather her wits, she heard Erran's excited voice, and without a second thought, she invited him in.

He was still dressed, although he'd abandoned his rumpled neckcloth and had unfastened his coat and waistcoat. Still sitting in her chair, she shouldn't notice how nicely he fit his trousers, but his hips were practically at eye level. She had to look up to see the book he was waving at her.

"This says your father sent copies of *all his documents* here to Wystan for safekeeping. He had doubts about the honesty of his English relations! There's apparently been bad blood between the branches of the family for generations."

She shrugged out of her blanket and stood to grab the book he was swinging so exuberantly. She laughed as he lifted it out of her reach, making her jump for it. "You should be happy more often. It becomes you. You're at risk of becoming a stuffy bore."

"A stuffy bore!" he cried, grabbing her by the waist and dancing her across the floor. "That's what lawyers are supposed to be."

She loved his arms around her too much. She wanted him to be happy like this always. Which was arrogant presumption.

She shoved from his arms and clasped her robe tighter to keep her heart from leaping from her chest. "You mad man! You dived straight into work and didn't bathe. There's a tub behind the screen and hot water on the grate. You have earned a celebration. Shall I call for brandy?"

His eyes lit as he glanced from her to the dressing screen. She didn't want to know what was happening in that powerful brain of his. Or if he'd gone as brainless as she had. She pointed at the screen. "After you fetch your clean clothes, I'll go in your room to give you privacy while you wash."

"You are a woman of rare understanding." He kissed her forehead, grabbed the last of her sandwiches, and leaving the precious book in her hands, returned to his room.

She hugged the book against her chest and let joy course through her. He liked her!

And soon, she would have the documents to allow her to return to Jamaica and save the plantation.

With the provocative male smell of him still clinging to her, she felt her heart begin to rip in two.

***

KNOWING CELESTE was only one room away, Erran bathed quickly, using his own soap to overcome the floral scent of hers. Her laughter sang in his ears. The joy in her eyes at his triumphant discovery lightened his heart. And the memory of her graceful, barely-clad figure in his arms would keep him awake forever.

He scrubbed at his hair and rubbed ruefully at his whiskers. No wonder she had shoved him toward the tub. He smelled and looked like a ruffian—but he'd wanted the proof to beat Lansdowne into the ground and had put work first.

He'd had the devil of a time concentrating on reading, knowing Celeste was only one wall away. He'd listened for every movement and heard only the howl of the wind. He'd wanted to check just to see if she were still alive.

That wasn't normal for him. His concentration had always been formidable.

She'd accused him of turning into a stuffy bore—and she was right.

Since he'd yelled a courtroom into obeisance, he'd kept his mouth shut and his nose to the grindstone. Duncan's blindness had only made life grimmer. Tonight had been the first night in forever that he'd felt like himself again.

He rubbed dry and yanked on clean breeches and shirt, then pulled his robe over them, not trusting himself to wear less in Celeste's presence. She was so naively unaware of his lust that he couldn't sully their *friendship*. She thought him a stuffy bore! That challenged him to change her mind—except she was far safer if he let her be. The devilish woman was addling his brainpan!

She met him at the doorway with her finger on a page of one of the books. "It says my parents sent witnessed documents of births and marriages to Wystan as well. Should we look for this marvelous repository?"

She had let her hair dry in a single thick braid that fell over her breast, and Erran couldn't make his thick tongue work. She was so exquisitely slender and fine-boned that he feared he would harm her just by touching, which he knew was ridiculous. But the notion was there, in his head, and he had to look away just to answer.

"We'll ask in the morning." He picked up the blanket she'd been wearing earlier and dropped it around her shoulders. "This place is too drafty to be wandering about at night."

The air seemed to sing with high-pitched voices. What the devil were the women doing upstairs?

Setting aside her book, Celeste looked around, as if she heard the sound too. And then, unexpectedly, she smiled. "The spirits are providing music. Perhaps they wish us to continue dancing!"

He wished to continue dancing. Knowing he would regret this shortly, still resenting that she thought him a bore, he bowed. "A spirit dance, my lady?"

The haunting song escalated, as if the spirits approved.

Celeste widened her eyes but accepted his offered hand. Instead of a waltz position, he placed his arms around her slender waist and drew her into him. Looking at him questioningly, she raised her arms to his shoulders. This was a kissing position—and she wasn't objecting.

The stuffy bore he'd become wanted to resist, to control his desire.

The man he'd once been lowered his mouth to hers and tested the sweet lushness of her lips.

The singing increased in rhythm and excitement, just as his pulse beat harder at Celeste's eager response. She parted her lips and allowed him access. He ran one hand lower, cupping her buttocks through the thin linen and lifting her into him. She was heaven in one beautiful package, and he plundered her mouth recklessly.

She didn't shy away.

She should. With reluctance, he pulled his head back, but he couldn't release her had he been offered a mountain of gold. "Slap my face," he bullied her with his Courtroom Voice. "Push me away."

Her eyes had turned a brilliant aquamarine, the color of clear oceans, beneath the thick fringe of her lashes. They were nearly luminous with wonder.

"I feel as if I've drunk your brandy," she murmured in her best seductive tone—and beneath it, he heard desire. "I don't think I can stand on my own."

The bed was right . . . *there.* He could just lift her on it and set her free. He need only make a single step . . .

Erran groaned and buried his lips in the sweet curve between

Celeste's throat and shoulder. She bent willingly into his embrace, her breasts pressing into him, her hips exactly where he needed her.

The singing multiplied into an angelic chorus, urging him to lift her, to push her back to that high bed, to take her as she was meant to be taken.

She fell into the down covers still holding onto him. As if by magic, he was standing between her legs while he continued to plunder her mouth. He stroked the gauzy lawn over her hips and covered her nose and eyes with kisses. Her gown slid up. His robe came untied. He could still stop. He could still push away—if she would just release him.

But her kisses whispered over his rough jaw, interspersed with siren murmurs. Those slender hands that sewed such tiny stitches shoved aside his robe and pressed their warmth through his shirt, and his cock surged in longing. Erran released her hips and spread his broad palms across her breasts, pushing them into ripe mounds so he could lean in and take them with his teeth through the thin fabric of her shift.

Her moan was more music to his ears than an angelic choir—promising heaven. No siren call could be more compelling . . . .

Before he could process the impact of that fuzzy thought, she moaned again and licked at a place beneath his ear. Lust swelled and irrationality claimed him. He needed to possess her, claim this perfect woman as his own and give her pleasure. She deserved happiness.

He opened her ribbons and found her bare breast. Suckling, he ran his hands back to her hips, lifting her more firmly to the mattress, pulling her into him again.

"Tell me to stop," he commanded with some still rational part of his brain. "Say the words."

"Stop," she said sweetly. But he heard that other voice, the real one, the one that said *go.*

Confused, he bent his forehead to press against hers, trying to gather his wits.

"Please," she whispered in her real voice. "Don't stop."

And this time, her words and her voice matched. But it wasn't her voice that compelled him. It was her hands sliding up his chest, her hips lifting into his . . . and maybe the music of the night . . . that drove him onward.

He covered her mouth with his and let their bodies speak. He could still rescue this situation. With just a little control ... He tugged her gown higher and pressed his thumb into the soft tissues between her thighs.

She cried out in a voice that was pure soul and need, and any thought of control fled.

Erran unfastened his trousers as if she'd demanded it.

Twenty-two

THE SINGING melted Celeste's heart and brought her such joy—she had never known such sweetness existed. She clung to Erran, the man who made the songs resonate with chords deep inside her. Until now, she'd never understood the physical attraction between man and woman. Yes, she admired his intelligence, enjoyed watching him at work, and craved his company. But until this moment, she hadn't understood how she needed him to *complete* what was missing inside her.

And suddenly, it was marvelously clear. She heard the command in his voice urging her to stop. She heard the lonely hunger behind the command telling her he needed her. And the songs blended the conflict into one whole—he cared for *her* more than his own needs. He wanted to stop for her sake, not his own.

She hadn't realized how much she'd missed having someone to care for her, to think of her needs above his own, so she must return the favor.

Her heart was no longer lonely. She nearly wept with joy as she ran her hands through his thick curls and returned his fervent kisses. When he caressed her *there*, she surged into him, needing more. She felt his need as her own, and the pressure to join with him was so strong, she could not deny him.

She bit her lip in frustration when he stopped to remove her shift, pulling it over her head as he lifted her more fully onto the bed. She grabbed his linen in retaliation, demanding the same. He obliged, and she savored the hard ridges of his torso, exploring the dark male nipples so different from her own.

She desperately needed to learn everything about him because not to do so would be devastating. It would be like not knowing her arms existed.

"Celeste..." he said in that warning tone that sent warm shivers down her spine.

"Erran," she replied mockingly, lifting herself to lick at his nipple as he had done hers.

Tomorrow simply did not matter. The joyous song told her so.

He groaned as she nibbled at his chest, and she *heard* his desire in that sound. She had never thought to experience a man's need, and it was delicious. He worshipped at her meager breasts, treating them with tenderness and respect while driving her to new heights of hunger. She parted her legs and lifted her hips and begged for what must surely follow.

He still wore his trousers, but they'd come undone. She could feel his raw maleness rubbing at her thighs, and she went a little mad not being able to touch.

"Please," she whispered as seductively as she knew how, even knowing he didn't hear her magic. *Magic.* The air was filled with it. Her womb stirred with the need for it.

He pressed his thumb to that *magic* place between her thighs, and she cried out her need. Her blood thrummed and pulsed, and when he inserted a broad finger and rubbed, she surrendered to the rhythm of the night, shuddering with shock and joy.

Her womb convulsed and liquefied, leaving her completely open and vulnerable. "Now," she whispered, without any need of using her charm.

Erran slid into her, filling her with the heavy maleness she craved. Ecstatic, she felt the pressure build again. She raised her hips, taking him deeper, crying out as his hard thickness thrust past a barrier and entered her completely.

The joining was so immense, that she may have lost consciousness for a moment. Her head spun with the high-pitched song wrapping around them. The phrases of the music mixed with words she'd heard and words that urgently demanded to be said.

"I vow to love, honor, and take thee in equality," she heard and chanted with the rhythm of her body and the night.

And the brilliant man who had saved her family's future joined her as thoroughly as it was possible for two people to join.

She couldn't hold back *anything*. All her life she'd been reserved, calm, in control of her passion. But tonight— she was a force of nature.

She cried out her ecstasy as her muscles convulsed and stole away his control as well as hers. Above her, Erran uttered a guttural growl of pleasure and thrust high to spill deep inside her, where her womb needed him. She wept again with the pleasure and felt as if she'd melt into the down of the mattress.

She shivered as a shadow slid between them and entered her womb, where his seed still burned. The music of the night exploded in triumph, followed by the wail of a newborn babe.

Awed by the moment, Celeste wrapped her arms around Erran's broad chest, kissed his muscled shoulder, and wouldn't let him go as he tried to take his weight off her. "This," she murmured senselessly. "This is why we're here."

He rolled over, carrying her with him, his strong arm capturing her waist and holding her close. "This is why they lock witches in towers," he said in amusement. "Both male and female, it seems. We enthrall each other and lose our minds."

"Minds can only take us so far," she agreed, *mindlessly*. She was too satiated and happy to actually think about what he was saying. In the morning, maybe, she'd have time for regrets.

"Live in the moment," he said thickly, drifting off to slumber— as if he'd heard her thoughts.

She wanted him again, but she could wait a few hours.

WITH A BEAUTIFUL, eager woman in his arms, Erran didn't need haunting songs to wake up aroused and ready in the middle of the night. It had been too long since he'd been with any woman, and Celeste . . . Celeste was far from any woman. She was made to fit in his arms, to respond to his caresses, and to blend with him in such harmony that it was as if they were really and truly one person as they climaxed together.

Magic, he thought again, as he cuddled her close and slept as he hadn't slept in months.

It was still dark when he finally woke and realized the room had no windows to let in daylight. Celeste stirred in his arms, and he wanted to see her more clearly. He had to satisfy himself with loosening her silken braid and watching those gorgeous almond-shaped eyes open to study him back.

"It wasn't a dream then," she said in wonderment. "You're really here."

"And willing to linger longer if I did not fear I've made you sore. Shall I call for another bath?" He waited for recriminations, accusations, and tears.

He had only one honorable choice. He simply feared it was the wrong one for her—she wanted to return to a distant island that held no place for him.

His cock grew harder as his eyes adjusted to the dim light enough to watch her run her hand unselfconsciously down her breasts and belly.

"I'm . . . I'm not sure what to say," she whispered, still sounding amazed. "I've never . . . I'm not . . ."

He kissed her brow. "I know. But you were miraculous, and I thank you from the bottom of my stuffy heart. I hope you will not regret the beauty of this past night when you are living in my cramped rooms without servants and fancy gowns while I traipse up and down the countryside, doing my brother's work."

Her long lashes flapped in dismay, and then she rolled from his arms to climb from the bed and stir the coals. "I'll heat some water."

Erran bit his tongue. He'd said too much already. He wanted her to know that he was more than willing to marry her, but he wouldn't force the decision—or give her delusions of grandeur in a life with him. Once they had the will in hand, her family would be wealthy again, and all society would be open to her. He couldn't take that away, if it was what she wanted.

Although he had a notion it might kill him if she chose to marry another. How had he come to this?

Aster had warned them . . . . And that notion was patently ridiculous.

He would not consider her admonition that his grandfather had been conceived here. Babies happened. They were the reason so many Ives were bastards.

Celeste covered her glorious brown beauty in a robe as Erran rolled out of the bed, naked. He couldn't resist tipping up her chin and kissing her. She flushed but didn't pull away. That was a good sign. She glanced down at his arousal as he reached for his own robe, and he felt the tug of desire as if there were a golden chain between them.

"We make magic," he murmured, brushing another kiss over her hair. "I have no understanding, but it's there. I'll go to my room and wash. Don't run too far."

She held her fingertips over her mouth as he departed.

Live in the moment, he told himself as he washed and shaved and dressed. He'd thought himself unprepared for marriage, but he knew a good woman when he'd found one. Yes, there were a thousand obstacles between them should he give it any consideration. Still, he wouldn't give her up easily. There had to be some way he could make this work—if she'd have him.

He feared she wouldn't. She wanted Jamaica and her home. He couldn't desert Duncan to his blindness and misery.

The memory of last night kept him strong.

He needed that strength when he escorted Celeste into the breakfast room filled with chattering women. They all looked up expectantly, as if angels might have descended from on high. When Celeste merely took a chair and Erran inspected the buffet, they returned to chattering.

Their babble didn't ease his anxiety any.

"Did you feel the energy last night?" one asked. "We should all deliver our babes on a full moon! It was as if magic was in the air. I think if my husband had been here, I'd be back in nine months, it was that powerful."

"Our ceremony did seem more than usually strong," another responded placidly. "The spirits were excited. If any of us is carrying a child, I would think they found their soul last night. I had that happen once. It's a very odd feeling but satisfying."

"I'd never thought of how closely the birthing ceremony resembles a fertility rite," another said. "Perhaps we should revisit the old songs."

"Not if it means the spirits of our ancestors can find a home in our children," a younger protested. "This is the reason we pass on our gifts."

Erran clenched his molars at this silliness and filled a plate for Celeste, who was mechanically sipping tea when he knew she preferred coffee.

"Is Lady Octavia well?" Celeste asked, changing the subject, as if sharing Erran's discomfort.

"She delivered a baby boy! They're ecstatic. I believe you brought good fortune with you."

Erran gave up trying to discern one voice from the other as they described the babe's miraculous attributes. It was as useless as listening to hens cluck since he barely knew one woman from the other. He kept his focus on Celeste as he set down their plates.

"Once we return to London, I'll sew some linens for the babe," Celeste said, keeping her voice unusually low.

He not only recognized her voice over the others, but heard her uncertainty and confusion. He couldn't remember the last time he'd been so in tune with anyone, much less a woman.

Not wanting to think about why she was uncertain, he stayed focused on their goals. "We've learned that Miss Rochester's father sent important documents here. Is there a place where papers are stored for safekeeping?"

One of the older women nodded knowledgeably. "We have a storage cellar that keeps paper remarkably dry. Only Malcolms are allowed entrance, however."

Erran considered himself an Ives, not a weird Malcolm, but beside him, Celeste snickered, understanding his dilemma. He needed those documents.

"His great-grandmother was Ninian Malcolm Ives," Celeste said, still looking at her tea and not at all the interested faces around the table. "And this *is* his family home."

She was using her persuasive voice. He watched with interest as everyone listening—which wasn't all of them by any means—nodded their heads.

"Saint Ninian," one woman exclaimed in admiration. "We still grow her herbs here. The village dries and sells them in the winter months. It keeps families in shoes and clothing. I don't suppose you inherited any of her herbal gifts?"

"No, I did not," Erran said gruffly, ripping off a piece of cold toast so as not to have to explain more.

"His gifts are more masculine," Celeste said in a voice laced with laughter. "But he is very good with law and documents, and that's what I need right now. My father was descended from one of Lady Ninian's cousins, so I believe I qualify, but Lord Erran will be better at finding what we need."

He was glad to hear that she was recovering from her earlier confusion, even if he was miffed that she found him an object of amusement.

But they'd gained the ladies' trust, and after breakfast, they were escorted to the locked cellar room where the family papers were gathered.

The windowless stone chamber wasn't exactly a romantic

bedroom, but the instant the door closed, Erran was painfully aware that he was alone with Celeste again, perhaps for the last time.

"I may have to ask you to leave the room," he muttered, holding up the lamp to look for dates on the various tin boxes stacked on shelves. "Looking for papers is the last thing on my mind."

"Same here," she murmured. "This whole tower is enchanted, I believe. Perhaps there really are spirits here."

"If so, then you may be carrying the spirit of my great-grandmother," he said cynically, finding the box he wanted and pulling it down.

She didn't respond. He tried to believe it was because she didn't wish to distract him while he searched.

He feared it was otherwise, but he didn't want to hear any more absurdity about spirits and ceremonies and . . . *fertility rites*. He didn't need to be reminded that one thing led to another. He couldn't afford a squalling babe and nannies.

He could very well have sacrificed the last of his freedom—and so had Celeste. His hands shook with guilt. He was a man consumed with the need to fight injustice—not a lady's man. How had he come to be caught on the horns of two wrongs?

She took the lamp, freeing him to sort through files of cramped handwriting and dozens of worthless receipts someone had thought valuable. He put that box back and started on the next.

At her continued silence, Erran halted, and studied her expression in the pale light. Without her voice to tell him how she felt, he was lost, but he could acknowledge the one thing that had changed between them. He knew what was expected of him, even though he feared she might have other ideas. As she'd said, Jamaica's customs were different from England. A woman who would wear trousers and ride astride might not think what they'd done so very important.

"You do understand that no matter what I find or do not find here, that I *will* marry you? You do not need to worry about all the inanity they were spouting upstairs."

She grew still, and her expression indicated her thoughts had drifted elsewhere. Then she shook herself, and seemed to return to normal. "They are right. This is a very odd place."

That wasn't precisely an acceptance of his proposal. But it hadn't been much of a proposal, either. He understood that she might not have done what they did last night if it hadn't been for the weirdness of the tower. Erran thought it an excuse for doing what they'd wanted to do, but he wouldn't argue if she preferred to believe they'd been enchanted.

"Ask Aster about the legends," he advised, returning to searching. "History doesn't have to repeat itself if we learn from the past. I, for one, do not wish to be supporting a dozen bastards as most of my family has done."

"I don't think you're in charge of that," she said pertly. "Women may have few rights, but they have the right to say no."

He hid his wince. "True. I shall remember that and keep my trousers buttoned."

Angry, he almost passed over the slashing handwriting of what he assumed was still another letter from some long dead solicitor. But the name on the address rang a bell, and he pulled it out to peruse it more carefully.

"By Jove, I think we've found it," he said in awe and delight.

Twenty-three

CLASPING the valuable documents to her breast, Celeste tried not to dance up the stairs. They had the will! They could chase Lansdowne's thieves from the plantation, and Nana and Jamar could be happy again! *Miracles happened.*

She wouldn't have to fret about an enchanted castle and a tempting man for another night.

Lord Erran had *proposed* to her! Very badly and only because it was the honorable thing to do, she acknowledged. Yet a noble Englishman had thought well enough of her to propose.

Only she held freedom in her hand now. She couldn't give up her dream of going home and restoring order. The people there *needed* her. Erran patently did not.

"Can we ride out now?" she asked in excitement. "It's not even noon. How soon can we be home? Will your friend sail us or must we take a carriage?"

Erran—her lover, her solicitor, her impossibly difficult *hero*— retrieved the packet from her hands. "If we leave now, we'll end up at the dreadful inn by nightfall. I don't think you want that. Besides, we need to make a good copy of these and have witnesses attest to the accuracy of the copy, then leave the originals here. Should anything happen to us, your family will still be protected."

The dratted man had a way of hitting her with reality. Celeste swallowed her alarm. He was saying Lansdowne might find some way of destroying her father's will—or *them.* "It's difficult thinking like that," she admitted. But she'd learned the hard way how precious a few pieces of paper could be.

Which meant another night in the tower . . . with Erran just one wall away. That raised a bewilderment of ambivalence.

She didn't know if she was ready to marry. She had never planned on it. She'd thought to sail straight home to Jamaica to set the plantation to rights and oversee it until Trevor had finished his studies.

But . . . Her hand strayed to her belly. What they had done

created babies. In her fever of desire last night, she'd not once given that a bit of thought. She had reason to think about it now.

She *still* wanted Erran in her bed again. She was horrorstruck to realize she was a shameless wanton. She didn't want to be a shackle on an honorable man who had made it plain that he wasn't ready for marriage. Neither was she—but what they'd done last night necessitated considering it, however reluctantly.

In terrified curiosity, she went upstairs to visit the newborn while Erran settled in the library with pen and paper and copied documents.

Babies were very peaceful when they slept. She rocked the cradle and ooohed and ahhhed over the sweet-smelling infant with the other ladies. When the babe awoke with a cry, she felt the tug in her own womb as Lady Octavia took her son to her breast.

It was natural instinct, she told herself. She had years in which to consider having a child.

When the baby wailed and flayed his small fists in infant frustration, Celeste hastily departed. She had no notion of how to care for babies. She couldn't even protect the family she already had. Adding more was out of the question.

The talk of fertility rites and spirits was all foolishness—and guilt for doing what she should never have done.

She kept her thoughts to herself as she read over Erran's strong handwriting that afternoon, comparing the documents word for word. She watched as the other men in the household witnessed the copy and applied their seals. And the most senior Malcolm matriarch attached her own affidavit—because in the world of Malcolms, women had the same authority as men.

Once they returned to London and filed the will, *she would be wealthy again*. The immensity of having her own funds staggered her imagination.

She would not need a man to support her, to tell her what she must or must not do. She could learn to be independent and do anything she liked . . . Except share Erran's bed again. She could not shame Trevor and Sylvia with wanton behavior.

Torn, she claimed headache after dinner and retired early. Once more, she felt change overwhelming her, change she could not affect by using her voice to charm. Change she could not control . . . and therein lay the crux of the matter.

When Erran entered her room through the connecting door, she felt the powerful tug she'd experienced the night before. This might be her last chance for the pleasure he had shown her . . . . He was such a beautiful man, and she could not force herself to send him away when he looked at her as he was doing.

"We cannot do this again," she murmured, hoping he'd tell her she was wrong.

"We can if we marry," he suggested. "We really ought to marry after what we did last night." He slid his arms around her.

"No," she said sadly. "I will not marry because I must, not if it can be avoided. I'm not even sure I want what my parents had, although their love was beautiful. I just don't think I can bear that kind of loss and helplessness again. I want to stand on my own." That he didn't insult her with an offer to be his mistress mitigated much of her shame.

He pressed kisses to her hair, and the strength of her need for him prevented her from shoving away. She had discovered a new weakness—desire.

"I can't claim to understand," Erran said. "But I hear your . . . pain . . . and confusion, except I'm also hearing what I want more than heaven." He kissed her lips.

She inhaled the bliss and felt the enchantment wrapping them again. This time, it was their inner voices urging them on.

"I have protectives," he whispered. "If it's children you fear, I can prevent that. Will you trust me?"

How could she not when her heart heard all the promises she needed to hear in his voice, overriding her mind's objections?

Erran was a magnificent specimen of man—all hard planes, taut muscles over wide shoulders and narrow hips. She would never know another to compare. This time, when they undressed, she dared touch the enormous part of him that grew hard and long when she stroked.

This was how babies were made. She was almost sorry when he covered that part of him with a sheath. She lifted her knees to take him, and she caught his hips to encourage his plunge . . . one last time.

They mustn't ever do this again, but just one last time . . .

As Erran thrust harder and faster with the pulse of their joined pleasure, it was as if her very being contracted in expectation. She

waited for that mysterious force that had joined them the prior
night, but caught up in the desire she heard in his voice as he
groaned his release, she shattered with her own.

In the aftermath, she accepted what had happened. This time,
their joining had been purely physical. The ladies had been right—
last night, she hadn't imagined the oddity of spirits entering her—
magic had found her womb.

She didn't need to wait months to know she carried his child—a
Malcolm child. It was just a matter of deciding what to do about it
should it survive these next difficult weeks.

Once again, life spun out of her control—but this time, she'd
been the one who had set it spinning.

ERRAN didn't know how to express his relief that Celeste allowed
him into her bed another night. He'd spent these past months
exerting a caution that didn't come naturally to him. With Celeste in
his arms, he didn't need to hold back his voice.

Other than to satisfy their physical needs—for which he was
immensely grateful— he wasn't at all certain why she continued to
allow him into her bed, especially after she'd rejected his proposal.

He should be stung that she'd turned him down after what
they'd done, but he understood that she was now a wealthy woman,
with a life half way around the world. He should be satisfied with
that. He *was* satisfied with that. Surely, some day, there would be
other women more suited to him.

That would be easier to believe if he wasn't existing in a state of
total lust for this woman and no other.

They set out at dawn in the chilly autumn air, but the clouds
and wind had died away. The cart carried their bags and enough
food for their luncheon, so they merely stopped at the inn at the
edge of the forest to return their nags and hire a post chaise.

Erran tried to draw Celeste out on her plans, but she returned
to her former restraint. He'd enjoyed their camaraderie on their
earlier ride and missed it now. He didn't have a great deal of
experience at gossip or chatter or whatever ladies preferred. He
didn't know how to find a topic she'd like.

So as the chaise traveled toward the town where he intended to stay for the night, he spoke of his family's interests and why he might spend the next months traveling on Duncan's business.

"The town where we'll be staying this evening has one of England's older worsted mills. The conditions there are different from those in the more populated areas in the west," he told her. "Because we have relations in the area who have reported the mills to Ashford, we're more familiar with them than some of Lansdowne's other properties."

She looked up with interest at mention of the earl. "He owns mills near here?"

"He doesn't own them outright. He's part of a consortium pretending they aren't dirtying their hands in filthy trade. They call it investing." Erran shrugged, trying to keep anger from his voice, even though he realized Celeste wasn't influenced by it. It still felt peculiar to express himself after these long months of keeping his lips sealed.

"That's drawing a fine line," she said with more spirit than she'd exhibited all day. "Since slave trading is no longer legal, one could say men owned slaves as a future investment against the time the commodity becomes increasingly rare."

Erran shot her a look of admiration. "You are quick. And Lansdowne's mills are not much better than slavery. Women and children work over twelve hours a day. The girls who started as little more than babies are physically deformed from spending long hours crawling underneath machines, then pushing treads before their bones are fully formed. They never get proper sun or exercise or nutrition. The boys . . . are deformed from the crawling, then denied the better jobs when they reach an age where they have to be paid a man's wage. They're incapable of working anywhere else."

"Women don't have to be paid a proper wage?" she asked, catching the nuance. "Bending over a sewing machine for hours is difficult work. If the mill machines are worse . . ."

"Sitting at any machine from dawn to dusk has to be excruciating," he agreed. "But every time Duncan tries to introduce a bill limiting the hours and raising wages, the mill owners scream they can't pay for their machinery if they do that, or they'd have to charge too much and lose sales. They say reform will bring about the demise of England's economy."

"Which is why the earl needs our money?" she asked in

perplexity. "In case he has to actually pay his workers?"

Erran made a rude noise. "That would mean planning to lose on the labor law. He built his wealth on the slave trade decades ago and has yet to find an income so lucrative to cover the expenses of that great monument to himself that he erected on his estate. He needs an influx of outside cash, and you're it."

"And I don't suppose he intends to pay back my father's estate with income from his investments," she said sharply. "That is like saying *he* is more important than *us*. Do all men of wealth consider their needs more important than those who work for them? That's arrogance."

Erran shrugged. "I call it thievery, but it is nothing new. Since well before medieval times, history shows that those who have, take, simply because they can. Human nature does not change no matter how civilized we call ourselves. Strong wins over weak and morality is viewed as the domain of preachers and women. Lansdowne will contest your father's will. You need to be prepared for that."

"But he will not prevail, will he?" she asked anxiously. "I want to believe we have some hope of repaying your family for their kindness. Goodness should be rewarded."

Erran thought guiltily of the house he'd planned to take from her once they won the case. "We are not all good or evil. Seeing Lansdowne defeated and justice prevail is its own reward."

"And if he has fewer funds, he will be less likely to support your candidate for prime minister?" she asked, groping to understand the situation.

"His vote is easily purchased. That is one of the reasons Duncan must come to town. A marquess wields more power than an earl. Surely you cannot be interested in politics?"

"I've never been given an opportunity to understand them," she admitted. "The island is small. A small group of men rule it. They met occasionally in my father's study, but I was not included. Now that I'm seeing how those meetings must have worked, I am rather appalled. It appears to my limited knowledge that all women and children and most men are slaves to those with the wealth and influence to negotiate away the rights of others. And if those men put themselves first—there is no justice in that."

"I had not carried the notion that far, but there is some truth in it." Erran admired how quickly she grasped what so many did not.

"Children, of course, do not have the understanding to have a choice in their welfare."

"There are those who believe women don't have the wits to deserve choices," she responded acerbically. "I've certainly learned my limitations under the law when a cousin I don't even know has the right to usurp all that is mine simply because he is male!"

Erran grinned. "Did men know there were women such as yourself, they might have second thoughts about leaving the vote only to men—but I cannot promise those thoughts would be positive in your favor."

She shot him a darkling look but must have heard his amusement. She offered a tentative smile. "You tease. I was not certain you could."

"There is much we need to learn about each other," he agreed, to his own shock. "I move too much in a man's world and too little in yours."

"You must show me your world," she suggested. "England is strange to me, forcing me to leave what is familiar and comfortable. But if I could look at it from a position of security . . . I might adjust."

Was she telling him that she might stay if he could offer her "a position of security"? And what the devil would that be? Not a solicitor's office, he felt sure.

He'd have to ask Theo how he'd persuaded Aster to take on a house full of obstreperous men.

But Aster had her own security—like a father who would crack whips if his daughter was harmed. Celeste had no one—and she must stand between her younger siblings and the world.

He was beginning to see the problem. He didn't have any more to offer than she did. In fact, if he won back her family estate, she would have more security and power than a barely employed third son.

In thoughtful silence, they rode up to the inn he'd chosen for the night.

Twenty-four

"IT IS EARLY yet. Would you like to visit the mill?" Erran inquired after they'd taken a single room under an assumed name at the inn.

Celeste had not seen the point in wasting Ashford's money in taking two rooms when she didn't wish to sleep alone. She would pretend she was a lady once she returned to the city, but for now . . . She wanted Erran's arms and reassuring presence for one night more, before she had to learn to be strong again.

She was surprised by his question. "We are allowed to visit?"

"The town is proud of their industry. They don't know who we are. A little reconnaissance mission might be enlightening. But I'll understand perfectly if you'd prefer to rest. It's been a long day."

Even after a day's travel, Erran looked every inch the gentleman and more. His square jaw, high forehead, and strong cheekbones depicted a man of intelligence and character. His wide shoulders and straight stance held authority. And his tailored coat and expensive linen . . . Celeste smiled. Those were vanity.

But as far as she could tell, his vanity only ran to his clothing. He did not seem to understand that a man of his integrity was a rarity to be treasured. She reached for her bonnet. "A stroll before dinner would be healthy, I'm certain."

His slow smile was such a glorious event . . . she wanted to throw off her bonnet again and steer him toward the bed. The knowledge that she could do just that with a man of his character was thrilling, but it was time she thought of someone other than herself. She could wait awhile longer.

She took his arm and let Erran lead her through the inn and down village lanes until they reached a hulking ugly building on the outskirts of town. The walls appeared to be no more than tin, and she shivered just imagining what winter must be like inside. She did not pity her own circumstances when faced with that of other people like this.

Her traveling skirt trailed in the mud as she walked across a stream on thin planks. The stench of sewage carried, and she thought it might be best not to look for the facilities.

The double doors were open to let in light and air, she supposed, although the late hour was chilly and there was no heat inside. They strolled through the entrance without anyone greeting them. The entire ground floor of the building seemed to be filled with rattling, bumping . . . *looms* . . . she thought. Each machine was run by a woman who sat with head down and gnarled hands feeding thread into wooden bars, peddling them back and forth, up and down. Not one looked up for fear of losing their rhythm.

She couldn't imagine how they saw what they were doing. It was dusk and the only light came from windows high in the walls. The air was full of dust, and she had to pull out her handkerchief to sneeze. How could they work without sneezing?

She watched, appalled, as small children wriggled on their bellies beneath the heavy lumbering cogs to gather balls of wool dust. "How do they keep from losing their heads?" she whispered in horror.

"They learn to be quick," Erran whispered back. "Or they end up like the two you took into your house. They need to eat, and this is the only way they can put potatoes in their pot tonight."

An officious, large-bellied man in open vest and rumpled linen hurried toward them. "Sir, madam, how might I help you?"

Celeste darted a glance at Erran when he did not reply. From the tightening of his jaw, he was fighting anger . . . *and his voice.* She hastened to speak for him. "My husband claims this is one of the finest old mills in the kingdom. I am quite fascinated by the . . ." she searched her brain. "By the machinery," she added weakly.

Her vocalization apparently soothed the mill manager. He nodded knowingly. "Amazing what the new technology has wrought, isn't it? In times past, it might have taken these women months to produce just one bolt of cloth. Now we can do it in days."

Celeste had never used her voice in anger. Charm and seduction were her strengths. She didn't know what would happen if she said what she thought right now. She bit her tongue, feigned a smile, and nodded.

"That . . . child . . . seems ready to give birth," Erran said in a low voice throttling any emotion. He gestured toward a reed of a girl with a big belly working with less speed and more difficulty than the others.

The manager shrugged. "They pop them out and are back to work the next day. I dock their wages if they can't keep up the pace. Teaches them not to dawdle with the layabouts in town."

The last time Celeste had screamed, she'd shattered glass. There was no glass here, but she feared screaming would cause harm in other ways. "I think you should tell that poor child to go home," she said in her most winning tones, burying her fury so deep that she nearly choked on it. "And that you'll pay until the babe is born. That is what any gentleman of morals would do."

She watched the fat toad struggle between his greed and her siren call. She caught Erran's arm when he seemed prepared to force the matter.

"Do be a dear and help that poor child up before she gives birth on the floor," she called in a voice that would reach the first row of machinery. She didn't care who responded, just that someone did.

To her surprise and delight, every woman within hearing, plus the toad, hurried to help the startled girl from her seat.

Beside Celeste, Erran chuckled. "I don't know what you will do with her, but I concede your method works better than me punching the pig in his snout."

"I don't think I should stop here," Celeste whispered, amazed at the notion that had materialized full blown in her head. "You may want to run."

For the first time in her life, she recognized the strength that her gift offered. This amazing man had given her the opportunity to learn, although he didn't know it yet—and probably wouldn't appreciate it since he thought her voice evil.

Erran looked startled at her suggestion, then narrowed his eyes as if about to give warning. Refusing to be stopped, she strode toward the women helping the frightened girl. Even the toad-pig was smiling that he'd done as she'd asked—or not fought it.

Raising her voice, Celeste applied every ounce of charm she'd ever possessed. "Thank all of you so much. This is how you should work together and help one another. Why don't all of you stand up now and walk out? He cannot run his shop without you. Do not come back until he agrees to cut your hours and double your wages. You are human beings, not oxen!"

Smiling as if she was strolling in the park, Celeste let the girl lean on her arm as she led her toward the doorway. The toad-pig still watched with approval, although his smile was starting to fade under a frown of bewilderment. The full effect of her words hadn't registered, just her charm. Ahead, Erran was struggling for dispassion. She couldn't tell if he wished to shout at her or kiss her.

He merely offered his arm to the girl and leaned down to whisper in Celeste's ear, "Don't look now, but they're all starting to stand."

She could hear the rustle and murmur behind her and felt the butterflies flapping anxiously in her stomach. But the charm needed confidence to continue working. She couldn't weaken now. She pasted on her smile, kept her shoulders straight, and spoke as if she'd done nothing singular.

"What's your name, my dear?" she asked of the girl stumbling along on their arms.

"Annie, miss," the child said, responding to Celeste's tone instead of her obvious fear. "What will happen to us, miss?"

The murmurs were louder. Chairs scraped. Feet shuffled along the wooden floor. Children piped up questioningly. Celeste stepped outside, into the fading sunlight. Erran nearly had to carry the girl down the steps and over the filthy planks.

"You will go home and have that babe, Annie," Celeste replied reassuringly. "And the others will find a few good leaders to speak with the fat toad-pig. What is his name?"

"Myron, miss." The child didn't hesitate over Celeste's description but answered with a touch of amusement. "He won't pay us if we're not working. We'll go hungry."

Now that she was across the planks and in the road, Celeste dared to turn around. Erran's arm circled her waist as they studied what she had wrought.

Drab gray-faced women of all ages streamed through the double doors as if their shift had just ended. Dozens of undernourished children tagged along. They all lifted their faces and blinked at the sunlight. Once realizing what they'd done, they began whispering nervously to each other and casting glances over their shoulders.

Myron wobbled in the doorway, looking as if he wished to shout but unable to do so.

"Better speak up," Erran warned. "You're losing them."

He was encouraging her! He believed she could do this. Celeste swelled with pride and relief and let another of the women support Annie.

Clenching her fingers into fists, she fought down the butterflies. "Why don't all of you go home, rest, and think about who you want to speak for you tomorrow? I'm sure Myron will be agreeable, won't you, Myron?" she asked as the manager stumbled after them, looking lost.

"Madge is a right 'un, miss," Annie murmured. "She'll know what's to do."

Celeste nodded and hoped the child was right. "Madge, could you speak to the others? You need to all agree on what you want before returning to work. Myron has no other choice but to listen, but you must be reasonable."

A tall, grim-looking woman of middle age stepped from the crowd. "I'll take Annie to her ma." She turned and scoured the crowd with her glare. "Tilda, Mary, come along with me. The rest of you, take the babes and go home. We'll be by in the morning."

Celeste nearly sagged in relief as the commanding Madge took over her charge. "I leave them in your good hands, madam. Make certain you demand time off to have your children. It may be a long time before we can make that a law, so it's in your hands."

Madge nodded curtly. "I don't know what trouble you've brought on us, but it was time, so I thank you."

Silently, Erran caught Celeste's elbow and dragged her away.

"I'm shaking with rage and admiration," he admitted once they were down the road. "I would have caused riots if you had not acted with such courage. But what you just did . . . is almost as dangerous. And I still can't believe I'm saying this. I must research Mesmerism. Is it possible to mesmerize a crowd?"

She knew nothing of Mesmerism, but Celeste started to shake at her temerity. She feared her knees would give out from under her before they reached the inn. "I had no idea . . ."

Erran caught her waist and practically carried her down the street. "And you had probably best not have more ideas any time soon. I'll arrange to keep you out of mills for a while. If anyone learns who did this today . . . It will not be pretty for you or your siblings. But I still applaud what you did. And I want to emulate it but can think of no way of doing so when all I do is intimidate."

Hearing his anger and fear, she smiled weakly as they entered the inn. "I think a form of madness took over me. I cannot imagine ever doing such a thing again." But as she climbed the stairs and recalled the horrid conditions of that mill, she regained some confidence. "It had to be done. I wish I could do it everywhere."

"*That* is a horrifying notion and one with which you'd better not tempt any of us again," he warned, opening the door to their room. "You saw the riots in town. England would end up in bloody revolution like France."

"England will end up there anyway," she argued, "if wealthy aristocrats do not stop stepping on the necks of free people. At some point, workers have nothing left to lose and start fighting back in the only way they know how—with fists and weapons. It's up to the educated to offer reform and help those who cannot help themselves. I fear the same will happen in my home if the slaves are not freed. Blood will be shed and people will die, and I cannot bear the thought."

A tumult of shouts and running feet penetrated the thin glass of the inn windows. Leaving her to seat herself, Erran crossed the bedchamber to look out.

"Are they coming to burn us at the stake?" she asked shakily.

He laughed. "No, the women are marching through town, waving brooms at the men who are shouting at them. You've fed their anger. I suggest we sneak away very early in the morning, before the magic wears off, and they all wonder what hit them."

He turned and his eyes smoldered in a way that left her weak with need. "I'll have our dinners sent up, shall I?"

"Tell them to take their time," she murmured daringly.

WATCHING the woman in his bed sleeping in the moonlight, Erran struggled with possessiveness, pride, and a horror of losing her to the impossibility of revolution. She had handled the mill today with amazing aplomb, keeping the situation under control with the serenity of her commands.

With experience, she could lead armies of workers on strike. That terrified the hell out of him.

Her voice could lead *insurrections*. The French had shown the disaster of that sort of upheaval. Britain had been fighting off the fear of revolt for decades. It was the whole reason London had finally agreed to a police force after centuries of fighting against the notion. This beautiful, intelligent woman would be despised and reviled by every person in society, should she persist in this new direction.

She would shatter the cautious life of reason and justice he'd been trying to build, and he couldn't even voice a good argument to stop her—because he had wanted to do what she had just done.

He wanted to march into Parliament and shout them into reform.

Celeste could be carrying his *child.* He'd always used precautions before. As far as he was aware, he'd not left a string of bastards across the countryside. But this time . . . he'd dishonored a lady. What the devil had overcome him?

If his Courtroom Voice was evil, then he'd have to say the devil made him do it. But he wasn't the one who had used the voice in the mill. Celeste had. And he was pretty damned certain the devil worked for the abusers and not the abused.

Fighting his conscience and cautious nature, Erran spent the night watching from the window for angry men to storm the inn. He'd prefer to wake up the woman in the bed and make love to her again, but he wasn't selfish enough to put his needs over her safety.

Small groups of men formed on the street, gesticulating angrily, but one by one, their wives came to drag them home. Several groups of women formed, glancing up at the inn with confused frowns, but they, too, gradually returned to their homes. He saw Myron enter the inn. Erran checked that his pistol was loaded, but other than drunken arguing below, no one stormed up the stairs.

Whatever *magic* Celeste had used may have worn off, but no one had associated the sweet-talking, polite lady with the walk-out. She'd simply left the village confused. How long would that last?

And would the women go back to work in the morning and forget everything that had happened? He didn't intend to take chances and find out.

Before dawn, Erran was up and ordering their post chaise. He had breakfast carried out in a basket before Celeste had time to don her cloak. He carried down their boxes and helped the postilion to tie them on back to speed the process.

They were on the road as the sun came up—before the villagers comprehended what had hit them.

"Will we ever know what happened to those workers?" his

witchy lady asked as the horses thundered down the road to the safety of Newport and their waiting ship.

"Only if anarchy explodes," Erran said, stifling his voice to a mutter for fear all his emotions would erupt with the same devastation as a riot.

"Perhaps we need better communication between mill workers." She crossed her gloved hands and seemed to be considering this madness. "Each location shouldn't have to reinvent the wheel."

Erran tried not to groan aloud. "I have created a monster. Isn't training workhouse inhabitants sufficient aid to the public good?"

Her bonnet prevented him from seeing her expression as she spoke. "That is Lady Aster's and her aunt's project. I am happy to help out for so long as I might. I suppose I cannot plan anything until I know whether or not we are staying in London. Our people at home really must come first."

Erran congratulated himself on not ripping the hair from his head. If she had to choose between returning to Jamaica and a possible slave revolt or staying in England and creating riots among millworkers . . ."This is the reason women shouldn't be allowed out of the house," he grumbled.

She prodded him with her elbow as if she thought he was jesting.

He could only undertake one obstacle at a time, Erran concluded. First, he must confront Lansdowne with Lord Rochester's will. That should cause riots of a different sort.

Twenty-five

THEIR SAILING RETURN to London was uneventful. Even Mrs. Lorna managed to knit and chatter through their journey. Erran spent most of his time in the engine room, discussing machinery, Celeste assumed. He'd returned to his tight-lipped, grim state, and she had to admit, he had reason to do so.

He thought he had to marry her. She supposed she ought to agree. But she was just discovering who she could be on her own. She didn't really want a man shutting the door on her world again, especially if she would soon have the means of supporting herself.

But the child deserved a father—if it survived. Celeste was well aware that many babes were lost in the first few months. Her own mother had lost several. And she could have just been dreaming that strange night when the spirits had walked the halls. She shouldn't act in haste.

She tried to smile normally when the ship docked and Erran came to fetch her—she needed to remember to call him Lord Erran now that they were back in society. His frown as he assisted her and Mrs. Lorna into a coach helped her keep her equilibrium.

It was dark already, and the docks were unlighted except for the lanterns hanging outside taverns. She swallowed her fear when Erran held his pistol in his hand as the coach traversed back alleys on the way to the main thoroughfare. Even her companion sat silently until they reached the better lighted districts.

She'd been attacked on these streets in broad daylight, so she wouldn't feel safe day or night. But surely no one knew of her return. Did she want to live in a city where people threw stones at her because she looked different? In a country where she was incensed into causing riots? There were so many things she needed to consider before she took any action.

When the coach rolled into their street, she could see lights in all the townhouse's windows. Celeste clasped her hands nervously, and Erran dropped the pistol back in his pocket.

"I doubt the reception committee is for us," he said dryly. "Mrs.

Lorna, would you like the coach to carry you home or would you prefer to stay here tonight and wait until daylight?"

"I'd like to be in my own bed tonight, if you do not mind, my lord. It looks as if the lady has family waiting up for her, so my job is done. It's been a pleasure traveling with you, but it's always lovely to be home again."

The front door swung open as the driver unloaded their boxes.

"Celeste, hurry! I think he is having a fit!" Sylvia cried from the doorway.

Erran muttered a few curses and shoved coins at the driver. Startled, Celeste picked up her skirts and hurried up the short walk.

Erran grabbed her arm before she could reach the step. "I doubt she's referring to Jamar or Trevor. Wait. I would introduce you properly." He gestured at the driver to carry the boxes to the front door.

Tired and bewildered, assuming he knew what was happening even if she didn't, Celeste waited for Erran to sort out the harassed-looking footmen who belatedly appeared.

Sylvia ran down the steps to hug her. "Did you find the journals? Can we go home now? The marquess is quite, quite mad."

That was the meaning of the uproar? Shocked, Celeste cast her escort a look of pure fear. "The *marquess* has arrived? I cannot think the construction is done! Where will we put him?"

Erran hefted his valise to his shoulder and gestured for her to precede him. "It would be exactly like Dunc to do whatever created the most havoc. We will leave him to camp in the parlor, if so."

"He is . . . very large," Sylvia said, following them inside. "Even Jamar will not go near him."

Her words were abruptly punctuated by a roar from the rear of the house. "Don't give me that twaddle, you sorry jackanapes! Bugger it!" A large object hit a wall with a resounding crack.

"I assume that's his valet with him?" Erran asked, setting down his burden and proceeding down the corridor as if violent curses normally permeated the air.

"I don't know, my lord," Sylvia whispered, hanging back. "We've stayed upstairs, out of his way."

"That won't do, you know," Celeste informed them. "We have paid for the exclusive use of this house. A guest is one thing. A berserk marquess is another."

More pounding and glass shattering accentuated her words.

"You slubber-degullion, not there!" the lion roared.

"Miss Sylvia, if you will direct the servants to carry up your sister's trunk, please. We'll see what we can do to quiet the Cyclops." Holding Celeste's hand on his coat sleeve, Erran dragged her toward the room at the rear.

"Leading the lamb to the lion?" she asked with a pinch of irony.

"More like the witch to the dragon. I expect fireworks," he retorted. "Keep in mind Duncan was an all-powerful marquess who commanded armies of men before his fall. Now, he can't even read the estate books or race his horse. I would probably have slit my throat. He prefers verbally slitting the throats of others."

"A subtle difference," she said as he rapped on the panel behind the stairs.

"No more swag-bellied hedge pigs," roared the beast. "Begone, the lot of ye."

"Shakespeare?" Celeste asked with interest.

"Is that where he gets it?"

"That last part. I'm not sure about the slubber-degullion."

"That's cant. I don't spend much time in the theater and didn't recognize the rest." Erran cracked open the door without permission and called around it. "If anyone is a hedge pig, it's you, oh brother mine. There is a lady present, so stow it until I can present her."

A shoe flew past his nose and hit the wall. An elegant but harassed looking servant appeared in the narrow aperture between door and frame. "His lordship has only just arrived and is not prepared for company."

"His lordship is never prepared for company," Erran said as if asking for a neckcloth. "Is he dressed? That's all I need to know."

"Erran, get your sorry arse in here, now!" the marquess shouted.

"Why, so you can fling a shoe at me? Or at our hostess? You do remember that you are here at the indulgence of the Rochesters? She will turn you out if you behave like an ogre to her and her family."

"If you will excuse me, I am not suitable company this evening, Miss Rochester," the marquess boomed from the darkened room. "Just send in my brother so I can remove his head."

"It is very good meeting you, my lord," Celeste called sweetly through the opening. "I do hope you are settling in nicely."

Silence.

Beside her, Erran winked and waited. He'd heard her calming charm.

"Another devious, manipulative Malcolm witch, I believe you said?" Ashford said without bellowing. "Come in."

Erran had called her a witch to his brother? With surprise as well as trepidation, Celeste cast Erran a quizzical glance. He nodded, offered his arm, and pushed the door open. She was relying on his strength again, but life kept heaving surprises at her, and she felt unbalanced.

"Ashford, may I present Miss Celeste Malcolm Rochester, part owner of a very large property in Jamaica. Miss Rochester, my hedge-pig brother, Duncan, Marquess of Ashford, Earl of Ives and Wystan, et cetera, et cetera. Dunc, she is making a very pretty curtsy even though she's been tossed about on a steamship these last twelve hours and more."

His lordship was an exceedingly large man, as Sylvia had noted. The marquess was not, however, taller than Jamar. He simply exuded an air of command and authority in just the way he stood— in shirtsleeves with hands on narrow hips, towering above the room's occupants. He still wore his knee-high boots and riding trousers, although Celeste assumed he had not ridden his horse to town. He stared blindly over her head, but he knew her direction.

"A curtsy is wasted on me, Miss Rochester, but the perfumed soap isn't. Nor the voice. Let me hear you speak again."

"Are you serious?" she asked, shocked enough by his bluntness to respond in kind. "You call me a devious, manipulative Malcolm witch and then order me around as if I'm a pot boy?" She used her best welcoming voice.

The red raw scar of Ashford's brow rose and his lips quirked in a manner reminiscent of Erran's—when he bothered to smile.

"By the devil, you've found another one, Erran, old boy. Does she collect orphans too? I heard something of the sort." Ashford stuck out his hand to his side in a demanding gesture.

The beleaguered valet hastened to place a walking stick in it. Ashford swung it about, apparently looking for a piece of furniture, Celeste hoped. At least he was not swinging it at them.

"We will discuss orphans at a later time. For now, we're weary,"

Erran said with annoyance. "What the devil are you doing here before the construction is complete?"

Celeste wanted to hear more about being a witch who collected orphans, but she supposed it was not smart to argue with the marquess who defended her family. Besides, Erran was right. She was too tired to think.

"Lansdowne is attempting to turn the party against me. I need to be here to take him down a notch or five. If you've found the documents the Rochesters need, we're taking him to court." Complacently, he took a seat in a large upholstered chair. "You will pardon my behavior, Miss Rochester. My leg still aches abominably."

"Of course, my lord," she almost whispered before she found her tongue again. "To court, my lord?"

"Yes. It has come to my attention that the earl is a thief and a liar and quite possibly a potential employer of murderous rogues. Erran, you will file the papers in the morning. I can't prove any of the other, but we can remove the Rochesters as a source of funds and show him to the world as the hog-grubber he is."

Hog-grubber? She would have smiled, but Erran looked decidedly grim. She thought perhaps this had not been his plan.

"We will discuss it in the morning," was all he said however. "I'm escorting Miss Rochester to her family. I will be back after we've had time to rest."

Celeste bobbed a half curtsy before she remembered the marquess couldn't see her. His presence was so striking, she'd almost forgotten his blindness. "Good-night, my lord. It was a pleasure meeting you."

He snorted rudely.

"You're in danger of becoming a curmudgeon, Dunc," Erran warned. Guiding Celeste from the room, he slammed the door so his brother would know they were gone.

"Court?" she whispered. "Why? I thought we only need present the will to the solicitors."

"Lansdowne has evidently thrown down some personal gauntlet to which Dunc objects. We'll find out in the morning. He'll have servants posted at the doors, so you should be safe now. I'll leave you to your family and see you in the morning."

He held her hand as if he didn't wish to let go. Breathless with the agony of releasing him, Celeste merely nodded. Their shared interlude had ended. Reality had returned far too rudely.

Checking the corridor to be certain no one lurked, he bent and placed a kiss on her cheek. Celeste almost begged him to stay—but she could not. Tears forming, she watched him stride toward the back door, evidently to check their security.

He was a good man. And she was in grave danger of loving him and ruining his life.

Twenty-six

"PASCOE and Lochmas have discovered Lansdowne has sold his vote and his pocket boroughs to a group of investors willing to loan him enough to cover part of his more pressing debts," Ashford said bitingly.

Workmen hammered and nailed next to the downstairs study, creating new chambers in the back of the house. Sitting at the ancient desk in his appropriated office, the marquess almost looked like his old self. Almost. The scar on his brow, Erran observed, had lost some of its raw redness, and the blind eyes didn't focus with the intensity they once had. But his oldest brother could snarl with the best of them.

How could he explain why he didn't wish to take Lansdowne to court? He couldn't tell Duncan that he would inevitably lose his temper, bellow his fury, and be thrown from every courtroom in the kingdom. With a little time, however, the Rochester issue could be resolved with appropriate threats and posturing without need of a courtroom.

Erran stretched out his legs and glared at his boots. "Still no proof that Lansdowne is behind the thugs who have been harassing the Rochesters? Or that he's working with your not-so-charming neighbors causing rural riots? I'd like to keep this civil and settle out of court, if at all possible." Dunc would laugh himself into a fit if he knew Erran feared turning a staid courtroom into a riot. Or worse.

"I have no proof other than that Montfort and Caldwell are siding with Lansdowne and the Tories. The hands of time can't be turned back, industry can't be halted, but they're fighting anything that resembles change." Ashford bounced a ball between his hands, successfully catching it despite being unable to see it. "If Montfort had his way, steam engines would be banned as the work of the devil, and we should go back to knights in shining armor—the good old days when the peasants knew their place."

"Lansdowne is more progressive than that. Politics makes strange bedfellows. That still doesn't persuade me," Erran argued.

"Lansdowne is a bully. He is too deeply in debt to settle for anything less than complete control of a very valuable asset when he sees the Rochesters as weak and unable to put up a fight," Ashford continued. "He is currently smearing Miss Rochester's name across town and is hinting that Lord Rochester is too dark to be English. That won't stop the court from deciding on the basis of the will, but it will influence solicitors. Try to settle, if you want, but proceed as if it won't happen."

Erran ground his molars. "Then we need to trot the Rochesters around town, introduce them as your wards, let Aster's family dote on them, and snub our noses at the old hedge pig."

Duncan snorted in amusement. "Or paint *hedge pig* on his door. The ladies will sort all that out, but they cannot fight the legalities. If there is any chance that Lansdowne can sell the plantation and its inhabitants, he will. I will not have people sold into slavery on my watch."

And there was the greatest fear—the Rochesters' servants could be sold and gone by the time Erran attempted settlements and moved on to courtrooms. Jamar had said the tenants and servants had gone into hiding, but that couldn't last forever. They needed food and housing, and they were deep into hurricane season. Anything could be happening to them right now. Any delay would worsen the odds.

"I'll get it done," Erran said heavily, pushing out of his chair. "We haven't had time to refurbish the house for entertaining. How will Zack work around you if you set up court in here?"

"Aster is working her magic in the front room. I can dictate letters anywhere I can sit. Not your concern. Take those documents and file them and start establishing the Rochesters' authority over their own damned property. If Lansdowne won't work for us, we'll leave him juggling so many debts that he won't have the ability to work against us." Duncan waved a dismissive hand in the direction of the door.

"The late baron's will left Miss Celeste as the guardian of her siblings until they come of age," Erran warned. "An English court isn't likely to accept that. Lansdowne will claim guardianship. I'll prepare documents for you to sign accepting them as your wards."

"At least I'm good for something," the marquess said bleakly. "Go, do what you must."

What he *must* and what he wanted were rapidly diverging. With a black cloud of doom hanging over his head, Erran headed for the front parlor, hoping for a glimpse of Celeste before he rode into the city. Should he woo her or leave her alone?

A woman wanted to be wooed, he thought. But what did he have to offer? He knew he was smart and could eventually earn his way in the patent business, if not as a barrister. But he was years from offering her the kind of wealth she deserved. She really needed an opportunity to meet men with titles and land before he tried to tie her down. That she hadn't responded to his proposal said she felt the same.

She wanted to return to Jamaica.

He was normally a cautious man. Erran didn't know how he'd plunged into this predicament. He'd like to believe in magic just to excuse his inexcusable behavior.

Celeste and Lady Aster had their heads together over a selection of fabrics in the salon. They looked up at his entrance, and his sister-in-law spoke to him, but all he saw was the worry in Celeste's eyes.

"I am going to file your documents with the court," he said after Aster's nattering quieted. "Don't go anywhere without strong servants. Better yet, don't go anywhere."

"If you were paying any attention at all," Aster scolded, "you would know I am having a dinner tonight to introduce Celeste to a few friends. We have invitations to my Aunt Daphne's soiree tomorrow. Celeste cannot stay home. You will simply have to come with her."

Go with them and act the part of polite but distant escort and pretend he hadn't spent the best nights of his life in her bed . . . Why didn't he just strangle himself?

He bowed. "Your wish is my command. I shall see you this evening, then."

"Please be careful, my lord," Celeste said, as if her voice could wrap him in a protective bubble.

He couldn't remember the last time anyone had expressed concern for his safety. Her casual comment struck a chord deep inside him.

He was about to file the papers that would give her the freedom to marry anyone in the kingdom or to return her to the other side of the world. That had been his goal from the start—remove her from the Ives townhouse so his family could return.

And he didn't want to do it.

He'd always been the peacemaking brother. But right now, he wanted to sling arrows and have fits of fury like Duncan, then get down on his knees and plead for Celeste to wait until he'd made his fortune.

Stiffening his spine, he marched out to the combat zone.

"YOU LOOK BEAUTIFUL, Cee," Sylvia said wistfully, straightening a sash on Celeste's new dinner gown. "Everyone will love you."

Celeste frowned at the looking glass, studying the effect of expensive fabric, excellent dressmaking, and a coiffure arranged by one of Lady Aster's maid trainees. Out of respect for her father, she hadn't wanted to wear bright colors, but those were the only ones she liked. It hadn't taken much persuasion for Aster to convince her that a simple cream and gold silk was sufficiently respectful.

She wouldn't know how she looked until Erran saw her. She was no judge of London tastes. She saw a tall, thin woman with boring brown hair, un-English tanned skin, a too-long neck, and a nose a trifle too prominent. She'd seldom wasted time over her looks before, but now they seemed crucial to making a positive appearance in aristocratic English society.

"You will sweep all the gentlemen off their feet when you make your come-out, Syllie, and you know it. So give me a chance first." Using the childhood nickname to reassure her sister, Celeste pressed a kiss on her cheek.

"If only I could believe it will happen," Sylvia said with a sigh. "The world may blow away before next year."

"Well, in that case, it will hardly matter if you meet gentlemen, for they will all be dead," Celeste countered pragmatically. "Matters are out of our hands now. All we can do is enjoy each day as it comes and hope for the best. What was Iveston like? Did you have a chance to wear your new gowns?"

Apparently accompanying her family to London had given the marquess incentive to leave the protective walls of his manor, from what she'd been able to determine. If a carriage was required for Sylvia and Nana, then Ashford could escort them in the carriage and salvage his masculine pride. His custom previously had been to gallop into town on his stallion, which he could no longer do.

It was good that they could be of assistance, she thought. She'd reserve her opinion until she learned how obnoxious the marquess intended to be now that he was installed downstairs.

Celeste studied her meager jewelry box and decided on her childhood pearls. She fastened the earrings while watching her sister in the glass.

Sylvia laughed. "Iveston was like living in a zoo with horses and dogs and sheep and goats. Trev rode out with a group of boys every day, so he was happy. But there are no women there, except a few maids and Lady Aster. We scoured the library for Malcolm journals and measured windows for new draperies. It was interesting, but I expected the home of a marquess to be more elegant."

"Well, you saw this place, so you shouldn't have expected better. Men take little interest in their surroundings, and it does seem to be an all-male household." Although Erran had been quick to note improvements needed here, but as a younger son, he didn't have the authority to change his brothers' careless ways. She thought he might be different from his brothers, given the chance.

That gave her something pleasant to think about when the carriage arrived. She was relieved to see that Erran accompanied it.

The marquess had retreated to his own quarters after the carpenters left for the day, leaving Jamar guarding the front door. Entering through the foyer, Erran doffed his hat and watched her descend the stairs, but he revealed nothing of his thoughts. Celeste was left hoping that was admiration in his eyes when he offered his gloved hand to assist her on the last step.

"I knew that gown would look excellent on you," he murmured as he lifted her hand to his lips. In front of Jamar, he could scarcely do more.

He stirred everything in her that was female. With Erran's approving gaze on her, she felt as if her breasts might actually be the perfect size, and that her height was ideal. None of that ought to matter, but somehow, it did. She lowered her lashes so he couldn't see the longing there, but her gown was so revealing, she feared he could see her breath catch.

"The gown does what it must," she admitted, trying to sound as casual as he. "The problem is in knowing what I must be to achieve the approval we seek."

He quirked his dark eyebrows, showing he understood. "Aster and Theo will only invite sympathetic guests. Their friends are scientists and intellectuals who will be intensely curious about your home, the charities you mean to support, and your politics. Try being yourself and see if I am not right."

"If only I could believe it so," she murmured. But so much rode on her making an impression that she didn't think she could do it, even if she knew who she was, which she didn't, really. It had been so long since she'd not had to disguise herself!

Erran knew the real her. He appeared to like her without need of her charm—which enthralled her far more than it should. She had little hope that he would follow her to Jamaica.

"Do you have additional footmen to send with us?" Erran turned to Jamar, obviously more interested in practicalities than the state of her foolish heart.

"Two who claim they can use pistols," Jamar replied. "Or I can ride on the outside."

"No, you need to be here with the others. The driver has pistols. We'll station one with him and the other in back. I don't expect trouble tonight. It's too soon. I just prefer to be cautious." Erran placed Celeste's hand on his arm. "I apologize for such harsh talk, but I wish you to be prepared as well. I don't think you will become missish on me, will you?"

"I think I shall," she said vaguely, producing a fan and flapping it to conceal her expression. "It is the only way to go about in society, isn't it?"

"Not in Malcolm society," he said with a laugh.

She swallowed, wondering if she could believe that, if she dared drop her deceptive charm and be herself.

Her maid brought her pelisse and Erran helped her don it. Then they were on their way to Celeste's first formal London event. She took comfort in Erran's assurance that her hostess would not invite anyone who would scorn her—unless one counted Celeste's own half-sister. The Guilfords had been invited.

Erran's prediction proved correct. Lady Aster and Lord Theo's guests asked politely after the marquess, then proceeded to quiz her on her own interests. Her half-sister Charlotte and her husband looked a little rural and out of place, but they were treated with the same respect as Celeste. In return, they barely said a word.

Celeste answered questions as honestly as she could, refraining from using her Other Voice, and no one appeared to object to her sometimes sharp observations.

"I feel horribly uneducated," she whispered to Erran as the evening progressed. "Everyone here has such fascinating interests! I sew and cook and keep house. I take it those are not done here?"

"You need only look beautiful and nod intelligently and they will be thrilled to make your acquaintance. You are doing just fine." He squeezed her hand beneath the table

After dinner, Celeste listened to the other ladies, spoke of her interest in Aster's charities, and did her best to blend in with the beautifully exotic withdrawing room. Lady Aster's tastes in decor reflected her eccentric interests, resulting in a London room that resembled an Indian jungle dotted with stars and moons and cats.

When the men joined the women later, the conversation took a more treacherous turn.

"The reports make preposterous claims that some female demon lured the mill workers out, then entranced them into making impossible demands," Celeste heard one of the political types say. "Superstitious rural sorts don't look for logical explanations, of course, but it *is* unusual for women to stand up for themselves."

Several of the lady guests raised objections to that assessment. Clenching her teeth in fear as well as in angry protest, Celeste let them speak for her. She really had not thought of repercussions when she'd demanded that poor mother be taken home. Although she would probably have done the same, even if she'd known the gossip would run straight to London.

Erran strolled over to stand behind her chair. She was grateful for his presence, but she had to learn to do this on her own—if only she knew what "this" was.

"The workers can't possibly win against the mill owners," one of the men argued. "They will all starve."

"Or start a revolution," another man warned.

"What do you think, Miss Rochester?" one of the women asked. "You are familiar with slavery. Would you say that the mill conditions are any different?"

"I have only ever seen one mill," she said, choosing her words with care. Erran had said to *be herself* with these people. That meant not sweet talking them into hearing what she wanted them to hear, or relaxing into the comfortable mood she might weave around them. "But if all mills are similar, then I would have to say that many slaves are treated better, though not all, certainly. Slaves are valuable property, so working them to death or deformity is a foolish waste. Whereas the mill workers are apparently expendable. That, alone, makes a difference, although not a moral one. People are people and all should be treated with respect."

She held her breath, waiting for tempers to explode and people to turn their backs on her. Instead, they dived into a much deeper discussion about the ills of slavery, the need for labor reform, and the economic advantages of income equality. Her head swam with the topics springing up around her.

Erran squeezed her shoulder and moved into the crowd.

"That was very nicely said," one intimidating lady said. "I wonder if you might speak at my salon someday? There is a bill being prepared to abolish all slavery on British soil, and you might sway a few influential people."

"I . . . Yes, of course," Celeste said, wondering if these people had heard the rumors the earl was spreading about her and didn't care, or if they hadn't heard.

"You will be attending the McDowell soiree tomorrow night, won't you?" a young gentleman asked. "I look forward to introducing you to a few people who will be delighted to meet a new face in town. We can look forward to a number of balls once the rest of Parliament returns for the vote. I will score a feather in my cap for knowing you first."

"Yes, I'm looking forward to meeting new people," Celeste agreed faintly.

She glanced at her half-sister and waited for Charlotte to repeat the earl's rumor about her being a bastard, but the Guilfords had cornered a gentleman who might press their ambitions in government and scarcely acknowledged her existence.

She'd survived her entrance into London society—but she had still done it with Erran's aid. Somehow, she had to learn to do it on her own. If she had learned nothing else this past year, it was that she could not always rely on others.

She needed to be in full control of her fate before she made any decisions.

Twenty-seven

AS HAD BECOME his custom, Erran entered the town house through the kitchen door early the next morning. The cooks ignored him. Usually Nana or Jamar was around to acknowledge him, but not this time. The one-armed potboy gave him a gap-toothed grin, and the lame little girl looked up from her seat at the table where she peeled potatoes. They looked healthier and better dressed than when they'd first arrived. That was how a fair world should work, and no magic had been involved.

Aster had apparently been by to check on them. The children now had kittens—in their laps and in a basket by the hearth. One tumbled out to investigate his boots before he could reach the stairs. Erran bent to rub the little fellow's head before preventing it from escaping up the stairs with him.

Pondering the best way of convincing Celeste to the insanity of marrying him to live in poverty in chilly England instead of returning to a plantation in sunny Jamaica, he strode upstairs to enter the chaos only his brothers could create.

Except, this time, Celeste's family and servants seemed to have joined with Aster's, and his brothers were more or less sidelined in confusion. Interesting.

Standing in the back of the hallway, Erran crossed his arms, leaned a shoulder against the wall, and simply observed the sublime folly. Aster's Aunt Daphne stood in the foyer, chanting and waving a lit candle as if directing an orchestra. Aster was reading from what appeared to be one of her family journals, sing-songing her aunt's chant and sprinkling dried herbs along the newly-built walls enlarging Duncan's chamber.

He could hear Celeste and her sister in the parlor. He couldn't detect the words but he could feel . . . prayer . . . in them. That was the only description he could apply. Such celestial voices had the power to make him feel as if he were in church.

He could use a little prayer to help him push the Rochester documents through the medieval maze of Chancery before

Lansdowne caught wind of them. Once the papers were filed, the old goat would have to sue Dunc to get his hands on the estate funds.

But even Erran had to admit that ramming the documents through the kingdom's slowest, most corrupt, court probably wouldn't happen without supernatural aid. Apparently Celeste and her family had concluded they needed the help of ghosts or the devil. He couldn't tell. His wearing a fashionable new coat and pleated shirt were as much superstition as chanting, he supposed. They wouldn't impress the court or sway a judge who already held him in contempt, but they gave him confidence.

Theo and Trevor weren't looking prayerful. They were wearing disgruntled expressions and waving flaming candles at the ceiling as they roamed from room to room. Erran couldn't see Jamar or Nana, but he could hear their mellifluous accents intoning along with the others from rooms along the corridor.

He could swear he heard his half-brother Jacques in Duncan's room, although it was hard to tell over Duncan's roars. Jacques had been more-or-less squatting in Aster's London home while hunting for directors for his plays. He would do anything Aster ordered him to do, and Jacques loved a good drama.

All the scene needed was their half-brother William's dogs and a sacrificial goat.

It wasn't Iveston or this house that was crazed—it was the whole damned family.

Erran waited until Aster had vanished into the parlor. Hoping Lady McDowell wouldn't notice him in the shadows, he steeled himself and strode down the hall. In the study he could hear Jamar intone a chant in a language that wasn't English. The ladies probably couldn't tell the manservant wasn't following the program, but Jamar seemed enthusiastically involved in whatever in hell was happening. Erran pushed open the door to Duncan's bedchamber.

"You've brought me to a nest of Bedlamites," Ashford shouted at the sound of the opening door.

"I didn't bring you here," Erran retorted, studying the situation.

Jacques was seated cross-legged in the center of the massive bed, presumably where Duncan couldn't whack him with his walking stick. His blond half-brother held a candle and read incantations from a script, ignoring Ashford's ire.

"I was the one who recommended that you *wait* until I had

removed the Rochesters to better accommodations," Erran reminded him.

Ashford was pacing the room, using his stick to fend off objects in his way. "If you're coming in here with more prattle about protective charms and enhancing the power of the ley lines, you can walk right out again."

"Do you happen to know what set them off?" Erran removed a tea tray before it fell victim to Ashford's counting of steps—his means of determining his location.

"Damned if I know," the irritable marquess growled. "No one tells me anything. I thought something must have happened at Theo's dinner last evening."

Erran thought about it. "I can't recall anything that would require protective charms. I told Theo I was taking the Rochester documents into the city today. Miss Rochester's half-sister was present, but I don't think they exchanged half a dozen words. Perhaps the spirits spoke to them," he said jestingly, although unease crept down his spine recalling the odd atmosphere of Wystan. Could he dismiss the possibility of spirits without scientific investigation?

Duncan waved a cantankerous dismissal. "Where are those contractors? Shouldn't they be finishing that wall?"

"It's early yet. They should be here shortly. Does Jones approve of his new chamber?" Erran looked for the valet but the man had apparently gone into hiding.

"He's out choosing wallpapers," Duncan complained. "He'll be gilding the ceiling if you don't take him in hand. Jacques, will you shut up the infernal incantations so we can hear ourselves think!"

As if the spirits had spoken, the entire household grew silent. Jacques crumpled up the paper he'd been reading from and grinned. "Oh, yes, my lord and master. I can feel the power now. I *shall* sell this play and make my fortune!"

"Balderdash. You'd sell it faster if you were actually talking to people who could buy it and not witches who think they can pull power from the earth. Go find out if anyone is fixing my coffee." Duncan smacked his stick against a bedpost.

"Aster says we're witches too," Jacques chortled as he sprang from the bed. "Or maybe sorcerers. I could use a little magic power. So could both of you." He strode off, whistling.

"The hell of it is, I think she may be right," Erran muttered, straddling a chair and prying out that admission for public humiliation. "And I think your Wystan property is haunted."

Ashford waved a dismissive hand. "Unless we can summon demons or angels to win this vote, I don't care if we're Merlin's descendants. Just get the Bedlamites out of sight before my guests start arriving. I'm holding a party meeting this afternoon."

Erran grimaced at Ashford's complete dismissal of his deepest, darkest secret. So much for thinking he had any importance. "*There's* the key to their ritual, lunkhead," he retorted. "The women have a lot riding on the election, and they're no doubt hoping to cast a spell of good fortune on you. You brought the fol-de-rol on yourself."

Duncan glared sightlessly at Erran. "Take your damned papers to court. Crucify Lansdowne and his cronies. That will help more than singing hymns."

"If you think they're singing hymns, you either need a physician to check your ears or you need a woman of your own to remind you of what they're like, old boy. I recommend the latter. You don't need eyes to bed them," Erran suggested cynically. "But I'd wait until we've moved out the Rochesters before you start trotting light-skirts through here."

He escaped before the book Duncan threw slammed into the door. The blind man was getting too damned accurate in his aim.

Erran wasn't entirely certain why he'd stopped by. He should have gone straight from Pascoe's house to the city, but he'd been up early and had the time and . . . he wanted to start his day by seeing Celeste. He found her in the front room with her family, all of them talking at once.

"I'll have Emilia look at the garden once the workmen are gone," Lady McDowell was saying as Erran entered. "The rowan bush is still alive, at least. I think if you place a few twigs in the corners of the house, you've done all you can. Your servants have a very powerful magic. I could feel the difference."

"I should speak to them before they return to their duties," Celeste said, catching Erran's eye and crossing the room toward him.

"Yes, of course," Aster said, although she smiled knowingly. "And be sure to tell Lord Erran that his mission has been enhanced to the best of our abilities."

He bowed silently, refusing to rise to her bait. "Good morning, ladies. I believe I saw Jamar in the study. I need a word with him also. Shall we greet him together?" He offered his arm and was rewarded with Celeste's ungloved hand on his sleeve and her floral scent easing his confusion.

He wanted her with every ounce of his body. He seldom craved anything the way he craved Celeste. He would concentrate on how to have her—except he was still uncertain that she wanted *him*. Not in the way he needed her—permanently.

He terrified himself thinking like that. Maybe he'd been infected by Wystan's spirits.

"Has there been more trouble?" he asked, rather than make a declaration he had no right to make.

"Nothing new. I have been recruited as hostess for your brother's meeting this afternoon, but that apparently means no more than greeting and offering refreshments and disappearing." She didn't sound worried by the task.

"Use your calming influence when Dunc starts bellowing," Erran suggested with a smile. "I think it works on him."

She shot him a sideways glance. "You don't think that's unfair of me?"

"I think creating calm is a good thing. It's riot that I worry about." At least Celeste would listen to his weird concerns, even if no one else believed him.

"I promise to create no riots," she agreed, looking relieved. "But your brother does need a calming influence. I shall see what I can do, now that I understand the importance of the legislation he wishes to pass."

"Keep that in mind when he roars the plaster off the ceiling. I expect to spend most of the day in the city, so I cannot come to the rescue. For that, I apologize." He bowed over her hand and left her in Jamar's capable care.

There were far too many people around to even dare a kiss.

AS THE DAY progressed, Celeste thought of a dozen different things she should have said to Erran when she'd had him so briefly alone. She should have wished him safety, above all. He held papers the earl might kill him for. But with luck, their father's cousin did not know they'd found the will. The troubles would come once Erran filed the papers and reclaimed their inheritance. How long would that take? And in what form would it come? Lansdowne had shown a nasty predilection for sneakiness.

She couldn't settle down while considering what might happen. She'd all but given up sewing. Nana and Sylvia turned out several shirts a day, just to keep occupied. Still, they were living off the marquess's largesse—or his rent, as his family called it. She didn't know how long that would continue.

They could scrape by on the shirt income should the inheritance case last for years, but she could not bear worrying about the servants at home living in danger. And *scraping by* wouldn't put Trevor through school or bring out Sylvia. She had to pray Erran could overcome the powerful earl's objections and put an end to this purgatory.

So she helped the Malcolm ladies rejuvenate the front parlor where the marquess would entertain his guests. She descended to the kitchen to ask for special treats for the company—and to hug the youngest members of the staff and play with the kittens.

Just thinking of what those children had been through put Ashford's irascible demands in perspective. She thought he needed to physically vent his frustration over his limitations, so she tried not to take his curses too seriously. If he could improve the working conditions of laborers and give slaves their freedom, then she needed to support him and his family in any way she could.

She rather liked the idea of being useful.

The first of Ashford's invited guests had been led to the front parlor when the potboy came racing up the backstairs shouting in distress.

"Jamar! They have taken Mr. Jamar!"

Chapter 28

STRETCHING THE LIMITS of his patience, Erran reached into his purse of coins and produced a silver one to wave below the clerk's nose. "I have told you, this matter is of great urgency to the marquess. It is a matter of life and death and could affect the entire ministry! I must have the judge's signature *now*."

He had known he'd set himself an impossible task—but he couldn't bear the idea of dragging Celeste into a courtroom setting where Lansdowne's lawyers would smear her name. Such a case could drag on for years.

He had this one chance, and this one chance only, to drive the baron's will through Chancery before Lansdowne heard about it. Once the will and the guardianship papers were filed—the banks would accept them. Lansdowne would have to be the one to file suit.

Today wouldn't end the conflict. It would just turn the tables. Establishing an executorship should be a simple thing—but not in this pathetic excuse for a court.

Erran kept his voice regulated, but he could feel his fury boiling—which only served to increase his frustration. All his life he'd done his absolute damned best to play the part of noble, responsible gentleman—and no one noticed or even cared.

While Lansdowne lied, cheated, and stole with impunity and no one stopped him. Justice was a damned elusive concept.

"His Honor is otherwise engaged, my lord," the obsequious clerk responded, managing to palm the silver despite his refusal to expedite matters. "I will see that he knows you are waiting."

"I have *been* waiting these last three hours. You are the fourth clerk whose palm I've greased, and I'll not be pawned off on another. All I need is a bloody *signature*." He'd drawn up all the papers necessary for Celeste to control her portion and be appointed executor for the estate. He had Ashford's signature agreeing to take her siblings as his wards because a judge would never deem a woman capable of caring for her own damned family.

All he needed was a signature from the court approving the

documents so they might be filed with the will. And the bloody damned judge he'd bribed his way in to see had wandered off to tup his mistress. So now Erran was on a mission to corner another judge.

"His Honor is in court, my lord," the clerk said apologetically, nearly cringing from Erran's suppressed fury. "I will send you to him as soon as—"

"My lord, my lord! Over here, my lord!" a boy's voice cried. "It's Jamar. They've taken Jamar!"

What?

Erran whirled around to gaze over the sea of faces in the crowded waiting room. In the doorway, a bailiff held a small boy by the back of his coat. The boy kicked and screamed and increased his cries when Erran looked his way—*a one-armed* boy.

"Sir, please! Miss Celeste says help!"

"Put that boy down," Erran thundered in his Courtroom Voice, not giving it a second thought.

The guard dropped the boy. Every parent with a son in the room did the same, although more gently. An infant began wailing.

"Oh, for pity's sake," Erran muttered. He needed to phrase his bellows better. "Tommy, make your way here, if you please," he said in a more moderate tone. "Explain yourself."

Although the boy's terrified cry had been explanatory enough. Erran simply needed a moment to cool his fury and panic.

"The lads from the tavern, sir . . ." the potboy said, gasping for breath. "They came to the kitchen looking for Mr. Trevor, said three big sailors carried off Mr. Jamar when he went to the market. Miss Celeste is crying. Mr. Trevor has gone off to find him."

Erran put a steadying hand on the weeping boy's shoulder, trying to calm himself as much as the boy. "You did brilliantly, Tommy, thank you. Are any of the lads out there now?"

Tommy hiccuped and nodded. "They showed me where to go."

Aware that the entire room was following this drama with fascination, Erran shoved his fury deep inside and feigned a composed demeanor. Thank goodness the boy hadn't used Trevor's correct title or the fascination factor would escalate given what he was here to do. "Wait for me on the steps. I'll be right out."

Sniffing, wiping his nose on his sleeve, Tommy nodded in relief and hurried out, past the bailiffs who had stopped him earlier.

"I have told you the matter was urgent," Erran said to the clerk in his most patient voice. "And now a respectable gentleman has been kidnapped and abused by a gang of thugs under the pretense of legality. These papers will end that pretense." Erran slapped the documents against the desk, his voice deliberately rising as he carefully framed the words. "I will see the judge, and I *will* see him now!"

Erran's forceful tone carried only as far as the clerk—who went wide-eyed as the papers *rose off the desk.*

He'd *levitated* papers—probably out of suppressed frustration. He'd probably be burned at the stake if anyone believed it, but they wouldn't. Even *he* didn't believe the evidence literally right beneath his nose.

"Poltergeists," Erran said curtly. "Don't anger them."

"Yes, my lord. Of course, my lord. If you will come this way . . ." Looking even more terrified, the clerk leapt from his chair, not touching the documents that flopped back to the desk.

The clerk actually *obeyed* his command! The floating debacle had horrified Erran as much as it had the clerk, but his appalled shock transformed to wicked elation as he grabbed the documents and followed the clerk's flight. Nothing like terrorizing clerks into doing their duty. He'd be following Cousin Sylvester to the Americas before long.

Hurriedly, the clerk led him down a corridor and opened a door to a chamber filled with dark-coated gentlemen. Inside, the judge was wearing his wig and robes but was obviously presiding over a meeting and not a courtroom.

Erran had no compunction about striding through their midst to lay his papers on a table in front of the judge. The last time he'd raised his voice to a judge, he'd been banned from the courtroom. He was likely to be banned from the bar now, but he no longer had time for noble patience. If he had the power to save a man's life, he had to conclude morality belonged to his side and not that of the errant court.

"A man has just been kidnapped because I cannot have these filed without your signature," Erran said in a reasonable tone, despite his fury. "If you wish to save a lady's family and fortune, you need only press your seal here, and here, Your Honor. If you want the entire story, I'll be happy to relate it. You will not be happy for these good fellows to hear it."

This time, he took no chances by following his noble conscience. Despite his calmness, Erran let his fury flow into his voice. If the clerk was any example, it was his anger that fed the compulsion. If this worked, he was being a bully, but he could hope the judge wouldn't know what hit him.

"Ives? Is that you? What is this about?" a querulous voice called from the gathering as the judge took the papers and affixed his seal without reading or even questioning.

His vocal coercion was actually working with an experienced man of the law! It certainly hadn't been his eloquent speech. Erran would examine his astonishment later. Right now, he needed to run before the judge regained his senses.

He turned to find the questioner. "Lord Montfort." Erran bowed while tucking the signed documents into his coat. "You may wish to reconsider which side your bread is buttered on. Lansdowne has committed the unpardonable this time. I will personally see him dragged through the streets."

Without lingering to see the effect of his declaration, Erran shoved back to the terrified clerk's desk in the front room and slapped down one of the signed copies. "Take care of this with your life. Have it filed as if the king commands it."

He added a gold coin as atonement for using intimidation. What purpose was Ashford's wealth if not to be used for the greater good?

As he walked out, Erran felt no jubilation at achieving what should have been—in a just world—accomplished months ago, when the Rochesters had first arrived and the head of their damned family should have taken them in.

He had stayed within the boundaries of the law. He refused to feel guilty for expediting what had been left unattended too long.

But if he couldn't save Jamar... There was no justice anywhere. What did he do then?

Tommy ran up the moment Erran stepped outside. "The docks, sir. One of the lads will show you."

The docks, of course. They'd drag dignified Jamar down in chains and be waiting for the next tide out. *Filth and damnation.*

Erran filled the boy's meager pocket with silver. "Pass this on to your friends. Have them keep me and Miss Celeste informed, if they can. We will find Jamar, lad, with your fine help."

The boy's eyes widened so far, Erran feared they'd fall off of his face. Then Tommy nodded and pointed out a grubby urchin kicking at dried horse dung on the corner. "That's William. He's the one what came calling for Mr. Trevor, says he knows which dock they're at."

"Can you return to the house on your own?" Erran asked. The court was closer to the docks than the house. He didn't want to go out of his way, but the boy was small and a stranger to the city.

"Trevor's lads will take me in their skiff," Tommy said proudly. "I'll give them your coins like you said."

Erran hoped Trevor had chosen his urchins well. He sent Tommy off and faced the older lad watching him warily. "To the docks, William."

He'd worry about how he'd board a ship on the river and fight an army of sailors once he got there—*nobility be damned.*

Justice obviously required leadership—or a good healthy shove off a cliff.

"MISS ROCHESTER, where the devil are you? Where are the d—, bl—" Ashford swore under his breath, swung his stick at a hall tree, and finally finished bellowing—"Servants?"

Wearing her riding apparel and tying on a cloak, Celeste breathlessly ran down the stairs to the tune of this tirade. "I do apologize, my lord," she called, as she rushed toward the front door.

The marquess stood commandingly in the arched doorway of the formal parlor. He stuck his walking stick across the hall to halt her. Behind him milled an assortment of gentlemen following their conversation with interest. She assumed they would observe anything the marquess did at this point. Watching a blind man taking his place in Parliament would be much akin to watching monkeys in a cage.

The fate of all Britain might rest on Ashford's shoulders. And still she could not abandon Jamar. Perhaps her newly developed backbone was in the wrong place.

"Where are you going?" the marquess demanded.

"Lansdowne's bullies have stolen Jamar," she said furiously, pulling on her riding gloves and shoving aside his stick. "They will claim he is part of the estate and *sell* him. It is not to be borne. You may tell your friends that slavery is inhumane. Who do they think they are, allowing human beings to be sold away from their families? The Roman Caesars and their armies are deservedly dead. Britain should not court their fate."

"I do not need a lecture, Miss Rochester," the marquess retorted. "I asked where you are *going*. Do you need the carriage?"

She tried not to gape in astonishment. "I believe a horse will be quicker, my lord. Trevor has gone to fetch some." She was terrified. She had never done anything like this in her life. But if she had any spine at all, it was because Jamar had showed her how to grow one.

And Lord Erran had given her the support to use it.

"And just what precisely do you hope to achieve by going alone? One assumes you are not carrying pistol or sword."

She had no idea what she hoped to achieve. A riot, perhaps. "I will not let Jamar believe he's been abandoned. I have my sewing money. I will find some way—"

"You have wits to let, Miss Rochester." The marquess turned back into the room. "You have your phaeton, George?"

BY THE TIME Erran reached the dock, a mob had formed. Carriages and wagons filled the cobblestoned roadway and the pier was milling with laborers.

His blood thundered in panic. He prayed Celeste had stayed home and not ventured into this crude sailor's hurly-burly.

But even as he thought it, he heard her crystalline angel's voice carry over the rumbles of the rough and disorderly crowd. "It is that ship right out there, the *Jolly Wench*. We cannot let it sail!"

Oh hell and damnation—did the woman not remember how a London riot deteriorated into violence?

Erran swung off his horse and hauled down the urchin who had directed him here. "My thanks, lad." He pressed a gold coin into the boy's palm. "We may need your help rescuing the lady, if you wish to hang about a bit."

Gazing at the coin in astonishment, the tough tested the metal with his teeth. "I can look after your horse for you."

Not looking back, Erran shoved his way into the mob, keeping his eye out for the blasted female doing her best to get herself killed. Or worse. The docks were no place for a woman alone.

He discovered Celeste standing on a pylon on the pier, balancing her tall, slender frame with delicate grace above the rough men with whom she pleaded.

One small shove—and she'd be dragged down into the tide, into the filthy sewer of a disease-ridden river. The mob was too close. One shove was inevitable with the fury she was raising.

He could hear her fear and fury. The mob heard only her command. Seamen were already leaping into skiffs and setting sails as if she were their general. She was damned well sending them to war!

Her hood had fallen back from her mahogany hair, revealing the full beauty of her brilliant eyes and slashing cheekbones. Half the men here were probably spell-bound by her captivating looks alone. Erran elbowed a filthy sailor out of his way in his rush to reach her.

"We must stop this piracy!" she called in a soaring voice that carried over the dock and probably the water. "A man should not be taken in chains and forced to abandon his home!"

Eminently foul word. Erran elbowed faster. She was describing the British system of punishment—chain up the thieves, heave them on a boat to the penal colonies, and forget about them.

The rumbles around him were that of agreement. These men lived with that threat every day. They didn't care about Jamar, probably didn't even know he was African or Jamaican. Prison ships, they understood. She was brilliant.

And her *magic* was terrifying. But it couldn't save her from the river. Her layers of petticoats alone would drown her.

He'd told her she was weak. He should have realized she was insane! Or maybe *he* was, for saying any such thing. Gut-wrenching horror had him elbowing a filthy deckhand larger than he was as he shoved closer to the pier.

More men leapt into boats. A flotilla formed on the filthy waters of the Thames. The tide depth was against the larger ship, but the little ones navigated this stream all day.

Erran wanted to tear his hair and bellow for everyone to go home, but he couldn't. He had to respect that the fool woman was doing precisely what was necessary for the occasion—even if she risked her own life in doing so. He was the inexperienced one in the Realm of the Wyrd.

But he damned well wasn't letting the brilliant, reckless female stand up there alone and unguarded. Keeping his hand on his pistol, he bullied his way to a space near her feet. Legs braced apart, arms crossed, he defied anyone to come close. He wasn't certain she saw him. She was concentrating hard on the right commands and not the pushing and shoving men milling at her feet.

To Erran's relief, Trevor eased up to his side, his hand on the grip of his sword. The boy had good instincts.

"Bring back the prisoner!" Celeste cried, gesturing dramatically with her cloaked arm, pointing at the ship.

More men poured into boats. A few leapt into the muddy freezing water and began stroking toward the middle where the *Jolly Wench* bobbed. Erran had to catch Trevor's shoulder to prevent the boy from leaping to this command.

"She's inciting a riot! Stop her, men!" a male voice abruptly bellowed from the cobblestones.

Celeste's eyes widened. Erran turned to see a phalanx of uniformed men marching through the crowd. These weren't bobbies, but hired forces.

He recognized the commander—*Lansdowne.*

In an attempt to retreat from the soldiers, the mob panicked and surged toward the river. Crushed between the edge of the pier and the crowd, Erran and Trevor stood shoulder to shoulder, attempting to stand strong against the wave of humanity, giving Celeste time to climb down.

She teetered helplessly, looking for footing as the crowd surged.

With a mighty bellow, Erran grabbed for her. Before he could clasp even her cloak, she lost her balance and toppled—*into the foulness of the Thames.* She would drown in that debris-strewn tide.

Watching such brilliance vanish beneath the murk was akin to seeing the sun explode and the heavens crash. Erran roared his anguish.

Caution be damned. He could not let her die. Bellowing for ropes and buoys, uncaring that objects leaped off the pier without human intervention, he tugged off his coat containing the valuable documents and shoved it at Trevor. Without noticing that his entire audience madly jumped into the water around him, Erran dived after his sunshine.

Twenty-nine

WATER AS THICK as pea soup closed over her head. Petticoats, cloak, and riding boots dragged her down through the murk. Celeste held her breath until she thought her lungs might burst and she started seeing stars. Frantically, she kicked, but fabric wrapped her legs, trapping her more surely than a river of seaweed. Something filthy bobbed beneath her nose. She fought to avoid it, and a rotted timber slammed into her arm. Panicking, she grabbed at it, but the board dipped from her hand and bobbed away. And she kept sinking. Her struggle against the current got her nowhere.

She sensed her parents in the water and air around her, frantically urging her to safety. She longed to reach out to them . . .

Abruptly, a barrage of large objects plunged into the water around her in a confusion of colors and bubbles.

Unable to hold her breath longer, she gulped for air. At the same time, her braid caught on an invisible hook. She almost screamed, except she couldn't. Choking, blacking out, she was barely aware of being hauled upward. Her cloak was ripped from her throat, and she felt immeasurably lighter. An arm grabbed her waist—

The muscular solidity was as familiar to her as her own frailty, jarring her back to consciousness. Why was he here? He was supposed to be in court, saving her family home. Was he dead, like her parents?

Frantic for his sake and for his child's, her spirit clung to this drowning body.

She wept and coughed as her head emerged from the water. She still couldn't breathe, but Erran's frantic pleas for her to live reached her through the veil separating her from life. She couldn't speak to tell him she was trying. Her voice was gone with her breath. She gagged desperately for air as he swam to the pier.

She could hear shouts of rage and panic and . . . concern? Maybe. She inhaled abruptly and couldn't think while gasping for breath and choking on water.

Hands hauled her upward until she sprawled along the pier planks, spitting up her lungs, soaked, and miserable. She tried to shove upright. She tried to shout Jamar's name, remind them they must rescue Jamar . . .

Erran sat on her rump. "Shut up. Just shut up for once. They've boarded the *Wench*. The mob is furious and out of control and turning on Lansdowne's thugs and will probably light fire to warehouses soon. The earl and his men are being mauled and driven back. You did a very good job of arousing ire. Just *stay down!*" He pushed her flat, then pounded and massaged her back until she indecorously heaved up half the contents of the river.

"Trevor, your handkerchief," Erran commanded when she had no more to heave.

A clean white square was pressed to her mouth, and the heavy weight lifted from her back. "You weigh twice of me," she muttered, scrambling to sit.

"And a good thing too," he retorted. "I went down faster."

"Like cannon shot," Trevor said cheerfully, although his voice hid terror.

She didn't *want* to hear other people's fear. She had enough of her own to last a lifetime. Shivering, she accepted someone's coat and leaned into an equally soaked Erran's reassuring embrace. She couldn't stop shaking. Or crying. She had to *do* something. She couldn't let Jamar—

A roar of triumph echoed over the water. She barely had the strength to lift her head and look.

She caught a glimpse of Jamar standing tall and proud on the ship's deck. Men swarmed over the *Wench*, dismantling the sails, carrying out trunks.

"Wharf rats," Erran commented, drawing her closer, holding her as if he would never let her go again. "They'll strip the ship clean now. It's blatant thievery, but I cannot condemn them if they demolish a slaver."

Neither could Celeste. She watched with hope as, unshackled, Jamar climbed down and into a waiting rowboat. At least one of the sailors appeared to be an honest man. Rather than wait for riches, he began rowing Jamar back to the dock.

"Justice takes a strange path," Erran murmured above her head. "I must condemn lawlessness, but if fighting among thieves brings justice, who am I to argue?"

Pistol shots rang out near the warehouses. The mob still on shore roared in rage and surged in several directions at once. She could hear fistfights breaking out and shuddered. "I should stop them."

"Take a look at yourself and say that again," Erran said in that disturbing tone she couldn't quite define.

While she glanced down at her seaweed draped skirts and soaked bodice—revealing everything they were meant to hide— he released her. She hadn't been fully aware that she'd been in his arms until she wasn't—he felt that much a part of her.

He was right. She couldn't stand up looking like this. People would merely see a madwoman. Wringing out her loosened braid, she watched as Erran stood and took the perch she'd commanded earlier.

"He got his new shirt wet," she said sadly, madly, admiring the way his lordship's finery plastered to his athletic build as he shouted at a rioting mob.

"He's lost his neckcloth," Trevor said, "and his boots will never be the same again. He encouraged a riot to save a nodcock like you."

For *her*. Not for the marquess. Not for riches. For her. The elegant, intimidating aristocrat she'd once regarded in awe had saved a pathetically useless wretch like her—as if she might actually have some value. Even after she'd used the compulsion he condemned.

As she watched Erran shouting in his commanding courtroom voice, accepting his gift and conquering his fear of becoming his evil cousin, she thrilled at the knowledge that he did this for her. Maybe, just maybe, he hadn't simply been being polite when he'd offered marriage. Was it possible a gentleman of his many talents could actually *care*?

She had been trying to pretend such a gifted man couldn't really want an ungainly spinster. She had sought to set him free. Instead, he was risking arrest, humiliation, and the ultimate destruction of his career for her, and for Jamar, and because her family would be devastated at Jamar's loss.

He had to be the most selfless man she'd ever met. And she loved him with every soggy fiber of her heart.

Her dripping, seaweed-adorned suitor stood like a towering,

waistcoat-wearing pelican on the highest pier post and bellowed for order in no uncertain terms.

And maddened men listened.

The chaos gradually died down, except for rowdies engaged in hand-to-hand combat with uniformed men. She could hear cries of pain and anguish and winced at what she'd done.

"Cease and desist!" Erran roared again. It was easier to hear him now that the worst of the shouting had stopped. "These men have a right to protest! Their voices should be heard. You have no power to arrest working men for enforcing the laws our wealthy aristocrats cannot and will not!"

"Protest? Is that what they are doing?" Celeste asked in confusion.

"Probably not," Trevor said with a shrug. "But there are soldiers beating up those fellows who were trying to help you, and I don't think we can explain tearing apart the *Wench* any other way."

She was grateful that her brother took her riot-inducing ability in stride.

She didn't dare stand up and use her voice if Lansdowne was still out there. There might really be a riot if she screamed her opinion of her father's dreadful cousin.

She and Erran did tend to approach riots from opposite sides, so it might be best if she let him handle this one. Besides, her throat hurt and her voice rasped.

"We are a kingdom of free men," Erran shouted—presumably at Lansdowne and his soldiers. Perhaps at the occupants of the expensive carriages watching the entertainment. She winced, remembering the marquess was in one of them. It was a good thing he couldn't *see* his brother. Hearing Erran would be shock enough.

"We have the *right* to speak our minds," Erran continued roaring as the noise died down. "These good men have been unemployed and underpaid and treated like human waste for far too long. Let them be heard all the way to the halls of Parliament!"

"Is that stopping the soldiers?" Celeste asked with curiosity.

"It's hard to tell," Trevor acknowledged, standing over her to keep her from being trampled. "There's an old man standing on a wagon, berating the soldiers and pointing at Lord Erran. I'd say that was Lansdowne. He seems to be turning purple. And there are more carriages filled with gentlemen who are shouting back. I think perhaps he's causing the *gentlemen* to riot."

"How very . . . original." She coughed and hacked some more.

Trevor stiffened at some sight out of her view. Frightened at his look of helpless terror, she struggled to sit up.

"He's aiming at his lordship," her brother said, shoving her down again. Before she could scream, she heard Erran thunder, "Put that gun down!"

A clamor of more than one weapon hitting cobblestones followed. Celeste watched in bemusement as a few of the guns seemingly slid of their own accord toward the water.

"I think his lordship has learned the purpose of his talent," she whispered in awe.

A gloved hand reached down to help her up. "Let's take the lady out of here, shall we?"

"Not without Erran," she argued, standing of her own volition to meet the eyes of Erran's blond younger brother Jacques.

He grinned. "You'll be good for the family, even if you're as tall as I am." He gestured at a few less filthy thugs and pointed at the orator on the post. "Haul his noble lordship off his pedestal and carry him along with the lady. The marquess is tired of waiting."

Celeste watched speechlessly as a couple of brawny sailors lifted Erran from his post and propped him on their shoulders. Erran continued waving and ranting and gesturing at the carriage surrounded by soldiers.

The mob parted to let them pass.

When Jamar finally caught up with them, he lifted Celeste into his arms and followed in Erran's wake. Despite her elation at learning her lover had come to her rescue, she despaired at the thought of a future without him.

Even a blind marquess couldn't accept a riot-invoking Fury into his household, not if he meant to win votes and influence Parliament. This was probably where he politely but sternly requested that she and her family find another home—far, far away. Well, that had been what she'd wanted, wasn't it?

THREE DAYS later and Erran still hadn't seen Celeste to determine how she felt. He knew she was alive because she'd been bombarding him with impersonal commands rather than face him. He paced the parlor with increasing dudgeon.

"You sorry dunghill, don't pigeon me with that claptrap! I may be blind but I'm not dead yet."

As Ashford's howl echoed down the corridor, Sylvia tittered and covered her mouth with her fingertips. Aster rolled her eyes and continued laying out bolts of cloth and studying the parlor windows.

Erran snarled and watched London pass by outside the hundred-year-old panes.

"Erran, swing your hide in here and make yourself useful," the frustrated marquess shouted from his newly completed apartment. "Tell this jackanapes the walls could be purple and the hangings fishnet, and I wouldn't give a fig!"

Aster raised one eyebrow at him. Erran wanted to toss her in the drink. "Where's Theo?" he growled. "Hiding?"

"Harvest, and swearing and scowling like the rest of you." She rolled up two bolts and opened another. "We need a miracle worker to fix Ashford's blindness so everyone can return to normal."

"He hasn't found a better steward yet?" Ignoring his brother's howls, he continued pacing up and down the parlor, listening for any sound from Celeste's chambers overhead. "It's not as if Theo was raised to ride the fields like Dunc."

"It will take time to sort out," Aster said with a shrug. "The stars aren't in the right house yet. But Ashford is doing considerably better. You should stage more riots. I think he enjoys them."

Erran refrained from rolling *his* eyes. He was not exactly proud of what he had done. He'd just known he'd had to stop Lansdowne from hurting the men who had saved Jamar. Perhaps this purgatory was his punishment for using his wyrd voice for his own purposes. Although dunking shotguns in the Thames hadn't been part of his plan.

Aster and her damned family had kept him from Celeste, saying she was too ill for male visitors. How could he even think if he could not see for himself that she'd survived her near-drowning intact?

They just thought he was restless. They didn't know what Celeste meant to him.

Maybe he should bolt up the stairs . . .

Jamar appeared in the doorway. Erran glanced his way in hope. The man merely shrugged. "His lordship requires your presence, my lord."

"You are not his butler nor his manservant," Erran pointed out. "You have the power and position of a respected majordomo who should be treated with dignity."

"As he treats you, an educated barrister?" Jamar asked.

"We'll tie him up and shove him in a closet." Erran stalked past Jamar and down the corridor to Duncan's chambers to confront the monster. His patience was at an end.

Duncan stood in the middle of his chamber, swinging his walking stick and pointing at the various workmen applying paint and plaster. Cousin Zack was working through a checklist and attempting to ask questions that Dunc apparently did not wish to answer.

"Erran, quit moping over that bird-witted female and explain to this jinglebrain that I just want his men *out*. I do not need plaster birds and cherubs or Wedgewood blue, whatever the hell that is. I want peace and quiet!" Duncan whipped his cane against the post of his mahogany tester bed, cracking the stick.

"We'll need a few timbers to carve out more canes for you to break," Erran said, shoving his hand in his pocket and surveying the scene.

Zack shot him an amused look. "Rotted wood, perhaps? Better to break the stick than heads."

"I am right here! Why does no one listen to me?" Ashford sat down on the mattress and bounced, testing it. "It's too soft."

"When you start saying something worth hearing, we'll listen, your noble lord and master. Do we bring in Goldilocks to test your beds now? We're all busy men. What, precisely, did you want of us that you cannot do yourself?" Erran took the list Zack handed him and began ticking off items with a pencil.

And, of course, there was the crux of it. Duncan couldn't check off the list to see what had been done to his satisfaction. He couldn't go out and order his own bed. He couldn't see the colors he wanted. Someone needed to deal with him with patience.

Right now, that wasn't Erran.

"I need a word with you without all the clamor about," Ashford complained. "How the devil am I to have a confidential meeting with a house full of witches and workmen?"

Zack snorted and took back the paper Erran had initialed. "Kick his valet in here to oversee the decoration, and use the valet's room.

I don't know what you do about witches."

"Dunking apparently doesn't work anymore," Duncan snarled, heading unerringly for Jones's chamber.

Erran followed into the dimly lit dressing room. Jones was tidily dusting his new furniture. The valet gaped at his employer's entrance and fled when Ashford pointed at the door.

"Terrorizing servants, nice, Dunc." Erran perched on the manservant's narrow cot and watched his brother pace off the chamber's dimensions. "What do you want of me?"

"Service to your country," he answered without hesitation. "Your exploits at the docks have been reported to Earl Grey. He thinks we need an orator on our side. I've a pocket borough you can fill for now. We'll consider a larger election after you've developed a feel for it."

Erran was glad he was sitting down. "You want *me* in the Commons? Have you run mad? Did you hear me speak?"

"A lot of people heard," Dunc said dryly. "Smart men would prefer to have you on their side rather than railing insurrection against them."

"Where they can control me." Erran nodded understanding even if Dunc couldn't see him.

There had been a time when he'd controlled himself out of fear. Now that he'd learned more of his ability, it was frighteningly tempting to use it. If word of the dock riot hadn't reached the court, another event would in due course. The judge hadn't acknowledged Erran's compulsion over the paper-signing, but there could always be a next time. Sooner or later, they'd ban him from practice.

Except now that Dunc dangled the opportunity—Erran discovered he urgently *wanted* this chance where his voice might make a difference. He had hoped to serve justice in the courts through legal means, but the pace was petrifying. Here was his chance to change the *courts*.

Only—if he couldn't trust himself in front of a single judge, how could he stand in front of all Commons and threaten and cajole and compel? "I'm not entirely certain I can be controlled. Or want to be," he admitted.

"Understood," Dunc said with unusual equanimity. "That's why you'll start in my pocket. If you don't work out, we'll not have invested a great deal. Are you interested?"

He was more than interested. He was trying not to float to the ceiling like a helium balloon. Here was his chance to offer Celeste more than a hope and a prayer. Of course, she still might not have him. Probably wouldn't, since she'd let her family come between them ever since the riot. She'd had him draw up papers that gave her the independence to return to Jamaica.

He couldn't think what *he* had done to deserve her rejection, but it wasn't as if he'd done much to deserve her acceptance either, except ruin her.

Remembering the moment the sun had abruptly vanished—Erran knew he had to fight to keep Celeste. He hadn't thought himself ready for marriage—but he knew he'd found the only woman he wanted to share his life. If gaining her required using his bully voice, then so be it. It wouldn't work on Celeste, though. For that, he had to rely on matters of the heart, a subject well beyond his comprehension.

Thirty

CELESTE ADJUSTED the folds of her new gown. At the time she'd ordered it, she had been trying to be demure while pleasing her need for color. She'd chosen a flowered muslin with an azure bodice that she hoped would match her eyes. Today, when her future was at stake, she would rather wear red, but even she knew that would be brazen. Perhaps a striped burgundy someday. She gazed critically at the result in her mirror.

"You look positively regal," Sylvia said in awe. "They will think you are a queen and do anything you say."

From her rocking chair, Nana emitted a snort.

On any other day, Celeste would agree that she could persuade lawyers to do anything she said. Today, of all days, however, *she couldn't speak.* The dunking in the Thames had given her a catarrh that had settled in her throat. She had hidden upstairs for days hoping the cold would go away. But she couldn't delay this meeting any longer.

She clutched her throat in an age-old expression of terror. Today was the day that set the rest of her life. She had to do this, had to know she had the backbone she needed to face Erran's proposal. If she kept remembering that her voice was a gift meant to help others, she could be strong.

Sylvia and Trevor trailed after her as she descended the stairs to the front parlor. The marquess now occupied the study, but he had offered his hastily refurbished front room for this meeting.

Jamar and Erran waited in the entry hall. She allowed Erran to escort her into the parlor. She held her breath as she clasped his arm. He was so solid, so confident . . . . . She wanted to simply hand him all her problems and rely on him forever.

For her own sake and that of her family and the people in Jamaica depending on her, she could not. She must show that she had the confidence and ability to direct her own life—and that of her siblings and an entire plantation on the other side of the world.

All their futures rode on today's outcome—*and she couldn't speak.*

She'd spent days frantically looking for ways to work around her lack of charm. If all else failed, she could do hysteria well. It wasn't the option she wanted.

A game table had been brought in to use as desk. Her father's solicitor, Mr. Herrington, stood and beamed genially at her. She had manipulated him into agreement last time. He must agree with her now on principle alone—not a simple task given England's preference to treat women as children or furniture.

Ashford's elderly solicitor nodded as they were introduced. Legally entangling her family with the Ives required an objective third party—not Erran. She had to overcome this man's objections with reason and by projecting confidence the way the Ives men did.

She swallowed hard and resisted the urge to flee.

Lansdowne's disapproving attorney, Mr. Luther, glared at her from over his spectacles. His animosity she could safely ignore. The angrier he became, the less anyone would listen, she hoped. Unable to use her persuasive voice, she'd developed another plan for dealing with him. The important part was that *she* dealt with him, not any man. She needed to know she could handle her father's affairs with the same competence as her father once had.

She took a seat on the sofa between Trevor and Sylvia.

In a fashionable gray morning coat, striped trousers, and red vest, Erran stood with hands behind his back on the far side of the parlor, away from the negotiating table. While she'd convalesced, she had sent him notes asking him to draw up the documents on the table now. He'd sent her notes of protest and notes requesting that they speak, but in the end, he'd done as she'd asked, to the dismay of her heart and the relief of her head. She needed to think straight, and emotions had a tendency to muddle her concentration.

Erran had the ability to stir every emotion she possessed, and some she hadn't known existed. Was lust an emotion? Because he inspired that too, and it was even less conducive to concentration than love. She deliberately looked at the gouty old men across the table rather than the handsomely aristocratic one making her heart race.

"Lord Rochester, Miss Rochester, Miss Sylvia," Mr. Herrington addressed them, once they were settled. "Lord Ashford and Mr. Brown, Ashford's solicitor, have consulted and decided as head of your maternal family, the marquess is in the best position to conduct your affairs until such time as the baron reaches his majority."

Trevor scowled, but nodded to what he'd known was coming.

"Miss Rochester, being of age, will have her share of the estate, understanding that other than her dowry, the rest will be as income from the Jamaican property. The property shall be maintained by the marquess of Ashford and his representatives until such time as the baron is of age."

Lansdowne's man rose to object. "He cannot usurp the rights of the father's family! The earl already has his men in place, as is his right—"

Celeste glanced to Erran. Her notes had told him what needed to be done. He'd agreed. As a confident man of the law, he could easily step in now and handle it for her, but she'd made it plain that she wanted to do it herself, to make these men understand that *she* was captain of her own fate now. Grimacing reluctant agreement, Erran waited for her to make her stand. He understood her need to establish her independence. For that alone, she could love him.

Once this was over, they needed to talk—about *them*. About his proposal. She had to block that from her mind. She could only take one enormous step at a time.

Drawing a deep breath for courage, Celeste gestured to indicate that Luther take his seat. Luther glowered and resisted. She had to save her voice for more important matters, and the lawyer wasn't important in the greater scheme of things. She found the document she sought on the table and held it out to Erran to read aloud.

He did so in a gloating tone despite the list being no more than a boring sum of the earl's rather extensive debts. Celeste took the list when he was done and produced a small pouch of coin she'd had Erran draw on her father's account now that the court had freed her funds. She picked up a pen, circled the debt owed to Luther's firm, and counted out the sum in coin. She shoved it toward the earl's solicitor.

"The lady is offering to pay your firm what it is owed for your oversight of her father's affairs these past months," Erran translated for her.

Luther looked wary. "In return for what?"

"In return for resigning Lansdowne's claim to the estate," Ashford's elderly attorney stated sonorously, at her behest.

"Lansdowne cannot pay you, even if he wished to do so. The Jamaican estate is a mere drop in the bucket of his debts. A suit will expose the details, making it obvious he is not the careful caretaker the court would approve. Such a revelation will almost certainly drive his creditors to demand bankruptcy. We have a judge's signature confirming the marquess's responsibility toward the family and their estate. We do not wish to drain the young baron's coffers with an expensive, protracted lawsuit—for which you will not be paid whether you win or lose. Sign the release and your hard work shall be recompensed despite your efforts to deplete the Rochesters' assets."

The list was a threat Celeste would have loved to deliver herself. The earl had attempted to steal everything they owned, but she wasn't facing the earl, just one of his lackeys. Her gesture would suffice in light of the more important task she still had to accomplish.

Once Luther's vociferous arguments had been defeated, and he had agreed to her payment, his involvement was moot. She'd done it! With Erran's aid and her suggestions, she'd defeated Lansdowne's representative—without need of her voice. She might have a backbone after all.

Triumph wasn't hers yet. She had thought long and hard about her future in deciding this next step—there were so many people counting on her! But she had found a solution that suited her and made as many people happy as possible.

Except possibly Erran. She hadn't told him. This was her decision and hers alone.

She now had to stand up to the men who sought to protect her— a much harder task than defeating a lackey. After the lawyers finished bickering over the details of the earl's resignation, Celeste gestured for Trevor to hand over the papers in his pockets.

Erran raised his eyebrows in surprise when she rolled out documents he hadn't prepared. She'd hated relying on him up until now, but for her family, she understood the necessity. For them, she would take no risks.

For herself—and the child she might be carrying—she must learn the confidence to act on her own. This was her declaration of independence.

"I would like the release of my dowry," she whispered as clearly as her voice allowed. She set the purchase agreement in front of Ashford's daunting solicitor. "To buy a house of my own. I will also need the return of my family's rents from the marquess, as my siblings will be moving in with me."

Sylvia and Trevor had been along when she'd visited the charming cottage Lady Aster had told her about. Both her siblings had agreed that if they were to stay in England, they couldn't continue sharing with the marquess. The cottage wouldn't be a grand London townhouse, but it would be *theirs*.

Celeste prayed Erran understood. Men liked to make big decisions, but if they expected a woman to make a decision as important as who she meant to spend her life with, then she should be able to decide on buying a home for her family.

She hadn't dared look at Erran to see how he was taking the news that she meant to stay in England, if only until she saw Sylvia and Trevor established on their own. Her heart had resolved the dispute between place and people. She didn't know if Erran would grasp what she was doing. She didn't know where his heart was.

"A young unmarried lady cannot set up her own establishment!" Mr. Brown said in horror, not even acknowledging that she wouldn't be returning to Jamaica. "It is not done."

"It is up to your husband to choose how your dowry will be spent," Mr. Herrington said nervously, polishing his glasses. "One cannot expect a young lady to manage her funds successfully in supporting her own household."

Celeste refused to back down. "The money is mine," she whispered as defiantly as she could. "I am independent in the eyes of the law. I have no husband to speak for me, so I speak for myself. I wish to establish my own household. I have an elderly companion who cannot make the return journey to her home, and she deserves a proper one here."

While the solicitors hemmed and hawed over costs and the wisdom of allowing a young lady such profligate use of funds destined for a husband, Erran stepped up to slap his hand on the document and call for silence. "The lady is of an age and intelligence to chart her own course without our guidance. Grant her request or I shall bring in Ashford so you might explain your objections to him."

After nearly fainting in relief that he agreed, Celeste laughed at the promptness with which the lawyers approved her request. Erran hadn't even used his compulsion. Just the possibility of Ashford's furious interference had cowed them.

She ought to be upset that she'd still needed him to help her, but the look he gave her was heated, and she quit thinking again. He understood. And her heart beat so quickly, she feared she might actually give into the vapors.

Thirty

ERRAN PROPERLY rapped Ashford's front knocker. A footman in gleaming linen and black coat opened the door and bowed to gesture him in.

So much formality would be off-putting if Erran hadn't been focused on one goal. He would not be deterred in his mission. "Is Miss Rochester at home?" He offered his card.

It seemed the height of idiocy to ask after weeks of coming and going through the kitchen and finding her when he liked, but after all his impropriety, he had to show her the respect she deserved. He smoothed his glove over his new morning coat and pleated shirt—to replace the one that had been ruined by the Thames. Celeste had seen him at his worst, but today, he'd dressed for her.

"I shall see, my lord. The marquess has requested that you make yourself known to him when you arrive. I will find you in his study, shall I?"

Torn, Erran glanced up the stairs, but there was no sign of Celeste. He prayed she hadn't moved out yet. With a grimace, he followed the footman to Dunc's study. Inside, he found Jamar reading a letter aloud in a sonorous voice that would have suited a judge's chamber.

Dunc looked up at his entrance. If nothing else, his brother had learned to listen. Jamar set down the letter when Dunc spoke.

"We need to send representatives back to Jamaica with Jamar to throw out Lansdowne's louts and bring the locals back into line," Dunc said angrily. "I want someone there who can monitor the slavery situation. It seems they're on the brink of revolt in surrounding plantations. We need to keep communications open and let Trevor's workers know we are on their side, working to eliminate slavery. Jamar can tell them, but we need to put a landowner's face on it."

"I trust you are not asking me," Erran said. "I will only go if Celeste wishes to go, and she's made it plain she is staying here with her siblings."

"And Nana Delphinia," Jamar said gravely. "She does not wish to make the return journey. We can send her daughters here, where she need not worry about them."

"I'm asking which of our misbegotten relations would be best for the task." Duncan tapped his desk with his pen as if he actually meant to use it. "There are enough idlers about who ought to be willing to go adventuring."

A few months ago after his first courtroom debacle, Erran would have happily volunteered. These days, he had new goals he was eager to pursue, including testing his voice only for good purpose—like fighting for the bill to end slave ownership. Celeste would help keep him from straying down Cousin Sylvester's path—if she would only have him. Which was why he was here, confound it.

He cast his mind over a list of relations as disaffected as he had been earlier in the summer. "Cousin Athan comes to mind. Now that Uncle Timothy has passed most of the estate responsibilities to his eldest, Athan is at loose ends."

"Loose ends," Dunc snorted. "Is that what one calls piracy these days?"

"Not piracy. Just smuggling. It's either that or the mines in Cornwall. He does not seem to have developed an aptitude for anything except leadership of thieves," Erran said with a shrug, listening for Celeste in the hall and not too concerned with the conversation. Dunc would do what Dunc wanted to do, regardless of all advice.

"A leader of thieves might be the best choice for this venture," Jamar said in amusement.

A footman scratched at the open door. "Miss Rochester is available in the parlor, my lord."

Nervously, Erran clutched his gloves and hurried after the servant.

She was wearing a celestial blue-and-gold striped gown that brought out the brilliance of her azure eyes. She cocked her head with interest as he entered, and he almost stumbled over his own damned feet. Only Celeste could make him aware of the man he was beneath the clothes he wore to impress. She saw right through them and stripped him naked. It was a daunting experience for a man who preferred his privacy.

"I have come wooing," he said. "How is your voice today?"

"Better," she said, with only a trace of huskiness. Her eyes crinkled in the corners, as if she might be laughing at him. "Thank you for asking."

Wanting to haul her from her seat and cover her with kisses and make his demands right here and now, Erran tamped down his impatience and continued to play his role. "Did you receive the flowers I sent?"

Her lush rose lips parted in a smile of delight. "I did. I cannot imagine how you found flamenco flowers in chilly England. They almost made me homesick."

"I have access to any number of conservatories. I just asked around a bit. I would not have done so if it makes you long for home," he said with concern. "I'd hoped to show you that your new home could have the same amenities."

"That is why Lady Aster was concerned that my new house must have a glass room," she exclaimed. "I can grow my own flamencos! Will you not take a seat? I can send for tea," she said with a trace of awkwardness.

"I know we are not accustomed to being so formal," he said to relieve her unease, "but I wanted to show you that I can be a gentleman and court you as you deserve. Would you care to go for a drive? I have borrowed Ashford's open carriage. It will be cool, but respectable. I don't wish to worsen your cold though."

Her entire face lit with pleasure—and mischief. "Court me! How enterprising. Let us go, please. I shall wrap warmly."

Within minutes he had her beside him on the carriage seat. She was wrapped in a wool mantle and bonnet as if it were winter. She let the bonnet dangle by its strings once the sun broke from behind the clouds. Erran had difficulty keeping his gaze on the horses and not her shining hair and laughing eyes.

"Let us see how the repairs to my cottage proceed," she demanded happily. "I cannot drive myself yet through these crowded streets, and I'm most eager to see the progress. Your Cousin Zach has most thoughtfully helped find the workmen, but I'm so impatient to have my own home!"

Erran had already made this trip several times to make certain the workmen were on the job. He knew the best routes through the city now. They were on Westminster Bridge in reasonable time, admiring the crumbling stone and not minding the heavy traffic.

As anxious as he was to determine his place in her new life, Erran kept his own hopes bottled and simply enjoyed Celeste's delight in her new home. She enthused over the beauty of Battersea's gardens and the room she would set up for her sewing. He thought perhaps she might be as nervous as he.

It had been weeks since they'd spent their nights together. Despite everything that had happened, he'd been able to think of little else since then. His all-male, mostly unmarried, family were of no help in telling him how to go about proposing marriage. He'd rather not do it the way Theo had—with angry families pounding on a locked door.

Although he could certainly see the advantage of locking up his intended until he had the answer he wanted, he would prefer to respect Celeste's newly-acquired independence.

The cottage they approached was one of the newer homes built after the bridge was finished—Georgian in architecture but well maintained over the decades. Graceful old trees and hedges lined the drive and gave an appearance of privacy, but she had neighbors to all sides of her. Property was less expensive on this side of the Thames, but he couldn't help noticing the distance to Parliament wasn't difficult.

"Have the workmen finished for the day?" he asked, tying up the horses and glancing around to see no activity.

"They are done entirely," she said in satisfaction as he helped her down. "We are to commence moving as soon as Lady Aster sends us her latest collection of almost-trained servants."

"Almost-trained," he said with laughter, escorting her to the front door. "You do realize you could be receiving reformed prostitutes and homeless soldiers, don't you?"

Even as he laughed, he realized what she was saying: no servants were on the premises. No workmen. They were all alone. His brainpan might just explode with possibilities.

She sent him an almost impish sidelong glance as she retrieved a key from her pocket. "I think irregular forces might suit, don't you?"

He hoped and prayed she included him in that suggestion. "You do not approve of propriety?" he asked, taking the key.

"I am thinking it is time we start a new propriety, one that includes all sorts of people. I cannot think I'd be happy sitting about my parlor, doing nothing for the rest of my life. Why should gentlemen have all the fun?" She stepped inside after he opened the door and whirled around in happiness in the sunbeam from the half-circle transom window over the double set of doors.

"If this is a test, is it dangerous for me to disagree? Gentlemen can't bear children, you'll remember. The thought of a woman heavy with child climbing ladders puts me in a state of utter horror." Accepting her dare to be different, Erran caught her slender waist and led her into the airy front room.

Airy because there were no draperies as yet. This room wouldn't suit.

She laughed and danced away from him. "The thought of men in high-heeled slippers attempting to wear skirts and petticoats on a ladder induces images of rolling on the floor in laughter. Women do many impossible things that men would not dream of doing."

"Fair enough," he agreed with equanimity, dragging her back to the stairs. "Women should have the freedom to explore their abilities. But you will admit that society creates limitations that must be overcome first?"

"Such as men fainting in horror at female ladder-climbing? No doubt." She broke away from his arm, lifted her skirts, and ran up the stairs.

He easily caught up with her in a corner bedchamber. An unadorned tester bed and linen-covered mattress were the only furniture as yet.

Erran didn't think she'd led him up here to show him the beauty of the bed's wood. Without asking permission, he lifted his Jamaican beauty and kissed her.

To his joy, Celeste flung her arms around his neck and kissed him back, with great enthusiasm. And much warmth. And all the passion his empty heart could desire.

"I do not ever want to let you go," he murmured, spreading his kisses to her jaw and the tender place between ear and throat. "You have no idea of the torment I've suffered these past weeks, not being able to hold you like this."

"It is as if we're bound by magic," she said breathily. "I thought I might pine away. Is that normal? I cannot think anything we've done is normal or proper, but I have missed you so!"

"We're the new propriety," he said with a smile. "May I have your permission to unfasten this very pretty bodice?"

"I sewed this one myself." She released the gauze wrap of her neckline to expose pretty buttons that appeared to be made of shells. To Erran's delight, they pushed easily through delicate holes to reveal the silk camisole beneath. "My father is not the only inventor in the family," she said proudly. "I see no reason why I must have a maid to unfasten all the silly hooks in back. And buttons are so much easier to undo than hooks!"

"I will attest to the immense intelligence and usefulness of this bodice," Erran declared in rapture as he gazed upon the plump curves of her breasts while unhooking the corset beneath. "Now, if only you could see fit to rid yourself of this benighted contraption . . ."

"As you would leave off this very pretty vest?" she asked, slipping her fingers beneath the fabric covering his chest.

"I will, if you like. What need have I of clothes?" He kissed her breast above her chemise and felt her shiver. "Say this means you'll marry me. I don't believe I can live knowing I can't have you beside me every day."

"You won't be beside me," she scoffed, abandoning his chest to run her hands into his hair. She gasped as he pressed his kisses deeper, but apparently she had a need to talk rather than give him promises. "I have heard Ashford say you are to be his minion in the Commons. You will be arguing with men all day just as he does."

"I will be gainfully employed," Erran protested without heat since she did not object to his pushing the gown off her arms. "And the Commons isn't in session all the time. I'm still in Dunc's employ, but I can stay here and improve your sewing machine and sell the patent and add to your already considerable income."

"Which will diminish if there is an uprising on the island," she said sadly. "So if you are marrying me for my money, you will be most disappointed."

He kissed her enthusiastically anywhere he could reach, until she laughed again.

"With you as inspiration, I will provide," he said fervently. "And with Ives to teach him, Trevor will find a way to sort out the plantation when his time comes. Let us talk of more important matters—like telling me yes, you will marry me. I know very little of love, but if what I feel for you is that emotion, it's turning me inside-out. Tell me yes and heal my confusion."

"What, you will cease to love me if we marry?" she asked archly, having succeeded in dragging his shirt tails from his trousers. "Or perhaps it is just lust you feel and that goes away when I become fat with your child?"

He groaned as she stroked her slender fingers over his nakedness. "Your size has no more to do with who you are than the color of your hair. You are the woman who understands me, who endures my fits and starts, who loves me with her eyes and makes me feel as if anything is possible. How can that be simple lust? Lust can be slaked anywhere. What I feel for you is . . . magic, as you said. A binding that cannot be torn apart."

"A binding that must be constantly woven and strengthened by deeds as well as words, my dearest love," Celeste whispered, pressing her kisses to his bared throat.

"That, I can do," he promised, laying her on the bed.

CELESTE had feared those glorious nights with Erran had been her imagination or the work of some mystical magic that had been woven in Wystan. She was happy to learn that her fears were groundless.

Not quite satiated but feeling more complete after their lovemaking, she basked in the glow of Erran's admiration—while drinking her fill of the man beneath the fashionable façade. Sunlight spilled through her bedroom window, giving her new appreciation of this man she had chosen.

He had wide, square shoulders and a broad chest that rippled with muscle. A trim waist and hips and powerful thighs gave evidence that he was not a man who sat behind desks for long. She gathered from his sun-tinted chest that he spent time outdoors in the heathen environs of his brother's estate where shirts were evidently not necessary. He propped himself over her on powerful arms that could hold her imprisoned—or offer the security she craved.

She caressed all that lovely man and wiggled her hips where they'd just been joined. To her satisfaction, he was already rising to the occasion.

"You have yet to say the words I wish to hear," he objected, rolling over and pulling her on top of him. "Are you having second thoughts about being courted by a mere commoner instead of a duke or earl? Am I depriving you of the debut you secretly long to make?"

She nibbled his shoulder and when that produced a reaction she enjoyed, began kissing any skin within reach. "You dare call yourself a mere commoner?" she scoffed. "A man who has better understanding of my eccentricities than anyone on earth? A man who exhibits such intelligence that he supports my beliefs and need for independence, allows me to do as I see fit, and otherwise suits me in every way, and is more handsome than he deserves to be? You think I should hold out for a portly duke who thinks women exist for making heirs? Do you insult *my* intelligence?"

He laughed and nibbled her ear while arousing her nipples with sensations that truly should not be allowed if this was a sin.

"I would not ask a stupid woman to be my wife. Any woman who marries me will require more indulgence and understanding than any ordinary woman. As you may have noticed, our family is noted for our unconventionalities, not our easiness to get along with." He lifted his head to suckle at the nipple he'd aroused.

Moaning, Celeste arched into him. "I find you very easy to accommodate," she muttered ambiguously.

He laughed and proceeded to tease her more with his ministrations. "Then say you'll be my wife, till death do us part."

"I think I already have," she murmured in wonder. "In Wystan. Do you remember the vow I made? It is an old Malcolm marriage vow. We have been bound ever since, by magic if not by law."

"I'll not explain that to my brothers if we have a six-month babe," he argued, stroking delicate tissues until she nearly cried out in impatience. "I need the legalities. Say yes, and I'll obtain the license tomorrow. We are not doing this again until I hear the words, my lady."

"Unfair," she laughingly protested, sliding her hand between them to stroke him as he was her. "That would be a true test of wills. I concede! Yes, I will marry you with whatever passes for legality in your mind."

He kissed her swiftly, thoroughly, then said in a voice hoarse with lust, "We'll talk to the vicar in the village, say the vows quickly, and avoid Malcolm insanity. You really do not want to wear a cloak and rowan twigs."

While she fuzzily tried to figure out twigs in a wedding service, he entered her, and there was nothing left to worry about. This man was her world now, and she would have him forever, in whatever way it could be done.

Thirty-one

"WEDDINGS are not about you, silly," Lady Aster proclaimed, pinning a circlet of rowan to Erran's thick curls. "You really did not think your bride would want to be married without her family around her?"

Erran really thought his bride considered them already married after uttering vows in a haunted castle, but he knew better than to try to explain that. He didn't intend to add to family legend.

Although Celeste had probably scribbled it in her journal for future reference.

His beautiful bride slipped her hand through the bend in his elbow and bobbed down so Aster could place a ringlet on her carefully constructed coiffure. A maid had wrapped all that glorious mahogany hair in a construction of curls and ringlets that Erran fully intended to take apart as soon as they were alone.

"I am glad this could be done quickly so Jamar could be with us before he sailed," Celeste murmured with all evidence of pleasure.

She slanted a look in Erran's direction that said what he'd already heard— for the sake of others, she was allowing this insane ceremony instead of the private one they'd prefer. He was the biggest sap in the universe because he swelled with pride that he had a woman who believed she belonged to him without need of formalities—and that she was a woman large-hearted enough to share her joy with others.

Erran glanced over the small churchyard. The vicar had accepted Erran's bribe to oversee this heathen ceremony, but he'd insisted it be held outdoors. That seemed to suit the party exceptionally well. Beneath the brilliant autumn colors of the trees, a vibrant swirl of guests milled. Nana Delphinia had donned her bright red African robes, and a colorfully printed bandana enswathed her graying hair. Jamar, too, had doffed his gentleman's coat for a long robe he referred to as a dansiki. His celebratory attire was a more sedate brown and gold pattern that Nana had sewn up for him. He wore it with a tight cloth hat that suited his distinguished mien better than the top hats the other gentlemen wore.

Rather than risk tripping on unfamiliar ground he couldn't see, Dunc sat in his open carriage, wearing his formal morning coat and top hat and looking like the wealthy aristocrat he was. The vicar had quit complaining the moment the marquess had arrived. Erran was grateful Dunc had made the effort. Celeste would now be accepted in the village as the person of importance that she should be.

Erran ignored the rest of the Malcolm women swirling about in billowing silks and lace, performing their family idiosyncrasies. As long as Celeste was at his side, he could endure whatever life flung at him.

"Tell them to come to order," his bride wickedly proposed. "See how many respond."

"If it will get us to the bedroom faster . . .?" He lifted his eyebrows suggestively. He had conquered his fear of his voice enough to try scientific experimentation, but he still preferred judge and jury to decide on its use.

She tugged him toward the vicar in answer. Trevor stood to one side to give her away. Sylvia giddily twirled her new gown, holding the bride's bouquet. Theo stood in for Dunc at Erran's side. His older brother leaned over and whispered, "Last chance to enjoy the misery of bachelorhood, old boy. Any second thoughts?"

Erran glanced down at the woman smiling up at him as if he were the moon and stars. "Not a one," he told his brother. Then straightening, he turned to address the chattering audience in his Courtroom Voice. "The service is about to commence, if you will please . . ." He almost said "take your places" but realized that could mean trees or London or anywhere but here. Instead, he added, "stand still and let the vicar begin."

Their audience immediately halted their milling. Ignoring his order, as usual, Celeste stood on her toes and pressed a kiss to his cheek. "I love your authoritative way with words."

He grinned. "And now, you may charm them all into believing you are modest and unassuming and would never think of starting a riot."

She beamed, and he could swear he heard a chorus of birds sing as if it were dawn.

Acknowledgments

As ever, it takes a village to create a book. Book View Café Publishing Co-op is one of the best villages I've ever occupied. Kudos to everyone involved for all the advice and encouragement and hard work. In particular, editorial advice from Mindy Klasky and Jen Stevenson, proofreading from Diane Pharaoh Francis, and above-and-beyond-the-call of duty formatting from Vonda McIntyre, and the tireless efforts of Pati Nagle for keeping us all organized!

And much gratitude to the newest edition to my group of tireless, hardworking associates, Ryan Zitofsky, who helps me find readers, wherever they may be.

GET A FREE STARTER SET OF PATRICIA RICE BOOKS

Thank you for reading *Whisper of Magic.*

Would you like to know when my next book is available? I occasionally send newsletters with details on new releases, special offers and other bits of news. If you sign up for the mailing list I'll send you a free copy of the Patricia Rice starter kit. **The books average 4.4 out of 5 stars and together usually retail over $15.00** Just sign up at http://patriciarice.com/

I am an independent author, so getting the word out about my book is vital to its success. If you liked this book, please consider telling your friends, and writing a review at the store where you purchased it. Reviews help other readers find books. I appreciate all reviews, whether positive or negative.

About the Author

With several million books in print and *New York Times* and *USA Today's* bestseller lists under her belt, former CPA Patricia Rice is one of romance's hottest authors. Her emotionally-charged contemporary and historical romances have won numerous awards, including the *RT Book Reviews* Reviewers Choice and Career Achievement Awards. Her books have been honored as Romance Writers of America RITA® finalists in the historical, regency and contemporary categories.

A firm believer in happily-ever-after, Patricia Rice is married to her high school sweetheart and has two children. A native of Kentucky and New York, a past resident of North Carolina and Missouri, she currently resides in Southern California, and now does accounting only for herself. She is a member of Romance Writers of America, the Authors Guild, and Novelists, Inc.

For further information, visit Patricia's network:

http://www.patriciarice.com

http://www.facebook.com/OfficialPatriciaRice

https://twitter.com/Patricia_Rice

http://wordwenches.typepad.com/word_wenches/

http://patricia-rice.tumblr.com/

ALSO BY PATRICIA RICE

Mysteries:
EVIL GENIUS, *A FAMILY GENIUS MYSTERY*, VOL 1
UNDERCOVER GENIUS, *A FAMILY GENIUS MYSTERY*, VOL 2
CYBER GENIUS, *A FAMILY GENIUS MYSTERY*, VOL. 3

Historical Romance:
WICKED WYCKERLY, *THE REBELLIOUS SONS*, VOLUME 1
DEVILISH MONTAGUE, *THE REBELLIOUS SONS*, VOLUME 2
NOTORIOUS ATHERTON, *THE REBELLIOUS SONS*, VOLUME 3
FORMIDABLE LORD QUENTIN, *THE REBELLIOUS SONS*, VOLUME 4
THE MARQUESS, *REGENCY NOBLES*, VOLUME 1
ENGLISH HEIRESS, *REGENCY NOBLES*, VOLUME 2
IRISH DUCHESS, *REGENCY NOBLES*, VOLUME 3

Paranormal Romance:
THE LURE OF SONG AND MAGIC, *THE CALIFORNIA MALCOLMS*
TROUBLE WITH AIR AND MAGIC, *THE CALIFORNIA MALCOLMS*
THE RISK OF LOVE AND MAGIC, *THE CALIFORNIA MALCOLMS*

About Book View Café

Book View Café is a professional authors' cooperative offering DRM-free ebooks in multiple formats to readers around the world. With authors in a variety of genres including fantasy, romance, mystery, and science fiction, Book View Café has something for everyone.

Book View Café is good for readers because you can enjoy high-quality DRM-free ebooks from your favorite authors at a reasonable price.

Book View Café is good for writers because 95% of the profits goes directly to the book's author.

Book View Café authors include NY Times bestsellers and notable book authors (Madeleine Robins, Patricia Rice, Maya Kaathryn Bohnhoff, and Sarah Zettel), Nebula and Hugo Award winners (Ursula K. Le Guin, Vonda N. McIntyre, Linda Nagata), and a Rita award winner (Patricia Rice).

bookviewcafe.com

Praise for Patricia Rice's novels

FORMIDABLE LORD QUENTIN

"another gem ...with touches of whimsy, astute dialogue, a bit of poignancy, passion and sensuality —fast-paced tale of love and laughter." – Joan Hammond, RT Reviews

"Rice has crafted her novel with plenty of witty, engaging characters and a healthy dose of romance. Clever Bell is a splendid protagonist, and readers will cheer her efforts to get men to take her seriously and treat her as an equal." –Publishers Weekly

MERELY MAGIC

"Like Julie Garwood, Patricia Rice employs wicked wit and sizzling sensuality to turn the battle of the sexes into a magical romp." -Mary Jo Putney, NYT Bestselling author

MUST BE MAGIC

"Rice has created a mystical masterpiece full of enchanting characters, a spellbinding plot, and the sweetest of romances." Booklist (starred review)

THE TROUBLE WITH MAGIC

"Rice is a marvelously talented author who skillfully combines pathos with humor in a stirring, sensual romance that shows the power of love is the most wondrous gift of all. Think of this memorable story as a gift you can open again and again." Romantic Times

THIS MAGIC MOMENT

"This charming and immensely entertaining tale...takes a smart, determined heroine who will accept nothing less than true love and an honorable hero who eventually realizes what love is and sets them on course to solve a mystery, save an entire estate, and find the magic of love." –Library Journal

MUCH ADO ABOUT MAGIC

"The magical Rice takes Trev and Lucinda, along with her readers, on a passionate, sensual, and romantic adventure in this fast-paced, witty, poignant, and magical tale of love." Romantic Times (Top Pick, 4 ½ stars)

MAGIC MAN

"In this delightful conclusion to the Magic series, Rice gives readers a thoughtful giant of a man who can bring down mountains, but with gentle touches can make the earth tremble for the woman he loves. This is a sensual, poignant, humorous and magical read." Romantic Times